Death by Dickens

Death by Dickens

EDITED BY

Anne Perry

BERKLEY PRIME CRIME, NEW YORK

A Berkley Prime Crime Book
Published by The Berkley Publishing Group
A division of Penguin Group (USA) Inc.
375 Hudson Street
New York, New York 10014

DEATH BY DICKENS

This book is an original publication of The Berkley Publishing Group.

Visit our website at www.penguin.com.

First edition: March 2004

PRINTING HISTORY
Berkley Prime Crime trade paperback edition / March 2004

Berkley Prime Crime trade paperback ISBN: 0-425-19420-5

Library of Congress Cataloging-in-Publication Data

Death by Dickens / edited by Anne Perry.
    p. cm.
    ISBN 0-425-19420-5
    1. Detective and mystery stories, English.   2. Detective and mystery stories, American.
3. Characters and characteristics in literature—Fiction.   4. Historical fiction, American.
5. Historical fiction, English.   6. England—Fiction.   1. Perry, Anne.   II. Dickens, Charles,
1812—1870.

PR1309.D4D38   2004
823'.087—dc22

                                                                        2003062890

PRINTED IN THE UNITED STATES OF AMERICA

10   9   8   7   6   5   4   3   2   1

Contents

Introduction

BY ANNE PERRY

SHAKESPEARE WAS THE master from whom to draw inspiration for a collection of mystery short stories. Who better to follow him than Charles Dickens? Was there ever a writer who created a finer variety of characters young and old, villainous and heroic, tragic and comical? His books abound with colour, variety, and emotion.

Eleven authors have been invited to write their own version of a Dickens-inspired tale, and these are they:

"A Stake of Holly" by Lillian Stewart Carl is one of the two stories of Scrooge, both of which have the morality and the hope of the original. This takes us many years ahead, to the conclusion Dickens did not write, but I think we all like to imagine, and it has a dark and satisfying mystery very cleverly woven into the book. Many loose threads are tied up, unfinished storylines explained and dealt with. In many ways it is a companion volume to *A Christmas Carol*.

The other Scrooge story, "The Holly and the Ivy" by Carole Nelson Douglas, has the same upbeat feeling to it, but the flavour is modern, tongue-in-cheek, and rips along at a wonderful speed. The ghosts are superbly inventive, all the elements are there, and the moral message is just as clear and as timeless. And of course it, too, has a very present-day murder solved by skillful detection.

Perhaps everybody's other favourite character is Mr. Pickwick. He is an institution not just national, but of the English language, and many other languages, for all I know. "Mr. Pickwick and the Body Snatchers" by Bill Crider is a rollicking yarn in highly Dickensian spirit; how could it not be with such a title? This is true Pickwick, but as I think you have never seen him before. I defy you not to grip the arms of your chair with the tension, and also find yourself laughing.

The other Pickwick tale, "Next Christmas at Dingley Dell" by Gillian Linscott, is a totally different affair. It begins slowly and you may well have no idea where it intends to go. There is a sweetness to it, a slow happiness of memory. Watch out for the end! You will see Mr. Pickwick as you have never seen him before, and I think that, like me, you will be immensely satisfied and amazed, incredulous even. But it will feel right to you. It will explain so much.

"Fagin's Revenge" by Brendan DuBois is the one story that has no reflection or companion in another. It is present day, quite different, and totally surprising. It makes suggestions I doubt will ever have occurred to you; they certainly had not to me! And yet, when you think them over, you will see how they fit exactly. That is why it is such fun to tell stories—the imagination is boundless, nothing is forbidden except that which doesn't work (or of course is libelous, which this is not).

"The House of the Red Candle" by Martin Edwards features Dickens himself as the detective and Wilkie Collins as his "Watson." It is a dark story. It captures the time perfectly, and perhaps echoes something of our own. It is Sherlockian in its subtlety and its comradeship, but there is an anger and a compassion in it which fire it with a different light, and gives it a warmth that prevents it from being too somber. I hope you will remember it with vividness as long as I will.

The other story using Dickens and Collins as detectives in a close friendship is "The Passing Shadow" by Peter Tremayne. Again it captures the seediest and most violent and dangerous part of London, swarming with characters who could have stepped off Dickens's own pages in all their passion and vitality, squalor, villainy, and heroism. I can see these two past giants of Victorian writing taking on whole new careers in literature—as protagonists in mysteries to come.

Two other stories that fall into a natural pairing are "Miss Havisham Regrets" by Marcia Talley and "A Long and Constant Courtship" by Carolyn Wheat. They both draw on characters from *Great Expectations,* but in entirely different ways, which shows how supple is the imagination of a writer, and how immortal are Dickens's original men and women. Miss Havisham in particular has passed into legend. It is hard to think that she did not really live, except in the minds of countless people: readers, actors, scriptwriters, and viewers. She is the embodiment of loss frozen in time. See a different side of her in Marcia Talley's alternative ending to *Great Expectations,* one which you may find you like very much.

"A Long and Constant Courtship" presents a different answer to Estella's origins, subtle, powerful, and filled with horror, sacrifice, and love. It is one I think you will go back to many times in memory, and still find intense satisfaction in it.

"Death in Dover" by P. N. Elrod harks back to a far earlier time, even before the French Revolution and the beginning of *A Tale of Two Cities.* A young Lucy Manette is taking a carriage ride to Dover and stops at an inn where remarkable things happen. I will not tell you who the detective is, or his clever observation that solves the crime, but you have no romance in your heart if it does not bring a smile to your lips. Ah—what fun it is to write stories!

"A Tale of One City" is my own contribution. I hardly need to tell you it is set in Paris during the French Revolution. What else could it be? It is a period I love, and any excuse to write a story there is good enough for me. Sydney Carton is my protagonist, unwilling hero, as seemed to be his fate. However, this is earlier than his great sacrifice, and he survives this adventure, in spite of barely missing the murder of Jean-Paul Marat (not a mystery to anyone, even at the time) and coming face-to-face with Maximilien Robespierre, the "Sea-green Incorruptible," and contriving to use him for his own ends.

We have all had a lot of fun, and I hope Dickens would excuse our liberties with his characters, his stories, and indeed with himself, all in the cause of further entertaining the reader and keeping his creations, his city, and his times alive.

Please enjoy it with us.

A Stake of Holly

BY LILLIAN STEWART CARL

Lillian Stewart Carl has published multiple novels and multiple short stories in multiple genres, ranging from fantasy novels like the Sabazel series to mystery, fantasy, and romance blends like *Memory and Desire* and *Lucifer's Crown*. More stories and novels are in the pipeline, but she's pretty much run out of genres. Since she particularly enjoys ghost stories—*Publishers Weekly* calls her *Shadows in Scarlet* ". . . an immensely readable tale . . . with some interesting twists on the ghostly romantic suspense novel"—she naturally chose Dickens's *A Christmas Carol* as her point of departure. She lives in Texas with her long-suffering spouse, in a book-lined cloister cleverly disguised as a tract house.

J ACOB MARLEY HAD been dead as a doornail, to begin with, and soon Ebenezer Scrooge would no longer be debating just why a doornail, rather than a coffin nail, was considered a fatal bit of iron-mongery.

Tim Cratchit bent over his benefactor's bed—it was his deathbed, but Tim was not yet ready to admit to that awful fact—Tim bent over Scrooge's wasted features and said, "You sent for me, sir?"

Scrooge's eyes fluttered open and took a long moment to focus, as though they were already inspecting the new world to which they were bound. Then they lit with a pleasure that plumped the deep furrows in his face and tinged its ashen color with pink. "Tim, my lad. Always a good lad, aren't you?"

"Thanks to you, sir." The young man pulled a chair, lately abandoned by the nurse, closer to the bed and sat down. "Your generosity to my family these nineteen years . . ."

Laboriously Scrooge waved his hand in the air and let it fall back to the counterpane. It made a thump no louder than that of thistledown. "What right have I to demand thanks for going about my business as a steward of mankind and fulfilling my responsibility to my neighbor?"

"Still," Tim insisted, "I owe you not only my health and my education, but my position with Lord Ector."

"No, no, no, pass your gratitude on to someone else. Teach your children. . . . But I assume you will be blessed with offspring, even though you as yet have no prospects?"

Tim ducked his handsome features shyly. "I shall find a wife, never you fear, Mr. Scrooge. I don't spend all my time cataloging Ector's collections."

"No, you spend your spare hours scribbling stories."

"Only the occasional tale for *The London Illustrated News* and the like."

"And fine tales they are, Tim. Take care, though, not to neglect the finer sentiments." The old man wheezed a moment, then coughed. "I was once engaged to be married, Tim."

Tim, having heard this story many times before, nodded patiently.

"Belle Fezziwig, she was, daughter of my old employer. I let her slip through my fingers, for I preferred the touch of gold to that of a human hand."

"Such was the curse of Midas," murmured Tim.

The apron-swathed nurse clattered about the room, building up the fire and making mysterious motions with vials, spoons, and porringers. "Don't be tiring him out now, young sir. He needs his rest, he does."

"Bah," muttered Scrooge. "Before long I'll have rest aplenty. We all come to the grave in the end, as the ghost, the Spirit of Christmas Yet to Come, reminded me. I can only hope that my efforts these last years have shortened the heavy chain I once dragged behind me and ensured that my death will be remarked upon with grief, not indifference, and never pleasure."

Tim had heard that story as well. Indeed, he remembered his own part in it as vividly as any occurrence of his childhood. Scrooge claimed to have been visited one icy Christmas Eve first by the ghost of his old partner, Marley, and then by three mysterious spirits, who had thawed his cold heart and softened his flinty disposition. Tim would have thought the story merely a fancy on the old man's part, save that Scrooge was the least fanciful man in the city of London. Save that Scrooge had manifestly changed his ways that Christmas, to the benefit of all.

"You sent for me, sir?" Tim repeated, sensing that his patron had matters burdening his sensibilities far and beyond the usual courtesies and reminiscences.

"Yes, so I did. Tim, I'd like for you to do something for me."

"With pleasure, sir."

"The three spirits, the Ghost of Christmas Past with its white dress and the jet of light springing from its head, the Ghost of Christmas Present, a jolly giant, the Ghost of Christmas Yet to Come, shrouded in a black hood. Were they dreams, thrown up not from a feverish but from a frozen mind? Or were they truly visions from another dimension of this familiar world?"

Scrooge's talonlike hand seized upon Tim's, with its ink-stained forefinger. "The ghost of my old partner Marley told me this: that if a man's spirit does not walk abroad among his fellow men in life, then it must do so after death. And, conversely, that a spirit working kindly in this little sphere of Earth will find its mortal life too short for its vast means of usefulness."

"There are the spirits paying penance," said Tim, elucidating the old man's words, "and those whose generosity of temper persists beyond the grave."

"Marley was one of the former. He told me this himself. But what of the other three ghosts? What events in their mortal lives sent them to me? Soon I, too, shall be a spirit among spirits. I would like to seek out those who came to me, and thank them most humbly for their efforts. I must know, Tim, who they were in life."

Tim had barely begun to digest this strange request when he felt a presence at his back, the bulk of the nurse looming over him like a great warship under full sail bearing down upon a dinghy. "Begging your pardon, sir . . ."

"Yes, Mrs. Gump?"

"If you're wanting to contact the spiritual world, there's none better at it than Mrs. Minnow in Bedford Square."

"A medium?" Tim asked. "I know that even Her Majesty has employed spiritualists, endeavoring to speak with her late consort, Prince Albert, but still . . ."

Scrooge's hand tightened upon his, grasping the young man's warm flesh as it had once grasped at gold coins, but to much greater effect. "Tim, I know not if this Mrs. Minnow could be of help to you, and through you to me, but if you please . . ."

"Yes," said Tim, setting aside his qualms as unworthy of both mentor and student. "Yes, of course. I shall do everything in my power to answer your questions, Mr. Scrooge."

"Bless you, my boy." Releasing Tim's hand, the old man settled back onto his pillow. The blush drained from his cheeks, leaving them the color of cold gruel. Still he smiled gently, even affectionately, up at his bedcurtains.

Tim took his leave, and walked out into a swirl of snowflakes with less spring in his step than steely determination in his soul.

*   *   *

Mrs. Minnow's parlor was all respectability. Not one hint of either charnel house or circus detracted from the sprigged wallpaper, the ponderous rosewood furniture, the circular table draped with a paisley-pattern shawl. The lady herself resembled a doll clothed in taffeta. When she told Tim to join those seated at the table, he did, even though he would have had more confidence in the spiritualist if either her apartments or her person had offered evidence of things, if not unseen, at least unsuspected.

With a sly silken rustle, Mrs. Minnow turned the flame in the oil lamp down to the smallest of flickers. "Let us all join hands," she instructed, putting her words into effect by taking Tim's right hand in her own soft grasp. He felt as though he were holding a mite of warm bread dough.

He allowed the bewhiskered gentleman on his left to clasp his other hand, and strained his eyes through the wintry gloom, but could see only shadows and implications, gray writ upon gray.

Another crinkle of fabric, and Mrs. Minnow began to murmur softly in what might or might not have been the Queen's English. She could as well have been summoning a waiter as summoning spirits, Tim thought. . . .

A sudden swish in the air above the table, and a spatter of ice-cold water droplets sent a ripple of surprise around its periphery. Like the gentleman on his left, Tim jerked in surprise. Mrs. Minnow did not.

The odor of pine boughs freshly cut in a snowy field came to Tim's nose. A masculine voice reached his ears, although it seemed to issue from the female shape to his right. "There is someone here who remembers a Christmas Eve long ago."

After a long pause Tim found his voice. "Ah—yes."

"I see a lad," said the voice, "a small boy with a crutch, sitting before a fireplace."

Now, how did Mrs. Minnow know of this? For a moment Tim entertained the thought that Scrooge and his nurse and Mrs. Minnow herself were conspiring in an elaborate joke at his own expense. But if so, why?

In for a penny, in for a pound, he told himself, and directed the— the spirit guide—to speak of Scrooge's past, not his own. "I was that boy. That I survived, nay prospered, and have achieved hale manhood I owe to a benefactor. It is on his behalf that I come here today. He is searching for the identity of three, er, friends who once did him the greatest of good turns."

Another silence. Then the voice, tentative now, as though pondering, said, "Fezziwig. Arthur Fezziwig."

"I beg your pardon?"

"Of Fezziwig's Chandlery, supplier of goods to His Majesty's Navy during the French wars."

Tim knew quite well the name of Scrooge's former employer, Belle's father. Again and again had the old man spoken of the Christmas parties held in Fezziwig's warehouse, of how much joy he and his fellow apprentice Dick Wilkins had found there, of how Belle had refused to dance with anyone but young Ebenezer Scrooge—difficult as it was to conceive of a man so withered by age ever being flush with youth. What Tim did not know was whether Mrs. Minnow or her spirit guide meant to name Scrooge's employer as one of his ghosts.

"If Arthur Fezziwig is one of my benefactor's friends," Tim asked, "then who are the other two?"

"Fezziwig's Chandlery," said the voice. "Christmas Eve. A pudding soaked in brandy and set ablaze. A sprig of holly. The gleam of gold."

Tim leaned forward, and the spongy hand in his drew him back. Mrs. Minnow's own feminine voice said, "You have had your answer, sir."

"But . . ." Tim began, and then stopped, sensible of the other ears ranged about the table.

A wobbly note of music sounded near the ceiling of the room, not the last trumpet, certainly, but one that was near to expiring. Again the male voice spoke from Mrs. Minnow's lips. "There is someone here who has recently lost a beloved brother."

The gentleman with the luxuriant whiskers stirred and spoke. "Yes, yes. Dreadful accident it was, the poor soul burned to a cinder in his rooms."

"Spiritous liquors," intoned the ghostly voice. "Fumes and fire."

Resisting the urge to inquire just which liquors were consumed by spirits, Tim retired into his own thoughts. If Scrooge's partner Marley could return from the grave to assist him, then why not Arthur Fezziwig? That, at least, Tim could credit. But a pudding garnished with holly, and the gleam of gold—if those were clues, they were maddeningly slender ones.

Fezziwig's Chandlery, though. There was a place, a time, and a person. While Tim very much doubted he had any answers as yet, he now had more specific questions.

The gleam of sunlight on the new-fallen snow made even the dirty, dingy streets of London shine as brightly as the streets of heaven. Each windowpane seemed to Tim to be gilded like the illuminated manuscripts in Lord Ector's library. Soon it would be Christmas yet again.

Passing beneath the weathered old signboard reading *Scrooge and Cratchit,* he opened the door to the countinghouse offices. There was his father, sitting at his desk, a ledger book open before him. Tim remembered how thin and careworn the man had once been, for many years supporting his family on fifteen bob a week, until at last Scrooge had his change of heart, raised his salary, and in time made him a full partner in the firm.

Now it was his hair that was thin, above a face lined with age, not care. Still, Tim could not remember a time when Bob Cratchit had not displayed a cheerful and confident disposition.

"It does my heart good to see you, Tim," said the old man, greeting his son with a clap on his shoulder. "Why, but for Mr. Scrooge I might not have you to see, and for that I am grateful not only at Christmas Eve, but on every day of the year. How fares our benefactor?"

"Not well. I fear his days have grown short."

Bob's face contracted to a pinpoint of sorrow and resignation mingled. "I wish there were some service we could render him, here at the end."

"There is," said Tim, and acquainted his father with Scrooge's request, and with the step he had already taken to fulfill it.

Bob tossed Tim's tale from thought to thought, then said gravely, "I remember when Scrooge saw Christmas merely as the one day of the year he could turn no profit. It was that same fateful Christmas Eve that I heard him say, 'If I could work my will, every idiot who goes about with Merry Christmas on his lips should be boiled with his own pudding and buried with a stake of holly through his heart.'"

"He tempted fate, then," said Tim, "and summoned the spirits with his own words."

"And yet, just what spirits were they? A fine question, an apt question. Surely, to have had such a profound impact on Scrooge's disposition, these ghosts were indeed friends and acquaintances, as you suggest."

"No, as Mrs. Minnow and her spirit guide suggest." Tim looked about the offices, shabby still. His gaze settled upon the ledgers mounting higher and higher up a tall shelf, until the topmost row of books made a veritable Himalayan peak of dust and cobwebs. "What happened to Arthur Fezziwig, Father? His business failed, didn't it?"

"Yes. With the defeat of Napoleon and the ending of the French wars the demand for his goods dropped away, and new means of production superseded the old ones to which he clung, as we all cling to that which is familiar. Fezziwig died impoverished in wealth but not in spirit, or so I heard."

"Aha," said Tim.

"Scrooge, I believe, considered his employer's fate to be a cautionary tale, and so made his fortune not by selling goods susceptible to spoilage and changes in taste, but by dealing in properties and making loans. Always he felt the shadow of insolvency looming over him, even though he had funds enough to buy and sell a business like Fezziwig's Chandlery ten times over."

"Could it be, then, that Scrooge's engagement to Belle Fezziwig was broken off because her father had been unable to bequeath her a dowry?"

"I believe so, although I doubt if even Scrooge at his most avaricious would have stated that so bluntly."

"Did Belle ever marry?"

"Oh, yes. After his miraculous transformation—and if ghosts or spirits were instrumental in that transformation, then it must truly have been miraculous . . ."

Tim smiled his agreement.

". . . Scrooge asked me to seek her out, to discover if she needed his assistance. But it was too late." Bob sat down in his chair, frowning slightly and drumming his fingertips upon his ledger. "What was her husband's name? Oh, yes, James Redlaw. He called in here one night, a full seven years before Scrooge's metamorphosis, seeking to borrow against his property and thereby pay his debts. But that was the night Jacob Marley lay at the point of death. Redlaw revealed a greater delicacy of feeling than Scrooge himself by going away without transacting his business."

"So Belle's husband also found himself a broken man?"

"Not only in finance, but in health—he died the next year, I'm told. In losing her father and then her husband, Mrs. Redlaw was obliged to support herself and her daughter on very little income. I can only suppose, then, that she despaired of this world and all too soon was taken up into the next." Bob shook his head sadly.

"When you went searching for her, you discovered that she was dead."

"Yes, and under most unfortunate and mysterious circumstances, although I don't know the full story. When I acquainted Scrooge with this fact, he said something about having seen her in his vision, well and happy with her family, and so he hoped that she was, indeed, in that bourn from which no traveler ever returns."

"Well, then," said Tim, properly saddened by the circumstances, and yet, at the same time, wondering if his clue had disintegrated in his hands like the ashes of a Yule log on Boxing Day. "What of Belle's daughter?"

"I believe she went into service, as a governess in the house of Sir Charles Pumphrey, the financier."

Another man of business, Tim thought. The gleam of gold did indeed illuminate his quest, although what the blazing pudding illuminated, he had not the least idea.

Still, perhaps he had made some progress. If Arthur Fezziwig had been one of Scrooge's spirits, then perhaps his unfortunate daughter Belle had also been. "I shall pay a visit to the Pumphrey household," Tim told his father.

"Very good. And may I suggest you also call on your brother Peter? The lawyer with whom he has partnered himself has worked for many years with properties, deeds, and wills—although I hope to heaven they are not chaining themselves behind him, as they did to poor Mr. Marley. There you may well learn more about the Fezziwigs and the Redlaws than I can tell you."

"Then so I shall." With a firm grasp of his father's hand—strange, how that hand was growing so increasingly frail—Tim settled his hat upon his head and his feet upon the icy pavement.

* * *

At the sound of feminine footsteps, Tim turned away from the black marble chimneypiece and its clock enclosed by a glass dome, as though time, like a jewel displayed in a shopkeeper's window, were a valuable commodity alloted only to those who could afford it instead of meted out to all humanity to use or abuse at will.

"Do I have the honor of addressing Miss Redlaw?" Tim asked the elegant woman who entered the parlor, the white square of his card seeming tarnished against the alabaster of her hand.

"I was once Miss Redlaw," she answered. "Now I am Mrs. Pumphrey. You are fortunate, Mr. Cratchit, that the servant who answered your knock has been in our employ long enough to know my former identity."

So the governess was now mistress of the house, Tim told himself. Had she married the Pumphrey's only son, and so restored herself to the position in life to which she had been born? Such an event seemed likely—her face and form, even in mature years, held just such a blushing beauty as he had always envisioned in Belle Fezziwig's. But that was one question he saw little chance of asking.

He sank onto the chair that Mrs. Pumphrey indicated. When she had spread her voluminous skirts across a horsehair sofa—which movement released a scent of spring lilac into the air—he identified himself, detailed his family's relationship to Ebenezer Scrooge, sketched out Scrooge's story of the three ghosts, and recited the results of his researches so far.

Save for a slight creasing of her brow, Mrs. Pumphrey's delicate features did not move for several ticks of the mantelpiece clock. Perhaps, Tim thought, she would condemn him for his effrontery in asking questions about her family. Perhaps she would order the servant who had seen him here to show him hence.

At last her pink lips parted. "I commend you for visiting

Mrs. Minnow. She has afforded me invaluable assistance by contacting the spirit of my grandfather Fezziwig, who is as hearty on the astral plane as he was here on Earth."

Tim made sure Mrs. Pumphrey did not notice the quick relaxation of his posture, and the sigh of relief that escaped his throat.

"As for my mother and father—well, as you perhaps already know, there is a tragic story. How it cheers me to know that they, too, are well and happy in the great beyond!"

"And perhaps Mr. Fezziwig and Mrs. Redlaw," Tim hinted in Scrooge's words, "after working kindly in this little sphere of Earth, find their mortal life too short for their vast means of usefulness."

"Yes," she said, coloring prettily, "I do believe so. You see, Mr. Cratchit, my mother regretted breaking her engagement to Mr. Scrooge, because, she said, if she had been his wife, she could perhaps have modified his miserly ways. And yet if she had been Mrs. Scrooge, she would never have been Mrs. Redlaw."

"It is a paradox," said Tim.

"But that was my mother, always thinking of others even when her—when our—position became dire. After my father passed over, Mother and I were reduced to the income from one rental property, a public house, and the interest from several India bonds. Still, though, there were others less fortunate then we, and Mother made sure that what we little we had, we shared."

Tim, having told himself that the ladies' income had no doubt been greater than fifteen bob a week, now congratulated himself for not stating this aloud.

"We took lodgings in a house owned by Dick Wilkins. Is that name familiar to you?"

"Why, yes," Tim said, sitting up straighter. "Was he not one of Mr. Fezziwig's apprentices and a boyhood friend of Mr. Scrooge's?"

The lady nodded, setting her curls to dancing. "That he was. Grandfather Fezziwig helped Mr. Wilkins establish a weaving mill, dyeworks, and clothing manufactory, which first supplied uniforms to our troops fighting the Corsican, Bonaparte, and then went on to provide ready-made clothes to all classes of folk. While Grandfather's business failed, Mr. Wilkins's prospered. As an old family friend, my mother was quite pleased when he offered her lodgings in his house."

"He rented out rooms?"

"Yes," Mrs. Pumphrey said, a slight edge entering her voice. "By this time he owned many properties, and lived with his wife Theodora—a foreign person she was, with the exotic beauty of a Gypsy—in a house that had once been a lovely villa, but which he had subdivided into many small flats, the better to turn a profit, I believe."

The gleam of gold, Tim repeated to himself, but said nothing.

The edge in Mrs. Pumphrey's voice was taking on the sharpness of that serpent's tooth mentioned in Scripture as belonging to a thankless child. And yet neither she nor her mother, Tim thought, was the person of whom she was thinking.

"Mr. Wilkins persuaded my mother to sell him her properties and bonds, in return for which he guaranteed her an annuity for life. The bargain was fair, she felt. What she did not realize—what none of us, mercifully, realize—is how soon one's life can end."

"What happened?" asked Tim, dreading her answer.

"My mother was found burned to a cinder, in her bed one Christmas morning."

Tim searched for some appropriate response, and found only a simple, "I am so very sorry."

Mrs. Pumphrey looked down into her lap, where her fair hands—white as the garment of the first ghost—were tearing Tim's card into shreds. "Mr. and Mrs. Wilkins put it about that my mother, in her despair, had turned to drink, for such spontaneous burnings do happen to those besotted with alcohol."

With spiritous liquors, thought Tim, realizing suddenly that Mrs. Minnow had been speaking not only to the gentleman with the whiskers but to himself. He should, no doubt, have kept an open mind and paid closer attention.

"My dear mother, though, while having her moments of despair, was still inclined to the positive outlook of the Fezziwig disposition, and took only the occasional glass of sherry." The lady lay the shreds of the card upon a marble-topped table and folded her hands. "Yes, Mother suffered from a cold that Christmas Eve. Mrs. Wilkins provided a counterpane from her own storage chest for Mother's bed, and smelling salts to clear the congestion in her throat that had rendered her speechless. But Mother took no drink, not one drop beyond the brandy soaking her portion of plum pudding."

"Was there an inquiry made?"

"The police made a brief inquiry, but brushed the matter aside, wishing to spare my feelings, they said, and those of the Wilkins family."

"But you suspect the Wilkins of taking some action to bring about your mother's death?"

"Indeed, while manifestly Mr. and Mrs. Wilkins profited by my mother's death, there are no means by which they could have accomplished it. I myself saw my mother alive, if not well, when I carried her pudding into her room on Christmas Eve, and I myself was breakfasting with the Wilkinses on Christmas morning when the maidservant came rushing in with her terrible intelligence."

Tim eyed the lady's bowed head with its trembling curls. So Belle had indeed died in unfortunate and mysterious circumstances, as his father had heard. Now he understood, with ghastly certainty, why it was that Scrooge's first ghost, the Ghost of Christmas Past, had appeared illuminated by a flame.

Collecting herself with a little shudder, Mrs. Pumphrey turned a wan smile upon her guest. "You may well ask, Mr. Cratchit, whether I have ever inquired of my mother, through Mrs. Minnow's spirit guide, exactly how she came to die."

Yes, Tim might well have asked that, had he not been reluctant to disturb the lady's sensibilities even further.

"To that, I can provide no answer, for my mother has spoken only of flames shooting suddenly up, and of merciful oblivion. I have more than once chided myself for not staying with her that evening, and yet there were guests downstairs and she gestured, smiling, for me to join them, and then, still smiling, reached for her bedside taper to light her plum pudding and make her own solitary celebration."

Tim sat in silent horror at the scene that rose before his eyes.

Clearing her throat, Mrs. Pumphrey went stoutly on, "I take great comfort in my mother's present happy circumstances, no matter how difficult her transition to them. And in her name my husband and I have provided for many charities."

The parlor door opened, admitting a young woman so fair, so charming, that her mother with all her comeliness seemed reduced to a crone before Tim's eyes. He stared, then remembered his manners and leaped to his feet.

Mrs. Pumphrey's eye glittered perhaps from unshed tears, or perhaps from maternal calculation. "Mr. Cratchit, may I present my daughter Annabelle."

"Miss Pumphrey." Making his most accomplished obeisance, Tim wondered if—Annabelle, what a lovely name—if she heard the sudden twang of Cupid's bow just as surely as he did. And yet how could he dare hope that such a lovely, nay such a stupendously beautiful, young lady could look with favor upon him?

She curtsied, the color rising past her exquisitely formed lips into her cheeks. A rose would surely have hung its head in shame at a comparison. "Mr. Cratchit," she said, in a voice resembling the song of a lark, "I trust you'll forgive me for listening outside the door. I am most impressed by the compassion of your quest, and would assist you in any way I can in its fulfillment."

Tim would have forgiven her for plunging a dagger into his heart.

"Perhaps," he said through his teeth, quelling a stammer, "you will permit me to call upon you again, so that I may share with you my discoveries. . . ." What discoveries he made, he told himself. If he knew she was waiting to hear them, he would make them, no doubt about it.

"How kind of you," Annabelle said.

Her mother rose. "And now, Mr. Cratchit, I'm sure you will want to continue making your inquiries."

Tim found himself floating down the front steps of the house in a trance—odd, how icy winter had suddenly turned balmy as spring. . . . Unbidden, his feet made their way toward the law offices of William Janders, Esquire.

Peter Cratchit regarded his younger brother's air of general discombobulation and laughed. "Who is she, then?"

Tim found he was, after all, capable of stringing words together and telling the tale yet again, this time appending its most recent chapter. Peter's expression went from laughter to bemusement to astonishment. At last he emitted a long whistle. "So you think old Fezziwig and Belle are two of Scrooge's ghosts, eh?"

"I suspect Belle of being the Ghost of Christmas Past with its crown of flame," Tim replied. "I suspect her father, Fezziwig, of being the Ghost of Christmas Present, for by all accounts he was a hearty soul who loved to celebrate the holiday."

"And the Ghost of Christmas Yet to Come?" asked Peter. "Who was, if I'm remembering the old man's tale aright, a much more sinister figure, hooded in black."

"That is where you come in, brother, you and your esteemed senior partner Mr. Janders. Can we trace these properties that Belle— Mrs. Redlaw—made over to Dick Wilkins, only to die so conveniently soon thereafter?"

"Why, yes." Peter conducted Tim into the next chamber, the book-lined office of William Janders, Esquire, himself.

The man's thick gray eyebrows, like caterpillars, lofted up his brow as though they would crawl onto the sleek hairless dome of his head and there set up housekeeping. "Well, then," he said, upon being familiarized with the facts of the matter, "there's no need to delve into the record books. I remember the case quite well. It all happened when I was but a clerk writing law in these very offices, younger and more junior than you are now, Peter."

"Pray tell me what you know," Tim asked politely, envisioning making his successful report not only to Scrooge but to the delectable Miss Pumphrey.

"The circumstances of Mrs. Redlaw's death were peculiar, quite peculiar. Spontaneous combustion is a well-known effect of excess drink, but, being a lady of fine breeding, she was hardly given to imbibing. Still, nothing could be proved."

That was as Mrs. Pumphrey had said, thought Tim.

"What is exceedingly interesting," Janders went on, "is that the next year Dick Wilkins was brought up on charges of murder."

Peter and Tim exchanged a significant glance.

"The circumstances were similar, save that this time the dead woman was a spinster. Again, though, she was of good family and modest property, which she had made over to her landlord, Wilkins. Her death was very obviously caused by poison. Poison in the plum pudding."

"Murder is vile enough," Tim exclaimed, "but to use an instrument of celebration in the commission of a murder!"

"Was Wilkins convicted of the crime?" asked Peter.

Janders nodded affirmatively. "That he was. And yet it was not he who prepared and served the pudding, and who then nursed the ailing woman until she died. There was some talk of charging his wife as well, but since wives are weak and subject to their husband's will, she was never tried. Not that Mrs. Wilkins struck me as being weak-willed, no, on the contrary."

Peter swallowed a chuckle, but not at this tale of murder most foul, Tim thought. Their mother was the strongest woman he knew, and Peter's own wife ruled their household firmly but fairly. There was something in the set of Miss Pumphrey's chin, Tim added silently, that told him she, too, was a woman to be reckoned with. As, in a very different way, no doubt, was Mrs. Wilkins.

"Dick Wilkins was hanged," Janders continued, "and without his guiding hand his business failed. I daresay he was guilty of abetting the murder, even initiating it. So justice was done. But as for the death of Mrs. Redlaw . . ."

"No charges could be brought because no one could prove that a murder had been done," said Peter.

"I am at as great a loss in the matter as you are." Janders took up his pen and dipped it in the fine brass inkwell that sat upon his desk. "Now, Peter, Tim, you will excuse me. . . ."

"Just one more question, please, sir," said Tim. "Do you remember Mrs. Wilkins's Christian name? Was she an Englishwoman?"

Janders considered a moment, tapping his nose with his pen. "Theodora, her name was. Yes, she was as English as you or me, but I do believe her father was a native of Greece. She was quite lovely, very young, with jet-black tresses and flashing eyes."

"Thank you."

Peter took Tim by the collar and steered him through the doorway and into the outer office. There he said, "There's a proper tragedy for you. Poor Belle! Scrooge will not be pleased to hear of her fate."

"No. And yet . . ." Tim's brows knit tightly. "Do you suppose that the visit of her and her father's ghosts to Scrooge had more than one purpose, not only to show him the error of his ways but to reveal the truth of her death? Her murder?"

"But how could the truth be revealed?"

"I wonder," Tim said, as his thoughts moved reluctantly from Annabelle Pumphrey's lovely face to the open page of a book in Lord Ector's library. *Christmas Eve. A pudding soaked in brandy and set ablaze . . .*

He took his leave of Peter and went back out into the cold afternoon air, this time directing his steps toward Ector House.

Lord Ector reminded Tim of an eagle, with his arched nose and small dark eyes always alert, whether to the movement of a mouse in the grass or to a ripple among England's allies in the east, no matter.

Now he turned from positioning yet another marble bust of some ancient worthy upon a pedestal in his library and answered Tim's question. "Yes, when I served as a diplomat in Turkey I did hear stories of the *tunica molesta,* the fiery cloak that brought the hero Heracles to his death."

"If I remember the story," said Tim, holding a step stool so that His Lordship might safely regain terra firma, "the burning cloth clung to him and could not be removed, nor could the flames be doused by water, so that he burned to a cinder."

"Indeed."

"But surely this story is only legend."

"Not at all," returned Ector. "You have heard of the Greek fire employed by the ancients—a mixture of quicklime, sulfur, naphtha, and saltpeter, that would cling to, say, an enemy's ship and only burn the fiercer when wetted."

Tim nodded, even as he tried not to let his imagination dwell too long on images of flowing, clinging, unquenchable flames. "And this chemical process could be applied to cloth?"

"Cloth is manufactured using the same ingredients: dyes and pigments can be made from sulfur and petroleum and fixed with a mordant of quicklime. Tar is used as a waterproofing agent. If such materials were ready to hand, one with knowledge of the ancient formula could impregnate a cloth with petroleum, sulfur, and lime. If it were stored away from the air . . ."

"In a chest," Tim murmured.

". . . it might well ignite at a very low temperature and continue to burn even when wet."

"And if the cloth were a counterpane say, covering a woman incapable of crying out for assistance—ah, what a diabolical plan!"

Ector would not have regarded Tim so quizzically had he started to speak in tongues. "A diabolical plan? Do you mean to say someone has committed murder using this infernal Greek recipe?"

"Yes, yes—the key to the murder is that it took place on Christmas Eve, when either a flaming pudding or the candle used to light it set the counterpane ablaze. The scheme would certainly turn upon Belle being alone in her room at the moment of conflagration. . . . Ah, yes. The guests downstairs would have insured that she was." Tim dashed his right fist into his left hand. "They even thought to provide smelling salts, to cover the odor of the chemicals in the cloth, which had, I'm sure, been manufactured in their own establishment. A clever scheme, but the circumstances did not favor its execution twice, and so did he—they, the souls of avarice—attempt a variation that worked less successfully."

"My dear fellow," said Ector, laying a restraining hand upon Tim's arm, "either you have quite lost your wits, or you have some wonderful tale to tell me—and no doubt, in time, to tell your readers."

"Yes, my lord, I shall most certainly tell all. And yet the tale is not finished, not quite yet."

Between his father's ledger books and his brother's legal documents, it took Tim only a day to trace Theodora Wilkins to a poor lodging house.

The old woman admitted him to her room, then seated herself beside a small fire, no more than a few coals piled upon a dirty hearth—the remains of another victim? Tim asked himself caustically.

Her beauty had long ago been sacrificed to age. Now her hair was sparse and drab, and she was as wizened as though she had gnawed nothing but the bones of avarice these long years. Reaching for the container of grog that was warming in the ashes, she drank deeply. The reek of the cheap liquor seared Tim's nose. He wondered whether she had used expensive brandy to soak Belle's pudding, and whether she had ever wished she had drunk it instead.

"Have a care," he told her. "You have heard of what happens to those who drink too freely, and then expose themselves to fire."

"Bah," she said. Her voice was like the scrape of bare branches across a windowpane.

A basket beside her chair overflowed with scraps of cloth and packets of thread and needles, leading Tim to deduce that she eked out a meager living stitching and mending. "You have always worked with cloth," he said. "Did you once make a counterpane for a woman named Belle Redlaw, who lodged with you and your—late husband?"

"What is it to you?"

"I am a friend of Mrs. Redlaw's friends and family. Her death was—mysterious. I'd like to know the truth of how it came to happen."

"She drank herself to death," Mrs. Wilkins said, and began to cough as rackingly as though she expelled smoke from her lungs.

Tim asked himself why he had come here. Did he hope to hear a confession? What if he did? What difference could it make, now? He felt sure that he stood looking at a murderess, and yet it was not his place to judge, either in this life or in the hereafter. For her crimes against humanity, Theodora Wilkins was now suffering the sharp bite of loneliness and poverty. He could do nothing else to her.

He could, however, do something for her. Had not Belle's ghost, and her father's, and yes, Dick Wilkins's dark ghost as well, carried a message of pity and compassion from the next world into this?

From his pocket Tim produced a gold coin. He held it in his hand a moment, warming it, then laid it down upon the mantelpiece. The beldame's rheumy eyes flicked upward, so that he could almost see the gleam of gold reflected in them. "Merry Christmas," he said, and left the chill, acrid air of the room for the frosty air of the city street.

The vapor of his breath hung in the air before him like a ghost. The windows of even the meanest shop and lowliest hovel glowed with a rosy, anticipatory light. Tomorrow would be Christmas Eve. He would join his brothers and sisters, by blood and by marriage, and they would raise a glass to Scrooge, the founder of the feast. And yes, they would eat plum pudding ablaze in brandy, with a sprig of holly adorning its round and savory top.

The bells of Christmas morning were pealing, setting the bedcurtains to shivering delightfully, like children first sighting their Christmas presents. And indeed, Scrooge had almost returned to a childlike state, opening his mouth trustingly as Mrs. Gump spooned gruel into it.

The nurse's gaze met Tim's. *Not much longer,* it said.

Behind him stood his father, and Scrooge's nephew and his wife, all kitted out in their Sunday best, for it was, after all, Christmas Day.

Scrooge tried to wave his hand and succeeded only in twitching his finger. Mrs. Gump, though, understood his meaning. Wiping his face with a corner of her apron, she vacated her chair.

Tim stepped closer to the bed. "I have the answer to your question, Mr. Scrooge. I know who your ghosts were. Who they are."

The old man's pale face seemed infinitesimally to brighten. His eyes turned in their sockets to where Tim stood. "Tim," he whispered. "Always a good lad, Tiny Tim."

Tim forebore to comment on his present height, but simply folded it onto the chair. He took Scrooge's hand between his own, gently, for it was as thin as a bird's wing. Slowly the old man's cold flesh began to warm. "The Ghost of Christmas Past," Tim told him, "of your past, is Belle Fezziwig. Belle Redlaw, as she was when she died. She is the spirit of former joys and former regrets."

"Ah," said Scrooge, summoning a blissful smile. "Belle."

"The Ghost of Christmas Present is Arthur Fezziwig, her father, the robust spirit of both gratitude and reproof. The spirit of every Christmas that has past and is yet to come."

"Fine old fellow, Fezziwig." Scrooge sighed, his smile abating only briefly.

"The Ghost of Christmas Yet to Come is your old friend Dick Wilkins. He was consumed by greed, sadly, and died with the black hood of the condemned criminal upon his head. Perhaps, though, by helping you his spirit was redeemed."

Scrooge's lips tightened to a narrow slit. "Poor old Dick. If only he had been visited by three spirits, as I was so fortunate to have been."

Tim nodded. "I have this very afternoon been invited to call upon Miss Annabelle Pumphrey, Belle's granddaughter, in whom Belle's beauty and compassion live on. I intend to take your advice, sir, and not neglect the finer sentiments."

"Good. We were not meant to be alone in this world, Tim." His hand twitched feebly.

Behind Tim's back Mrs. Gump was chatting with Scrooge's niece, a woman of sprightly disposition and great interest in the doings of mankind: "I heard it on my way here this morning, madam. The poor woman went at her pudding so greedy she ate the sprig of holly stuck in its top and choked to death upon it."

Tim glanced round. Of all the women in the city of London, surely . . .

"Her name was Wilkins, too, so I hear. Dead as a doornail, the undertaker said, as sure as though someone had driven a stake through her heart."

"Not now," said Scrooge's niece, quelling the nurse's gossip.

Too late. Tim looked down at his strong young hands cradling Scrooge's blue-veined and fragile one. Had those same hands, then, brought justice at last to Theodora Wilkins, however unwittingly? Had she died—no. Even though she had died unredeemed, her spirit would now be walking abroad amongst her fellow human beings. Perhaps she would find peace at last, as her husband had done. As their victim had done.

Scrooge's eyes widened, beholding another vision. "I am light as a feather, I am as giddy as an angel, I am as merry as a schoolboy." His voice cracked and then steadied. "I hear old Fezziwig now: Clear away, Dick. Clear away Ebenezer. It's Christmas, a time to celebrate. . . . Why, Belle, you wish to dance with me? Gladly, my dear. Gladly."

Tim felt the others gathering close. Their hands, too, reached out for Scrooge's. He smiled, brilliantly. "God bless us, every . . ." And he sank back upon the pillow, giving up his own ghost.

Tears started in Tim's eyes. Carefully he laid Scrooge's hand down upon the clean white counterpane, and leaned his head back against his father's chest. Perhaps Scrooge would also find his mortal life too short to spread the compassion he had learned—and learned very well—nineteen years ago today.

"He would not think it sad to die upon Christmas Day," Bob said softly, pressing his son's shoulder. "Not Ebenezer Scrooge."

"No," said Tim. And in his heart he repeated the words that his own childish mouth had once uttered, as fine an epitaph as any man could wish: *God bless us, every one.*

Mr. Pickwick vs. the Body Snatchers

EDITED BY BILL CRIDER

Bill Crider is the author of more than fifty published novels and numerous short stories. He won the Anthony Award for "best first mystery novel" in 1987 for *Too Late to Die* and was nominated for the Shamus Award for "best first private-eye novel" for *Dead on the Island*. He and his wife, Judy, were nominated for an Anthony for their collaborative story "At the Hop," and they won the award in 2002 for their story "Chocolate Moose."

IN WHICH MR. SAMUEL PICKWICK, HAVING RETIRED FROM ADVENTURES, HAS ANOTHER ONE QUITE UNEXPECTEDLY.

"I wants to make your flesh creep."
—JOE, MR. WARDLE'S Servant in *Pickwick Papers*, CHAPTER 8

WHEN MR. SAMUEL Pickwick left his rooms at the George and Vulture to settle in the house he had chosen for himself in Dulwich, it was his firm intention to spend many quiet years in peaceful retirement and to go no more adventuring in the frivolous pursuit of novelty. But even a man of Mr. Pickwick's determination cannot remain idle forever, especially when within his breast there beats the heart of a man less than half his age. And so it was that Mr. Pickwick was quick to spring to the aid of his friend Mr. Wardle when called upon, though the cause was gruesome enough and the errand itself a still more grisly one.

But we are forgetting the true beginning of the adventure, which occurred some days earlier when Mr. Pickwick received a note from Mr. Wardle informing him of the death of that gentleman's mother, who had lived for many years at Dingley Dell and with whom Mr. Pickwick had enjoyed many a game of whist, during the course of which the old lady's impaired hearing would often improve immensely, especially if she were winning.

"And at the worst time of year for a death in the family, too," Mr. Pickwick said, brushing away a sympathetic tear, for it was the season of Christmas, that happy interval when the thoughts of most good Englishmen turn to feasting, merriment, hospitality, and the company of friends; when the Yule log burns brightly as the members of a scattered family gather once again around the table to remember the blest days of other years before the hairs on their heads were as white as the snows on the ground; when generosity and kindness abound. But had Mr. Pickwick thought further, he might have been reminded that Christmas is also a time of sad reflection when we remember those who can no longer join us around the fireside though we held their hands in ours only the shortest time ago; when we recall the bright eyes that shine no more for those who through them saw our cheerful smiles have now entered through the low doorway of the earthen house that awaits us all at the end of our journey; when we remember the jests and jollity of those who will laugh and jest no more.

"It's a worser time than you know," said Sam Weller, Mr. Pickwick's servant, whose own thoughts had turned to things far removed from the mind of his master. "The old 'un told me just the other day that the carters 'as carried some strange freight over the last few weeks, and it might be that some of it came from Dingley Dell."

Now Mr. Pickwick was well aware that by "the old 'un" Sam meant his father, the elder Mr. Weller. But as to the rest of Sam's meaning, Mr. Pickwick was completely in the dark.

"Pickle barrels that hadn't a pickle in 'em, if you take my meanin'," Sam said when Mr. Pickwick made his puzzlement plain.

"I do not take your meaning," Mr. Pickwick said. "In fact, your explanation has, if anything, left me more bewildered than before."

"I don't mean to be the cause any confoozlement," said Sam. "But the medical schools is in session, and 'tis the season for cuttin' things up, as the butcher said to the hog just before he slit its throat."

Mr. Pickwick understood then what Sam was getting at, and that excellent man was of course brought to a righteous rage by the thought of bodies being unlawfully exhumed for dissection by students even though he knew they needed to study the course of veins, the play of muscles, the connections of bones, and the sites of internal organs if they hoped to be surgeons or treat injuries.

"You cannot be suggesting," he said, "that the body of Mrs. Wardle might be wantonly disturbed by those creatures known as body snatchers! Why, the very thought is repugnant to any man of feeling."

"I don't know about feelin's," Sam replied, "but I know that when sack-'em-up men are after money, there's little that will stop them from gettin' it if it lies within their means to do it, no matter the shame attached to the way they go about it."

"I am afraid that you are correct, Sam, as much as it pains me to acknowledge the venality of my fellow man. That such a thing could happen in Dingley Dell, that has more than once been my haven from the cares of the world, is almost more than I can bear to contemplate. But it will not happen this time if it is in my power to prevent it."

"I don't know about the prewentin' on it," Sam said. "Just 'ow would you go about doin' that?"

"We shall see what we shall see," said Mr. Pickwick, and that was all he cared to say about the matter at the time.

Mrs. Wardle was buried in the cemetery beside the church she had attended for many years, and the service was eminently satisfactory. The weather was cold and clear, the mourners were dressed all in black, the minister read the psalm and said the proper words of comfort, and the dear departed was sent to what all those gathered there, and especially Mr. Pickwick, hoped to be her eternal rest with the good and the great, with dust to dust returning. Even the sexton, a man quite accustomed to death and funerals, wept. And to cap all, when the services were concluded and the funeral party was gathered at the home of Mr. Wardle, Mr. Snodgrass, once a noted Pickwickian and now married to Mr. Wardle's daughter Emily, declared his intention of writing a Shakespearean sonnet in honor of his wife's deceased grandmother. And although it is quite true that while Mr. Snodgrass had often declared his intention of writing a poem on this subject or that, no one had ever actually seen the result of his efforts, yet everyone was pleased to know that his empathetic soul had been so affected by the day's events that he was moved to poesy.

It must be noted, however, that even in such calming and comforting circumstances as the excellent meal of hot meats, cold meats, meat pies, bread, and boiled vegetables that awaited the funeral party on their return to Dingley Dell, not everyone appeared quite comfortable with the outcome of the rites so recently completed. Indeed, Mr. Wardle appeared to Mr. Pickwick to have a countenance that was even more troubled than the sad circumstances warranted.

"There was a person there," Mr. Wardle said when Mr. Pickwick questioned him about his apparent perturbation, "a person whom I did not know, a woman, heavily veiled, who walked all around the grave and talked closely with the sexton."

"But she was a person who knew your mother, surely," Mr. Pickwick said. "If not recently, then in happier days."

"That is possible," Mr. Wardle admitted, "but unlikely. My mother had lived with me here for many years without visitors beyond the family. I am afraid that the person I saw today was there to see if the grave might in any way be rigged out with a spring gun, or whether the plants were arranged in a particular way so that I could tell if they had been moved. In short, I fear she may have been a spy."

Mr. Pickwick did not have to ask for whom the woman might have been spying. His earlier conversation with Sam Weller on the topic of body snatching had already prepared him, and he was dismayed to hear that Mr. Wardle harbored the same suspicions that had been aroused in Mr. Pickwick's own breast. However, he hoped that such suspicions might be quieted by the application of logic.

"The cemetery," he said, "is well protected by its high fence and sturdy iron gate. It would be difficult indeed for anyone to enter or leave it, and in the darkness of night, more difficult still."

"You do not know the kind of men of whom we speak. They will overcome any difficulties to win the prize they seek and the nine or ten guineas they will receive for it from the butchers to whom they deliver it. Were it not for this cursed gout, I would be beside my mother to watch over her this very moment. If only there were someone I could trust to guard the grave tonight," and here Mr. Wardle looked at Mr. Pickwick with especial attention, "I would count him my friend forever."

And so we come to that grisly errand to which we alluded at the beginning of this account, for Mr. Pickwick could not help but come to the aid of a friend in such need as Mr. Wardle. It was not in the Pickwickian nature to refuse a friend's urgent request, no matter how bizarre the request might be, as long as it arose from genuine feeling and distress.

"Have no fear," Mr. Pickwick said, "for I shall do my utmost to stand guardian over the grave of your departed relative. As long as I remain awake and alert, no foul hand shall disturb the mortal remains of Mrs. Wardle. You have my word on it, and there is no need to raise objections on any grounds at all."

This last was spoken even though Mr. Wardle had made no move to raise objections of any kind and indeed appeared more than eager to fall in with the scheme that Mr. Pickwick had so impetuously suggested.

"I will help you make ready," Mr. Wardle said. "Joe! Where are you, Joe! D—e but that boy must be asleep again."

And indeed that was the case. They found Mr. Wardle's servant in the kitchen, leaning against the wall as if standing there waiting to be called, but motionless and with his eyes closed in peaceful slumber.

"'e's been like that ever since downing a pigeon pie in one gulp," Sam Weller announced, looking at Joe with a critical eye. "'e went from wide awake to soundly asleep in less time than a cat."

Mr. Wardle walked over and gave Joe a sharp jab in the ribs with a stiffened finger, and the boy's eyes popped open. As soon as they did, Mr. Wardle told him Mr. Pickwick's plan and commanded Joe to accompany him.

"But it will be very dark and cold," Joe protested, "and the ghosties will be walking there tonight, as like as not, for they like to prowl at Christmastime."

"You can fortify yourself against the cold, and the ghosties will not bother with the likes of you," Mr. Wardle told him. "I will not allow my friend Mr. Pickwick to pass the night there alone."

"And what would cause you to think he'd be alone there?" Sam Weller asked. "As if there was any kind of a chance I would not be with him all the time?"

"I would not ask it of you, Sam," said his master, "for Joe is right about the cold if not about the ghosts, in which I do not believe."

"We can cover ourselves 'ead and ears, and take brandy against the cold," Sam said. "And if the young brock'ly over there can stay awake, 'e can help us watch for ghosties or ghoulies or whatever else may come along in the dark o' the night."

Joe did not appear to be much encouraged by these words, though he managed to remain awake to hear them, a not inconsiderable accomplishment when one realizes that he had not a single bite to eat for several minutes. Mr. Pickwick, on the other hand, thought Sam's words quite fine and declared the matter settled.

"We will go and guard the graveyard," he said. "And not all the body snatchers in the kingdom shall prevail against us."

Mr. Wardle now uttered several more high-flown protestations, but all to no avail. Mr. Pickwick was determined, and when Mr. Pickwick was determined, he was more adamant than any stone. And so, in a short time, he and Sam and the glumly somnolent Joe were making their way down a twisting lane, their path lit by a lantern carried erratically by Mr. Pickwick, who sent its rays searching among the branches of the trees and along to the side as well as occasionally behind. Joe and Sam carried food and drink, though in truth Sam had imbibed much of his share of the latter already, as the redness of his face might have attested had the light ever fallen on it.

"We are near to the church now," Mr. Pickwick said, extinguishing the lantern and plunging the three at once into the deepest of darkness, for it was a winter's evening and the sky was covered by heavy clouds that kept the moon and stars well concealed behind their inky cloak.

"If we're near to anythin', I can't see it," Sam said. "Nor can I even see you, sir, for that matter."

"We must go carefully," Mr. Pickwick replied, making no move to relight the lantern whose bail he still gripped in his right hand.

"We do not want to be seen by anyone who might not have the right understanding of our business here."

"No 'un'll see us, for certain," Sam said as they ventured forward in the darkness, bumping into each other with every other step.

Each time Joe was bumped, he jolted into awareness and emitted a small outcry not unlike that of someone whose bare foot has been trod on by a thickset man wearing hobnailed boots.

"They might 'ear us, 'owever," Sam said, but Mr. Pickwick took no notice, intent as he was on not wandering off the path, which he did anyway, though he realized it only when he came into contact, nose first, with the thick stone wall that surrounded the cemetery.

After he had rubbed his stinging nose, he announced his discovery of the wall, and the three felt their way down the stone enclosure to the gate, realizing only when they arrived at it that it was locked tight and that they had no key with which to open it.

"Then we will climb over the wall," Mr. Pickwick said. "I have climbed walls before, and I can climb this one as well. And if I can climb it, so can the others we wish to prevent from doing their vile business. We will go in as they would."

Sam's memory of the former wall-climbing adventure was not quite the same as that of Mr. Pickwick, but he did not say so, for he knew he would be wasting his words. So he simply put his burdens on the ground, bent over, and said, "You can stand on my back, sir, if you can see it."

Mr. Pickwick set the lantern down and after much fumbling managed to locate Sam. Requesting the aid of Joe, he endeavored to clamber up on Sam's back, and he succeeded after falling only three times. Even standing on his servant's broad back, however, Mr. Pickwick could hardly have seen over the wall even in the daylight, as his eyes were still about one stone below the top.

"Put your feet on my shoulders," said Sam when he was informed of his employer's precarious position, "and hold on to the top of the wall. I vill try to stand. Joe can help you to balance, and I hope you can pull yourself over quickly, as you're rayther heavy, sir."

Somehow Sam did manage to stand, and with Joe's hands steadying Mr. Pickwick by holding on to his legs, the worthy gentleman contrived not to fall. He found himself now conveniently higher than the wall, and with a great effort and much heavy breathing and scrabbling with feet and hands, he pulled himself atop it.

"I shall drop down on the other side," he said, "and the two of you can join me."

Joe and Sam heard a noise as of someone dropping a heavy sack of sand, followed by a loud "Ooooof."

"He's done it," said Sam to Joe. "It's my turn now, young boa constrictor, so give me your back."

Joe, who was cold, hungry, and uncomfortable, said, "Then can I go home?"

"No, you cannot go, for you are pledged to join us in the wigil we keep. I will pull you up ven I reach the top of the wall."

First, however, Sam threw his pack and Joe's over the wall, having no desire to be without food and liquid refreshment for the duration of what he knew would be a long and weary night of watching. Then, not without an abundance of groans and sighs and heavy breathing, he attained the top of the wall, after which he helped Joe to do the same. Had anyone else been passing by the graveyard at that time, surely he would have believed that the ghosts of all the departed were having a romp through the headstones and tombs. But as no one was passing by, their exertions went unnoticed by all except Mr. Pickwick, who was well aware of the source of the noise.

After a while Sam and Joe joined Mr. Pickwick at the base of the wall. When Sam suggested that Mr. Pickwick light the lantern so that they could find their way to the grave they were seeking, Mr. Pickwick admitted that he no longer had the lantern, having put it down to climb the wall and not being able to reach it once he had gained the other side of the wall.

"I thought you might have thrown it over to this side, along with the food," Mr. Pickwick said.

"It wasn't packed up like the wittles and drink," said Sam. "It would have broke all apart had I done that, but I didn't, because I could not have found it in the dark."

"No matter, then," Mr. Pickwick said with his usual good cheer. "We can find the grave if we just find the flowers laid atop it. Perhaps we can smell them."

Sam reminded him that flowers were quite difficult to find in the English winter and that, as Mr. Pickwick must remember, only a few puny green plants adorned the grave. The plants, Sam said, would not be easy to smell, at least for him, because "All's I can sniff is the frost that's hangin' on the tip o' my nose."

Mr. Pickwick was deterred by neither the darkness nor the cold, nor did Sam's reference to the frost daunt him. He marshaled his small troop into a semblance of order, and they searched by feel and instinct, bruising their shins and stubbing their toes on the headstones as carven angels watched with their frozen stone faces. After a while, Mr. Pickwick stumbled across the fresh grave. He communicated his discovery to the others, and Sam said, "That's all to the good, but the wind is getting stronger and bitin' through my clothes. There's a tomb nearby where we can find shelter if I'm rememberin' it aright."

He was indeed correct, and soon the three were sitting on the cold ground, their backs leaned against the rough stone sides of the tomb, out of the wind. But also out of sight of the grave, had they been able to see it in the black night. However, they were sure that they would remain alert and wary of visitors, so they began to partake of the kindly spirits packed up to warm them. The imbibing went on for quite some time, and the brandy, along with their earlier exertions and the lateness of the hour, contributed to the slumber that crept upon Sam and Mr. Pickwick, though not Joe, who needed no such excuses to drop into the arms of Morpheus; and as the hour drew close to midnight, the only sounds that could be heard in all the cemetery were the gentle susurrations of the wind, and of the snoring that came from behind the tomb.

Mangle, Miggs, Pooch, and Snubb entered the graveyard quietly and without incident, opening and closing the iron gate as if it were freshly oiled.

Miggs was the oldest of the four, an ill-favored man of near forty, with a hooked nose and a dirty scar that ran from one ear to the other in a ragged line, a result of a sad misunderstanding that might have ended even more unpleasantly for Miggs than it had if the knife of his attacker had been as sharp as the anger of the one who wielded it. Miggs carried with him two wooden shovels, the better to dig quietly, without clanging into stone or metal. The shovels were pointed like daggers to cut through the fresh earth. Miggs was the chief digger, and he would see to it that they started digging at the head end of the grave, uncovering only about one-third of the coffin, so that the dirt that remained on it would act as a counterweight later on. Over his clothing he wore a heavy dirt-soiled apron, as did the others.

Of the four men, Snubb was the smallest. He had a small head and small eyes, small hands and small feet. He was wrapped up in his ragged clothing like a mummy from the tombs of Egypt, and of his face, only the eyes could be seen. Over his shoulders were looped coils of stout rope to the ends of which were tied iron hooks. When the grave had been opened, it was his job to climb down with the coffin and force the hooks under the coffin lid. When the lid had been broken, Snubb was the one whose job it was to fasten another rope around the neck or shoulders of the Thing, as the grave robbers called it, so that it could be pulled up from the hole.

Pooch was the strong man, with a thickset body and shoulders an ax handle could not span. He was characterized by his doglike face and his doglike devotion to Mangle, who had taken him from the streets and taught him the lucrative if unsavory trade of body snatching. After Snubb forced the hooks under the coffin lid, Pooch would pull on the ropes until the lid, counterweighted by the earth that remained atop it, split apart.

And then there was Mangle, the leader of the crew. He carried the canvas that would be spread beside the grave to take the earth as it was shoveled out. He would see to it that when the earth was replaced, not a jot remained on the grass to betray the fact that any of it had been removed. He also carried a lantern with the lens partially blocked so that only a bit of light was emitted.

" 'Ere now," Mangle said when they reached the grave. The others stopped, and Mangle set down the lantern and spread the canvas. Miggs indicated the head of the grave, and Mangle said, "Get busy."

Miggs and Pooch took the wooden shovels and began to pile the fresh earth on the canvas. Mangle watched for a moment before he took a drink from the flask that he carried with him always. He did not offer it to Snubb, who stood beside him respectfully and silently.

In only a short time one of the wooden shovels struck the coffin, and soon the top third of it was uncovered. Miggs and Snubb clambered out of the grave, and Snubb took hold of the hooks before sliding back down into it. With the skill that comes of long practice, he wedged the hooks under the coffin lid before scrambling out again.

Pooch grasped the ropes in his huge calloused hands and began to pull. Had he not been wearing heavy clothing against the cold, one could have seen the muscles bulge in his arms. His scarf hid the cords in his neck, and the darkness hid the way that his face reddened with his exertions. His frosty breath hung heavy in front of him as he strained. Every few seconds he would take a deep breath, renew his grip on the ropes, and pull even harder. Eventually his efforts were rewarded with the sound of a loud *crack!* as the coffin lid split apart, and as soon as it did, Snubb slithered back into the hole with another rope. His clothing, like that of the others, was well protected by his apron, and he was careful not to get any more dirt on his clothing than was necessary. Like the others, he was a professional and proud of his abilities, and like a professional he slipped the rope around the neck of the Thing in the box.

Mr. Pickwick had been dreaming of something peaceful and lovely, like Dingley Dell in the springtime, and the noise of the coffin lid's cracking woke him with a start. He looked around blindly, not precisely certain of his whereabouts. The cold, the darkness, and the snoring of Sam and Joe soon reminded him that he was in the cemetery, and he thought that he must have heard thunder. He did not relish the thought of being out in a storm of rain and sleet.

He listened for more thunder, but he heard instead the sound of voices. Joe and Sam were still snoring; he could see their lumpish forms beside him, and he knew the voices must be coming from the other side of the tomb. And he knew that they were not the voices of ghosts but must be those of the very men he had come there to prevent from stealing Mrs. Wardle's body from the place of its final rest.

They shall not have it, thought Mr. Pickwick, nudging the dark shape of Sam with his toe. Sam, too, must have been dreaming, but perhaps his dreams were not as serene as those of Mr. Pickwick, or perhaps Mr. Pickwick's nudge was not as gentle as intended. At any rate, Sam jumped to his feet with a cry, looking about for whoever or whatever had goaded him, and in the process he stumbled over Joe, who sprang up like Jack from his box and fled in panic, waving his hands and yelling about ghosties.

Now Pooch was generally a very steady man, and he was certainly a very strong one, but he was a bit superstitious by nature, and the job of robbing graves had always been a matter of apprehension to him. So when he saw a dark figure run screeching from behind a tomb, it should surprise no one that he momentarily lost his grip on the ropes he was holding, allowing the coffin lid to fall back several inches just as Snubb was slipping the rope around the neck of the Thing in the hole.

Now Snubb had been in many graves and had popped many a Thing from its casing, but he was taken aback by the unexpected noise somewhere above him, and when the movement of the coffin lid animated the Thing and made it seem as if it were trying to squirm back into its coffin, Snubb lost his composure.

"It's alive!" he screamed, and scattering the freshly turned soil without heed of the canvas placed to receive it, he scrambled out of the grave, much to the consternation of Pooch, who was already somewhat discombobulated by the appearance of Joe, who was now running straight toward the grave as if his earnest desire was to dive directly into it.

Miggs and Mangle were a bit more matter-of-fact than their companions, having worked longer at their peculiar occupation than they. Mangle calmly capped the flask from which he had been nipping. He slipped the flask into a pocket and held out his hand to Miggs, who gave him one of the shovels. With a nod to Miggs, Mangle prepared to use the shovel as either a club or a spear, as the occasion demanded, and advanced on Joe.

At that moment Mr. Pickwick and Sam stepped from behind the tomb, though in the darkness it may have appeared to one of a superstitious nature that they emerged from inside it. The spectral effect was increased when Sam, who stubbed his toe on a low footstone, let out a low cry of pain.

That guttural moan gave increased impetus to Joe, who fairly flew over the ground, colliding at the edge of the grave with Snubb, who was just climbing over the side. The two of them disappeared into the ground in a tangle of arms, legs, and exclamations of astonishment and fear.

Pooch, meanwhile, had released the ropes and run to join Mangle and Miggs, or rather to take up a position somewhat behind them, as he preferred their company to that of Joe. Mangle and Miggs stood unafraid, their feet planted firmly and shovels at the ready to confront Mr. Pickwick and Sam.

The noises that came from the grave were quite disconcerting to Mr. Pickwick, as were the dimly seen figures that struggled there. First Joe's head would appear above the edge and then Snubb's as they struggled to escape the Thing, each refusing to allow the other egress from the hole. But Snubb at last prevailed, kicking Joe on the point of the chin and scuttling over the edge and across the frozen grass like a giant crab across the shore. He did not slow down when he passed his comrades but rather increased his pace, rising to his full height and passing out of the gate and into the dark beyond without so much as a fare-thee-well, his rags flapping as he ran.

At that point Pooch seemed to see the sense of Snubb's honorable retreat and followed him. His devotion to Mangle had evaporated into the night air in the face of Snubb's flight and the preternatural sights and sounds that filled the graveyard.

Miggs and Mangle had no desire to fight without their friends to aid them, so they, too, turned and left as swiftly as they could, though it was painful to Mangle to leave behind his canvas, ropes, hooks, and lantern. He paused only long enough to lock the gate behind him as he left, feeling that it would give him some measure of satisfaction if his tormentors were trapped inside or had to climb the wall to get out.

For their part, Sam and Mr. Pickwick hardly realized what was happening, other than that coming from the grave were sounds as terrible as any they had ever heard.

"I don't s'pose you are a-feared," Sam said to Mr. Pickwick.

"Indeed, I am not," Mr. Pickwick said. "I believe our adversaries have fled, and unless my eyesight has betrayed me, it is Joe in that grave."

"And is he the one makin' those 'orrible sounds?"

"I pray that it is so," said Mr. Pickwick.

Sam went to where Mangle's lantern sat on the ground and brought it to the edge of the grave. He turned up the flame, and he and Mr. Pickwick peered into the grave, where they saw Joe in the macabre embrace of Mrs. Wardle, with whom he had become entangled during his struggle with Snubb. Joe was wailing as if he were being pursued by the hounds of Hell.

"I don't b'lieve I've ever seen the young vetch-table so alert," said Sam.

"We must get him out, Sam," said Mr. Pickwick, and so Sam descended into the grave, separating Joe and Mrs. Wardle and allowing the latter to return to her repose. Even with that done, it took Sam quite some time to bring calm to Joe, and he might have taken a great deal longer had not Mr. Pickwick fetched the remaining brandy, which Sam administered to Joe in draughts that eventually had a comforting effect.

At length Sam was able to assist Joe's removal from the grave. The ropes were pulled up with their hooks, and the coffin lid was replaced, though not screwed down.

"No one need know," said Mr. Pickwick. "I have no fears that Mrs. Wardle will walk abroad."

"No need to be worried on that score," Sam agreed. "If we had one of them shovels, we could put that dirt back in."

"We shall do our best with our hands," Mr. Pickwick said, and they did. Joe joined in with a will, appearing not to have quite as much faith as the others that Mrs. Wardle would remain in her coffin unless there were a certain weight of dirt atop her. His teeth were still chattering, either from fear or the cold. Sam rather thought it was the former.

When they had done as well as they could to cover the coffin, Sam wiped his hands on his already dirty pants and said, "We oughter be leavin' now, but I don't know as to how unless we climb the wall again."

"The intruders did not have to climb," said Mr. Pickwick. "Are they phantoms that they could pass through the wall unimpeded?"

"I don't b'lieve they are phantoms or anything like," said Sam, and he went to have a look at the gate, which was now locked securely. He ran a fingertip over the hinges and rubbed fingertip and thumb together. "They got away slick," he said.

"And we will not be able to bring them to justice," said Mr. Pickwick, "as I had hoped."

"I would not be sayin' that, yet," Sam told him. "We will see as we will see. Now let's us gather up our packs and go about climbin' that wall."

The constable was a stern-faced man with large mustaches and glittering black eyes, but he had no hope that the body snatchers would ever be found.

"They works in the dark, and nobody sees 'em," he said to Mr. Pickwick the next day when they met at Mr. Wardle's house.

"Those that sees 'em don't see enough of 'em to recollect their faces."

That seemed true enough. Neither Sam nor Mr. Pickwick could describe any of the men they had encountered, and Joe could as yet hardly talk for the chattering of his teeth, which had persisted throughout the night and into the morning; and it was doubtful that he could have described anyone other than Mrs. Wardle, with whom he had been in close communion.

But Sam said, "There's some'un as sees 'em."

The constable gave him a look filled with suspicion. "And who'd that be?"

"The one 'oo keeps the gate 'inges oiled and the same one 'oo let 'em into the graveyard."

"Who would perform such dastardly work?" Mr. Pickwick asked.

"Who's the one with the key?" Sam responded. "I'd say it was the gravedigger, myself, the church sexton, who vas cryin' crocodile tears just yesterday at the funeral."

Sam went on to explain that to his way of thinking, while the minister might have a key to the gate, he was much less likely to have allowed the body snatchers into the cemetery than the sexton, who was the man charged not only with digging the graves but with the upkeep of the grounds. He would know all about the arrangement of the grave and whether there was such a thing as a spring gun set to fire if it was disturbed.

"That's why the stranger woman was talkin' to him," Sam said, "and also to give 'im 'is payment for slippin' her the key to the gate. Fact is, I would not be surprised if the woman weren't no woman at all but one o' them we met last night, wearin' a dress and a veil. There's not a one of 'em that wouldn't stoop to it."

Mr. Pickwick had no doubts about the perspicacity of his servant, and he urged the constable to act on what Sam had said. The constable agreed, and later returned with the news that not only was the sexton guilty but that he had admitted his crimes, a confession that all believed would soon lead to the apprehension of his confederates. Mr. Wardle thanked Mr. Pickwick profusely for all that he had done and assured them of their welcome at Dingley Dell, no matter the time or season. Mr. Pickwick accepted his friend's thanks graciously, but insisted that Sam was the one who was the more deserving.

"And," said Mr. Pickwick, "there was your own servant Joe. Without him, we would never have overcome those terrible men."

"D—n that boy," Mr. Wardle said. "He is sound asleep in the kitchen, but still his teeth are chattering."

For fear that Joe's teeth could continue to chatter until the young man grew old and entered his own low house in the sod, Sam forbore to elaborate on his own suspicion that the body snatchers had been associates of the sexton for quite some time and that more graves than one lay empty in the cemetery by the church.

That evening, word came from the constable that the sexton had confessed all and that those he had aided would soon be caught. Mr. Wardle fed his friends well, and Mr. Snodgrass proclaimed his eagerness to write a poem about the shrewdness of Sam Weller and the greatness of Mr. Pickwick. As to whether he ever completed, or, indeed, even began the poem, no more is known. But as to the greatness of Mr. Pickwick, there was no one to deny it then, nor will any deny it now, though the days of his adventures are long past.

Editor's note: It is both a privilege and an honor to have been asked to edit this posthumous Pickwick paper. As all Pickwickian scholars know, Mr. Pickwick, after his retirement to Dulwich, recorded his adventures in various memoranda, often having his servant, Sam Weller, read them aloud. As the events Mr. Pickwick described in these memoranda occurred after the dissolving of the Pickwick Club, the papers remained unedited and thus were not included among the accounts of that august body. These anecdotes might have been lost entirely had not Mr. Weller preserved them out of his affection for the old gentleman he served. They were handed down to Mr. Weller's heirs so that later generations could both appreciate and learn from the qualities of the extraordinary Pickwick until at last they came into my hands through an intermediary who has asked to remain nameless. In preparing this account, I have updated the punctuation lest the reader find himself stumbling through veritable thickets of commas springing up everywhere in the text. I have also emended some of the spelling, especially in the dialogue, so as to render the characters' words more easily comprehensible to the modern eye and ear.

Death in Dover

BY P. N. ELROD

P. N. Elrod is the author of twenty novels and as many short stories. She's usually on another planet but maintains citizenship in the state of Texas for tax purposes, and lives quite comfortably with her dogs, Sasha and Megan, and a full-size Dr. Who TARDIS she once built when she had too much time on her hands. (We'll gloss over the K-9 in her living room.) Her hair remains red nearly all the time, except when it's on fire because of a deadline. Everything else is subject to rewrite. Check out her Web site at www.vampwriter.com.

Dover, England, November 1775

I VENTURED TO pull back the flap of the coach window for a glimpse of what lay ahead and was disappointed by the near-unrelieved darkness. The only glimmer I caught emanated from the distant gray sea, which stirred restlessly under a wind out of the bitter north. Some of that cruel zephyr cut its sharp way round the stuffy interior of our swaying conveyance, causing a large, red-haired, red-faced woman to make a most indignant remonstrance against my curiosity.

"Faith, Mr. Barrett, if you've pity in your heart, spare us from your gawping lest we all perish of cold. You'll be seeing the town soon enough. It's been there for hundreds of years an' not like to run off now, is it?"

As a gentleman it was my lot to meet harsh speech—at least when it flowed from female lips—with humble apology. I tied the flap back into place. "I do beg your pardon, Miss Pross, and yours as well, Miss Manette."

By this I acknowledged the smaller, younger lady who seemed to be her mistress. Miss Manette had caught the attention of all the gentlemen since she first came aboard with her forceful companion. The coach's confines were such as to kindle interest in any member of the fair sex who happened to be there, but her delicate blond beauty would command attention even in a great throng. In Miss Pross, though, she had so fierce and wild a protector that none had been able to draw her into polite conversation.

The passing of pleasantries was difficult anyway. The most innocuous of exchanges had to be conducted at the top of one's lungs because of the rumbling of our wheels. The violent rocking as we tumbled over broken and muddy roads kept most of us occupied hanging on to leather straps to avoid a degree of intimacy not generally shared by the average English subject with his fellow countrymen.

There were seven of us crammed in rather tight: the two ladies, my good cousin Oliver, myself, and three other gentlemen. The fellow next to Oliver was Sir Algernon . . . something. I'd missed his whole name. He was a tall, handsome specimen, but very dolorous of aspect and dressed in the deepest mourning. Traveling with him was his son—a boy of no more than eleven years—also impeccably dressed for sorrow. Because of this outward declaration of a private tragedy we left them to themselves. The man was disinclined to speak, and the boy miraculously slept, leaning against the third gentleman. This was M. Deveau, a Frenchman who was the boy's dancing and sword master, the male equivalent of a governess.

He and the boy, Master Percy, had the misfortune to share the opposite bench with the females. I say misfortune, for the lady next to Percy was the redoubtable Miss Pross, who acted as a bastion of protection for her delicate charge, who was on her other side. Though it was clear by manner and dress that none of us—for we were one and all clearly gentlemen—would presume to make unwelcome overtures to the young lady, Miss Pross seemed to have decided we were rascally adventurers of the worst sort. I was certain she had a pistol, or at least a leaded cudgel, concealed in the large traveling bag she clutched to her lap, and was equally certain she would find a use for it if she determined any of us to be the least importune in our behavior.

"Are there no lights in the town at all?" I asked. Even the most squalid parts of London had lamps here and there.

Oliver barked a short laugh, which roused Master Percy from his slumber. "Oh, lots, but they don't get much use. It's a rare lamplighter who makes aught else but a poor living in our coastal hamlets on certain evenings. Haven't you something similar on your Long Island?"

"Smugglers, is it?" They preferred a pitch-dark night for landing their goods on shore. Any fellow lighting a lamp would be looked upon most unkindly by such free-traders, often to the point of violence. Indeed, it was said that the lamplighters, unable to make a fair wage, were themselves in on the smuggling. "I'm positive we do, but the family estate is set well inland, so I've not had opportunity to make a firsthand observation. Of course, one hears tales, and the place has a dark history. It was a haven for Captain Kidd, you know. They say his treasure is buried somewhere along one of the beaches, but none have found it."

As I'd hoped, the mention of that name caught the interest of Miss Manette (and the boy). She peeped shyly at me, her blue eyes bright in the dimness of the coach. "Do you speak of the infamous pirate, Mr. Barrett?"

Had there been space to do so, I would have made her a proper bow of courtesy. As it was, a partial one from my seat had to serve. "Indeed I do, Miss Manette. Long Island was a favorite hiding place for his stolen booty."

"Where is this island?"

"It is part of the colony of New York in the Americas," I replied.

"And you are then an American?"

"A loyal American subject of our good King George, God save him." Since coming to England to complete my education at Cambridge, I'd learned to answer similar questions with that phrase and hopefully avoid social complications. Things were unsettled enough between Mother England and some few of her wayward children in the New World, and I did what I could to assure my countrymen that I was *not* one of those troublemakers.

A murmur of "amens" went round the interior.

"Why are you come to England, then, sir?" Miss Manette asked. "And Dover in particular?"

"Hush, my ladybird," admonished her companion. "Vex not the gentleman" —Miss Pross emphasized that word slightly—"with idle questions. I'm sure he has other things to think about."

Her incivility put the devil in me, so I smiled and bowed as well as I could to her, and in such a way that she couldn't possibly object without looking out-and-out boorish. "Not at all, dear lady. I am here to read law at Cambridge. My cousin, Mr. Marling, who is to be a doctor, and I are merely come to Dover to conduct of bit of private business."

Young Percy, who sat next to Miss Pross, stifled an unexpected guffaw. I took that to mean he well understood our errand, which made him very perceptive for his age. The noise of the wheels served to disguise his sudden burst of humor, so the ladies quite missed his reaction. Not so for M. Deveau, who, from the glint in his eye, also knew the truth of the matter.

"Will you be proceeding to the Continent?" asked Miss Manette.

"I think not. Is that your destination?"

"I believe so, sir."

Under the hard glare of Miss Pross, I knew an inquiry over why the ladies would hazard the Channel in this unsettled season would be too direct. "Then I wish you a very easy and uneventful journey."

"You are most kind, sir, but 'uneventful'?"

"Indeed, miss. It is a gracious fate who allows us to be free of cares when traveling. I was half bored to death when making my crossing to England, but see it now as a blessing. All travelers should be afflicted by absolute boredom, for that means a safe passage."

I was rewarded with a smile for this and might have pursued the topic further, but for being interrupted by a change in our pace and a shout from the coach driver. Our arrival was at hand. I burned to have another look as we rolled into town, but Miss Pross wore a glower sufficient to discourage a saint from praying, so I forced myself to have patience until we came to a stop.

The head drawer for our hotel—which happened to be the Royal George—pulled open the door, welcoming us to Dover. The ladies gathered themselves and were the first out. Sir Algernon was next, then followed my cousin Oliver, with me straight behind. The boy had politely indicated I should precede him, and M. Deveau was last. I think Master Percy wished to avoid a continuation of his proximity to Miss Pross. She was shouting in a most challenging manner for people to make-way-make-way for her "ladybird," though the only ones about were the driver and the drawer, who showed no concern for this display and went about their business of unloading the coach.

The chill night air was deadly damp as only England can make it and rife with the slimy stink of dead fish. Still, it was better than the coach. Thunder grumbled angrily in the distance, and I was thankful we'd arrived ahead of what promised to be a wonderfully malicious storm. I stretched my cramped and cold body, feeling a certain shakiness in my limbs that inevitably follows the abrupt cessation of a long, uncomfortable ride. Oliver was in a similar state of shock from the change.

"I say, Coz," he said, distracting me from looking about. "Let's have something hot to restore the flow of blood, then I'd dearly like to put myself around a joint of beef if they have one."

At this reminder I realized I was quite hollow. As Miss Pross pointed out, Dover would not be running off. It struck me that wandering about in a strange town rife with smugglers would be as unhealthy as the dank air.

Oliver had stayed at the hotel on previous journeys, and after sending up our bags, led us to the coffee room, which was very large, the long, low ceiling stretching far away into shadows. It smelled divinely of that hot, black brew, and we availed ourselves of a curative dish each, well-laced with good French brandy. With it, we threw off the rigors of the road, along with our cloaks and hats, and took up a post before a very large fireplace. The ladies and their baggage were conducted upstairs to more private quarters. Sir Algernon and Percy took themselves to a dim corner, giving their order to a waiter, content with their own company. M. Deveau was elsewhere, probably securing rooms for his master and young charge. The only other occupant was an orderly looking man of sixty or so, dressed all in brown, which made an odd contrast to his shining, flax-colored wig. Another waiter approached him respectfully.

"Miss Manette has arrived, sir," he said. "She says she would be happy to see the gentleman from Tellson's, if it suits your pleasure and convenience."

"So soon?" asked the man in brown.

The waiter's response escaped my hearing, for I noticed the father and son both looked up at the mention of Tellson's, a name I did not recognize. The brown fellow left, unaware that they marked his departure.

"What's Tellson's?" I asked Oliver, who also noticed the exchange.

"Bankers," he said. "Very old and so fearfully respectable even my mother has nothing to say against them."

"They must be truly formidable. Wonder what's afoot to bring one of their people out to meet with the fair Miss Manette?"

"No business of ours or so that Pross creature will tell you. You've not a hope with the young one, dear Coz. Besides, what would the beauteous Miss Jones say if she knew your attention had wandered from her?"

I pretended to be unconcerned by that prospect. "Wandered? I was only making conversation to pass the time. You had plenty of chance to have a try, but you didn't, so I stepped in."

"Oh, bother, I never know what to say to proper young ladies, especially when they are so closely chaperoned. It's dangerous, too."

"How so?"

"One stray remark about the weather, a cordial smile, and before you know it you're engaged. I've seen it happen countless times. Those London girls are the most frightful predators you'll find this side of any wilderness. They can't abide the sight of an unmarried man, and from birth are set up and schooled for the sole purpose of getting a fellow under wedlock-and-key."

"What's this? Has your mother found another prospect for you?"

He shuddered. "I shall have to engage myself in some sort of revolting tomfoolery so she won't speak to me for the next few months. By then the wretched girl will have moved on to stalking another victim."

"Take care what you wish for." I thought about the delightful Miss Manette and our too-brief exchange. "I don't think she's English-born, though. Did you not notice she had some other accent? Very slight."

"French, I'll warrant, considering the name. She's probably off to Calais to meet up with relatives, and the banker's here to provide her with a bit of spending money and perhaps protection for it. Though God help any thieves trying to get past the Pross."

"Indeed."

The waiter came to us in turn, inquiring what we would like in the way of food.

Some short while later, replete with half the contents of the kitchen inside our bellies, we were in a wonderfully lethargic mood. The *café noir* made us wakeful, though. Instead of going up to the room prepared for us, we idled before the fire, content to slowly roast, smoking our pipes.

"When?" I asked Oliver.

He looked at his pocket watch. "Not too much longer. Word will be about. We can expect someone at any time."

"And you'll be able to trust him?"

"Certainly not, but that's what makes it so amusing."

M. Deveau had returned to break bread with his master, and that party lingered at their table for a time until Sir Algernon retired upstairs. Young Master Percy had schooling to do, though. He and Deveau produced books and papers and went to work. I caught enough to hear a French lesson in progress. Percy had an excellent accent, speaking as rapidly as a native. Mine was quite rusty by comparison, and though I had a good and careful tutor at his age and after, I wasn't up to his rapidity of speech.

Our digestion was abruptly cut short by some sort of disturbance upstairs.

"What's that?" Oliver asked, stirring from his near-doze. "The Pross raising the devil?"

"Or fighting him," I put in. "What a row."

A moment later the owner of the George came quickly into the coffee room and, upon spying us, approached. "Mr. Marling?"

Oliver sat up straight. "Yes?"

"There is a—that is—the young lady—has become suddenly ill, and Miss Pross says that you are a doctor. . . ."

"Well, not quite yet I'm not, but I can have a look at her if you like."

The man seemed supremely relieved. Oliver, perhaps anxious to prove himself already worthy of practicing the physician's art, took himself off with a cheery wave to me.

The disturbance temporarily halted the French lesson. M. Deveau closed the book they were using. "Ah, M. Percy, this is of little interest to you when some real adventure takes place only a room away, is that not so?" His English was as superb as the boy's French.

"Indeed, sir," responded Percy, his gaze fixed on the door where Oliver had gone. In the distance one could still hear Miss Pross carrying on.

"Then go satisfy your curiosity while I have a pipe."

For all his obvious eagerness to leave, the boy bowed to each of us before departing, as grave and formal as any gentleman thrice his age. Then he clattered upstairs, a child again.

"May I join you by the fire, Mr. Barrett?" asked Deveau.

"Please."

He rose and came over, prepared his pipe and lighted it, then stood silhouetted before the flames warming his back. The storm had arrived in force by now, and some of the rain made its way down the chimney to fall hissing on the burning wood. It made one humbly grateful for the pleasures of being under a solid roof with good food and ready warmth at hand.

"You English have a most excellent idea of how to build a proper fire," he remarked affably. "There are homes in France where such a space would be used as a receiving room instead."

I enjoyed his exaggeration and offered a share in a bottle of wine Oliver and I had been working through. He accepted with thanks and asked when we expected to place an order for more. Deveau had rightly deduced the nature of our errand to Dover.

"Soon," I said. "We're to look for anyone coming our way wearing a red flower in his hat."

"That is the game of it. A certain color flower for some, a handkerchief for another. You have dealt with the gentlemen before?"

That must have been his term for those who made a living on the free trade of wines and spirits. "My cousin has done this many times and will see to the details."

"That is good. Many of the fellows who avoid the king's excise men are rough by nature and bear watching."

"You know something about it?"

His gave an expressive, wholly non-English shrug. "It was a family concern once upon a time. My father was a French captain, so I grew up with it. My English mother was not fond of the dangers of the sea and encouraged me to less perilous pursuits, and so I am here."

Deveau seemed to think this to be sufficient explanation of himself, and, for two travelers sharing a pipe and a sip of wine, it was exactly right.

Master Percy returned just then, full of news, but so self-possessed that he did not forget his position as a young gentleman and offered a proper greeting to me. This required that I stand up and return his bow and invite him to partake in some of the wine. He was a bit young, yet, for smoking a pipe. He declined and reported that there was indeed considerable excitement upstairs, most of it coming from Miss Pross.

"Miss Manette was speaking with the Tellson's banker, a Mr. Lorry," he said. "He must have had some bad news for her, for she fainted dead away. Miss Pross discovered what happened and is herself in a state, running about blaming everyone, especially Mr. Lorry. You'd think there was a war begun, the way she's carrying on. All the maids and waiters have made themselves scarce lest she fall on them like the storm outside."

"An interesting picture, young sir," I said. "How fares my cousin Oliver under the assault?"

"Oh, he's ignoring her and looking after the lady. Most calm he is."

Oliver had had much practice at ignoring loud, fit-throwing females, what with his own mother being an exceptional example of that ilk. He would make a fine doctor. "Did the banker say what caused her to faint?"

"Not a word, sir, but then bankers are like that and bankers from Tellson's more than most. By coincidence, my father's estate is in their charge. When my father and I heard that the man was from them, we thought he might have some business with us, but we were wrong."

I was framing a polite query on just who his father was, but an interruption—three of them, in fact—barged into the coffee room, dripping wet and complaining about the foul weather. Deveau gave one and all a narrow, careful look. A rough lot they appeared to be, too. Though their clothes were acceptable, they brought to mind a pack of ungroomed plow-mules dressed up in polished royal harness. Each wore a red flower of one kind or another in his hat.

"Is your cousin acquainted with any of these fellows?" Deveau murmured from the side of his mouth as they scrutinized us in turn.

"No," I replied. "He was going to speak to whomever came tonight and pick the best bargain of the lot."

"As Mr. Marling is elsewhere, may I put myself forward in his place?"

This from a man who grew up in the trade. I gratefully accepted his generous offer. Percy took Oliver's chair and watched the exchange with sharp interest.

The three tradesmen, not gentlemen, came over, and each presented himself to us: Captain Shellhorse, Captain Keech, and Captain Talmadge.

Keech was the largest, most pugnacious of them and put himself to take the lead. His hat's red flower was made of paper. It being late in the season for fresh blooms, that struck me as a clever substitute. He and Deveau stepped off to the side and spoke quickly in low tones for several minutes, then Shellhorse, who wore a much-faded rose, had his turn, then Talmadge, whose scarlet blossom was so small as to be easily overlooked. They each retired to separate tables as Deveau returned to confer with me.

"How much brandy are you planning to buy?" he asked.

I told him. Brandy, wine, and a long list of other items.

His eyes went wide. "So much? Are you buying for the royal palace?"

"Er, no, just for my house at the university. With Christmas and the new year coming up we'll want a good stock in place for the celebrations of the season."

"How many are in your house?"

My answer astonished him.

"So few? For so much drink?"

"Well, that's university men for you. We require ten times more than other chaps."

He found that most amusing, as did Percy. "I shall see what I can do."

Deveau returned to his task of interviewing each of the captains. Not one of them blinked at the quantity of my order, but a disagreement broke out between Shellhorse and Talmadge over who could deliver the quickest. It looked as if it would come to blows until the owner of the hotel, perhaps drawn by the noise, made an appearance. Clearly he commanded their respect, for the argument instantly subsided. I got the impression that he turned a very important blind eye to their trade, allowing them to conduct business under his roof—providing no trouble came of it. It was to everyone's mutual advantage to behave.

But when he left, Keech put himself forward, declaring that he had better quality stock for a better price. Deveau expressed interest, but Shellhorse and Talmadge instantly made lower bids. Keech waited until they'd exhausted themselves in their auctioning in reverse, then underbid them both. He got a murderous reaction, but they eventually backed down.

"Ye'll leave yersel' penniless an' starving at tha' price," said Shellhorse with satisfaction. "Me an' Talmadge'll be selling for double that to the next man down the road. You see if we don't!"

Talmadge spat on the floor, his way of showing agreement.

Keech seemed unconcerned. "Aye, but what I 'ave now is mor'n what I started out with this dawn. I'm pleased with my lot."

As was I, for I instinctively knew that Oliver would not have gotten a better price for the goods. At this point I was able to take over and sort out the details of delivery and payment. We determined that money would be exchanged once the kegs and bottles safely arrived at our Cambridge house. Keech had a man who could be trusted with the task, but I was not as confident.

"Worry yoursel' not over 'im, sir," he said by way of assurance. "'E does 'is job 'onest or 'e gits to wear 'is smile down low." To illustrate, he tilted his head back and drew his finger slowly across his throat. Some of this show was obviously for Percy's benefit. The boy shuddered appreciatively, eyes bright.

At this point Shellhorse bellowed a laugh. "If that be yer usual man, then ye best ride on the cart with 'im and not shut yer eyes the whole trip."

"Tha's my brother yer talkin' idle about! You don't know nuffin' on 'im!" said Keech, going red in the face.

"Oh, so *you* can talk of cuttin 'is, throat, but no one else is 'lowed a word agin 'im?"

"Tha's right, Bob Shellhorse, so you keep yer dirty mouth shut!"

"'Ere now, stifle that," put in Talmadge, coming between them. "We don' want the drawer to be throwin' us out."

But a scuffle followed, with much grunting and cursing, all strangely quiet, as each tried to assert himself as quietly as possible so as not to draw official attention. Deveau, alert to trouble, plucked Percy easily from harm's way as the trio staggered into the lad's chair, knocking it over. Shellhorse fell, dragging the other two with him, and there was a highly entertaining show as the small mob rolled across the floor of the coffee room.

It was at that moment that Oliver chose to return. His long face went longer with astonishment, and he nimbly avoided being caught up by the nautical juggernaut by a quick, wide leap.

"I say!" he crowed, delighted. "What's all this about?"

I spread my hands wide, shaking my head and laughing.

"Perhaps we should stop them," Deveau suggested. "This is a respectable hotel, not a bear-baiting pit. If Captain Keech is in gaol . . ."

That was enough to induce me to enter the fray. I grabbed a coat collar at random and hauled back, Deveau and Oliver stepped forward, each making a successful catch. The combatants were winded by now, but we still had our hands full keeping them apart.

"Git yer dirty 'ands off me, ye damned Frenchy!" cried Keech, trying to shake off Deveau's grip, which was apparently very strong. "If you were a gen'leman, I'd call you out!"

Deveau released his man in the direction of the door, somewhat forcefully. Keech, who wore a cutlass like his fellows, now drew it, waving it toward Deveau. That man, in turn, darted smoothly to one side of the door, where a line of pegs held a collection of cloaks, coats, and hats belonging to hotel guests. In a tall container next to them were a number of walking sticks. He seized one as though it were a sword, rounded on the captain, and in a move so fast that I could scarce follow, sent the cutlass flying across the room. It struck the wall with a startling pot-metal sound.

Keech was in a red-faded fury, eyes blazing, then suddenly seemed to realize that his hand was empty. He stared at it, then at the cane. He had been neatly disarmed, not by a sword, but by a simple length of wood, wielded by an obvious expert.

Deveau smiled gently. "Sir, if you have quarrel about my ancestry, I shall be most pleased to offer you satisfaction at any time of your choosing."

With a remarkable effort of will, Keech collected himself. "Tha' is to say . . . I mean . . ."

Deveau was generous. "Perhaps the captain was caught up in the heat of battle? It is my understanding that the English are born warriors. How difficult it must be to curb so great a predisposition."

The speech might have been delivered in an insulting manner, but Deveau was at once conciliatory and full of admiration. I wasn't sure if Keech grasped the words so much as the tone of voice. It worked on him, though. Perhaps he comprehended that it was a poor businessman who quarreled with his customers.

"Come, sir," said Deveau. "Let us toast this excellent trait with some fine English ale. You would honor me greatly if you would permit me to buy you a pint."

While the rest of us—including the other two captains—fairly gaped, Deveau and Keech left arm-in-arm like the best of friends to seek out the hotel's tavern.

"*That* was as smooth as ice," declared Oliver in a hushed voice.

"Aye," agreed Shellhorse, also caught up in the performance.

Captain Talmadge shrugged free of my grip and nodded. "That be old Deveau's get an' no doubt of it."

"You know his father?" I asked.

"Father an' son both, and the lad's the dead spit of his sire. I ain't clapped eyes on either of 'em for years, but there's some men as ye can'ts ferget. What's the boy doin' playing fancy to the gentry, I wonders?"

Master Percy now stepped forward. "Captain, sir, M. Deveau is my tutor in French, Latin, dancing, and the sword, among other things."

He nodded. "Well, young sir, you pay special mind to his swordwork an' no one'll get the better of you in a duel when the time comes. If he's that handy with naught but a stick, what might he be doin' with a real blade? I'd pay good money to see!"

*   *   *

The remainder of the evening was considerably less exciting. The storm lashed the town with more rain than was rightly necessary, and thunder boomed like siege cannons. The three captains took rooms and departed each to his own, and by the devil's own luck the hotel owner remained ignorant of their altercation. We later learned that Miss Pross had kept him fully engaged upstairs with complaints and suggestions of how to better run his trade. The only reminder of the occurrence was a small red flower left on the coffee-room floor, fallen from one of the captain's hats. Percy took it as a memento of a grand occasion. M. Deveau wisely cautioned him that mentioning the incident to his father might result in ill consequences for all, and thus obtained a solemn promise of silence.

Oliver and I retired to our room for the night, each pleased with the success of our trip. He was in particular happy at the bargain that Deveau had struck in his stead. "What a square fellow he is. I daresay he must be more English than French. Let's invite him to our Christmas celebration. Think you that Sir Algernon can spare him?"

"I've no idea, Coz." I'd left my coat and waistcoat over a chair, removed my traveling boots, and dropped into bed. "Ask him in the morning."

"Ask who? Deveau or Sir Algernon?"

"Both, either. Sir Algernon, I suppose."

"One hates to bother the poor fellow. I heard stories about his sad plight. Married a beauty and two years later she slipped into hopeless madness. Not raving, mind you, but the quiet kind. The family's been living on the Continent all this time. He's looked after her, best doctors and all that. She's recently died, as you might have guessed."

I grunted, staring at the bed canopy. The story sounded eerily similar to my own father's plight. He'd married a beauty as well, and she also had slipped into a kind of madness, but not the sort for which one is locked up. Hers was a willfully cruel and controlling agitation that she was careful to reveal only to her immediate family. We few, we happy few.

"For all that," Oliver continued, "it's left Sir Algernon quite brokenhearted, for he loved her dearly, I hear. Saw him in the hall during that business with Miss Manette. Looked half-distracted himself. Good thing he's got a solid sort like Deveau looking after the boy."

"Is the lady all right?" I asked.

"Oh, she'll be fine, an ordinary fainting spell. I don't know what brought it on, but gathered that the Pross won't allow it to happen again."

"Excellent. I want no more rows, only a good night's rest."

"We'll get it here, my lad. You won't be kept awake by bedbugs in these sheets, I'll warrant."

"Good. My God, look at the hour, half-past nine if it's a minute, no wonder I'm tired."

He dropped down onto his side, and we had a small contest for the lion's share of the covers before finally settling with equal halves. To my annoyance, he shut his eyes and almost at once began snoring. I preferred to be the first to fall asleep, for then his nasal dissonance would not keep me awake. I prodded him to turn over, hoping to curtail the noise, then turned as well, seeking sweet slumber.

It was not to be, though. I was jolted wide awake by a most dreadful shriek, and it seemed to come from beneath our very window. What terrible mischief was that?

Staggering from bed, I rushed over and pushed the shutters wide, staring out into the blackest of nights, the rain and wind cutting my face. With a terrible thrill I saw that devilry was indeed afoot. Exactly below me two men—shadows thrashing about among thicker shadows—were engaged in desperate struggle. One of them had already come the worst of it, for he was clearly weaker and no match for the other. He seemed to be hanging on to prevent the other's escape, and once more there came from him a second unearthly cry of pain and anguish that turned my bones to jelly.

I roared out something, I'm not sure what, and that had an instant effect on the attacker, who wrested violently away. His lesser opponent clutched at him, but was brutally struck down. I heard the sickening crack of wood striking bone. One shadow fell to the ground; the other stumbled and came near to falling. Then he regained his balance and hurtled away as though caught by the wind.

It was some moments before I was aware of Oliver dragging me clear to have a look himself. "Dear God, but it's murder!" he shouted.

He wasn't the only one aware of the row. The screams without had roused all this wing of the hotel, and the passage was full of people in various stages of dress, clutching blankets and shawls to their shoulders, their white faces full of questions. I pulled my boots on again, grabbed my smallsword, and pelted downstairs. Oliver was ahead of me, bringing his doctor's bag along with his own blade.

There was a crowd knotted by the front doors, and the landlord refused to open them. Oliver and I were not to be thwarted, though.

"There's a man dying outside, sir!" Oliver cried, indignant.

"Aye, an' he might have more company," came the chill reply.

"Bother that!" Oliver pushed past, turned the key, and in a moment we were outside blinking in the storm. "This way!"

We raced 'round the corner. Several more men were at our heels, grooms, waiters, guests, and the like, one of them brought a lantern. We quickly found the victim of the attack. He was sprawled flat on his face in the mud, and when the light was brought near, there was a collective gasp at the terrible wounding on his head. Blood was everywhere, and the poor man's skull looked to be caved in. Oliver felt for a pulse, but there was no doubt that this patient was quite dead. With a grimace we turned over the body. The far-seeing, yet empty eyes of Captain Keech stared up as though searching for his swiftly fled soul.

* * *

The storm grew more violent, matching the foul and unsettled mood of everyone sheltering under the Royal George's roof. One and all, guests, hosts, and servants, gathered in the great coffee room. The body of Captain Keech, shrouded by a tablecloth, lay in an improvised state in one of the small parlors, and his sudden demise was much discussed. Several times I was subjected to close questioning to ascertain who I had seen under my window. To their unanimous chagrin, I refused to divulge a single word of what I'd witnessed. Not that there was much I could say, but I insisted it was best to wait until the authorities were sent for and then make my rather thin declaration to them.

For all I knew *anyone* in this hotel—saving myself, Oliver, and Percy, who was too small—could have murdered the man. I could not discount the females, for Miss Pross was a very tall woman whose temper was certainly belligerent enough to do violence to a man if provoked. It was easy to imagine her attacking anyone who might have insulted her friend, Miss Manette.

I was thankful for Oliver being there, not only for his support, but his good sense, for he brought me a large brandy that helped bolster my thoroughly shaken disposition. It is not every day one sees— and *hears*—murder being done. No matter whether you know the victim or not, a fellow creature has fallen before his natural time, and the sheer brutality of the act inflicts a profound devastation upon the spirit. I stood close to the huge fire, yet felt no warmth.

The owner of the hotel was also in something of a state, doubtless fearful that such a crime would either drive away custom or attract the wrong sort of guest. He many times stated that such a thing had never before happened in his house, and when it came to the truth of things, the matter occurred *outside* the hotel, and therefore had nothing to do with his business.

The banker from Tellson's, Mr. Lorry, quietly reminded him that Captain Keech was a guest, and therefore . . . but he was not allowed to finish. Miss Pross cut in and confidently asserted we would be murdered in our beds if the miscreant was not immediately caught and gaoled. Lorry looked fearful, but of Miss Pross, not the prospect of being bludgeoned in the night by some deranged assailant.

At this point Captain Talmadge revealed that a duel had almost taken place between Keech and Deveau, and that the latter had used a walking stick as a weapon. Such a stick had been found only yards from the body. Instant silence followed this disclosure, and all eyes turned to Deveau, who was still fully dressed, unlike the majority of the company.

"What of it?" he asked. "We did not actually fight, and afterward I bought the man an ale to mend things. The innkeeper will bear witness for me that we were amiable the whole time, and when he left I came in here to enjoy the good fire and a pipe."

"Alone?" asked Mr. Lorry.

"Yes." Deveau was obviously chagrined at this admission.

"Then you mayn't be telling us ever'think," said Talmadge. "We don't knows if that be the truth. Easy enough to get Keech drunk as a tinker, for all Dover knows 'ow fond he were of 'is own wares. Then you takes 'im outsides an' *whack*! 'E's done in like a bullock at the butchers."

Deveau went very red in the face at this, not from guilt, but rather suppressed fury. "Captain"—he spoke very quietly for all his ire—"I will draw your attention to the fact that I not only had *no* reason to inflict harm upon Captain Keech, who was otherwise a stranger to me, but also that I am quite dry from top to toe, a state I would not be in had I been out in this Noah's deluge. You, however, are quite soaked."

"As are a dozen other men who went outside," said Mr. Lorry. "Based on that, I am cautiously inclined to believe him, but we need the authorities here to sort this out in a proper and legal process."

"There's no need fer sortin'!" put in Shellhorse. "It were the dirty Frenchie what dun fer 'im! 'E changed 'is clothes is all!"

As a man raised with a wide ocean between himself and ancestral grudges, I was unprepared for the vehemence of ill feeling between the English and the French in this otherwise civilized setting. It was as though their ancient quarrels down through the centuries had taken place only that afternoon, so strong was the wave of animosity that rushed through the room to break squarely upon M. Deveau. I stood up and called for reason, but was unable to make myself heard above the others. Catching Oliver's attention, he hurried to my side, and we both took up posts next to Deveau, prepared to defend him from what promised to turn into a mob.

Then unexpectedly, Sir Algernon took charge. He had been somber and silent through the arguments and accusations, but now when he stood—an imposing figure he was with his great height—all eyes turned to him. In his black mourning he reminded me of a hangman.

He had a very piercing gaze, and it touched on all present. "Good folk, I agree with Mr. Lorry that this matter must be looked into by the proper authorities. Someone will guide the way for me, and I will fetch them myself. Until then, I require that everyone retire to their several rooms and compose themselves to cooperation, not vituperation. I would also suggest most strongly that prayers be said for the departed soul of the poor man. As for the guilty one who committed this violence, his sins will find him out, you may be sure of it."

Sir Algernon did not look at any one man for very long, perhaps wary that it might inspire riot, but I did notice who he paid special attention to: the remaining captains, M. Deveau, Oliver, and myself. I felt a flush creep into my cheek at this scrutiny, along with the fear that I might also be unfairly and unreasonably accused. Sir Algernon then took the arm of the hotel owner and moved him purposefully toward the door.

Master Percy, who had stood on a chair to view the madness of the adults, dropped down and rushed to his father, drawing him to one side for a whispered conference. The boy was agitated and earnest, but Sir Algernon clearly had other matters on his mind. He patted his son on the shoulder in an absent way and departed on his errand. Percy stared after him, then next went to M. Deveau.

"Sir! I must show you something important!" he cried.

"What might that be?" Deveau bent slightly to see.

Then Percy launched into very rapid French, which was possibly the worst thing he could have done in that still-restive crowd.

"Frenchie spy!" shouted Talmadge. "'E's leadin' even the lad astray!"

A few others took up this chorus, rounding on Deveau. Had he been the devil himself they could not have been more outraged.

"He's no spy!" I roared. This time I was loud enough to make an impression, halting them. They were still on the edge, though; I had but a moment to turn them back to common sense again. "And I know he is *not* the murderer!"

This was met with derision from the two captains, their opinion backed up by a few other men demanding proof of my declaration. For the first time I noticed that a number of rough-looking fellows had gathered close to them. *Shipmates,* I thought. A chill of unease crept up my spine that had nothing to do with my wet clothes. They, too, were soaked from the rain from having been outside not a quarter hour ago, but one of them might have been out longer than the rest to do his evil work, then joined our party as we rushed to aid his victim. I tried not to shiver.

"Who did it, then?" demanded Miss Pross, her voice cutting across the length of the room.

I felt a sudden tug on my waistcoat and glanced down. Master Percy's bright gaze fairly burned through me. He held one hand to his chest, closed into a fist. He moved this hand, opening it slowly so only I could see. I stared at what lay there, not comprehending its import.

Deveau softly murmured, "Not now, sir. They'll tear us to ribbons. Trust me on this, I know them well."

"Who *is* the Cain here?" shouted the Pross, looking around. "Who has so wickedly slain his brother?"

I was at a loss for an answer, but happily fate intruded. The delicate Miss Manette, who stood next to her, suddenly fainted. This set the Pross off again. She vented a loud scream of distress for her charge and swooped to aid her, calling for water and a cold cloth and a dozen other remedies that are necessary when a lady collapses. Oliver started forward, but I grabbed his arm and muttered for him to wait.

"What?"

"A moment, you'll see."

Pross took charge like a Caesar, sending the servants hither and yon, and commanding that several of the maids lift her companion and bear her up to their room instantly. She bellowed fit to captain a whole fleet of ships herself, ordering the roughest of the sailors aside.

"Make-way-make-way for my poor ladybird!" she shouted, pushing men twice her size from her path. Bless me if they did not move quick as spit.

"Now!" I said, and urged Oliver forward.

He caught my intent. "I am a doctor! Let me through!"

Next I nudged Deveau, who allowed himself to be swept along in the general movement. I trusted that Percy could look after himself, as lads often have an instinct to place themselves where they most want to be no matter what obstacles may stand between.

As I hoped, the confusion of the moment served to protect us, and in a very short time we were up the stairs and in Miss Manette's room along with a dozen others caught up in the parade. The Pross spied Oliver and dragged him over to see to the young lady, then shooed the excess gapers out the door. That would have included myself, Deveau, and Percy, but her charge abruptly wakened from her swoon and gently requested a cease and desist.

The Pross was decidedly full of opposing feelings about this turn, but was finally persuaded to back down. She regarded us with undisguised suspicion, but when asked by the girl, who swore it would fully restore her, left the room to fetch a pot of tea. Oliver was told—ordered, rather—to act as chaperon, the Pross apparently trusting that as a prospective doctor, he was a sober, responsible sort. How little did she know.

After the door shut, Miss Manette favored us with a small smile. "Please forgive her. Her heart is in the right place."

"Of course, mademoiselle," said Deveau, with a bow. "Are you unharmed by your misadventure?"

"I am very well, monsieur. But you should know that it was a sham."

"Indeed?"

We favored her with increased interest.

She continued: "It is true that I did faint earlier this evening, but not again in the coffee room just now. My earlier event gave me the idea for it, though. Mr. Barrett seemed in need of help, and it was the only thing I could think to do. I knew my dear friend would make a great fuss, and that it might change the situation, but it grieves me to have troubled her so."

"Mademoiselle's conclusion was correct," I said. "I am most humbly in your debt for the timely rescue." Now was I able to execute a proper bow, including a little flourish with my smallsword, which was still in hand. "And please do not trouble yourself about Miss Pross's feelings. It's quite obvious that she enjoys making a fuss. You have provided her with considerable happiness."

"Before she returns, please, sir, will you tell us what you know? If there is a murderer under this roof, then it is our duty to catch him."

"I would be glad to tell all, but I know so little. The darkness and weather hid his face from me as perfectly as any mask."

"But I thought—"

"I know, but I was trying to distract that crowd from doing harm to M. Deveau. It's certainly plain to me he is innocent, he was the only dry-shod man in the room, but they weren't of a mind to hear sense."

"I believe," said Deveau, "that one of them was very much of a mind to falsely blame me for the crime and thus escape himself. I also believe that Master Percy holds the proof of it in his palm, do you not, young sir?"

Percy, who had slipped in unnoticed, now stepped forth. Again he open his hand. I stared at the small red flower there as did the rest.

"That's proof?" asked Oliver. "Bless me, but I don't see it."

"The hats," I said, with sudden inspiration. "This flower fell from one of the captains' hats in their scuffle tonight. I remember Percy saved it."

We then had to explain to Miss Manette the business about red flowers being used as a sign by certain ship captains wishing to conduct private business. We did not specify what that business might be.

"Still don't see it," Oliver repeated.

"The hats," I repeated in turn. "Talmadge and Shellhorse were still open for trade. They had red flowers in their hats."

"So?"

Percy said, "Captain Talmadge lost his flower earlier. I have it here. But he found another. Made of red paper. I saw it when we were in the coffee room."

The significance was unknown to Oliver, for he had not noticed what sort of flower was worn by each captain. He'd not dealt with them, after all. "So Talmadge murdered Keech for a paper flower?"

"I haven't a clue as to why he murdered," I said, "only that he took Keech's paper bloom."

"Or his hat," suggested Deveau. "Much more likely."

"Ah." That *did* make more sense. "They each lost their hats in the fight, and then he grabbed the wrong one. I remember the man who fled stumbled. He might have been picking it up instead, and I mistook his movement."

"Indeed, but a man can't be charged on anything so feeble as that. Your English courts must have stronger proof before they hang the guilty."

"Well-a-day, then we shall just have to find some."

Miss Pross returned, armed with tea, bread, and jam, and decided that our presence was no longer required. Even Oliver was summarily turned out, though he raised no objection. The only disappointed face belonged to Miss Manette, who would now not hear what I had in mind to resolve matters.

Since Oliver had stayed there before, I asked what he knew of servant's stairs in the building.

"I suppose there must be some, there always are, but bless me if I know where to find 'em."

"Come, sir," said Deveau. "I learned to navigate most of the harbors on both sides of the Channel by the age of twelve; I'm sure together we can find the back stairs here. What then, Mr. Barrett?"

"We find the servant's entry to the parlor where poor Keech is and slip in there."

"For what purpose?"

"To find his hat."

I explained—after the four of us, with young Percy eagerly in the lead, found the stairs—that it wasn't enough to point out the detail of the flowers to the authorities, but we had to be certain that Talmadge just didn't find a paper bloom elsewhere. In a very few moments we quietly entered the dim parlor where the dead captain lay stretched upon a long table. We lighted more candles to better see. His muddied shoes were visible beyond the hem of the tablecloth shroud, but the rest of his large form was carefully covered. Most important, someone had placed his hat on his chest. Sad relic it was, battered, damp, and also muddy.

Picking it up, I examined it for a maker's mark, but found none.

"Now what?" asked Oliver.

"Nothing pleasant. We see if it fits his head."

He wanted none of that, but saw the sense of it. With somber respect he drew back the tablecloth enough to expose as little as necessary. Master Percy stood a little closer to M. Deveau, but maintained a man's stout bearing through the course. While Oliver partially lifted Keech's head, I attempted to fit the hat to it. The article in question kept falling off.

"That settles it," said Oliver, wiping his hands on one end of the cloth afterward. "Not his bonnet, to be sure."

"But it may be argued that the damage to his skull altered the shape of it." Deveau pointed out.

"Not unless it had been thoroughly crushed—like a boiled egg that's been stepped on. I'll take an oath that that's not what happened here. 'Tis true he has a fearful and fatal wounding, but the greater portion of the bony structure is intact, and so his own hat would still fit. Unless he preferred a loosely fitted one."

"A ship's captain with a loose hat?" questioned Deveau. "Never. He would have it snug tight to his head or lose it in the wind. Look at his forehead. The line is still there that marks where he was accustomed to wearing it. I saw Mr. Barrett bring the other hat well over that line, therefore it does not belong to Keech. But we still have a problem of proof. Talmadge could claim that in the confusion of carrying the body inside that he got his hat mixed with Keech's. Forgive me, but in light of the strong feelings running here between my shared countries, it is more likely his word will be believed over mine. I am but half-English, and he is an Englishman bred and born."

"As am I," said Oliver. "And I'm ashamed to call him countryman, but you are not without allies. Jonathan and I will vouch for you, and certainly Sir Algernon will have a great influence in the matter."

"That will serve to keep me from the hangman, but how to bring the guilty to justice?"

"We find out why Talmadge would want to do for the fellow."

Deveau made a throwing-away gesture. "Many of these captains are honorable men, but there are some who resent the success of others and are always ready to remove the competition. I would hazard to say that Talmadge took exception to Keech's winning this night and acted upon it. I would think with Keech out of the way, he would then approach you later on with an offer to sell you spirits."

"Grim way to conduct a trade," I put in. "He said that he remembered you from when you were a lad."

"I do not recall. I think he was not a captain, for I knew all their names. One had to, but back then he could have been a first mate, perhaps."

"Sir!" cried Percy, who had been examining the hat close by the light of the candles. "See what I have found!"

We gathered near. There was a much-weathered ribbon on the outside running between the brim and the crown, and Percy had peeled it back. Within was a store of small reddish flowers.

"I sometimes hide things in my hat this way," said the lad. "I wondered if it might be the same here and so it is."

Oliver clapped a hand on the boy's shoulder. "And so it is. That's brilliant of you, young sir. As soon as your father returns—"

"'E'll 'ave other things on his mind, I'm thinkin'."

As one, we beheld the depressing visage of Captain Talmadge, who, with a muddy hat in hand, stood blocking the doorway that opened to the main hall. Crowded behind him were several of his men. They were smiling—a singularly alarming sight. Deveau quietly put Percy behind him, and I sensed him marshaling for some immediate action against this threat. However, Talmadge drew a pistol from his coat and aimed it at him.

"There'll be no mischief from you, Frenchie. "Ever-un keep shut and quiet as little mice an' we'll finish up 'ere an' be gone an' no 'arm done, eh?"

"What do you want?" asked Deveau.

"I'll thank ye to return me 'at, then we'll be off. You fine gentl'-men'll keep shut or it'll go 'ard on the lad."

Percy had slipped to a little off to better see, and his young eyes went wide as Talmadge swung the pistol in his direction.

Deveau kept his voice steady. "You harm that boy and there will be no safe port for you anywhere."

"The world's a wide place. Come now an' show sense. Ol' Keech 'n me 'ad a quarrel, an' I won the day. None of it's yer concern, so we'll just be off after I gets me rightful property. An' to make sure you behaves while we leaves, the lad's comin' along 'til we're clear. 'Less 'e'd perfer ter see the world. We're short a ship's boy and this 'un looks a likely sort. . . ." His gaze shifted suddenly to me. "You be droppin' that blade, Mr. Barrett, or you'll 'ave innercent blood on yer soul."

I'd been easing to one side, hoping to be able to lunge with my sword and disarm him, and froze. Deveau shifted ever so slightly, and I feared he would charge the lot of them, collecting a pistol ball for his trouble. Perhaps if I offered a substantial bribe and got their attention on me . . .

Percy suddenly made a strong snapping motion with his wrist, sending the hat spinning right into Talmadge's face. It was a fine dis-traction, but the man still pulled the trigger of his pistol. There was flat crack, strangely muffled. Providence had smiled on us; the damned thing had misfired. Talmadge's threat had come to naught, and before he could react to his change of fortune, Deveau leaped upon him like a tiger. I thrust my blade at the nearest of the henchmen, wounding his arm. He yelled and fled along with two others, which was most gratifying.

Oliver's blood was also up, for he roared like a savage and charged one of the men, a fellow who topped him in size by a good half foot. Nonetheless he won his contest, for Percy dropped low and curled himself tight behind the man's legs. When Oliver slammed into him, the wretch went tumbling over this unexpected obstacle. By the time he caught his wind, his captain was also on the floor, knocked insensible by Deveau's good right fist.

The row brought a crowd, of course, and it was some while before everything was properly sorted out, even when Sir Algernon returned with the authorities. It was nigh on to midnight before things were settled and the guilty and wounded were marched away to be locked up. The landlord was guardedly pleased to have the trouble in his house resolved, and stood us a round of brandies. It served to remind me that Oliver and I would now have to deal with Captain Shellhorse to complete our errand, but I was not unduly put out by the prospect. Indeed, Oliver and I faced the likelihood of having many more brandies and invitations to tell the tale of this night's events once we were back in Cambridge. If not for the ghastly event of Captain Keech's demise, we might have counted this as an excellent adventure to share to our friends.

"That was dangerous business with that hat, though," I said to Percy. We were again gathered before the fire in the coffee room, along with most of the hotel. "He could have killed you but for the devil's own luck that his pistol did not fire."

Standing on a chair, Young Percy flushed under the admiring scrutiny of the adults. It must have been a heady experience to him, for we had pledged that he was the hero of the hour for his action, perilous as it was. "It was not luck, Mr. Barrett, only logical reasoning," he said with much dignity.

"Indeed? How so?"

"It's a very wet night out, sir. Captain Talmadge was soaked coming here in the first place, and more so when he was outside quarreling with Captain Keech, and again when he helped bring in the body. It struck me that the rain would have made his pistol very safe, so I—"

"Brilliant!" said Oliver, and he called for a toast to Master Percy

Blakeney's—only now did I collect the family's full name—very good health and wits, and suggested additional celebration was in order.

The boy's somber father even looked pleased, but gently reminded us that the hour was late and the morning would be early as it always must be for travelers. Deveau agreed with this, and Sir Algernon preceded them toward the door; Deveau and his charge close behind. Their progress was slowed by a number of well-wishers who patted the boy on the head or, in the case of ladies, bent to kiss his cheek. He squirmed a bit under that particular type of reward except when it came to Miss Manette. He seemed to rather like her.

Before they quite made it clear, Percy gave a little cry and hurtled back to the chair he had been standing upon, and from it retrieved a by now very crushed specimen of the flower that had been Talmadge's downfall. The boy hurried to Deveau with his unique trophy.

"What the devil sort of weed is that, anyway?" Oliver called after him.

Percy paused, at a momentary loss until Deveau stooped and whispered discreetly in his ear. "It is called a scarlet pimpernel, sir!"

"Deuced peculiar name for a plant," muttered my cousin as they left. "Who'd have thought so little a thing could make such a thundering great mischief?"

I clapped him on the shoulder. "Well, never again will it happen if we live to be a hundred. Come, good Coz, let's have another brandy to celebrate and be thankful for small favors."

Author's Note: The character of Jonathan Barrett is the hero of my "Jonathan Barrett, Gentleman Vampire" series. Obviously this tale takes place prior to his toothy transformation. The Barrett books are scheduled to be reprinted soon by Ben Bella Publishing. You may learn more from my Web site, www.vampwriter.com.

The House of the Red Candle

BY MARTIN EDWARDS

Martin Edwards was born at Knutsford, Cheshire, in 1955, educated at a grammar school in Northwich, and continued at Balliol College, Oxford University, where he took a first class honors degree in law in 1977. He was trained as a solicitor in Leeds and moved to Liverpool on qualifying in 1980. He published his first legal article at the age of twenty-five and his first textbook—on the legal aspects of buying a business computer—at twenty-seven. He is married with two children, and they are all now living in Lymm. His series character solicitor Harry Devlin has appeared in seven novels. He is also no stranger to anthologies, having edited thirteen, including *Northern Blood* and *Northern Blood 2, Perfectly Criminal,* and *Whydunit?*

TO THE END of his days, Charles Dickens forbade all talk about the slaying of Thaddeus Whiteacre. The macabre features of the tragedy—murder by an invisible hand; the stabbing of a bound man in a room both locked and barred; the vanishing without trace of a beautiful young woman—were meat and drink to any imaginative mind. Wilkie Collins reflected more than once that he might have woven a triple-decker novel of sensation from the events of that dreadful night, but he knew that publication was impossible. Dickens would treat any attempt to fabricate fiction from the crime as a betrayal, an act of treachery he could never forgive.

Dickens said it himself: *The case must never be solved.* His logic was impeccable; so was his generosity of heart. Even after Dickens's death, Collins honored his friend's wishes and kept the secret safe. But he also kept notes, and enough time has passed to permit the truth to be revealed. Upon the jottings in Collins's private records is based this account of the murder at the House of the Red Candle.

A crowded tavern on the corner of a Greenwich alleyway, a stone's throw from the river. At the bar, voices were raised in argument about a wager on a prizefight and a group of potbellied draymen caroled a bawdy song about a mermaid and a bosun. The air was thick with smoke and the stale stench of beer. Separate from the throng, two men sat at a table in the corner, quenching their thirsts.

The elder, a middle-sized man in his late thirties, rocked back and forth on his stool, his whole being seemingly taut with tension, barely suppressed. His companion, bespectacled and with a bulging forehead, fiddled with his extravagant turquoise shirt pin while stealing glances at his companion. Once or twice he was about to speak, but something in the other's demeanour caused him to hold his tongue. At length he could contain his curiosity no longer.

"Tell me one thing, my dear fellow. Why here?"

Charles Dickens swung to face his friend, yet when he spoke, he sounded as cautious as a poker player with a troublesome hand of cards. "Is the Rope and Anchor not to your taste, then, Wilkie?"

"Well, it's hardly as comfortable as the Cock Tavern. Besides, it's uncommon enough for our nightly roamings to take us south of the river, and you gave the impression of coming here with a purpose." He winced as a couple of drunken slatterns shrieked with mocking laughter. The object of their scorn was a woman with a scarred cheek who crouched anxiously by the door, as if yearning for the arrival of a friendly face. "And the company is hardly select! All this way on an evening thick with fog! Frankly, I expected you to have rather more pleasurable company in mind."

"My dear Wilkie," Dickens said, bating his teeth in a wicked smile. "Who is to say that I have not?"

"Then why be such an oyster? I cannot fathom what has got into you tonight. You have been behaving very oddly, you know. When I talked about Boulogne, you didn't seem to be paying the slightest attention."

"Then I apologize," Dickens said swiftly. "May I thank you for your patience."

Collins was not easily mollified. "Even when you mentioned your jaunt with Inspector Field the other night," he complained, "it was as if your mind was elsewhere. May I finally be allowed to know what lies in store for us during the remainder of the evening?"

Dickens pushed his glass to one side with a sweep of the hand as though, after wrestling with an intractable dilemma, he had at last made up his mind. "Very well. I shall enlighten you. Our destination lies at the end of this very street."

Collins frowned. "By the river?"

"Yes." Dickens took a deep breath. "You cannot miss it. There is a fiery glow in the window of the last house in the row. In these parts, people call it the House of the Red Candle."

"Ah!" Collins's eyes widened in understanding. "I take it that the name speaks for itself?"

"Indeed. Unsubtle, but you and I have agreed in the past that even the most refined taste can have too much of subtlety."

"Quite." Collins chuckled. "So you favored a change from the houses of Haymarket and Regent Street?"

"Even from those of Soho and the East End," Dickens said quietly.

"A writer must indulge in a little necessary research!" Collins laughed, his cheeks reddening with excitement. "Whatever strange resorts it takes him to. Do you recall telling me about your experiences at Margate, years ago? Margate, of all places!"

Dickens shrugged. "At the seaside there are conveniences of all kinds."

"And you knew where they lived! Very well, tell me about this House of the Red Candle. Come on, spare me no shocking detail!"

"Later," Dickens said. "I have no wish to spoil your anticipation."

Collins belched. "Really, I must complain. You should have mentioned this an hour ago. I would have been more abstemious if only I had realized the nature of the entertainment you had up your sleeve. You old rascal! I wondered why you were wearing such a mysterious expression and only taking ladylike sips from your glass!"

Suddenly Dickens leaned across the table and stabbed a forefinger toward his companion's heart. "Tonight, Wilkie, tonight of all nights, whatever happens, I beg you to repose your trust completely in me. Do you understand?"

His massive forehead wrinkling in bewilderment, Collins exclaimed, "Why, my dear fellow!"

"I must have your word on this, Wilkie. Can I rely upon you?"

A light dawned in the younger man's eyes. "Oh, I think I understand! Go on, then, you rascal! What is her name?"

Contriving a sly grin, Dickens said, "Ah, Wilkie, you are always too sharp for me."

"Go on, then! Her name?"

"Very well. Her name is Bella."

"Splendid! And is she as pretty as her name?"

"She is beautiful," Dickens said softly.

"Ah! I do believe you are smitten. Now, don't forget you are a married man, Charles, old fellow. How long have you known this—Bella?"

"I have answered quite enough questions for the moment," Dickens retorted, springing to his feet. "Come, it is time for us to be away."

Outside it was bitterly cold and fog was rolling in from the Thames, smothering the dim light from the sparse lamps. As Dickens led the way down the cobbled street at his customary brisk trot, Collins heard the restless scurrying of unseen rats. He knew this to be a part of the city where life was as cheap as the women, but he found the temptation of the unknown irresistible. Like Dickens, he always felt intensely alive during their late-night wanderings in dark and disreputable streets and alleyways. One never knew what might happen. For a writer—for any man with red blood in his veins—that shiver of uncertainty was delicious.

Just before they reached the river, they paused in front of the last house. A red candle burned in the ground-floor window, its flickering light the only color in a world of gray. The curtains at all the other windows were drawn. Dickens tugged at the bellpull beside the front door, but at first there was no response. Collins shivered and rubbed his hands together.

"I shall be glad when I am warmed up!"

"Patience, Wilkie, patience. I promise you one thing. You will not readily forget tonight."

Collins was still chuckling when the door creaked open. A small and very fat woman peered out at them. Her hair was a deep and unnatural shade of red—Collins surmised that she wore a wig—and perched on her nose were spectacles with lenses so thick that they distorted the shape of her porcine eyes.

"What d' you want?" Her voice was as sharp as a hatchet.

"Mrs. Jugg? Splendid!" Dickens greeted her with gusto. "My friend and I have been given to understand that you have a young lady lodging with you by the name of Bella."

"What if I do?" The woman had several chins, and each of them wobbled truculently as she spoke.

"Well, the two of us are eager to make her acquaintance."

"Bella's a lady," the harridan hissed. "A proper lady. She has very expensive tastes."

"Expensive and exotic, I understand," Dickens murmured.

"There's no one like her. If you've been recommended . . ."

"We have."

"Then you'll know what I mean."

Dickens glanced over his shoulder, making sure that he was not observed by prying eyes. They could hear the rowdy harpies, presumably tired of baiting the sad woman with the scar, spilling out of the tavern in search of better entertainment. In the distance hooves clattered, but the fog was a shroud, and anything farther than five yards away was invisible. Satisfied, he put his hand inside his coat and extracted a wallet, from which he made a fan of banknotes.

"My friend and I are not without means."

The woman took a step toward them, as though keen to check that the money was not counterfeit. Collins caught the whiff of gin on her breath as she grinned, showing damaged and discolored teeth.

"Well, you look like respectable sorts. Proper gentlemen. I have to be careful, y'know. Come with me."

She shuffled back inside, the two men following over the threshold and into a long and narrow passageway. The air reeked of damp and rotting timber. She led them into a cramped front room where a slim scarlet candle in a dish burned on the windowsill.

"So you both want to visit Bella at the same time?" she asked with a leer.

"You read our minds, Mrs. Jugg." Dickens contrived to step backward onto Collins' toes, stifling his companion's gasp of surprise as he passed a handful of banknotes to the brothel keeper.

The woman's myopic gaze feasted on the notes for a few seconds before she secreted then among the folds of her grubby but capacious dress. "That's very generous, sir. Very generous indeed. You'll both be wanting to stay the night here, I take it?"

"Not exactly," Dickens said. "I am on good terms with a man who keeps an inn not far away from here, and it would please us if Bella accompanied us there."

The fat woman frowned and indicated their surroundings with a wave of a flabby hand. "This is her home, sir. She doesn't care to go out much."

Dickens said with animation, "But this is our one and only night in the locality! Who knows when we will return? My friend and I wish to enjoy a memorable finale to our sojourn south of the river!"

He passed her another sheaf of notes, and the woman caught her breath. So did Collins. Clutching the money tightly in her fist, as if fearing that he might change his mind, the brothel keeper whispered, "Well, sir, the circumstances are obviously exceptional. Very exceptional indeed."

"I'm glad we understand each other. Now, if we can be shown to Bella's room?"

The woman glanced at a battered old clock on the sideboard and let out a snort of temper. "I'm sure she won't be long. Perhaps you'd like to make yourselves comfortable in the parlor while I see what's what?"

She shuffled back into the malodorous passageway, and they followed her into a rear hall, from which a narrow flight of stairs ran up to the floors above. Opposite the bottom of the staircase was an open door leading to another room. A bald unshaven man in shirtsleeves, heedless of the chill of evening, was standing there, a tankard in his hand. He glanced at the two visitors, but seemed more interested in savoring his ale. Collins surmised that he was a "watcher," retained to keep an eye on the girls and customers of the House of the Red Candle.

Someone was coming down the stairs, taking them two at a time, stumbling over her skirts so that it seemed that she might at any moment trip and fall head over heels. The fat woman demanded, "Where d'you think you're hurrying off to, Nellie Brown?"

Nellie came to rest at the foot of the stairs. She was a stooping, round-shouldered woman in a lace cap and a maid's uniform. Pulling a handkerchief from a pocket, she blew her nose long and loudly.

"Nowhere, m'm," she croaked.

"I have two gentlemen here with an appointment to see Bella. You took His Lordship up a good three quarters of an hour ago. You left the key with him, didn't you?"

With eyes downcast, Nellie said, "Yes, m'm."

"Well, he never needs longer than thirty minutes. What are they doing up there?"

Nellie, evidently reluctant to meet Mrs. Jugg's gaze, bowed her head and declined to speculate.

"Lost your tongue, girl? Why, he was supposed to be out of there a good fifteen minutes ago!"

"Yes, m'm."

"I can't abide cheats, whatever their airs and graces! He paid for half an hour, no more. If he wanted longer, that could have been arranged."

Nellie's shoulders moved in a hapless shrug as she considered the threadbare carpet.

Dickens shifted impatiently from foot to foot, and the woman snapped, "Well, I can't keep these two gentlemen waiting. You'll have to rouse her."

Nellie darted a glance at Bella's visitors before shrinking away from them, as if fearing a slap, or worse. Collins thought she was afraid of Dickens; he had a fleeting impression of dark, secretive eyes and a disfiguring mark on her left cheek that she was striving to shield from his gaze.

For a moment Dickens seemed taken aback, but then he said,

"Yes, my friend and I have made a special journey. We prefer not to waste our time."

Collins was disconcerted by the sudden urgency in his friend's tone. His mood of excitement had given way to fascinated apprehension. The whole evening had taken on an *Arabian Nights* quality. Dickens had a hedonistic streak, but his taste did not usually extend to houses of ill fame quite as unsalubrious as this.

"Take them up with you, Nellie," the fat woman commanded. "Bang on the door until he leaves her be. I don't care if he hasn't got time to button up his trousers, d'you hear? He's long overdue!"

"But . . ." Nellie sniffled. Her distress was unmistakable.

"At once, or it'll be the worse for you!"

The maid began to drag herself up the stairs as if her limbs were made of lead. At a nod from the old woman, the two men followed. When they reached the landing on the first floor, Collins whispered in his friend's ear, "Both of us with the same girl? Taking her to a nearby inn? For Heaven's sake! What are you thinking of?"

"I asked you to trust me," Dickens muttered.

The only illumination came from the faint glow of the moon through a skylight. The ceiling was low and a taller man would have needed to bend to avoid banging his head against it. Three doors led from the landing. From two of the rooms issued the unmistakable cries of men and women in the throes of ecstasy. Nellie halted in front of the third door, and it seemed to Collins that a tremor ran through the whole of her body.

Dickens hissed, "Is that Bella's room? Come, there is no need to be frightened. You can see we are gentlemen! I swear, we mean her no harm."

She shot another glance at them, taking in Dickens's extravagant clusters of brown hair and Collins's fancy yellow waistcoat. Her lips were pursed, as if she were thinking: *not quite gentlemen, actually*. Her dark eyes, misty with suspicion, held something else as well. Collins realized that it was terror. Did this pitiful creature really believe that she would be called to join Bella in satisfying their lusts? The thought had the same effect as a drenching by a bucket of ice water.

"My friend is right," he said. "And we mean you no harm, either. What are you afraid of, Nellie? That Bella's customer will want to punish you for disturbing him? We won't allow it, do you hear? We simply won't let him take out his anger on you, will we?"

Dickens nodded. "The sooner the blackguard is gone, the better."

Tears began to form in Nellie's eyes. "But, sir . . ."

Dickens patted her on the shoulder. "I am *sure* you are a good friend to her, Nellie," he said meaningfully. "So let me tell you this. The sooner you introduce us to Bella, the better for everyone."

The maid seemed to have been paralyzed. Even when Collins gave her an encouraging nod, she did not move an inch.

"He has the key to this room," she said. "All I can do is knock. If he don't answer . . ."

Dickens took a step toward her. "Does he hurt her, Nellie?"

She choked on a sob. "I . . . I can't say."

"We must stop this," he said. "Will you knock at her door?"

"Sir, I—"

She was interrupted by a sound from inside the room. A low groan. And then, unmistakably, a man's hoarse voice.

"Please . . . help me!"

As the voice fell silent, Nellie screamed. Dickens leapt forward, hammering the door with his fist. "Let us in! For pity's sake, let us in!"

Collins rushed to his friend's side and pressed his ear to the keyhole, but he could detect no further sound from inside. The door was locked. Nellie's head was in her hands and she had begun to weep. Dickens put his shoulder to the door in an attempt to shift it, but to no avail.

The commotion must have roused the watcher down below, for a coarse voice roared, "What's to do? What's to do?"

One of the doors to the landing was flung open, and a half-dressed man appeared. "What's happening, for God's sake? Are the peelers here?"

Within moments the place was in uproar. The man who feared the arrival of the police was fastening his britches with clumsy desperation. A grizzled old fellow emerged from the second room, wheezing so frantically that Collins feared that he might succumb to a heart attack at any moment. The bald ruffian from the parlor was lumbering upstairs, with the fat brothel-keeper trailing in his wake. Looking into the other rooms, Collins could see two naked girls cowering in the shadows. Their clients jostled past the bald watcher, the younger man taking the steps two at a time in his haste to escape.

The watcher grabbed Dickens by the arm. "Causing trouble, mister? Why did she scream?"

"We heard the voice of Bella's client," Dickens said. "He sounded frightened and in pain. But the door is locked and I cannot force it open."

The man pushed him aside and heaved against the door. Timber splintered, but the lock held. Puffing furiously, the fat little woman arrived on the landing.

"What's all this to-do?" she demanded, turning furiously to Nellie. "Where's Bella?"

The maid was sobbing piteously and unable to speak. Fearing that the fat woman would strike her servant, Collins interposed his squat frame between them and said, "We heard her visitor. Something—is very wrong."

The watcher grunted and took a step back before charging at the door. They heard the wood giving way. He charged again and this time the door yielded under his weight. Bella's room was no more than twelve feet square. Apart from a tall cupboard and a double bed, the only furniture was a cracked looking glass and a battered old captain's chair on which were piled a pair of tweed trousers and an expensively tailored jacket as well as a man's underthings, evidently discarded in haste.

Stretched out on the bed lay the body of a naked man. His wrists were tied to the bedstead by lengths of rope, his glassy eyes staring sightlessly at the ceiling. Collins had a sudden fancy that he saw in them a look of horrified bewilderment. Tall and broad-shouldered, with heavy jowls, the man had a shock of jet-black hair. His lips had a sensual curve. Blood dripped on to the sheets from a gash in his stomach, an inch above the navel.

The watcher uttered an oath. "She's done for him!"

"Murder!" the fat woman cried. "Oh, Bella, you stupid little bitch!"

Behind them, Nellie retched. Dickens was the first to move. He rushed into the room and bent by the corpse, searching for a pulse. After a moment he said, "Nothing. Nothing at all."

"There's her weapon," the watcher said, pointing to a pair of scissors lying on the floor. They were dark with blood.

The brothel-keeper lifted the man's coat from the chair. A leather wallet tumbled from one of the pockets. She picked it up and folded it open. They could all see that the wallet was empty.

"So she's a thief as well as a murderess! I'll swing for that precious little bitch, just see if she won't!"

Only four of them were in the room: the fat woman, the bald man, Collins, and Dickens. Outside the door Nellie was wailing, her head in her hands. Of Bella there was no trace.

"She must be in there!" the fat woman cried, waving at the cupboard.

The two friends held their breath as the bald man flung open the cupboard door. Collins was not sure what he expected to see: a cowering woman, stripped and covered in blood, he supposed. The cupboard was crammed to overflowing with gaudy gowns and dresses. As well as a pair of tasseled boots, there was a mass of lace and ribbons piled high on the cupboard floor. The watcher tore the clothes aside, as if to unmask his quarry, lurking behind them. But there was no sign of her.

The room had a small rectangular window set high in the wall above the end of the bed. Collins could detect no other means of egress. The watcher ripped the blankets from the mattress, but found nothing. He got down on his hands and knees and peered underneath the bed, discovering only dust.

Unable to help himself, Collins cried, *"Where is she?"*

The fat woman clasped a podgy hand to her heart. "The window is bolted shut. Besides that, there are bars outside."

"Could the bars have been tampered with?"

The bald watcher clambered onto the bed and shoved at the window. There was no hint of movement. Shaking his head, he said, "I couldn't move 'em, never mind a young slip of a girl like her."

"How can she vanish into thin air?" Collins demanded. "This Bella, is she a wraith, a phantom?"

"All her clothes are in the cupboard," the fat woman gasped. "Every stitch. But where is the key?"

"The girl must have it," the watcher said. "She is hiding somewhere."

"Not in here," Dickens murmured.

Beyond argument, he was right. Dickens pointed to the corpse. "This man came here alone, I take it?"

"Oh, yes. He was one of her regulars. Always paid handsomely for her time."

"When he arrived, you handed him the key and asked Nellie to escort him up to this room?"

Mrs. Jugg nodded. "Ain't that right, Nell?"

The maid, still sniveling out on the landing, managed a grunt.

Dickens said, "You saw him enter the room?"

"As he put the key in the lock," the maid croaked, "he told me I could go."

"So you did not see Bella herself?" Collins asked.

The maid shook her head, but the fat woman said impatiently, "Of course, Bella was in the room, waiting for him. She was here all evening, same as usual. Nellie brought her up and locked her in, same as always. The gentleman had an appointment. He called upon her every Thursday at nine, regular as clockwork."

"She must have done him in and then locked the door on him," the bald man said. "It's the only way."

"If she'd come down to the ground, you'd have stopped her, wouldn't you, Jack my lad?"

"She could never get past me," he boasted. "She's tried it once or twice and I made her pay for it, so help me."

"Then," Dickens suggested, "if she is flesh and blood and not a poltergeist, she must be concealed in one of the other rooms on this floor."

"He's right," the watcher said.

"What are you waiting for, then?" the fat woman demanded. "Let's find her, quick!"

They hurried out and into the adjoining bedroom. Dickens moved swiftly to Nellie's side and whispered something to her before returning and pulling the door shut behind him.

"What did you say to her?" Collins asked.

Dickens was staring at the pale flesh of the dead man. "Do you recognize him, Wilkie?"

"The face seems familiar, but—"

"This is the Honorable Thaddeus Whiteacre. You heard the woman refer to him as 'His Lordship'? He liked to play up his noble origins. Besides that, he fancied himself as something of an artist, although to my mind his daubs were infantile. John Forster introduced me to him a year ago at a meeting of the Guild for Literature and Art."

"You are acquainted?"

"Regrettably. *De mortuis*, Wilkie, but he struck me as one of the least agreeable men I have ever met. I recall a conversation in which he sought to convince me of the pleasure that could be gained from inflicting pain—and having pain inflicted upon oneself."

Collins shivered as he considered the corpse's face. Even in death, the saturnine features seemed menacing. He found it easy to imagine that they belonged to a man with vile and sinister tastes.

"Do you believe that Bella killed him?"

Dickens put a finger to his lips. "Come, let us join the search."

The watcher and his mistress were opening and slamming shut cupboard doors and drawers scarcely large enough to accommodate a box of clothes, let alone a full-grown woman. It was absurd, Collins thought, to imagine that the missing girl could have taken refuge in a room where a colleague was entertaining a client—but where might she have concealed herself? The brothel-keeper was cursing and describing in savage terms what she would do to Bella once she was found. Nellie had scuttled off downstairs, while the shivering prostitutes hugged each other in a corner and tried not to attract the fat woman's attention.

"She's been spirited away!" one of the girls said. Her face was blotchy and tear-stained, her body covered in yellowing bruises. Collins doubted if she was yet sixteen years of age. "It's the Devil's work!"

"Bella would never hurt a fly!" the other girl cried. "Someone else has done this! Or some*thing*. Killed His Lordship and then kidnapped Bella!"

"Shut your mouths!" the brothel-keeper shouted. "Bogeymen don't stab strong fellows to death with scissors. And as for you, Jack Wells, don't think I've finished with you—not by a long chalk!"

"I told you, she couldn't have passed me," the bald man said mutinously. "I never take my eye off the stairs when there are visitors in the house."

"Then where did she go? I've been by the front door ever since Nellie roused me at five."

"You reside on the premises, I suppose?" Dickens said.

"In the basement, that's right. But it would have been impossible for her to get down there. Jack or I would have seen her. And there aren't any windows she could have climbed through to get out of the building. Besides, her boots were in the cupboard. That's her only pair. She can't have got far without her boots!"

"The fact remains," Dickens said, "that Bella has vanished. It is as if she never existed. Yet my friend and I have not enjoyed the privileges for which we paid handsomely. May I ask for reimbursement of—"

The bald man took a couple of paces toward them and seized Dickens's collar. "So you want your money back, do you? Well, you'll have to whistle for it!"

"That's right!" the fat woman shouted, as if glad to find a target for her fury that was made of flesh and blood. "If you two know what's good for you, you'll clear off now like those other lily-livered bastards!"

"Please assure me," Dickens said, rubbing his neck as the bald man released his grip, "that there is no question of your summoning the police."

The fat woman stared at him. "Think I was born yesterday? No fear of that, mister. Them peelers would like nothing better than to pin something on me."

"But the body—" Collins began.

"Jack will find a graveyard for it," she interrupted. "Don't you fear."

"At the bottom of the Thames, I suppose?" Dickens said.

The bald watcher scowled at him. "You heard what she said. It's as easy for me to chuck three bodies in the river as one."

Dickens caught his friend's eye and nodded toward the stairs. "Very well. We will go."

"And don't come back," the fat woman said. "You've brought trouble to this house, you two. Theft and murder. Now, Jack, you see to the body while I get Nellie to help me look for that murderous little bitch."

Dickens hurried down the stairs, with Collins close behind. As they reached the ground, they heard the brothel-keeper calling Nellie's name, but Collins could not see the maid in the parlor. He presumed that she was in the front room, where the red candle burned. Dickens caught hold of his wrist and manhandled him down the passageway and out into the fog.

An hour later the two friends were ensconced in the more congenial and familiar surroundings of the Ship and Turtle in the heart of the City. Exhausted on their arrival after racing from Greenwich, they had quaffed a couple of glasses of ale to calm their nerves with scarcely a word of conversation.

"An extraordinary evening," Collins said at length. "Expensive, too."

Dickens shrugged, his expression shorn of emotion. So energetic by nature, he seemed in an uncharacteristically reflective mood. "For the Honorable Thaddeus Whiteacre, undoubtedly."

"Well, I realize you are a man of means, old fellow, but you must be bitter at having spent so much for so little reward."

"Oh, I'm not so sure about that, Wilkie."

Collins stared at his friend. "I really think that it is time that you were frank with me. Your behavior tonight has been most extraordinary. I thought that we were out for a little innocent amusement. . . ."

"I agree that what happened was neither innocent nor amusing."

". . . and instead we ended up running through a pea-souper, fleeing from a madam's hired ruffian. Even since we've arrived here, you've spent most of the time staring into space, as if trying to unravel the most ticklish conundrum."

"In which endeavor I believe I have succeeded. You are right, Wilkie. I do owe you an explanation. But first—let us have another drink!"

"You almost sound as if you are celebrating a glorious triumph," Collins grumbled as a waiter replenished their glasses.

"In a sense," Dickens said calmly, "I am. Your health, dear Wilkie!"

"But we have been present at the scene of a brutal slaying!" Collins protested. "What is worse, the circumstances are such that we cannot inform the police. I might be a young nobody, but you are Dickens the Inimitable, the most famous writer in England. Not even your friendship with Inspector Field could save you from disgrace if the truth came out. He could not hush up your presence at the scene of the crime, even if he wished to do so. The author who patronized a house of ill repute on the night of a murder—how the scandal sheets would love that story!"

"True, true."

"You have not yet told me how you became acquainted with Bella," Collins grumbled.

"Forgive me, Wilkie," Dickens said. "Undoubtedly you deserve an explanation for the night's events."

"In so far as you can explain the inexplicable."

"Oh, I shall do my best," Dickens said, with an impish smile. "I met Bella one night when my nocturnal ramblings took me to that God-forsaken tavern the Rope and Anchor. I was sitting just where you and I sat this evening. Looking round, I noticed a young woman in the company of Jack Wells, whom you met this evening. Her profession was apparent from her dress, if not from her demeanor, yet I was struck by her quite astonishing beauty. She is no more than seventeen, Wilkie, but her face and figure were as fine as any I have seen in a long time. More than that, there was an innocence and purity about her that I found mesmerizing. It was as if, by some miracle, she had yet to be tainted by her profession. But it was plain that she was in the depths of misery, above all that she was in mortal fear of her brutish companion. I surmised that she was a dress lodger and that the madam of the house where she plied her trade had instructed Wells to keep an eye on her."

"That is the way these people run their business, is it not? A watcher dogs the dress lodger's footsteps to make sure that she does not run away from the brothel."

"Exactly. As I studied the girl, I found myself speculating about her history, imagining the sequence of events that had reduced her to such dire straits. It can happen easily enough, you know." A dreamy look came into Dickens's eyes. Collins had seen the same expression when he acted before the Queen at Devonshire House, throwing himself body and soul into his part, so that any deficiencies in thespian talent were amply compensated by the intensity of his imaginative investment in his performance. "A young woman, perhaps an orphan, becomes destitute and is 'rescued' by an apparently kindhearted older lady. She is offered salvation in the form of board and lodging, only to learn—too late!—that the price is higher than she can afford. Possibly she is accused of a petty theft—a put-up job, with the threat of criminal prosecution supposedly bought off by the bribing of a bogus police officer. By whatever means, the madam ensures that the victim stays deeply in her debt. The poor wretch must repay by selling the only wares that she possesses. Oh, yes, Wilkie, there are female slaves in plantations across the ocean that enjoy liberty for which a dress lodger in a mean London brothel can only offer up hopeless prayers."

Collins swallowed a mouthful of beer. "It is pure wickedness."

"Indeed. I hold that a woman is free to sell herself, just as a man is free to buy. That is the way of the world, and has been throughout history. But when all that the woman earns goes to the harridan who keeps her in thrall . . . well, emboldened by drink, I decided that I must do something. This young woman might only be one of a thousand dress lodgers in this city, but I vowed to myself that I would set her free."

"But you knew nothing of her."

"Only what I had seen in her lovely, wistful face. Yet it was enough, Wilkie. I decided to bide my time and when the watcher succumbed to a call of nature, I approached the girl. I urged her to come with me and escape from her guard while she had the chance. But she was terrified and suspected a trap. I could see in her eyes that she yearned to believe that I was offering her a chance to start a new life, but her fear of Jack Wells and his mistress was stronger than the faith she could muster in the words of a complete stranger. Within a minute I realized it was no good. I had time merely to ask her name and where she lived."

"Bella, from Mrs. Jugg's lodging, the House of the Red Candle in Greenwich," Collins murmured.

"Precisely. Even as she gave me those few details, a look of panic crossed her face, and I realized that Jack Wells was returning to take charge of her. I made myself scarce—but not without whispering a promise that I would see her again and set her free."

"Hence tonight?"

"Hence tonight." Dickens sighed. "I had not reckoned that Fate would intervene in the sordid shape of her regular client, the Honorable Thaddeus Whiteacre."

"I suppose he abused her terribly."

"No doubt," Dickens said softly. "Yet Bella does not lack spirit. She did not trust a stranger in a tavern to rescue her, but she was prepared to save herself. So she conceived an audacious scheme of her own, to kill Whiteacre and escape with all the funds he kept in his wallet."

"You are sure that she did murder him?"

Dickens gave him a pitying look. "Who else?"

"Indeed. But *how*?"

"There, my dear Wilkie, I can only speculate."

"For the Lord's sake, Dickens, you can't leave it at that!"

For a moment Dickens eyed his friend, scarcely able to contain his amusement. "Very well. If you wish to hear my theory, then I shall be glad to share it with you. I make just one condition."

"Name it."

"That, after tonight, we never speak of this matter again. No matter what the circumstances. Can I trust your discretion?"

"Naturally," Collins said in a stiff voice.

"I mean it, Wilkie. We must hold our tongues forever. Two lives depend upon it."

"Two?"

"Those of Bella and the maidservant Nellie Brown."

Collins frowned. "It was hardly the maid's fault that she led Whiteacre to his death and that Bella contrived to flee from the House of the Red Candle. If indeed she did escape."

"Oh, I think she did."

"But *how*?"

Dickens finished his ale and put the tankard down on the table. "I helped her to escape."

"We have been together all evening," Collins said. "How could you have done so?"

Dickens grinned. "When I saw the chance for her to get away, I whispered that she should seize it. My fear was that she might be overcome by remorse at the enormity of her crime and confess her guilt to the madam. I do not condone the taking of life, but tonight I am tempted to make an exception."

"But I don't—"

"She masqueraded as Nellie Brown," Dickens interrupted. "You saw the real maidservant yourself. She was waiting at the Rope and Anchor for her friend. Remember how the drunken women mocked her, and all because of the scar on her cheek?"

"That was Nellie?"

"I am sure of it. Bella had borrowed her clothes, so as to fool Mrs. Jugg. I suppose they slipped out of the house while Mrs. Jugg was dozing and under cover of the fog sliding in from the Thames, Bella put Nellie's garments on under her own dress. Once she was back in the upstairs room, she reversed the outfits. She must have strapped her bosom down—I recall that she was quite formidably endowed, Wilkie!—and used cosmetic preparations to mimic the scar on her friend's cheek. She is a couple of inches taller than Nellie, and she needed to stoop and kept her head bent so as to avoid close scrutiny. She was relying on Mrs. Jugg's poor eyesight and Jack Wells's lack of imaginative intelligence. When, in Nellie's character, she showed Whiteacre into the room and then revealed herself as Bella, no doubt he was amused by the impersonation, perhaps even excited by it. We can speculate as to the inducement she offered to persuade him not only to strip for her, but to allow her to tie him up. When he was at her mercy, she stabbed him, but with insufficient force to kill him straight away. Then she stole his money. Knowing Whiteacre's penchant for heavy spending, I suspect she found enough to keep her and Nellie out of the brothels forever and a day. She committed a wicked crime, but I cannot find it in my heart to condemn her for it."

"She must have been trying to escape when we saw her coming down the stairs."

"One can scarcely imagine her feelings when she was forced to take us back to the room," Dickens said softly.

"And when she heard her victim's dying words. No wonder she vomited when faced with the horror of his corpse. But how did you guess what had happened?"

"Guess?" Dickens raised his eyebrows in amusement. "The scar was my clue. It bore such an uncanny resemblance to that which disfigured the woman in the Rope and Anchor that the whole scheme revealed itself to me. But Bella made one mistake."

"Which was?"

"When she put on the makeup, she forgot that she was applying it to an image in a looking-glass. And so her scar ran down the right cheek. But Nellie's was on the left."

A Long and Constant Courtship

BY CAROLYN WHEAT

For twenty-three years Carolyn Wheat lived in New York City, where she practiced law and wrote mystery stories. Three years ago she began a new life traveling around America, where she spent some time in Boulder, Sonoma County, San Diego, and then Oklahoma, where she was artist in residence for two years at the University of Central Oklahoma, helping student writers to live their dreams. She now lives in California. Her latest book, *How to Write Killer Fiction*, is a *Writer's Digest* Book Club Selection.

"The law is a jealous mistress and requires a long and constant courtship. It is not to be won by trifling favors, but by lavish homage."
JUSTICE JOSEPH STORY

"HE'S AS DEEP as Australia," old Mr. Wemmick told me on my first day in Mr. Jaggers's employ. "If there was anything deeper, he'd be it."

I had no reason to doubt his words. Indeed, I had myself witnessed Jaggers's triumphal progress—there could be no other word for it—from the Old Bailey to Bartholomew Close. At every step along that lugubrious way, he was accosted by clients, would-be clients, families of clients, all importuning him, all begging a crumb of reassurance from the table of his enormous competence.

No such reassurance was forthcoming—and the lawyer's fierce black brow and forbidding demeanor, his complete refusal to offer one single word of kindness, only served to reinforce that faith in his ability that bordered upon heathen superstition. To one ragged pleader, he thundered, "*You* thought? How dare *you* think! *I* think for you, that's enough." To a woman sobbing into her dirty shawl over a son charged with petty theft, he growled, "I am for him, what more can you want?" To a supplicant who attempted to whisper fell secrets into his ear, Jaggers said sharply, "I want to know no more than I know. I am not curious. Tell me nothing save for one single, vital fact."

The man's eyes widened. He looked terrified; whatever Jaggers wanted to know, he *must* provide, or his brother would surely hang. "Have you paid Wemmick?" The man nodded. "Then you may go." The man went, shaking his head, not as might be supposed, in despair, but with a look of stunned wonder upon his face. One paid Wemmick and one's brother did not hang. Justice was, after all, a simple thing.

I was about to become the solicitor's first articled clerk. Old Mr. Wemmick, who wished to retire to the country within the year, would teach me all I needed to know about making fair copies and handling pleadings while Jaggers would educate me in the sinuous path of the law. After a suitable period of years, I would emerge a second Jaggers, able to take instructions from clients, conduct police-court trials, and advise barristers on my own. Always a man of caution, Jaggers agreed to take me on a month's trial before agreeing to sign the articles my father wished to purchase for me.

At first, I thrilled to the life of the law. I found even the dank, dismal corners of Newgate Prison exciting beyond measure, for each told a story, each represented a passionate moment in a human life.

That so many of our clients were patently guilty bothered me not at all, a circumstance that delighted my employer. "Judge not, lest ye be judged" appeared to be his favorite maxim. We judged not, and we did our best to persuade juries to judge not as well.

My favorite moments were those I spent in the crowded police-court, watching Jaggers cross-examine witnesses. In truth, it was difficult to tell whether the witness in question was his own or the prosecution's, for he put his questions with such force and power, such an air of knowing something discreditable about the hapless individual in the witness-box, that even citizens who had come to offer testimony on his own client's behalf hung in dread rapture on his words, and shrank when his massive eyebrows turned in their direction. "I'll have it out of you!" was his thunderous cry, and "Now I have got you!" struck witnesses dumb. Whenever a word seemed to go against him, he thundered at the court clerk to "take it down."

He ground the whole place into a mill. I sat in wondrous admiration, daydreaming of the time when I, too, could command the courtroom with such incisive questioning. I had no other ambition but to follow my new profession with zeal.

At last a day came that I had begun to suspect must come. I had seen Jaggers preparing a witness for testimony before, but I had never observed the proceeding from the beginning; that is to say, I had viewed my employer questioning a person already dressed for his appearance at trial. This may strike some as a trifling distinction— what, after all, does it signify if a witness wears his own habitual attire or strives for that respectability which a court appearance ought to stimulate? The difference was soon to become clear to me.

I was accustomed to the throng of supplicants who lined the street leading to Jaggers's office, but this time the place directly before the door was taken up by three enormous brutes, each one larger and more menacing than the last. I recognized one of them as the brother of the client whose trial was to start on the morrow. "Hello, Bill," I said as I took my place beside him and waited for Wemmick to arrive with the key.

He replied with a grunt and then, lowering his voice and taking me into his confidence, asked, "Do ye think these will do, sir? Do you think Mr. Jaggers will approve of them?"

"Approve of them for what purpose?" I suppose I deserved the blank, baffled look that greeted my words.

"Why, approve of them as witnesses for Jem's trial, o'course," he said. "They can swear as to character or alleybye, sir, whichever is needed."

I was not so green as to think our client possessed a character that could be sworn to by anyone with a straight face, and one look at the prospective witnesses belied any pretense to their being able to swear to anyone's good name. They were brutes of the sort habitually involved in drunken brawls, as evidenced by several bruises on each broad face.

As to providing Jem with an alibi, I had, in my innocence, believed a witness actually had to have been with the accused at the time of the crime in order to offer testimony of that nature. It was clear that Bill had no such conviction; for him, anyone who was willing to swear to Jem's having been with him on the night in question would suffice.

I had no doubt that Mr. Jaggers would send Bill packing, and that his tongue would be exceedingly sharp when he did so.

He did no such thing. "Alibi, is it?" He looked the two brutes up and down, frowning and biting his finger, his heavy black brows knotted in thought.

"You," he said to the one nearest the door, "have you ever worked as a butcher?"

"I were a butcher's apprentice when I were a nipper," he replied, astonishment in his face.

"Can you obtain a butcher's apron?" The man nodded, obviously mystified by the lawyer's questions.

His companion was quicker on the uptake. "I been a bricklayer," he volunteered.

"Excellent," Jaggers said, rubbing his hands together. "You will both appear at the Old Bailey tomorrow in the accoutrements just mentioned."

The witnesses would not lie about their professions; their clothing would lie for them. The jurors would see, not two hulking brutes ready to swear to anything that would save their friend, but two honest workingmen taking precious time from earning their livings in order to speak the truth about their friend's whereabouts on the night of the crime.

That they were nowhere near Jem that night was a fact known to them, but not *known* to Jaggers. He might suspect it, he might believe in his deepest soul that it was true, but he would not know it because he chose not to know it. I now had the full meaning of his cryptic phrase "Do not tell me. I do not wish to know more than I know." He often said to me, "Take nothing on its looks. Take everything on evidence alone. There is no better rule." I now understood why he distrusted looks and understood to his very core how misleading they could be.

If I were to become a second Jaggers, would I have to develop the same highly calibrated set of scruples? Would I be obliged not to know a great many things, and to dress my witnesses in a respectability they did not in actuality possess? Was I to lose all moral sense in order to make a living in the legal profession?

Would I, like my future employer, scrub my hands with scented soap after dirtying them in the service of the law? Would I wash my clients off my hands, scrape my cases out of my nails with a penknife, and repair to a lonely retreat after a day's work?

These questions nagged at me as I made my way to a tavern on Fleet Street where lawyers and newspapermen alike repaired for a healing glass after their day's work. I downed an entire pint of best bitter in a matter of minutes, and still my head pounded with the force of my thoughts.

As I quaffed my second pint, almost as quickly as my first, I became aware of a small, elderly man standing beside me at the public bar. "You're Jaggers's boy, aren't you?"

I should have liked to deny being anyone's boy, least of all my employer's, but after what I had been through that afternoon, I felt myself a child, and a slow one at that. "I work for Mr. Jaggers," I replied shortly, not wishing to prolong the conversation.

"You're articled to him, I understand."

"Not yet," I said, and that answer provided the only glimmer of hope I'd had all day. "My articles are not yet signed."

"I am glad to hear it," my companion replied. "Then there is still time."

The little man's words coincided so completely with my own sentiments that I turned to stare at him in wonder. He was a sparrow of a man, with tiny bones and sharp features. His hair was white and thinly spread over a scalp as pink as a ham. His black suit was shiny with wear and his neck cloth needed washing. Yet his speech was so refined, so educated, that I was certain he had fallen from a higher station in life, and, from the smell of his breath, I deduced that a love of alcohol played some role in his decline.

"I know Mr. Jaggers, you see," he said in a low, confiding tone. Since everyone in a ten-block radius of the Bailey knew Jaggers, I hardly felt this was a great distinction. I was about to say so, when my companion went on, "I knew Jaggers when he was scarcely older than you are now. I knew him before he took the case that made his reputation."

I confessed myself intrigued. Although two pints had hitherto been my limit in the Bench and Bar, I ordered a third and one for my new friend and motioned him toward a table in the private bar.

"Tell me about Mr. Jaggers," I said once we were settled near the fire, our pints brimming with foam.

"Oh, he was green. Grass green. As verdant as the sticky new leaves of spring was our Mr. Jaggers in those days." The old lawyer, for such I decided he must be, lifted his glass and drained it in one long pull, then gave a great, deep belch of contentment, either as tribute to a noble brew or indication that another would not be entirely unwelcome.

I could not imagine a young Jaggers. So intimidating was that worthy, so beetled his brow, so biting his tongue, so cutting his cross-examination (and Mr. Jaggers was a man whose very good morning was a form of cross-examination) that I am sure my countenance wore an expression of complete disbelief.

"Are we talking of the same Jaggers? The one whose office is in Bartholomew Close?" My rheumy-eyed companion assured me that we were.

"What happened to him to make him as he is now?" I asked.

"It was a case of murder, a very popular murder indeed." I understood the reference; some murders went unnoticed by the general public, while others gave rise to cheaply printed broadsides and much tavern speculation. "Jaggers represented a woman named Molly." The old man called for another round. I begged off, having scarcely touched my pint. "She was a Gypsy, as beautiful as she was treacherous, and she killed another woman in cold blood."

The immediate prospect of his client's being hanged concentrated Mr. Jaggers's mind wonderfully. He felt he had never really been alive before, so fresh did the air seem, so brightly colored and fragrant the flowers in Hyde Park. Knowing that he was at last about to embark upon a trial of such magnitude, with such irrevocable consequences, sharpened his senses and focused his brain. On the one hand, he profoundly regretted that he had been unable to convince the police to free her without a trial; on the other, the keen blade of his legal mind longed for the whetting of a court proceeding that promised so much.

His client was accused of strangling her rival with her bare hands. Gypsy blood, the newspapers hinted, was at the root of her passionate nature. Gypsy blood was evident in the blackness of her hair, the flashing dark eyes, the spirit with which she denied the crime. She was a woman of low birth and lower habits; her trial was of interest to the public only because of the sensational aspects of her crime. For a woman to kill her lover in a hot-blooded rage was one thing, but the killing of another woman was a crime so depraved that the London papers made a feast of it.

⌗

"Jaggers was engaged in those days," the little man went on.

I could not help myself. "Who would marry a man like Jaggers?"

The old storyteller countered with the only possible reply: "He wasn't a man like Jaggers—yet. He was a young man with a young man's hopes and dreams, a young man's power of address, a young man's eye for the ladies. He was engaged, as I said, to a respectable young woman named Clara, daughter of a local doctor and quite beautiful, with three hundred a year to recommend her over and above her lovely face."

"Jaggers engaged!" I shook my head in wonder. I knew him as a man of regular habits, living alone in Soho save for a housekeeper some said he'd once got off on a charge of murder. The thought that he might have married struck me dumb.

* * *

Clara Scrivens thought her affianced the most intelligent of men. It seemed her life held no higher goal than to be married to a successful lawyer. It is true she would rather he devoted his time to respectable clients; she often suggested he seek out more like Miss Havisham, whose affairs he managed in addition to his criminal work. On the other hand, she believed with her whole heart his pronouncement that in acting for the defense he embodied the very bedrock of the British system of justice.

That is to say, she felt all these things until Jaggers took on the case of Molly the Gypsy. Molly's case unnerved her in ways no previous trial had done. Drunken men fighting outside pubs, robbers stripped of their booty by stronger robbers, even the case of the landlady who poisoned her lodgers failed to stir Clara's moral scruples as did the woman who put her hands around her rival's neck and strangled her. Clara begged Jaggers to refuse the case, and once the woman was committed for trial, she implored him to let trial counsel take the lead.

"You have such powers," she told him, her dark eyes filled with admiration. "Surely your penetrating cross-examination should be reserved for those clients truly worthy of it. You mustn't waste it on guilty defendants but use it only in the service of justice."

"If I did that, my dear Clara," he replied with a tolerant smile for her feminine sentimentality, "we would starve within the year. I cannot set myself up as judge and jury, you know. I must take my clients as they are and do my best for them, no matter my private beliefs."

Clara was not a stupid woman; she understood this principle, and yet the image of the raven-haired, hot-eyed Gypsy placing her thick fingers around her rival's neck and squeezing the very life out of her was enough to deny her sleep. Or perhaps her real source of anxiety was the words Jaggers appended to his remarks: "Besides, this case will make my reputation. If I can succeed in convincing a jury that this virago is not guilty, then I can command any fee I choose for my services. My name will be synonymous with court-room victory, and I shall become the most sought-after counsel in the entire police-court." Clara knew enough not to point out that this glory would only lead to more guilty clients; it was clear Jaggers understood that part of his devil's bargain only too well.

⁂

"A more sensitive man might have forborne from talking of Molly to his affianced bride," my companion allowed, "but Jaggers was, as I said, grass-green. He gloated over his future success with these ill-advised words: 'She is so patently guilty, my dear, that obtaining her acquittal will be especially sweet.'"

I had found myself entertaining the same thoughts about certain of my own clients, even if I hadn't quite been prepared to put perjurers in the witness-box to secure those acquittals. I could hardly blame the young Jaggers for the same sentiments. "Clara begged him to withdraw from the case, but her pleas were in vain. He would defend Molly, he would acquit Molly, and he would stand before all London as the lawyer to be sought out in the most desperate of cases. Clara would see, when all was said and done, that her husband-to-be was right."

⁂

Newgate Prison, that gloomy depository of the guilt and misery of London, became a second home to young Mr. Jaggers. At first, to be sure, the stone walls, as massive and forbidding as a medieval castle, loomed over him with a menacing bulk, and the narrow windows that admitted but a fraction of light served only to deepen the dark-ness that entered his soul whenever he passed through the gates of the prison. The death masks and leg irons that served as decoration in the dismal warder's office did nothing to dispel his low mood (how surprised he would have been to learn that his own clerk's office would one day boast two death masks taken from his own clients' faces after hanging!).

The women prisoners occupied the right wing nearest the Sessions' House. They lived, ate, drank, slept, and conferred with visitors in a bare but spacious common room, whitewashed and heated by a fire in the grate. Pegs were hung beneath a shelf that ran the length of two sides of the room, from each hook hung a sleeping mat, and above it on the shelf sat the woman's rug and blanket. The women ate their meals and did their needlework at a large deal table near the fire.

As he grew in prosperity and reputation, Mr. Jaggers would come to be accorded the honor of meeting his clients in the governor's house, but at this time in his practice, he stood at the bars like everyone else visiting a prisoner. Next to him an Irishwoman berated her daughter for leaving honest ways, while several yards away a prisoner whose red shawl marked her profession spoke loudly with a like-attired friend about the prospect of getting off.

Gypsy Molly stood tall, looking as unconcerned as if her days in prison were nothing more than a visit to the seaside. "Who's going to say I killed her?" she demanded. "Answer that, Mr. Lawyer. Who's going to dare say I struck her down?"

Jaggers was young and inexperienced, but not so raw that this mode of speaking went past him. "If you are trying to say that you've threatened any witness who might come forward, let me tell you now that I won't have it. Do not tell me anything of the sort." ("You will, no doubt," my companion said with a sly smile at this point in the narrative, "note the subtle wording of the lawyer's admonition: he did not say, 'Do not threaten a witness,' he said, 'Do not tell me that you have done so.' Such is the artfulness of our breed.")

"Who said I threatened anybody? Did I say I threatened anybody?" Molly spread her arms wide and invited her fellow prisoners to take part in the conversation. As they had little else to occupy them, several joined in with vociferous assent.

The prison bars were spaced wide enough for a cat to slip through. Jaggers's arm, swift as a cat, reached in and grabbed Molly's wrist. He pulled it to his side of the bars and, with his other hand, peeled back the sleeve of her dirty gown.

The women standing around Molly gasped as Jaggers revealed a hand and wrist deeply scarred, as if scored by sharp knives. The wrist was thick and strong; the Gypsy's sinews strained at her lawyer's grasp.

Lifting his client's arm so that all could see, Jaggers raised his voice. "Who among you, having seen the strength of this woman's arm, having heard that she once threatened to strangle the deceased, having now seen the marks of the dead woman's fingernails on Gypsy Molly's wrist—who among you would find her Not Guilty?"

"She did for Long Liz all right," a slattern with rotten teeth and foul breath said.

"I never seen such a wrist on a woman," another said, half in fright and half in admiration.

"You're for it now, Moll," a third prisoner said, her tone thick with anticipation. "Them scratches will do you in, they will."

Molly wrenched her arm away from her lawyer's grasp. "It's your job to see they don't."

"And that job I shall do." Jaggers faced his client, his demeanor as cool as hers was hot. "You will wear the dresses I bring for you. You will stand in the dock with your hands at your sides, and the sleeves of those dresses will cover your wrists at all times. You will not stand to your full height, but bend your knees slightly and hunch your shoulders. Your task is to look as small and delicate as possible. You will not react in any way to what is said in court by the witnesses. I will have no outcries, no protestations of innocence, no shouts that the dead woman deserved what she got."

"She did, all the same," muttered the Gypsy.

"That sentiment must not appear in your face," Jaggers said in a cold voice. "I will allow only one emotion to appear upon your face, and that emotion is a single tear. You may shed that tear at any point in the trial, so long as the jury believes it is shed for the dead woman and not for your own plight."

"I'm to crawl, then."

"If you care to walk out of here into Newgate Street instead of leaving by way of the gallows, yes."

Mention of the gallows took the starch out of Gypsy Molly. Four men had hanged, all in a row like Christmas geese in the poulterer's window, that very morning. "I will do as you say," she whispered.

"And be sure to let your hair out of its pins," Jaggers added. "Let the jury see how young you are, and how . . ." He did not finish; he did not dare say "beautiful." The realization that the tall, pale woman with the abundant, flowing hair and flashing eyes could have been a famous beauty had she been born in a different station was one he dared not dwell upon.

⟨∽⟩

One week later Jaggers sat behind his counsel at the defense table in the Old Bailey. The woman who stood in the dock accused of mur-der wore a gown of pale blue muslin dotted with sprigs of violets. With a lacy collar caressing her throat and matching lace frills at her wrists, she looked to be the daughter of a respectable merchant. Instead of pulsing with life, she stood quiet as a wax figure, and her height seemed to have diminished by several inches.

"This woman," Jaggers whispered to the barrister who would actually question the witnesses, "this frail creature is charged with the murder of a woman ten years older than she, and much larger and stronger. Put it to the police witness that she could not have overcome the dead woman's strength."

"What of the scars on her hands?" The barrister was well known as a lazy man who tended to dwell upon the strength of the prosecution's case instead of his own.

"Brambles," Jaggers reminded him. He'd chosen his own trial counsel so that he, sitting in the place reserved for instructing solicitors, might control the cross-examination, but he was beginning to regret having selected someone so vague and forgetful. "She crawled through brambles. Remember, the police found brambles in her cuts, and they also found blood and shreds of her dress on the brambles. We can definitely establish brambles as the source of the scratches."

"But what of her jealousy?"

Jaggers sighed. Not for the first (or last) time in his long legal career did he regret that he had neither the birth nor the financial wherewithal to take silk himself. How much better it would be if he could stand before the bench, address the jury, and convince them instead of relying upon a surrogate! It was one thing to add the salt and pepper to the defense case, but he would so dearly have loved to cook the whole meal.

For two days the trial followed the lines Jaggers intended it to follow. Partisans of the deceased painted a portrait of Gypsy Molly as a perfect fury jealous of any woman seen talking to a man she fancied. For the defense, Jaggers had an equal number of witnesses prepared to swear that Long Liz had numerous enemies of both sexes, and that any one of them was just as likely as the prisoner to have killed her.

Then Lightfinger Tom stepped into the witness-box and dropped a bombshell so shocking that several London newspapers scrapped their front pages to run lurid accounts of the retired pickpocket's testimony.

"She was so jealous of Liz taking up with her man that she done for her own child out of revenge," Tom said. "Killed her own daughter to get back at her man, she did. Everyone in Seven Dials knew it."

The barrister hung his head so low his wig slipped to his eyebrows. Jaggers sat stiff as a board, unwilling to show by even a twitch that this news rocked him to the core. For her part, Molly obeyed her lawyer's instructions and stood as though carved of wood instead of flesh and blood. Jaggers hoped he was the only person in the courtroom who saw the glint of triumph in his client's dark eyes.

⁓

As soon as the court adjourned for the day, Jaggers made his way from the Bailey to Newgate Prison. The barrister, by choice as well as custom, refused any contact with the prisoner; he repaired to a local tavern to mourn his impending defeat with stout and sausages. The sun was lowering itself behind the massive stone buildings, and the dome of St. Paul's loomed overhead like the very personification of Divine Judgment.

That Molly the Gypsy had strangled Long Liz Jaggers had long been accepted. That she had killed her own child was something he could scarce imagine. Yet that glint of triumph told him the accusation was true. She'd done it and she was proud of it, and no jury in England could possibly forgive her for it.

On this visit the admiring crowd of women surrounding Molly was absent. Whatever any of them had done to bring them within these walls, they still felt morally superior to one who had murdered a child. Jaggers faced her, boring into her with his implacable eyes. "Is Tom telling the truth? Did you murder your daughter?"

The prisoner gave a toss of her magnificent head. Dusky curls moved seductively over her honey-colored throat, and her nostrils flared. Despite the coarseness of her speech and the horror of the allegations against her, Jaggers still felt a stirring whenever he was confronted by the sheer animal passion inside her. "So what if I did?" she asked. "That's got nothing to do with Liz's death, has it?"

"Strictly speaking, within the law," he replied, choosing his words carefully, "it does not. But few jurymen will be capable of separating the two crimes. They will convict you of the one if they believe the other."

"They shouldn't ought to, though, should they? I mean," she went on, cunning narrowing her black eyes, "it's my right to be tried for what I done to Liz, not for the baby. The baby's nothing to do with this crime."

"The prosecution says it shows how jealous you were. It says you killed your child to spite your husband for going with Long Liz." He drew in a long breath, hoping she'd deny the charge, call the child's death an accident or tell him it died of fever. God knew, children died of natural causes every day in the foul den where Molly lived.

"Before I let that bastard see her ever again, yes, I did." Her defiant stare told him she regretted nothing. "He took from me what was mine, so I took his child from him. He had it coming."

"But—" Jaggers hardly had the words to continue. *But the child wasn't his or yours*, he wanted to say. It belonged to itself, its life was worth something regardless of anything its parents had done.

And yet the creature standing not five feet away from him at this very moment belied his own thoughts. She was a girl of no more than fourteen, thinly clad and shaking with cold. Her pinched, half-starved features were twisted into an expression of cunning quite at odds with her youth. Born in neglect and nurtured in vice, she had never known a childhood, never heard a father's loving voice or felt a mother's loving touch. Reared into her profession of pickpocket, she faced a short, unhappy life without remorse or hope. Into just such a life would Molly's child have matured, had her mother allowed it. Was death, even death at the hands of a cruel, vengeful mother, so much worse than this girl's death-in-life?

The eccentric Miss Havisham wanted a child. For what fell purpose

Jaggers could scarcely imagine, nor did he wish to dwell for long upon the lonely life a child reared by that broken woman must lead. Miss Havisham wanted a child, and, whatever her faults, she could provide for a child. No child in her care would ever go hungry or want for a warm cloak in winter. No child of hers would stand in the freezing London rain holding flowers in its shaking hands, begging passersby to purchase a bedraggled blossom. No child raised by her would spend its formative years learning to sneak its tiny fingers into pockets and lift the contents, then hide them in her clothes and run away.

For Jaggers, that was enough. The child might never know a loving touch, but that fate awaited it in Seven Dials. If love was impossible, then food must suffice. He would deliver a child to Miss Havisham as soon as Molly's case was concluded.

Jaggers began his lonely walk from Newgate to his lodgings in Gerrard Street in a funk of gloom that surpassed even the dense fog off the river. Slowly, gradually, as his deliberate pace sped up, an idea formed in his great brain, an idea so bold, so audacious, that it took his breath away. No longer was the child's murder an obstacle to Molly's acquittal. He had seen a way to turn it to his advantage, to use it as a sword instead of attempting to shield her from its consequences.

A child whose mother is trying to kill it will scratch.

A child will scratch, and a mother's hand will show such scratches.

"'Brambles or the dead woman's last desperate attempts to stay alive?'" The old lawyer's quavery voice rang with a passion I could never have imagined in him. "'We say brambles caused the scratches on our client's hands, but if you will insist that they were made by fingerprints, could they not have been made by the child clinging to its mother and begging for its life? Can you state beyond a reasonable doubt, as the law instructs you to do, that this woman killed Long Liz?'"

My companion lifted his glass and took another swallow of the third pint I had seen him drink. "That was only one part of the argument, of course. The other waved the flag, so to speak. I can remember is as if it were yesterday." The faded blue eyes seemed very far away as the old man intoned, " 'You and you alone, gentlemen of the jury, stand between our country's greatest achievement, the common law, and utter barbaric degradation. Convict this woman because you believe she killed her child and you will condemn this beloved land to a lawless rule unequaled since the time of the Huns.' "

A twisted smile turned the corners of the old man's mouth as he finished. "You've heard the Hun speech, I take it."

I had. Fool that I was, I had been impressed by it. I had thought it a fine and admirable way to appeal to a jury's reason. Now the fine words sat like a lump in my stomach. For all the beer I had drunk, I was as sober as if it had been lemonade.

How the *London Herald-Tattler* came to the attention of Miss Clara Scriven can only be imagined. It was not the sort of periodical that should have graced the parlor of a young lady of her rank, and yet that she became acquainted with its contents cannot be denied. The article concerning Molly the Gypsy dominated the far right side of the periodical, which referred to Molly as a "Hounslow Heath Medea," a reference lost upon the vast bulk of its readership, but not lost upon Miss Clara.

Clara's response to this awful story: she slipped the engagement ring off her finger and handed it to Jaggers without a word. He pocketed it, also without a word, and left her father's house for the last time, his poor dreams of a happy family life dashed forever.

* * *

"You remember this case in great detail," I said. "You must have been in the courtroom when it was tried."

"Indeed I was," my companion replied. The sadness in his watery eyes told me the truth I should have realized earlier: the lazy barrister who had voiced Mr. Jaggers's questions and delivered his summation was the very man who sat across from me in the snug.

"Why have you told me this?" My voice was a raspy whisper. I felt as if I had been given a glimpse of Hell.

"She killed her child. She killed her child, and not only did Jaggers get her off, he took her into his house. Gypsy Molly is his housekeeper to this day. Every day he looks at her, he must be reminded of the horrible thing she did to her own flesh and blood, and yet he is so depraved as to take his breakfast from her hands. Is that, my young friend, the kind of man you wish to be?"

The old man was mad, of that I was certain, yet I could not deny the force of his words. If I stayed with Jaggers, if I allowed my father to sign my articles with him, I would lose my soul.

"No," I said, my voice hoarse but determined. "No. I will not stay with Jaggers."

"Then buy me another drink by way of thanks," the old man said.

In the ordinary way, Jaggers would have dismissed Gypsy Molly from his mind and proceeded to the next case on his desk. Instead, he walked to Newgate Street and stood outside the prison, waiting for his client's release. When she stepped through the heavy iron gates into the straw-strewn street and freedom, he stepped in front of her and blocked her way with his menacing bulk.

"We had an agreement, Molly," he said in his softest, and therefore most dangerous, voice. "I was to secure your acquittal and you were to deliver your child to me."

"She's dead," Molly said in a flat voice. "Didn't you tell the jury as much?"

"You and I both know she is not. You concealed her and convinced her father she was dead. You even convinced me—for a brief moment." There was no sign in the lawyer's face or voice to reveal that Molly's deception had cost him so much. "But then I confronted you with the truth and put before you a proposition: I will do my best to bring you off, but I must have your child. If you are saved, she is saved. If you are lost, I will still save your child. It is now time for you to honor that agreement."

"I saved her from her drunken filth of a father, didn't I? I did what I had to do to make sure he never saw her again. And now you want to take her away from me?"

"For her own good," Jaggers pointed out. "What can you give her? What life can she have here in London?"

"London's good enough for the likes of us," Molly said sullenly. Her dark eyes had ceased to flash with anger, and she stared at the muddy street as if realizing for the first time how squalid her surroundings were.

"Good enough for you, perhaps," Jaggers said in a cold voice. "Good enough for Elsie—think, woman. Think of someone besides yourself for once in your miserable life."

Now the black eyes met his. Molly's Gypsy blood was up; her cheeks flamed red and her eyes burned with a rage so hot it should have raised blisters on his face. "I thought of her when I hid her from her father. I thought of her when I told everyone she was dead."

"No." Jaggers shook his large head solemnly. "No, I don't believe you did. You hid her out of revenge, not love. All you wanted to do was hurt your husband."

"Husband?" Molly's voice became a fishwife's shrill, derisive cry. "You think that man was my husband? Over the broom, that's the kind of husband and wife we are. Churches and weddings aren't for people like us."

"All the more reason to give Elsie to someone who can raise her properly."

"Raise her to look down on her own mother, you mean." The challenge hung in the air. A lesser man would have denied the charge, would have equivocated and used fine, cajoling words.

"Yes." The lawyer stood his ground, piercing brown eyes meeting hot black ones. The fire of her passion filled her face and voice; the deeper, hotter flame of his own lay banked yet fully stoked.

Molly recoiled as though struck. "I won't have it. I won't have you taking my child and turning her into a toffee-nosed snob. You can't make me give her up."

With a move as swift as it was unexpected, Jaggers reached out and grabbed Molly's wrist. "With these hands, you strangled a woman. With the power of these hands, you took a life. If for no other reason than that, you should not be allowed to keep your child."

"The jury found me innocent." Molly bent all her strength on trying to pull away from the lawyer's iron grip, only to find herself more firmly held than before.

"They did not find you innocent." Jaggers bit off every word as though tearing into a cut of beef. "They found you not guilty. There is a world of difference in those two things, and you'd do well to remember it. Every man of them knew the truth, knew what you'd done and hated you for it. They acquitted because I made them see that the law itself is more important than any one individual. They did their duty, and I am now going to do mine and take that child to a place of safety."

If Molly had shed tears, it is doubtful that Jaggers would have prevailed. But the lack of tears, the insistence upon her own rights without any pretense of love for her daughter, put the final nails in the coffin of Jaggers's resolve.

That very night a carriage pulled up to Satis House, and the lugubrious butler opened the door to a strange sight: Jaggers, dressed in black and wearing his most forbidding expression, stood in the doorway. In his arms, sleeping, with her tiny thumb in her mouth, lay a little girl of three years old, dressed in rags yet with a face so lovely that even the butler smiled at her.

Within five minutes Jaggers sat in the musty parlor sipping tea, while Miss Havisham gazed hungrily at the child, who lay under a blanket in the chair nearest the fire.

"Her name is Elsie," Jaggers said.

"Her name," countered Miss Havisham, "is Estella."

Miss Havisham Regrets

BY MARCIA TALLEY

Marcia Talley was born in Cleveland, Ohio, but spent the first eighteen
years of her life bouncing about the planet—from Ohio to California,
China, New York, Virginia, Kansas, and Taiwan (sometimes more
than once)—as the eldest of five daughters of a career Marine officer.
Back in Ohio at last, she received her B.A. from Oberlin College,
where she met her future husband, Barry. After graduation the couple
moved to Baltimore, where Marcia taught sixth grade and Barry
earned his doctorate in music. In 1971 they settled in scenic, historic
Annapolis, where Marcia earned her M.L.S. from the University of
Maryland and subsequently held several different library positions.

In January 2000, she took an early retirement from federal service
to accompany her husband on a six-month sabbatical, living on a 37-
foot sailboat and sailing down the Intercoastal Waterway from
Annapolis to the Bahamas and back. She now writes full-time and is
the multi-award-winning author of the Hannah Ives mysteries series:
Sing it to Her Bones, *Unbreathed Memories*, and *Occasion of
Revenge*. *In Death's Shadow*, the fourth in the series, will be published
in September 2004. Her latest novel, *I'd Kill for That*, is another serial
effort with other authors, and her short story "Too Many Cooks"
from *Much Ado About Murder* won both the Agatha and Anthony
Awards for Best Short Story of 2002.

IT WAS JOHN Forster who, in his *Life of Charles Dickens* (1874) first revealed that Dickens had written a different ending to *Great Expectations* at the urging of his friend, the novelist Edward Bulwer Lytton. A proof of an earlier version and part of the manuscript have since been discovered. It wasn't until 2002 that an American scholar, researching the life of Anthony Trollope among the papers of the Ternan family at the University of London, uncovered yet a third ending to Dickens's classic tale. Experts have identified the handwriting as that of Ellen Lawless Ternan, who met Dickens in 1857 while she, her mother, and sister were acting in a charity production of *The Frozen Deep*. Ternan was Dickens's mistress until his death in 1879 and almost certainly served as the model for the heroines of his last three novels: Estella (*Great Expectations*), Bella (*Our Mutual Friend*), and Helena Landless (*The Mystery of Edwin Drood*). Whether this third ending was written at the suggestion of Miss Ternan or by Miss Ternan is a matter open to debate.

As an aid to the scholar, text matching the
1861 edition of *Great Expectations* is printed in *italics*.
—EDITOR.

"Tell me as an old, old friend. Have you quite forgotten her?"

"My dear Biddy, I have forgotten nothing in my life that ever had a foremost place there, and little that ever had any place there. But that poor dream, as I once used to call it, has all gone by, Biddy, all gone by!"

Nevertheless, I knew while I said those words, that I secretly intended to revisit the site of the old house that evening, alone, for her sake. Yes even so. For Estella's sake.

I had heard of her as leading a most unhappy life, and as being separated from her husband, a pompous lout named Bentley Drummle, *who had used her with great cruelty, and who had become quite renowned as a compound of pride, avarice, brutality, and meanness. And I had heard of the death of* Drummle, *from an accident consequent on his ill-treatment of a horse. This release had befallen her some two years before; for anything I knew, she was married again.*

The early dinner-hour at Joe's left me an abundance of time, without hurrying my talk with Biddy, to walk over to the old spot before dark. But, what with loitering on the way, to look at old objects and to think of old times, the day had quite declined when I came to the place.

There was no house now, and the cleared space it had once occupied had been enclosed with a rough fence. *Looking over it, I saw that some of the old ivy had struck root anew, and was growing green on low quiet mounds of ruin. A gate in the fence standing ajar, I pushed it open and went in.*

A cold silvery mist had veiled the afternoon, and the moon was not yet up to scatter it. But, the stars were shining beyond the mist, and the moon was coming, and the evening was not dark. I could trace out where every part of the old house had been. "Its name is Satis House," Estella had told me once. Greek or Latin or Hebrew— she didn't care which—for "enough."

Enough. Sufficient. Adequate. No, hardly adequate, for it had been a sad and deserted place even then. I recalled an overgrown garden tangled with weeds; an empty pigeon-house in the brewery yard, blown crooked on its pole by the wind; unoccupied stables; a vacant sty; a wilderness of empty casks upon which Estella and I had once, as children, played, watched from an upstairs window by Estella's adoptive mother, Miss Havisham, who had, over the years, grown ever more eccentric and reclusive.

All were gone, long gone, and even the courtyard, which had

once been paved, had disappeared under a sea of mud, potholed and rutted by the constant to and fro of the removal carts.

At the far end of the lane, a wooden gate in the high enclosing wall stood open. I picked my way carefully along a furrow—for little else was left to mark where the lane had been—and was astonished to discover, when I passed into the old brewery yard, that the latch on the gate was new and the brewery had not been pulled down.

Where once the odor of malt and hops had lingered on damp and molding wood, the premises now fairly gleamed with promise. Bright paint lacquered the doors, the sills, and the window casements; even the mullions had been decorated in the same cheerful blue, as if word had been received that the Queen, in her golden coach, might at any moment be passing by. Gaps in the brewery's foundation had been repaired with new stone, its brick and stone-faced walls had been repointed, and a roof, part gabled and part gently arched, lead onto a new four-sided chimney nearly forty feet high, its sides neatly tapered and faced with brickwork fluting. The grime-encrusted windows through which I had once fancied a ghostly vision of Miss Havisham hanging from a wooden beam and beckoning to me—an apparition from which I, then a common laboring boy, had fled in terror—had been cleaned and glazed anew. As I stood there, entranced, a skylark began its cheerful song and I thought, as it sang, that all might be well.

Who in the village, I wondered, had the resources to revive the old enterprise? As I drew closer, I spied a sign, newly painted, propped against an open door and girded round with rope, ready for the workmen who would hoist it into position on the iron scrollwork that crowned the archway. The sign bore a picture of a sheaf of wheat, and beneath the sheaf, black letters spelling out the words "Wm. Pumblechook, Ltd."

So, I chuckled, Joe's Uncle Pumblechook, that pompous old seed merchant, he who had taken shameless credit for every happy rise in my social condition—even though he had nothing whatever to do with it—had invested in the old brewery. Perhaps Pumblechook had tired of his hot gin and water, or he had grown weary of having his ale sent round from the Boar. I resolved to call at the Blue Boar on my way back to Biddy and Joe's to quiz Squires, the landlord, on the particulars of the matter.

Twilight was closing in as I left the brewery behind and passed back through the gate. I was strolling *along the desolate garden walk, when I beheld a solitary figure in it.*

The figure showed itself aware of me, as I advanced. It had been moving toward me, but it stood still. As I drew nearer, I saw it to be the figure of a woman. As I drew nearer yet, it was about to turn away, when it stopped, and let me come up with it. Then, it faltered as if much surprised, and uttered my name, and I cried out:

"Estella!"

"*I am greatly changed. I wonder you know me, Boy.*"

"I should always know you, miss," said I. *The freshness of her beauty was indeed gone, but its indescribable majesty and its indescribable charm remained. Those attractions in it, I had seen before; what I had never seen before was the saddened softened light of the once proud eyes; what I had never felt before was the friendly touch of the once insensible hand.*

We sat down on a bench that was near, and I said, "After so many years, it is strange that we should thus meet again, Estella, here where our first meeting was! Do you often come back?"

"*I have never been here since.*"

"Nor I."

"*I have very often hoped and intended to come back, but have been prevented by many circumstances. Poor, poor old place!*"

The silvery mist was touched with the first rays of the moonlight, and the same rays touched the tears that dropped from her eyes. Not knowing that I saw them, and setting herself to get the better of them, she said quietly:

"Were you wondering, as you walked along, how it came to be left in this condition?"

"Yes, Estella."

"The ground belongs to me. It is the only possession I have not relinquished. Everything else has gone from me, little by little."

"Indeed. My Uncle Pumblechook, it appears, has acquired the brewery."

"He has," said she, a frown unaccountably darkening her face. "He made me a generous offer. Restoration is well underway, as I'm sure you noticed, although how that silly man can make a success of it when none has done before, is a mystery to me."

"But I have kept this." She tapped her foot upon the ground. *"It was the subject of the only determined resistance I made in all those wretched years."*

"Is it to be built on?"

"It was, but . . ." She paused, and a tear fell, unchecked, upon her cloak. "Oh, Pip, Pip, whatever shall I do?"

"Estella, dearest!" A frenzy of unhappiness welled up within me. I clasped her hand to my breast and cried, "What is wrong? You must tell me!"

"Just when I thought myself to be free"—and by that I presumed she referred to the untimely death of her boorish husband—"that horrid man, Compeyson, long the author of my family's misfortune, has encroached again upon my happiness."

My heart began to hammer like a drum within my chest. Compeyson! The scoundrel who seduced Miss Havisham, played upon her affection, and by vile trickery joined with her wastrel brother, Arthur, to cheat her of her inheritance, and more. *The marriage day had been fixed, the wedding dresses were bought, the wedding tour was planned out, the wedding guests were invited. The day came, but not the bridegroom. He wrote her a letter, which she received at twenty minutes to nine, when she was dressing for her marriage, the very hour and minute at which she afterward stopped all the clocks.* Compeyson! The betrayer responsible for the death of Abel Magwitch, my friend and benefactor and whose hated name I believed to have been struck for ever from my lexicon as I watched him sink into the muddy waters of the Thames.

"But that's impossible!" I cried, taking but little time to consider the matter. "Compeyson is dead! He fell overboard with Magwitch and both were sucked under the keel of a steamer."

"Alas, he survived," wept Estella.

"But his body washed ashore," I forged on, despite the hopelessness that was invading my brain, "and was identified by certain papers in his pocket, still quite legible, despite having been weeks in the water."

"The papers may have been Compeyson's, but the body was someone else," Estella sobbed. "That wretched man called at my home in London—for I live in Chelsea now—and threatened to reveal the awful truth about . . . about . . ." Her terrified tears fell fast upon my hand.

Estella's sobs tore at my heart. "There, there," I soothed in a gentler voice. "This will pass. Even if he lives, Compeyson is a fugitive and can hardly afford to make his presence known."

Estella turned her red and tear-filled eyes toward me. "He intends to flee to New South Wales, and for that he requires assistance," she said. "I'm to give him five hundred pounds or he threatens to publish the truth about my mother!"

I had long ago extracted, as one would a tooth, the truth about that delicate matter from Jaggers, our mutual lawyer and friend. I almost smiled, but recomposed my features when I sensed that a smile on my face, at that moment, would do nothing to mitigate the abject misery that contorted hers.

When I had pressed Jaggers for information about Estella's mother, he had spoken in parables and endless put-the-case-that's, all the while exchanging odd looks with his clerk, Wemmick, until I'd guessed the truth of Estella's parentage and we'd ended our conversation by touching our lips gravely with our forefingers.

And so, "I know about your mother," I confided to Estella, and before she could object, I touched my hand to her damp cheek to silence her.

Her dark, luminous eyes searched my face. "You know?" she exclaimed at last. "But how?"

"I discovered it of an evening while dining with Jaggers," said I. Longing to erase all doubt from her mind about the specific knowledge that I held, and in hope of bringing a smile to her lips once again, I said, "I know that you are the daughter of Molly, Jagger's maid."

"Molly!" Estella's hands flew to her face. "Molly isn't my mother, dear fool! Miss Havisham is!"

I felt my face flush with surprise and shame. I had been so *hot on tracing out and proving Estella's parentage,* that in my haste, I had jumped to unwarranted conclusions. How could I have been persuaded when Molly served us at dinner that Molly's hands were Estella's hands, and her eyes Estella's eyes?

Once, I had detected in Estella's looks and gestures a tinge of resemblance to Miss Havisham which I dismissed as being acquired as a child from a guardian with whom she had been much associated and secluded. But, as I studied Estella now, I realized how wrong I had been. In the moonlight, and with the patina of age soft upon her features, she resembled her mother, Miss Havisham, without any doubt. Whatever child Molly had borne to Magwitch, it had not been Estella.

"Then who . . .?" I began, before swallowing my words, as the answer came as clearly as a bolt of lightning in the night sky. "Compeyson is your father."

Estella nodded. "He used my mother most cruelly. First he robbed her of her maidenhood, then her money, then, for all intents and purposes, her very life."

I recalled Miss Havisham as I had last seen her, lying upon the banqueting table under a loose, white sheet, her grievous burns covered from foot to throat with white cotton wool. All around her had lain the ruins of that ancient banquet, dominated by the rotten bride cake, shrouded in cobwebs.

"At first," Estella continued, "Miss Havisham stayed within the house to hide the undeniable fact of her pregnancy. Jaggers sent a maid trained as a midwife to attend her, and after I was born, I was removed and placed, with great secrecy, in a convent to be raised with other well-to-do orphans. On my third birthday Jaggers brought me back to Satis House and introduced me as Miss Havisham's ward."

Where once she had been Miss Havisham in name only, Estella was now Miss Havisham by right of birth.

"But why do Compeyson's threats trouble you so?" I inquired. "Surely, it's preferable to be Miss Estella Havisham, daughter of the late Miss Havisham of Satis House in Kent, than of Molly, a maid in service, who has stood trial for murder?"

"I can hardly find the words," Estella replied. "Compeyson, though married, was a deceiver. He sowed seeds of his deceit everywhere."

"Please, Estella. We are old and dear friends. Kindly speak to me plainly."

"Compeyson taunted me." She lowered her head, and even in the early December light, I thought I saw a flush upon her face. "I am not his only love child, he told me. Love child! As if what passed between that villain and my mother could be dignified by the gentle name of love!"

My involuntary start occasioned her to lay her hand upon my arm. "No!" she cried, imperiously stopping me as I opened my lips. "You must hear all."

"Do you recollect my late husband, Bentley Drummle, who fancied himself next in line to a baronetcy . . .?" She laughed derisively. "Bentley, too, was conceived on the wrong side of the blanket, to Katherine Drummle and her secret lover, Compeyson."

I dropped my face into my hands, but was able to control myself better than I could have expected, considering the agony it gave me to hear her say those words. When I raised my face again, there was such a ghastly look upon Estella's countenance that it impressed upon me the awful truth of what she had just revealed to me.

Estella leapt to her feet and began pacing back and forth in front of the bench, her handsome dress trailing upon the ground. "For all I know, I may have tens of brothers and sisters in the shire. Hundreds! Thousands!" She leaned forward and placed a hand of each of my shoulders, then peered deeply into my eyes. "You know what this means, don't you, Pip? It means that I married my brother!"

I drew a ragged breath, fearful that I'd need to thrump my chest with a fist to start my heart beating again. Married to her half brother! Thank God there had been no children of the union. I struggled to find some comforting words for my darling Estella, but none at all came.

Estella was the next to break the silence that ensued between us.

"To settle this matter, I've arranged to meet Compeyson at the Blue Boar, where I'm lodging, on Tuesday. He's traveling under the name of Gerrard."

My mind was racing furiously. Something had to be done to stop him!

After several minutes I found my voice, and a plan. "I'm lodging nearby, at Joe and Biddy's." I took Estella's hand and pulled her down onto the bench next to me. "You'll prepare a note to 'Gerrard.' In the note you'll instruct 'Gerrard' to meet you here, at the brewery, at eight-forty."

The significance of the time was not lost on Estella. She nodded.

"I'll post the note to 'Gerrard' in care of the innkeeper. On the appointed day you will slip quietly out of the inn and meet me at the forge. You will arrive at the forge no later than eight o'clock."

Again, she nodded.

I stood, drew Estella up to stand before me, and with my mouth close to her ear, told her what I planned to do.

⌘

But for his shock of black curls, I should not have recognized him. From a window I watched Compeyson stride, with confidence, along the muddy path that lead to Pumblechook's brewery, inside which I had concealed myself. Compeyson's body was the same height and girth of my recollection, but the clothes he wore were brown and rough, like those of a farmer. His face was disfigured. A red welt bisected an eyebrow and meandered in a jagged path down his cheek, and his nose was flattened like a pug. Compeyson disappeared from my view for a moment, and then the door yawned wide, and he entered.

"Miss Havisham?" he called.

It was not Miss Havisham, but I, who stepped from the shadows.

The wretch staggered back, startled. "Pip! I didn't expect to see you here."

"No, I don't imagine you did, Compeyson." I wrapped my fingers more tightly around the hammer I had borrowed from my brother-in-law's forge and ventured closer, with a confidence buoyed only by the weight of the weapon clutched in my hand. "So tell me," said I. "How is it that the dead can walk?"

"Your friend Magwitch is responsible for this," said he, indicating the scar that marred his once handsome cheek. "Although gravely wounded, I managed to swim ashore." He laughed, an ugly sound that rang harsh and hollow in the vastness of the deserted brewery. "A kindly farmer's widow nursed me back to health." Then he leered. "Shocking, isn't it, when a gentleman can't travel the Queen's highway on legitimate business without being set upon by vagabonds?"

Never had I hated another human being as much as I hated Compeyson at that moment.

He indicated his jacket, which upon closer inspection proved to be a faded tattersall. "Her husband didn't need it anymore."

I gasped, a dread suspicion seizing hold of my brain. "You didn't . . .?"

"Murder her husband for his clothing? No." He sneered. "Just let us say that the poor sod who washed ashore wearing the jacket that bore my papers didn't have much need for his body anymore."

While we were talking, Compeyson had circled round until he stood between me and a copper boiling vat. I controlled an almost irresistible urge to erase the smirk of self-satisfaction off his face with a single blow of Joe's hammer, but I wasn't done with Compeyson yet, and neither was my clever Estella.

"What's that?" I inquired suddenly, tilting my head at an angle like a spaniel who'd sensed a rabbit in the underbrush.

Compeyson shrugged, stared at me silently for a moment, then pulled a watch out of his ragged pocket and flipped the case open. "What do you want, old chap? I haven't got all day."

"I'm certain I heard something," said I.

From far above, in the rafters of Pumblechook's deserted brewery, came a peal of laughter so crystalline, that even Compeyson could not fail to hear. He glanced upward, his eyes traveling from the copper vats on the wooden floor before him to the mash tuns on the level above, up yet again to the water tanks on the upper floor, and across to the iron stairway that led to a storage room and a high, open-worked gallery upon which Estella—Miss Havisham—now stood.

She was dressed all in white, and she had bridal flowers in her hair, from which a long white veil depended. Jewels sparkled at her throat and upon her fingers. A bridal slipper was on one foot, but the other foot was unshod.

"Who is that?" cried Compeyson.

"I must have been mistaken. It's nothing but the wind," said I, as if my life's love were not standing fifty feet above my head wearing a wedding dress that had belonged to my deceased sister, Mrs. Joe.

The laughter pealed out again, and Compeyson's jaw grew slack. Comprehension dawned on his startled face, and I said a silent prayer to Magwitch who had been the unwitting author of my plan.

As Magwitch told the tale, Arthur Havisham, Estella's uncle, had been Compeyson's willing partner in forgery and swindling; yet when Arthur lay raving in Compeyson's house, driven to insanity by visions of his dead sister in her wedding clothes—Compeyson spoke hardy, but never came nigh himself.

Now Miss Havisham's ghost had come again, and this time, Compeyson would have to face her.

Yet, to my great surprise, it was not fear that seemed to drive him now. Eyes glued to the vision in the gallery, Compeyson, his voice choked with emotion, croaked, "Mirabella!"

Now it was my jaw that dropped, as I had never heard Miss Havisham called by her Christian name.

"Mirabella?" Compeyson cried again. "I must explain!" He turned and bolted up the stairs, his rude farmer's boots clattering on the iron treads. I followed close behind.

As Compeyson neared the gallery, Estella extended an arm, as I had instructed, and shook out a shroud. "I'll put it on you at five in the morning," she sang, in a clear, high soprano.

Compeyson covered his head with his arms, pleading, "Take it away from her, take it away! But instead of lifting himself up hard and dying, as Arthur had done, Compeyson screamed, "There's blood, blood!" and staggered backward against a water tank, stumbled over a bag of malt, tumbled over the railing, and fell into a mash tun, where he lay, twitched thrice, then once again, until he moved no more.

Estella sank to the floor, sobbing, Mrs. Joe's wedding gown pooled in a silken puddle around her. I gathered her into my arms and stroked her hair, as Miss Havisham had once done when Estella was a child—*I wanted a little girl to rear and love, and save from my fate.* "It's finished," I said. "The circle is closed. Her revenge is complete—for poor, mad Arthur, for you, for Magwitch, and, yes, perhaps even for me."

"Let me take you back to the Boar," I said. "A hot toddy is just what the doctor ordered."

"I'll be arrested!" she shuddered.

"For murdering Compeyson? How can you have murdered Compeyson?" I asked reasonably. "He's already dead. Drowned in the Thames before witnesses, including a boatload of constables." Besides, I added gently, "Any inquest would rule it an accident."

My eyes shifted, on their own volition, to the motionless form in the mash tun below. Compeyson would lie there until spring, at least, when farmers would fill Pumblechook's till with money for seed. Longer, perhaps for all eternity—food for vermin, like Miss Havisham's bride cake—if Pumblechook's investors couldn't raise the funds he needed to continue construction of the brewery.

I assisted Estella down the stairs, wrapped her in her cloak, which had been hanging in the room that was to be Pumblechook's office—if the oversize desk and chair were any indication—and we walked, arm in arm, back to the Boar.

Although it was early in the day for hot toddies, Squires fixed her an ample one, adding an extra bit of lemon to ward against a chill. "Here 'tis, miss. Good for what ails you!"

I sat with Estella by the fire until her mug was empty, then saw her to her chamber and urged her to rest. I promised to join her for lunch the following day, after which we'd catch the afternoon coach to London.

The day dawned crisp and clear and the sun shone warm upon my head as I walked briskly to the Boar, carrying my satchel and dressed in my traveling coat. As Estella had not yet come down, I shook off the chill, poked up the fire, and ordered an ale.

"You here to see the young lady, Mr. Pip?" asked Squires as he drew me a pint.

"Yes, Squires, I am."

"Why, she left on the morning coach," said he, "but asked me to say if you called"—and here he cast his eyes upward as if reading Estella's instructions off the wooden beams—"I'm to say: 'Miss Havisham regrets she's unable to lunch today.'" Squires reached into the pocket of his grimy apron and withdrew an envelope. "And here's a note, sir." *It was addressed to Phillip Pirrip, Esq. and on top of the subscription were the words:* To Be Read at Satis House.

I took the note from his hand and, with a heavy heart, returned to the ruined place where Satis House had once stood, the scene of my greatest happiness and greatest sadness. Once again I took the garden path that lead to the bench we had so recently shared, sat down upon it, and opened Estella's letter.

"I have often thought of you," wrote *Estella. "Of late, very often. There was a long hard time when I kept far from me, the remembrance of what I had thrown away when I was quite ignorant of its worth. But, now I have given it a place in my heart. I little thought,"* the note continued, *"that I should take leave of you in taking leave of this spot.* Yet, when the innkeeper inquired this morning if "Mr. Gerrard" had found me well, I thought it best to leave. When Compeyson's body is found, as surely it must be found, I will be far away, beyond reach of the law.

"You once said to me, 'God bless you, God forgive you!' And if you could say that to me then, you will not hesitate to say that to me

now—now, when suffering has been stronger than all other teaching, and has taught me to understand what your heart used to be. I have been bent and broken, but—I hope—into a better shape. Be as considerate and good to me as you were, and tell me we are friends. And will continue friends apart."

Disconsolate, I remained on the bench for several hours, the stone hard and cold beneath me, rereading Estella's words, as if by study, or rearrangement, they might contain some secret clue to as to where she might be found. Then I folded the letter and slipped it into my pocket, next to my heart, and with new determination, walked *out of the ruined place.*

And, as the morning mists had risen long ago when I first left the forge, so, the evening mists were rising now, and in all the broad expanse of tranquil light they showed to me, I knew I would countenance *no shadow of another parting from her.*

Scrogged: A Cyber Christmas Carol

BY CAROLE NELSON DOUGLAS

Ex-journalist Carole Nelson Douglas is the award-winning author of forty-some novels and two mystery series. *Good Night, Mr. Holmes* introduced the only woman to outwit Sherlock Holmes, American diva Irene Adler, as a detective, and was a *New York Times* Notable Book of the Year. The series recently resumed with the *Chapel Noir* and *Castle Rouge* duology, which proposes a new candidate for Jack the Ripper. Forthcoming is *Spider Dance*. Douglas also created contemporary hard-boiled PI Midnight Louie, whose Runyonesque first-furperson feline narrations appear in short fiction and fifteen novels featuring a quartet of pro-am human crime-solvers unknowingly aided by this Sam Spade with hairballs. (*Cat in an Orange Twist*, etc.). She collects vintage clothing and stray cats, and lives in Fort Worth, Texas.

MARLOWE WAS DEAD, that much was certain. Dead certain. The TV news channels had harped on that fact for almost a week now. Dead by his own hand.

Ben Scroggs could hardly believe it, although much that was shown on the TV news was pretty unbelievable these days. Marlowe dead. Killed instantly when he threw himself from the balcony atop the three-story entry hall in his Rivercrest mansion, his brain smashed to smithereens on imported Italian marble, a brain that had been so agile in life, so admirably ordered.

Not that Scroggs had been a particular friend of Marlowe's. Scroggs had few friends at the company. Better not to get involved in office politics during off-office hours, especially the frivolous socializing that led to overdrinking and sometimes even adulterous affairs. None of that nonsense was for Ben Scroggs. And, of course, if he *had* been a particular friend of Marlowe's, it would be *his* figure the news cameras would be tracking as he left the police station after questioning, instead of his higher-ups, dashing in and out amid clusters of high-powered lawyers, their Society Page faces now hidden beneath hasty tents of Armani camel-hair trench coats and *Houston Chronicle* Lifestyle sections.

No, Ben Scroggs was a very small fish in the corporate shark tank, thank Anderson Accounting, and dedicated to doing his job (and saving it) by getting small notice. That strategy—and, honestly, it was more a temperamental preference than a strategy—stood him in good stead now that the nation had its hungry eyes on Axxanon and its executives and all their works. And especially all their *workings.*

That was why at this dread time of unprecedented corporate accountability, Scroggs, the quintessential accountant, still sat at his old mahogany desk, enduring among the husk of stricken employees and absent executives that Axxanon's self-important skyscraper had become. He was working this Christmas Eve as he had all the others, even while the lower-level employees scurried away like mice for their foolish materialistic celebrations they thought honored an infant, but instead honored only the Bottom Line that is the true heart of all business and industry in the civilized world as Ben Scroggs knew it.

His own "personal assistant"—what a ludicrous and largely untrue title! Scroggs allowed no one to become personal with him, and no one could assist him to his satisfaction—was just visible through the open office door, her broad back clothed in cheap Kelly-green polyester.

She was on the telephone, as usual, and on a personal call, as even more usual.

He shook his head. Why would a woman in these enlightened days allow herself to become the mother of four young children with no legal father—or should he say *fathers?*—in sight? Small wonder one of them had been born with some exotic disease she was forever on the phone about. She was, of course, the politically "correct" profile for a corporate personal assistant these days: black and female. At least the pittance they paid her reflected reality.

"Sir," she was saying on the phone to some harried banker, as were most of the support staff at Axxanon these days, "there must be some way to save my 401K."

Four-oh-one Kayo! What did these financial dunces know, except that the Company was supposed to bail them out of their own ignorance? Scroggs felt no pity for them. He had not opted for employee stock options or any of that slippery nonsense. He kept what he had squirreled away where only he knew about it, and none of it was in get-rich-quick schemes, even if they were disguised as a corporate pension program.

"Merry Christmas!" cried a voice in the outer office. *What?* Was there still some idiot in Houston who could possibly think there was anything to celebrate this December of 2001?

With chagrin, Scroggs recognized the upbeat voice: his own dead sister's son, a ne'er-do-well as seasoned at it as her late husband, the trailer trash from Biloxi. Ah! Nephews.

The fool came barging in to his inner sanctum, spouting, "Merry Christmas!"

"Screw Christmas!"

"Say, Uncle! You don't mean it! The kids love it."

"I don't love the kids, so how is it my affair? Christmas is social extortion, and you ought to know it, Jimmy Joe Scroggs. It's a scheme to keep the poor thinking they have a future, and spending it on gimcracks of the season. Great business, but worthless sentiment. What a scam! You and your naive wife from the wrong side of the tracks are some of the poor who happily will be plucked buck-naked as a turkey this season, all in the name of that ancient invitation to bilking the public, 'Merry Christmas.'

"Aw, Unc, have a heart. You're welcome to come over and eat brisket with Bobbie Rae and me and the kids."

"Brisket! I can't believe they chose to serve that lowbrow stuff at Disneyland France. Meadow Muffins! Might as well sit in a pasture and swill what the bulls put out. Eat barbecue with sticky-fingered brats and their stupider parents? I'd rather rot in hell first. And a Happy New Year to you, too, Jimmy Joe."

"I know this scandal must be freezing your pumpkin patch, Uncle Ben—"

"Do not call me by that commercially compromised brand name! No pumpkin pie for me, either, overrated slush! Out of my sight! I've bigger things to tend to."

"Nothin's bigger than a time when people reckoned themselves small in the face of a miracle. I'll still lift a home brew in your honor on Christmas Day, Uncle, for my maw was your sister and she was all right through and through. We're sorry for your trouble. It can't be fun to be an Axxanon employee these days. And I'll say it again, 'Merry Christmas!' We'll keep the hot sauce warm for you tomorrow besides."

At this the young man was on his way, pausing in the outer office to plant a yellow rose on Lorettah's desk.

"There's a pair of idiots." Scroggs offered his opinion to the air. One was about to be goosed and loosed by her employer, and the other had no employer, not even a defaulting one, to speak of. Odd jobs, indeed.

He was appalled to see two more holiday mendicants entering against Jimmy Joe's departing tailwind: a pair of Houston society grande dames, lacquered and enameled and furred to their spa-applied single eyelashes. They looked like Carol Channing moonlighting in a *Star Trek* movie. But Seven of Nine they were not. More like Majel Barrett.

"Mr. Scroggs," one said cheerily, entering his Holy of Holies. "How reassuring to see you at work on Christmas Eve, even though the house around you falls. We have no doubt that your sterling reputation will survive the current deluge, and a bit of prominent local charity could only burnish your community standing."

"My house is perfectly fine."

"Oh," said the other, "Chantelle wasn't speaking literally. We just thought how this was the perfect time for you to put your house on display for charity. Interest has never run so high in executive Axxanon residences. It's a 'New Hope for the New Year' tour at the end of January, and the Children with AIDS project needs support."

"Better their parents had supported them by having the discipline *not* to have them, or what led to having them!" Scroggs grumbled.

He was pleased to see Miss Personal Assistant Lorettah Craddick stiffen at her desk. Overpaid and underfunded. All this indignation at lower-level employees' losses was bleeding-heart liberalism. What about his investment of every minute of his life in the company? What was he to get out of it but early retirement?

"But they are here, and suffering, Mr. Scroggs."

"Send them back."

"To where? They did not ask to be here."

"To wherever this foul disease originated. Not in my house, I assure you, ladies. Good day."

"It is a good day," one called back as she was ushered out by Scrogg's determined advance. "It's Christmas Eve and I know that there will be happy children tomorrow morning under every Christmas tree in Houston, no matter how poor."

" 'The poor ye have always with you'. . . . forget changing

things! Good-bye and remember, Christmas is not merry, it is a marketing opportunity!"

Scroggs retreated to his den of an office. When Axxanon was not being besieged by the media, it was having its bones picked by do-gooders. No doubt someone was already on eBay, coveting Scrogg's Aeron chair, not that he had wanted the blamed thing, an obligatory Axxanon office toy, more like a blown-up mesh kitchen implement than a seating piece.

A hulking presence on the threshold to his office interrupted his reverie.

"Everything's done, sir. I was hoping to leave a bit early."

Scroggs regarded what passed for secretarial help in these days. "Four-thirty P.M., Lorettah?"

"My sitter has family and Christmas doin's of her own. I thought—"

"If you thought you would not still be in such a menial position. Why should you go home while I remain working at the office?"

"You don't have much family, sir, and I do."

"And that is what's wrong with society! You have an armful of brats that a high-earning man like myself must pay taxes to support. All right, but I don't have to let you short-sheet the company, and I won't, even though it's sinking like a stone."

"I lose a lot, too. My job, my pension—"

"Piddlely winks! Nobody's put in more hours than I have. That's the key to success. And will you be in the day after accursed Christmas, asking for more handouts?"

"I'll be in, sir. This is the only job I've got."

"For now. Go on, then! No one has any dedication anymore. There are Kmart trinkets to shower on your brats, no doubt, and I wouldn't get half a minute's attention from you anyway."

She paused before stiffly saying "Thank you," then turned in the doorway before she left. "There's no one waiting at home for you. I can see why you'd be reluctant to leave. Still, I wish you . . . joy of the season."

She had scooped her overstuffed cheap purse from the desk and left the outer office before he could muster a retort: "Joy is not a seasonal thing, it's a delusion!"

He muttered it anyway, fully deserted now, by the highest and the lowest of his fellow employees.

And so Ben Scroggs went home in the December Houston mist, cursing traffic and department-store Santas and vehicles with last-minute trees tied on top by fools who should have saved their dollars, and bottom lines that somehow became lethal when they were only pretty numbers, all in a row, like Christmas tree lights—no!

There was nothing light about the Christmas season, a ridiculous concept in Houston anyway, he thought as he motored through neighborhoods sodded in dry yellow grass. Christmas tree lights draped houses like ersatz icicles and outlined every gabled, overdesigned detail on each massive facade (which is what Axxanon had proven to be, a massive facade of the business sort) until the Lodge seemed a gingerbread development inhabited by witches awaiting gullible Hansels and Gretels.

"You kids will get sick on Christmas!" Scroggs shouted to the upscale mansions as he drove by in his Volvo. "You will overeat and die!"

But the kids in the Lodge had never died yet, and still ran over his lawn in summer and shouted names at him all year 'round.

Scroggs hit the remote control for his driveway gate and drove his elderly black station wagon through. The other Axxanon executives had sniggered at his modest choice of vehicle, but he had never risked a carjacking in it. No, he had been immune to all their easy and obvious temptations now so much in the news: expensive cars, clothes, houses, women, and wine.

Still, he had been forced to buy a home in the "right"

neighborhood. His corporate peers and superiors wouldn't have tolerated that much eccentricity. Yet his house was a remainder of the days before the land became an exclusive gated community called the Lodge. It had been built in the 1930s, and the only pleasure Ben got out of owning such an overpriced property (for its neighboring estates were worth multimillions) was equipping it with all of the high-tech devices his computer nerd's heart desired.

He paused to gaze up at its Art Deco Italianate two-story facade. The city's most chichi decorators of dubious gender and the annual Designer House committee makeover hags had been itching to get their French-manicured hands on Scrogg's house to "reinvent" it. From the outside, it looked shabbily elegant, neglected almost to the point of a visit from the Lodge's Community Aesthetic Standards Committee, but not quite. Ben had learned long ago never to let his personal habits show enough to invite meddling from outsiders.

He was considered a business genius, and a certain eccentricity was tolerated . . . in him, at any rate. He kept the numbers dancing the can-can in their designated rows, just as the CEO and CFO and all the other high muckety-mucks had liked and wanted. He had never looked up to see the bigger picture, and that's what he would tell them if subpoenaed. He had seen only his pixels and his numbers and what wrong was there in that? That is what a Chief Accounting Officer is supposed to do: keep an eye on the bottom line. CAO. That was Scroggs. . . .

He paused at his front door, a copper-painted coffered affair with a showy brass knocker of the masques of comedy and tragedy. (The home's builder had been a Hollywood silent star who had married Texas businessman and retired to Houston to haunt charity affairs and install her dubious Cecil B. DeMille taste wherever she could.)

Odious things, those twin masques of twisted features. Even the masque of comedy seemed to be screaming.

Scroggs reached for the keypad at the door's right. He needed no primitive knocker or key to enter, for he kept no servants, despite the house's size. It was bad enough that he had to overpay the Merry Maids every two weeks. He punched in his code, and the thing burped them back at him. The LED numbers looked utterly alien until he realized that they broke down into a date: 12/24/01. 122401. Ridiculous. He punched the keypad again, harder. Again: 122401. 12/24/01. That was today, the date that employee 401Ks officially dissolved, though even now their assets were frozen, what there was left of them, as their salaries would be frozen soon.

Scroggs made a fist and punched the entire contrary keypad with his bare, cold hand. Investing in costly leather gloves in a climate such as this, which only flirted with winter now and again, was ridiculous. It was cold this night, though. Maybe that's what made him shiver when his punch delivered a response . . . a deep, distant tolling of bells. It sounded as if it came from inside the house, but of course it was some stupid church calling the ovine faithful to some Christmas Eve service.

Near him, someone groaned. He studied the Hollywood twists bracketing his door for lurkers, but the pines with their jagged arms remained still. An odd phosphorescence played over his front door, brightening the age-blackened brass of the grotesque masques for which Houston's leading interior designer had offered him $5,000 . . . . They seemed to spring to life and, despite their distorted features, resembled somebody Scroggs couldn't quite place, but whose features frightened him.

Heartbeat thumping through his spare, computer-stooped frame, Scroggs heard them groan and scream with pain and searingly hysterical laughter, like living things being tortured beyond even the dead's endurance. . . .

He shrank back from his own door, but suddenly it popped ajar as it was supposed to. The keypad's red warning light had turned green, and the alien numbers had vanished.

"Nerves," Scroggs muttered to himself.

He moved through the house, past spare rooms with polished

wood floors furnished in leather and steel Barcelona chairs and other minimalist modern pieces. As he passed through the rooms, the controlling computer system switched lights and music on and off. The house's sleek, impersonal interior reminded him of the clean electronic order inside a computer. An interior elevator door was open to waft him up one floor to where he really lived, the master bedroom suite. Instead of piping in Muzak, the elevator sound system offered the high-pitched bleeps of high-tech equipment chattering to itself.

Scroggs moved into the carpeted upper hall, passing the home theater . . . passing, then stopping and returning to stare through its open padded double doors to the huge screen on which black-and-white people moved. The drone of dialogue made him frown. The theater wasn't programmed to go on automatically at his passing. It was operating now, a three-foot-high face in close-up, a dead actor looking troubled fifty-some years after he'd filmed the scene. Who was it now? He didn't watch much anymore, just hunkered down in his bedroom for microwave meals and professional reading material.

Jimmy Stewart, that was it! Mr. Nice Guy. Scroggs blinked at the dialogue. . . . No, not that treacly movie again. Of course! It was Christmas Eve and *It's a Wonderful Life* was a staple of the season! What was so wonderful about being financially ruined through your own fault and attracting the unwelcome attention of some self-appointed guardian angel determined to make you see the bright side of business ruin? This was worse than panhandling socialites in his office. He darted into the darkened room, hunting the controller, but when he found it on the arm of a theater seat, it refused to shut off the movie, or the whining Jimmy Stewart/"George"! Scroggs pressed buttons in a panic, not wanting another syllable of cheap and manipulated sentiment to hit his ears . . . when the image faded. At last.

But the thing wasn't totally off. It showed an office . . . an office at Axxanon! And seated at the desk was another familiar figure—George Marlowe! In black-and-white, like Jimmy, but otherwise as live as he could be.

"Marlowe!"

The man stood and came forward to perch on the desk edge like some latter-day Walt Disney selling Disneyland. "This is my last will and testament," he said, staring straight at Scroggs. "I guess you could call it my 'unliving' will."

"That's right, Marlowe! You're dead, so you get off my movie screen."

"Can't. Guess this is my purgatory, or limbo, a limited engagement at your home theater."

"You're seven days dead."

"I suppose you were expecting advanced decay by now. No, I just turned . . . pale. This two-dimensional existence is pretty painful, though."

"You're a delusion."

"But I'm your personal delusion, so you might as well sit down and listen. I've come to warn you, Ben."

"We were never friends in life."

"We weren't enemies, which is saying a lot at Axxanon."

"I don't get it. You were an honest and decent man. You had the least to hide of anyone. Why did you of all of them—?"

"When the truth came out, I saw that I was a part of the conspiracy, unwittingly maybe, but it was all a vast network of links and nodes. I saw in an instant all the thousands of hapless employees whose pensions had been financed in company stock, whose futures were tied to the company's stock-market value, who suddenly had nothing, and all those hundred of thousands of ordinary souls, retired workers whose pensions had been invested in the glittering, rancid bubble that was Axxanon, who'll now be working into their eighties to survive."

"Neither of us had much to do with it."

"We were there!" Marlowe thundered over the high-end Bose

speakers, sounding like Charlton Heston's Moses on the mount. "There is no escaping such facts in the afterlife. I may not be blue-faced and dripping seaweed or rattling chains or sliming unsuspecting mortals like a *Ghostbusters* wraith, but I wear an invisible cloak of regret as heavy as stainless steel. I'm imprisoned in shades of gray forever, mocked by others you thankfully cannot hear or see. So hear *me*, Scroggs! You face the same eternal fate unless you do something about it."

"What?"

"Three spirit guides will visit you tonight. You must go where they take you and face what they show you."

"Spirit guides! I don't believe in that New Age claptrap."

"Believe, or you will linger in a limbo worse than any you could imagine, half-seen, half-heard, but sensing everything around you as if it were felt through steel wool. It wounds, Scroggs, to know your own failures so well, to see the hapless, hopeless, helpless faces of your fellow humans and know you put the agony into their features. It is more than I can bear!" Here the figured moaned and wailed with a sound so like a garbage disposal crossed with a demon that Scroggs put his palms to his ears. Still he heard Marlowe's voice even as it descended into guttural howls. His image twisted and melted into that of a Great Dane, an ancient woman, Jimmy Stewart's.

"You of all of us did the least wrong, Marlowe! You couldn't help it that our superiors used our cleverness with numbers to defraud our fellow workers and the stockholders."

"I could have helped it! It was my job to have 'helped it.' I answer here not to Axxanon, but to every last one of those faceless fellow workers and stockholders we took no notice of until government investigators and newswriters told us how they had paid for our indifference and arrogance."

"Humankind has always suffered, on the whole. Those people were not our affair. Our jobs were our business, and doing them satisfactorily."

"Humankind was my business! Their welfare was my business! The company existed to supply numberless people with services, and jobs, and some modicum of financial security, not to make its top executives wealthier than Greek shipping magnates. We have sinned, Scroggs, and will pay for it after death, as I should know most painfully."

"I don't know why I should believe the word of a suicide, a man who couldn't face his own music now asking me to face something I don't believe in. Spirit guides! As much mutter about the 'spirit' of Christmas. As you point out, Christmas is only for the rich and the greedy, and as much as you and I were paid for our services, we are minnows in the shark tank. I have nothing to atone for."

"Believe in me," Marlowe's voice thundered again. "And I wasn't a suicide, Scroggs. I didn't kill myself, else I'd be in some even more horrible lower hell. I was murdered."

"Murdered! My God, man! Murdered?"

The image blurred, then Jimmy Stewart was poised on a bridge, about to leap to his own death, when a guardian angel named Clarence appeared by his side. The only Clarence Scroggs could remember was a clown on some children's show in his foggy, foggy youth. Or was that Clarabell? Either way, the name was a silly abomination, and irrelevant.

Scroggs wrung his hands on the controller as if to break its plastic neck, punching buttons with the same impotence as he had belabored the keypad by his door.

"Murdered," he whispered to himself as the screen went blank, leaving the room pitch dark. "Spirit guides? Hardly. Indigestion, more like it! Too many Taco Bell lunches. I'll go to bed and finish dreaming there."

Scroggs scurried to his bedroom hideaway, ate a can of cold mushroom soup and three Oreo cookies, and called it Christmas Eve. Then he lay down in his bed, a circular affair with a built-in TV in the gray flannel canopy that had cost as much as a good car. Axxanon required its employees of a certain level to live up to a certain level. Scroggs chose his excesses to match his misanthropy.

Marlowe murdered. Now, that was news, Scroggs thought as he muted the nightly news show, leaving footage of his former bosses being paraded in and out of courtrooms silent, like a Keystone Cops short subject from the twenties. Pity no one would know but he. Nor would anyone believe it, if he was so rash as to say such a thing. Scroggs burped, then shook his head. Indigestion. With the cursed season as well as his diet.

The lights in his bedroom brightened like the rising sun. He sat up blinking. He hadn't ordered this blinding, and expensive, blitz of kilowatts. His built-in stereo system was wailing out Christmas carols. And somewhere an old-fashioned clock chimed. And chimed. And chimed. He owned nothing but modern, and quiet, timepieces, but Scroggs thought he counted thirteen chimes of the clock.

A baker's dozen that added up to 1:00 A.M.

On the sleek stainless-steel portable refrigerator that served as a nightstand (and which held what was left of the mushroom soup, for Scroggs's stomach had been a tad unsettled after the Marlowe episode) perched an aged waif, looking rather like a child with that premature aging disease the TV news shows were always showing to revolt people and loosen their purse strings for medical research. Purse strings? That was a strange way to put it. To lift the contents of their crocodile wallets and 401Ks was more like it.

"I suppose you represent yourself to be a 'Spirit Guide.'" Scroggs snickered. "You look rather old to be a Boy Scout."

"I am a boy and not a boy any longer," the creature answered with a certain melancholy. "I am the Ghost of Christmas Past." A small, wizened hand reached for Scroggs's fingers, which looked knobby and old even to his own eyes, yet clutched the down comforter like a child's. "Come with me."

Before Scroggs could say yea or nay, the ghostly hand had seized his own like icy, oozing Silly Putty and was dragging him toward the metal-blind–shrouded window.

"We'll crash!" Scroggs cried. Instead he felt a cold bracing wind, and then he was treading thin air hand-in-hand with the spirit. And him wearing only Neiman-Marcus boxer shorts.

Houston's high gleaming buildings—Axxanon's A-shaped mirrored plinth among them—flashed beneath them like a river of fireflies. Only the chill high stars remained. Scroggs took pleasure in their remote placement, as predictable as numbers on a spreadsheet.

But soon the pair were plummeting back to earth, humble east Texas earth, pockmarked by stands of piney woods and reedy swamps.

Scroggs saw battered pickup trucks plying the rutted country roads—few SUVs here, and no Humvees—and they plunged low enough over the one beacon in the darkness, the lit-up Dairy Queen, to hear arriving and departing diners wishing each other "Merry Christmas" and "God bless."

"Meadow muffins!" Scroggs grumbled, but, as the ghost pulled him on, he recognized more than the terrain. "Why . . . this is my hometown. I'm amazed that toad puddle is still here."

They were plunging down to the very center of it, the Baptist church. This was a simple wooden building very proud of its one dinky spire. It had been a hardscrabble town and life, and the religion had been demanding and sometimes cruel.

"There is a child below debuting in the Christmas pageant; perhaps you'd like to see."

"Oh, God, no! I was just some dribble-chinned Joseph hanging over a manger, not knowing why. Having children is overrated."

But the ghost swooped low and Scroggs with him, until they were hovering over the hovel Scroggs recognized from his youth. Someone was shouting. Scroggs's ears shriveled at that angry din, though he was not the object of it, and instead sat silent in a corner, in some craven way happy to be the observer rather than the object of the tirade.

Daddy was drunk and Daddy drunk was usually mad, but this time he had something serious as the object of his fury. He railed at Scroggs's sister Fran, a frail girl trying to grow into a woman on too little food and no love. She cowered against the paper-patched wall, her thin arms wrapped around a slightly swelling stomach, like a young pine bent by the wind but not quite breaking. The word *slut* peppered the air.

"Fran!" Scroggs cried out. Now he would go to her defense. She had always stood between him and the Old Man, and seen to his clothes and his snotty face. He didn't understand, then, what the problem was! If only he had been big enough to defend her.

He saw her now, again, while he quailed like the ten-year-old he was at Daddy's big hands and Daddy's big voice. She was sixteen, he remembered, a shy, pretty girl with something stronger beneath their mutual fear. Something in her was better and braver than he ever could be.

"Take me away, ghost! I'll never see Fran again on this earth, and I can't stand seeing her berated again now!"

The ghost bent a sharp eye on Scroggs's face, and saw the horror and unhappiness.

For after that searing scene, Fran was gone forever, and Scroggs heard no more of it or her until he had escaped on a scholarship to Houston and the university. He learned later that he couldn't have defended her that night even if he had mustered the will, that he had a young nephew he never knew, and a dead sister he'd never known was ill. He learned it from his mother, a shadow not much different from a ghost that he'd never paid much mind to, just like everybody else, after his father had died.

By then he had Latin words awarded with his accounting degree. *Magna cum laude.* By then he knew what they meant, which no one in his hometown could claim except the Catholic priest with his tiny congregation among the born-agains of the county. At university his classmates had dismissed him as a "grind," but he landed a good position with a family hardware business . . . until the chain stores of Home Despot put it out of business.

The ghost floated with Scroggs over the dead carcasses of many businesses of his memory . . . the old single-screen theater with the Art Deco marquee . . . Nathan's Drugstore, where you could call in an emergency and a pharmacist would get out of bed to assist you . . . the old hardware store that smelled of oil and rusty metal instead of the modern tang of chrome carts and computerized checkout stations.

"It's gone," Scroggs mourned, "all of it. My sister, my youth. Take me home, ghost. I can't stand to see these places of my past. . . ."

So the ghost did, wafting Scroggs and his N-M shorts over the topless towers of downtown Houston, Axxanon the highest and sharpest, like a paper spike on an old-time desk, except it was made of shining chrome and heartless glass, reflecting only ambition and envy and greed.

"I was not like that," Scroggs wailed. "Once."

But he looked at the ghost and saw it had changed, metamorphosized, and now it was as gigantic as a jolly gray giant, a great floating jellyfish of ectoplasm in the sky, wreathed in perhaps six thousand dollars' worth of Christmas icicle-lights. Scroggs's accountant brain knew what his neighbors' Christmas excesses cost down to the last twinkling Rudolph the Red-nosed Reindeer lawn ornament.

"Ghost, who are you?" he cried, for by now all this nocturnal floating had convinced him that he had either eaten Oreo cookies doctored with LSD, or he was dreaming or dead, and he was beginning to hope for the latter. Better dead than misled.

For the first time he got a glimmer of how Axxanon's employees and stock investors might feel.

The ghost laughed so heartily that the illuminated faux icicles shook like a bowlful of luminescent spaghetti. Scroggs's stomach lurched, a victim of heights, bright lights, and motion.

In an instant they were plunging down again, onto a peaked roof the size of a small county, that Scroggs recognized as Chairman Lao's principal residence of some seven luxury hideaways worldwide.

There was no shouting and bullying under that immense roof . . . or, rather, it was disguised under the cloak of jollity and a rather perverse celebration of infamy. For Scroggs recognized the Axxanon Thanksgiving party at Chairman K's he had not attended. Parties bothered him, you see, always had: the noise, the crowds, the loud voices . . . for the first time he saw that it was not festivity he shied away from, but the memory of noise and loud voices from his past. Fran! Why had he never followed her, tried to find her? Being ten years old was no excuse! She had been his champion, and he had shrunk from the idea of championing her.

This ghost was a solid, middled-aged sort of soul. His grip was almost physical as he yanked Scroggs down through the acres of slate roof—*Oof*! That felt like being buffeted by a steel surf on South Padre Island!—and into a massive Great Hall filled with Axxanon employees.

It wasn't really a Great Hall, it was just your average Houston executive mansion of 15,000-square-feet.

They were making merry, though it wasn't Christmas. Scoggs had remembered hearing about this party. He had been invited, of course, but he never went where invited. And well that he had not attended. The event had been the usual extravagantly boring affair designed to celebrate the triumphs of Axxanon's upper-echelon management. Scroggs was decidedly under-upper management and happy to be ignored . . . overlooked as he had been at home when the punishments had been handed out. Somehow that had translated into being ignored when the rewards were being handed out, too. He had to admit that at least he hadn't benefited from these shameless sorts of rewards. He's always tried to do a day's honest work, unlike most around him. When had that day's work become dishonest, and why had he failed to notice?

They were laughing below him and missing him not at all. The room was full of attractive female support staff and trophy wives, no wonder *Playboy* had leaped to do a "women of Axxanon" photo spread. Scroggs snorted his disgust as the ghost let him drift over a cluster of executive wives with shellacked blond hair and crimson fingernails. "She's asking a hundred and forty thou a month maintenance in the divorce," said one. "That includes ten thou a month on jewelry," another noted. "And," said another, ticking off the items on her clawed fingers, "nine hundred for a personal trainer, six hundred for a makeup person, eight hundred for a hairdresser—"

"She certainly didn't get her money's worth." Another hooted with laughter.

"They say his mistress got a hundred and fifty thousand a month."

"The one in Paris or the one in Belize?"

Thankfully the ghost pulled him away. The wives had sounded more like accountants than mates.

There were silly skits and musical interludes that made much ado about nothing, to Scroggs's mind. The President was there, not in the flesh, but on videotape, but he hadn't been President then, only governor. Maybe that's why he'd made the videotaped appearance, he saw the future, as Scroggs was now seeing the past, caught as he was now in the grip of Christmas Present.

"This isn't present," Scroggs objected.

"Yes, it is. It's making all the newscasts now. Merry, merry," trilled the spirit.

The men were clustered around the huge plasma TV screen, hearing how much the Axxanon executives had supported the presidential dynasty of the past, present, and future.

Uber alles Axxanon!

Scroggs watched, with an accountant's dismay, a skit showing the departing Axxanon president play a doubting Thomas (though his first name was Rich, a telling abbreviation) as he told his successor, Billings, "I say, old man, I don't think you can pull off six hundred percent revenue growth after I leave."

"Hah!" Billings retorted. "We've got HPV on our side."

HPV? Was that like HIV? Scroggs wondered.

"HyPothetical-future Value accounting," Billings chortled. "We'll make a killing. We'll add a billion dollars to our bottom line."

Scroggs writhed in the grasp of the Ghost of Christmas Present. "Release me, spirit! Let me fall to my death like poor Marlowe! I see now what he saw! I contributed to the insanity. I made the figures balance on the head of a pin, when there was nothing there but air, as is under me now. Let me drop! I am not worth holding up. Always I retreated to the corner and let the worst do the worst to the best. Let me go!"

"I cannot let you go," the Falstaffian ghost's voice boomed louder than the din of the partying crowds below. "You must face one last spirit, and he may indeed fulfill your wish. But first you must see others celebrate the season, grim as it is for them."

Swooping downward, Scroggs was soon a fly on the ceiling at the cramped but crowded apartment of . . . his nephew Jimmy Joe.

"You actually stopped by the geezer's office?" a plump young man was asking, laughing rather.

"He *is* my only living kin, crabbed as he might be in that empty office of his. I said 'Merry Christmas.' It's no more than I would have said to a Salvation Army Santa outside the mall."

"But that Salvation Army Santa would be doing some good in the world," a young woman dressed in not nearly enough put in, "and your uncle has been part of the worst rip-off of the American worker the century has seen."

"It's a new century now, Bobbie Rae." Jimmy Joe shook his head, with its too-long hair. "He's a weird old bird. Never had a thing to do with family, not that ours was worth much socializing with. But my mother always had a soft spot for him, kept telling me what a rotten childhood he'd had. Hell, the old man's alone in the world, and so am I. I thought I'd say a kind word to my only kin."

"And he snarled at you," Bobbie Rae said, both teasing and lecturing.

"Snarling dogs don't bite. They just hurt themselves because no one will want to go near them. I give up. You're right. Uncle's a lost cause. There is no Spirit of the Season, at least not in his office or house or world. So . . . Merry Christmas to what friends and family care to share it with us!" Jimmy Joe lifted a bottle of Shiner Boch beer.

"I used to drink that in college!" Scroggs cried. "When I drank, which wasn't long. Accountants who wanted to be trusted didn't drink. Or do drugs. Or . . . date. I don't know why I didn't do any of that after a while. It just seemed . . . too much trouble."

The ghost was dragging him down again, under another humble roof that would hardly occupy the square footage of his entry hall at the Lodge. His empty, sparsely furnished, unwelcoming entry hall . . .

"Ghost, I'm beat. I can barely see straight, and this journey has been like riding the Viper roller coaster at Six Flags AstroWorld. Let me rest."

"One last stop, Scroggs. One last visit to the one person who is closest to you now."

"Close to me? Who?" Scroggs couldn't think of a single soul who would fit that definition, and while he was searching his memory banks, the ghost pulled him down into the meanest, smallest domicile yet.

A woman was sighing. She was hanging up a phone receiver.

Why didn't she have a cell phone, like all civilized Houstonians?

"That was M. D. Anderson," she said, referring to the famed cancer facility and turning to show the face of his personal assistant, Lorretah, ridiculous spelling! There was nothing ridiculous about her expression, a sort of resigned despair that Scroggs recognized as his late mother's most consistent mood. "They can't," she was saying, choking on the words, "or won't take Little Lanier. They're sympathetic, they hate the system. But if we don't have the money and we don't qualify under the right programs . . . would you believe, honey, that my 'good' job at Axxanon is an obstacle, as they put it? Oh, I don't know what I'm going to do!"

Scroggs turned away as Lorettah buried her face in her hands and then in her friend's shoulder. "What's wrong with the kid?" he asked the ghost.

"A puzzling leukemia, but not puzzling enough to merit scientific investment."

"Is that the child?" Scroggs nodded at an ashy-skinned little boy sitting close by the artificial fireplace—abominable invention—as if for warmth. The child in the corner, he thought, and shivered despite the image of a flaring fire.

"*Yesss,*" the ghost hissed on a sigh. "You see the walker beside him."

"Poor little tyke! He hasn't a chance."

"But he has a happy family. Look."

Scroggs was gazing down on a tiny, people-crammed kitchen about the size of his guest closet. Friends and family were lifting aluminum foil from a scant few bowls and platters of food. Elbows struck elbows and, er, rears chimed with rears like cymbals clashing as piping dishes were laid out on the chipped countertops. There were candied yams, rich and yellow-orange; beans awash in mushroom soup and bacon bits, the lucky New Year's pot of black-eyed peas; mashed potatoes, collard greens; a snacking bowl of pork rinds, but no main course, no ham or turkey.

"This'll get Little Lanier grinning." A woman who looked like Lorretah's sister bumped hips with her sibling as if they were doing a cha-cha. "Good food will overcome anything."

"No, it won't!" Scroggs cried. "Why do they deceive themselves? I've run the numbers on everything from this year's profits, which are fantasy, to the future in worrying about the future. Nothing computes but losses. I've lost everything, why shouldn't they? How dare they be happy when they have nothing and I have everything and am not?"

His cry, however heartfelt, did not appear to impress the Ghost of Christmas Present. In a dizzying instant Scroggs was dropped with a *thump* back onto his massive king-size bed, which he now knew for both oversize and empty.

Moaning, he passed out.

A nagging alarm awoke him. Not his pretimed awakening gong via the smart-house computer, but a *bong-bong-bong* like a hammer on a hungover head. Scroggs had not been hungover since freshman year, when he had decided it was not a good career curve.

A skeletal hand attached to nothing else human was reaching out for him.

This time Scroggs was not playing along. *Hell, no, he wouldn't go.* Pity he hadn't said something of the sort to Axxanon years ago, but he hadn't.

"Go away," he ordered the spirit. But ghosts, like hangovers, leave in their own sweet time.

Once again Scroggs was jerked from his bed and his attuned-to-his-body-temperature electric blanket. Once again the dark of night embraced him like a chilly ebony shroud as he was wafted over rooftops and finally down to a stark concrete building that crouched like a machine-gun pillbox in a hill on some featureless, lightless, unoccupied land.

"This is it," Scroggs intoned, trying not to let his voice shake. "Hell at last."

"No, Benjamin Scroggs," a voice intoned, eerily sounding like it came over a loudspeaker, though all Scroggs saw was the bony hand still clasping his wrist like a cold ivory handcuff. "Hell is too good a destination for you and all the things you left undone in life. This is your heritage."

Scroggs gazed around at the featureless dark. Where was there this much undeveloped land near Houston, for the flight had been far faster than his first journey back to East Texas? Apparently even spirits faced transportation traffic jams.

An answer came to him: the city dump.

The grasping hand pulled him down until his icy bare feet touched cold hard ground in front of the austere building.

"Here, Benjamin Scroggs, is your destiny. Here will you go, and no farther." In the distance a bell began to toll. Houston had a good many churches, but the biggest were far too fashionable for anything so downscale as a single bell: ominous, tolling bells. A passing bell, as used to be rung for the dead, one toll for every year of life. Uh . . . this must be three, four, five—

"You are the Ghost of Christmas Future, aren't you?" Scroggs asked, still mentally and frantically counting. His preternaturally developed left brain totaled the bell tolls like a mathematics program running in the background on a computer whose foreground programming had gone buggy and crashed.

"Don't leave me here alone! I know my sins now. I know I have withdrawn from all that is human and humble in myself. I've treated my fellow man—and woman—as if each had only numerical worth, and low figures at that. I may not have schemed to defraud, but my vanity and my self-sufficiency allowed me to be used to shatter the lives of hundreds of thousands. I do not deserve to live, Ghost, I know that! But . . . somehow I still want to, and more than ever. There are things I must do, and foremost among them, I beg you, let me live long enough to testify, as poor Marlowe was never able to! I *will* do good. You'll see." Scroggs gazed entreatingly into the empty air two feet above the disembodied hand. Well, maybe you won't *see* exactly—"

"Silence! You always read numbers, and put your faith in numbers. Now read those."

The hand released him and Scroggs fell to his frozen knees. Where the skeletal finger pointed, he saw phosphorescent lettering on the building's dark plain wall.

DECEMBER 1, 1933–DECEMBER 25, 2003

"My God! It's my birthday and . . . my death day. Today! It's too late! It's *too* late." His eyes lifted above the damning numbers, even more damning than the numbers he had calculated endlessly for Axxanon, and saw his name very neatly etched in the bronze plague. At least someone had paid for that, he thought numbly. Who?

Scroggs collapsed on the ground, his fingernails clawing the hard Texas clay. He'd been cremated, burned in hell just the same. No doubt this spirit and he were the only people, souls, who had yet come or would ever come to mark this proof of his presence on earth.

There was nothing left to lose. He bawled out his horror and sorrow. He moaned like a ghost—would he become one now and drift like poor tortured Marlowe? He bewailed the past he could not change a jot or tittle or decimal point of. He bid life adieu like a mewling baby, but all remained dark and cold and unutterably lonely.

Finally, exhausted, he opened his eyes.

He lay on a hard cold surface . . . but— He pushed himself up on his elbows, looked around. It was his bed! The computer system had failed and the air mattress had deflated to granite-hardness and the electric blanket was stone-cold dead.

There was no wall before him but the blank, giant liquid-crystal TV screen on which he ran accounting programs.

On it he saw, in his mind's eye, himself groveling before his own epitaph, an epitaph that recorded only name and dates, nothing of his life but the factual parameters of it. And why should it? He had never lived beyond his factual parameters. And he heard his slobbering self sob, "Is there nothing I can still do, to help others if not myself?" And the bony forefinger pointed to an adjoining bronze rectangle. Those almost-forgotten phosphorescent letters and numbers glowed again on the dark unactivated screen before his eyes.

George Marlowe
April 23, 1948–December 21, 2001

Now, in his unheated, unfriendly bedroom, where even the resident computer program had deserted him, Scroggs understood the mute message. He must testify as poor Marlowe had intended, testify against his superiors who had turned out to be so morally inferior.

This he could do, if he could live. Scroggs pinched his forearm flesh. It was icy but registered the burn of pain, mortal pain, something he had not felt in the flesh or in the mind or in the heart for decades. Yes. Perhaps he would die as soon as he completed the task, but then there would be something to put on his bronze marker besides name and dates: whistle-blower. Well, after the fact, but better late than never. Scroggs struggled upright in the icy linens, rubbing his upper arms, and wiggled his numb toes.

No, there was something else to do. Something that nagged at him, that had nothing to do with spirits and other bad companies. *Heh.* A small joke. *Heh. Heh-heh-heh.* He was alive. Cold as hell, but not *in* hell.

He clapped his hands at the screen and saw the opening image blossom to fill the frame like a painting. A spreadsheet. Scroggs pulled the portable keyboard he always kept by his bed onto his thighs— *oooh,* cold!—and began clicking keys, going into the operating systems desktop properties menu.

Clickety-clickety. He'd never noticed it before, but a keyboard had a cheerful chirpy sound. Snickering, he raced through all sorts of options. Nothing quite matched his mood, but he found an image of falling snowflakes on a sky-blue background to use as new "wallpaper." It would have to do until he could customize something . . . perhaps photographs of friends and relatives. He hardly had any. Well, he would.

He went into the house's programming and turned on everything again, everything that ghostly hands had somehow turned off. Last, he brought up *It's a Wonderful Life* on the big screen and programmed it to play the last few minutes, the happy part, on a loop. Around him the house whirred into its low-key electronic life, heating, humming, breathing. He could hear an echo of the *Wonderful Life* sound track from the big screen in the home theater.

"Good old house!" Scroggs chortled. "I've kept you to myself too long. How'd you like some company? Not just decorators, but parties all year 'round! Party, party! They wanted in, I'll let them in, but only if they donate to the charities I back."

He finally had the courage to push his cold feet down to the rugs on his floor. They felt warmer already, but still chill enough that he hot-footed—that expression made him titter despite his bitter coldness—his way to the big window overlooking the street, where he pushed the button that opened the metal blinds.

They obediently swiveled to reveal no winter wonderland, but the cool pale pink glow of dawn breaking over the slate rooftops as high as mountains. Christmas lights still twinkled over every surface, as did stars above, for the moment vying with each other. Both would soon fade and grow as invisible as the warmth of a man's heart when the sun came fully up, but the sun was indeed coming up.

He cracked a door to the balcony that he had never opened (it was not computer operated because Scroggs never intended to open it, never feeling the need to look out on his neighbors and neighborhood and the world, but today he did). The facade of the house was old if the contents were not, and he had to fight the latch and push against time and disuse to get himself out in the crisp predawn air. There was no snow on the ground, but the rising sun had painted the yellowed sod a gracious shade of pink, burnishing everything like a blush.

Scroggs inhaled such a deep gasp of fresh air that he choked on it and coughed and realized that he'd attracted the attention of the sole person outside right now besides him: a woman below in a red velour sweat suit and stocking cap and white earmuffs with white angora gloves and black hiking boots, her cheeks flushed cherry-red.

Why, it was a lady Santa Claus!

She stared up at him, gaping. For one thing, no neighbor had ever seen hide nor hair of him. For another thing, he realized he was wearing nothing but his Neiman-Marcus shorts.

"Mr. Scroggs?" she said as if she'd just seen a ghost.

He laughed. "Out for a walk so early on Christmas Day? It *is* Christmas Day?"

She seemed befuddled at what to answer first. "I always walk at six-thirty, and, yes, it's Christmas Day, and aren't you going to catch your death?"

"What? Oh, my, no! No, I'm not going to catch my death." Scroggs couldn't help laughing, but he could tell it was an unprecedentedly merry laugh and, wonder of wonders, the woman started laughing with him. "Catch my death? Not now, no, sir! Er, no, ma'am!"

He clapped his hands on his skinny arms and reflected, a bit mournfully, that he was at an age and in a condition when the sight of his bare upper torso would not frighten strange women but inspire concern. He'd better retreat, but before he did . . .

"Merry Christmas, neighbor!"

She waved a red-mittened hand as he ducked back inside, still chuckling.

He had plans to make for the day. Many plans.

Jolly old elf. That's what Mr. Claus had been called in that delightful Christmas poem he had used to hate the sound of. Mice and sugarplums, indeed. But that's what Scroggs felt like, a jolly old elf, after he dressed and began planning his first Christmas Day party schedule.

First he hacked into the company computers . . . for the employee information. Then he hacked into the city hall files, for more information, laughing all the way. He had no time for regular channels, and besides, they were all closed for the Christmas holiday. *Halloo, hooray!* That suited his plans perfectly.

It was 10 A.M. when he and a crew from Delectation Catering showed up on the Craddick doorstep. The apartment building was as shabby as the side of town it occupied, but on the door a ragged wreath's candy canes crossed as spiritedly as swords.

Scroggs wore his best suit and had insisted on buying a festive red muffler from the catering manager for fifty dollars, although she had kept muttering "Target" as if they were in a shooting gallery. The catering crew was grinning, because he'd paid twenty-five hundred for their food and the service and had promised they'd be home to their families by noon, cab fare on him.

A small child opened the door, clad in pajamas. A small black boy who looked too small for his age. An older child, a girl of twelve or so, came up behind him fast. "Lanier," she was starting to rebuke him and then she spotted Scroggs and his party of five, not to mention the wedding-reception-size pans and dishes and trays they bore. "Mama!"

Behind her appeared Lorettah, wearing a caftan in some African fabric and long wooden earrings that dusted her shoulders and looked pretty impressive.

"*Mis-ter* Scroggs!" she said, half-exclamation, half-question.

"Call me Ben," he said. "May we come in? I've got a bit of Christmas cheer."

She glared over his shoulder at the corps de kitchen. "Delectation Catering? But aren't they closed for Christmas?"

"They were." He peeked beyond her to a living room with a decorated pine tree straight ahead and a floor strewn with wrapping paper. "Just show us the kitchen and the crew will get you set up and be out of your way in a twinkling. As will I."

"Scroggs?" asked the preteen girl behind her mother. "Isn't he the old grouch who kept you overtime and never paid it?"

"Be quiet, child," her mother ordered, and was obeyed.

"What a delightful girl. Frank and not afraid to speak up. Yes, my dear, I am that old grouch, but I've had a change of heart. Christmas dinner is on me, and, Ms. Craddick, a raise is long overdue for you. It may not be at Axxanon, I'm afraid, but I'm sure another position can be found at a more upstanding company. In fact, I will make that a condition of my testimony."

"Testimony?"

"I'm going to blow the whistle . . . after the fact, perhaps, but blowing nevertheless. I never meant to participate in such heartless and illegal doings, and I *am* Mr. Numbers, aren't I? I am liable for much ignorance and indifference, but I can do a lot of damage to those who actually meant to harm in their hearts."

"Mr. Scroggs," she said again, only this time she sounded like a stern but—was it possible?—loving aunt. "You just get your skinny ass in here and let your people go to work and stay out of my kitchen and take a look at our Christmas tree and such. Now sit."

And he did, and was besieged with a lot of what he had used to call "brats," who, it seemed, had no preconceptions about him at all except that he was responsible for the fragrant smells coming from their kitchen.

The little one, whom he knew must be the sickly child, leaned against his knee and watched him like a hawk. "We said grace for you last night," he finally confided. "Everyone said it was a loss but Mama, who said you were the means of our money no matter what and we should be thankful. And I sincerely tried to be thankful and I guess it worked."

"Being thankful always works," Scroggs said, lifting the boy gingerly to his lap. He weighed hardly more than an inkjet printer. "And we should be thankful that Houston has so many first-rate medical centers, for I'm sure that they'll find a present for you in the near future."

Meanwhile, Lanier's siblings crowded around, proudly showing plastic gewgaws from Wal-Mart. Scroggs discovered he had a sneaking desire to play with some of them, although it would be beneath his dignity. Dang dignity!

And so he was happily playing with some fool computer game on the floor amid the wrappings when the Delectation staff marched out and Mrs. Craddick invited him for Christmas dinner, for now there was a clove-dotted ham, a glazed turkey, roast beef, and fried chicken.

"Just a smidge," he said, standing and looking abashed. "I'm expected elsewhere."

But he hadn't been expected elsewhere, his only lie so far, and a benign one. Knocking on Jimmy Joe's apartment door late that afternoon was the hardest thing he'd ever done. He brought nothing but himself and his goodwill for the future, which didn't really show, as the best goodwill doesn't.

He brought humble pie, he supposed, and that was invisible, too.

The girl opened the door, and her face fell.

Amazing, he'd never met her, but his reputation had preceded him. Well, his disapproval. How was she to know that he had disapproved of everything?

"Jimmy Joe," she called, like a woman asking her man to banish some disgusting vermin that had gotten into the house.

Even in his new good humor, Scroggs could hardly muster a sheepish grin. He wasn't welcome here, and why should he be? Beyond the door he saw a roomful of young people. Young people? When had they become "they" and he had become so opposite to them, so full of sour instead of sweet, fatalism instead of hope, drudgery instead of enthusiasm?

He was an old, cold man. He didn't belong here.

"Uncle!" Jimmy Joe was standing before Scroggs like a portrait of his dead mother, face flushed with Christmas cheer. "Good God!"

"I've . . . come to wish you Merry Christmas. That's all." He wanted to do more than that for his nephew, but realized that he would have to earn the right. Just saying your were sorry was not enough.

"Merry Christmas? Well—"

"You young folks need to get on with your partying, but I wanted to stop by."

"Stop by and, and step in, uncle. We're playing Trivial Pursuit and I suppose . . . someone your age might be pretty good at it."

"You mean an old geezer like me."

Jimmie Joe clapped him on the back and shot a glance toward his girlfriend that was half-plea, half-command. "Christmas is a time for all generations, and we are a solid bunch of Gen-Xers. I guess we could use some mixed company. Want something to drink?"

"I don't dr—" Scroggs looked around. "Beer would be good."

A young guy in a Harley-Davidson T-shirt jumped up. "Beer for the geezer! Ebenezer Geezer has arrived."

Ebenezer Geezer. Nobody had ever bothered to give him a nickname before. He liked it. Might have a T-shirt made with just that on it. Yes, sir.

Finally, full as a tick but sober as a judge, he drove back to the Lodge. It was the short end of Christmas Day, and dark had fallen.

He entered a gated community transformed into a fairyland of blinking lights. He'd driven past the displays before, but he'd never seen them, or believed in them.

Poor nerdy Rudolph's red nose beamed from several rooftops, leading the leaping reindeers and Santa's sleigh. *A little child shall lead them.* Sometimes the little child that led them had to be the lost little child in ourselves.

Scroggs thought of Lanier Craddick and prayed that he would grow from a little child into a man who had not lost himself, as Scroggs had.

His own house stood dark and unfestooned. This year. Next year would be a different story.

But there was another house he needed to visit. This was the last visit of Christmas Day. He had become the Ghost of Christmas Future, with a new role to play.

Now, Scroggs's heart ached, for he knew that numbers no longer sufficed. Every "one" had a human being at the other end of it.

He drove to the only other dark house in the Lodge and parked out front.

Had the spirits who visited him felt this sad, heavy lassitude? This reluctance to bring retribution on a day made for salvation?

But retribution *was* salvation. He saw that now. Only repentance would redeem, and people were astoundingly willing to forgive if you admitted that you needed forgiveness.

Scroggs slammed the car door behind him and approached the door. He thought he saw three spirits cavorting on the roof, drawing a sleigh bearing a fourth spirit burdened, not with Christmas presents, but bound with electrical cords trailing computer monitors of guilt and regret.

Only Scroggs could liberate that fourth spirit from the terrible death and afterlife it had experienced.

He rang the doorbell and glanced at the redundant knocker, a pretentious mass of costly brass. Pretension. That had been the sin of Axxanon. Everyone pretending to greater glory and more money and vacation homes and high-end cars and power and a hard, glittering diamond of interior emptiness that was as big as the Ritz.

After a long while a light came on, shining through the glass side-lights on either side of the impressively coffered double doors.

The door cracked open. "Yes?"

"Mrs. Marlowe?"

"Who else would it be? I can't afford servants anymore."

"It's Ben Scroggs."

"You weren't at my husband's funeral."

"I'm . . . I was . . . a recluse. But I was at his funeral. His real funeral. May I come in?"

"Sure. Share a Christmas toast. I'll be outa here in two weeks. Foreclosed. The bastard's life insurance doesn't pay for suicide, and the bastard police are sure that's what happened."

"I'm sure it wasn't."

The door swung wider. The woman standing there held a wide-mouthed martini glass tilted in one hand. Her figure was as svelte as liposuction could make it, and her hair was streaked to the color of champagne. She looked no more than thirty, yet her face sagged with four or five decades' worth of unhappiness. Scroggs would guess that it had mostly showed up in the past month.

"So who are you?" she asked, her words slurred.

"Ben Scroggs," he repeated patiently. "I worked with your husband at Axxanon."

"You and eight thousand others. Who cares?"

"I do. I believe George's death wasn't suicide."

"Wasn't a suicide? Then . . . then the insurance would pay off, and I wouldn't lose the house and . . . everything."

"If the policy regards murder as payable, no."

"I'd keep the house?"

He nodded cautiously, but she waved the hand holding the almost-empty martini glass and welcomed him in.

The entry hall had a domed ceiling three stories high and a marble staircase winding along it to a skylight high above and black with night.

"My God, Scroggs, is it? He may have mentioned you. Yeah, you're the numbers nerd with your head in the clouds. My George had his head in the clouds, too. He was going to rat on them, all the big cheeses. The top executives who sold every little investor and employee down the river. Why not? It's just get all you can and flash it. If you don't have the house or the car or the best hairdresser or twelve residences all over the place . . . George was a loser, you know? But if I get the insurance money, I won't lose. I'll keep the house and the address and my hairdresser—they're that ones that know for sure, they say?—and I'll be all right. I'll keep my friends. So you can prove he didn't off himself? You're a godsend, Mr. Scroggs, a damn godsend. Let me call the insurance company investigator, irritating prick. You talk to him. You tell him."

She snatched a cell phone from the entry hall table, a slab of glass that balanced atop two stag heads, with antlers. She barked her name at whomever answered.

"Arlene Marlowe. I don't care if it's Christmas. I don't care where you are. Listen to this. I got proof."

Scroggs took the phone, pressed it to his ear. Somewhere, perhaps with angels we have heard on high, he heard—saw—the three spirit visitors of his Christmas Eve.

They had come on a deadly mission, with bad news, but somehow it had become the Good News.

And the last figure he saw was Marlowe, dragging his lost life and opportunities behind him through eternity.

Scroggs took the phone. He introduced himself. He explained his position at Axxanon. He found a plausible way to mention what he knew to be the truth.

Mrs. Marlowe screamed. She dashed the martini glass against the marble floor. She collapsed on the first step of the grand spiraling staircase to the second and third stories, and to the unlit Santa sleigh on the roof and to all the ghostly overseers up above, including her late husband.

Scroggs slowly explained to the insurance investigator. "She couldn't stand to lose the status that her husband's money and position gave her. She was terrified what his testifying to his boss's malfeasance would do to her social standing, their worldly goods. She killed him. It was her bad luck that it was presumed to be a suicide. Even the wives at Axxanon were infected. It was an epidemic of greed. Scroggs. Ben Scroggs. I'll be testifying for the prosecution. You're welcome. What? Oh. Merry Christmas."

He looked at Mrs. Marlowe, sprawling across the bottom step of her Cinderella staircase, behind the massive facade of a Rivercrest mansion, under the unlit ghost of a Santa sleigh, and he felt as sorry for her as no one had ever felt for him. Behind every cold grasping soul is a fearful lost child with a heart as chill and deep as death.

Suddenly the silence was broken. Distant voices echoed in the entry hall. The noise startled Mrs. Marlowe out of her stupor. She looked around wildly, then laughed.

"Just the damn home theater. George must have preprogrammed it before he died. He was always doing things like that. A gadgets geek. I suppose I'll have to listen to *that* all night."

Scroggs listened, expecting *It's a Wonderful Life*. The lines were familiar, but were being spoken by British actors, not *Life*'s all-American cast.

He left and shut the double doors behind him. He could hardly expect the police to bring charges on the basis of a hunch and a drunken confession. Marlowe would remain unavenged.

He looked over his shoulder. The Marlowe knocker was glowing phosphorescent green. For an instant Scroggs saw an anguished face. The brass must be reflecting the neighbors' outdoor Christmas lights, he concluded.

And then he realized what film had been playing uninvited on the Marlowe's expensive, oversize television: the old Alistair Sim version of *A Christmas Carol* that he had seen at the college dorm one year.

He glanced up at the dark and star-sprinkled sky. Empty.

Still, could unwanted spirits pay unexpected visits on Christmas Day, too? The night *after* Christmas instead of the night *before*?

Smiling, Scroggs walked to his car. He began humming a tune he was barely conscious of. It was, of course, a Christmas carol.

The Passing Shadow

BY PETER TREMAYNE

Peter Tremayne is the fiction-writing pseudonym of Celtic scholar and writer Peter Berresford Ellis whose work has been published in nearly twenty languages around the world. His work has received much critical acclaim, and in 2002, being born of Irish parentage, he received the accolade of being only the second living writer to be bestowed as an Honorary Life Member of the Irish Literary Society at the hands of its current president, Nobel Literary Laureate Seamus Heaney. Peter began to publish fiction under the Peter Tremayne pseudonym in 1977 and has authored many books in the fantasy genre, based mainly on Celtic themes. In 1993 he began a series of short mystery stories featuring a seventh-century Irish religieuse—Sister Fidelma—which were instantly acclaimed. There are now twelve Sister Fidelma novels and one volume of short stories published. The books appear both in the UK and USA and are translated, so far, into six other European languages. Peter's work covers a wide field and demonstrates his many interests. There is now an International Sister Fidelma Society, supportive of Peter's work, with members in twelve countries.

"And talk of Time slipping by you, as if it was an animal of rustic sports with its tail soaped."
—"THE PASSING SHADOW" IN *OUR MUTUAL FRIEND*

THE TWO MEN sat opposite each other, either side of a dark oak table in the dark, tiny snug of the Thameside tavern. There were no windows in the curious three-cornered little room. A gas burner, jutting from the wall above the solitary table, gave a curious flickering light, reflecting reddish on the red oak paneling. The elder man was in his early fifties, small of stature, immaculately dressed and coiffured, his curly hair receding from a broad forehead. A small "goatee" beard and mustache gave him the appearance of an intellectual, perhaps a professor. The other man was younger, in his thirties, fair of skin, with wide blue eyes and auburn hair. His handsome features had an indefinable Irish quality about them, although when he spoke, his soft, well-modulated tones were clearly those of someone educated in England.

There had been a momentary silence between them while a young girl had brought a tray into the snug on which reposed a decanter of port and two glasses. She had placed it on the table between them and left with a bobbed curtsy, for she was well aware of the identity of the older guest who now sat gazing moodily at the cut-glass decanter as the gaslight caused it to flicker and flash with a thousand points of light.

"I think you are worried, esteemed father-in-law," the younger man broke the silence with a smile.

The elder man turned with a disapproving frown and commenced to pour the port into the glasses.

"You know that I hate being addressed as father-in-law," he reproved.

The young man shrugged.

"Since I married your daughter, Kate, I have been at odds as to how to address you. Since I am called Charles and you are called Charles, it would sound like some echo in the conversation if we hailed each other with that mode of address."

The elderly man's eyes lightened with humor.

"In that case, let us agree. I shall call you Charley and you may address me as Charles, otherwise we shall have to resort to the formal Mr. Collins and Mr. Dickens."

He pushed the port across the table, and his son-in-law dutifully raised the glass.

"Your health, Charles," his son-in-law toasted solemnly.

"Yours, too, Charley. I hope your new novel sells well."

"*Straithcairn?*" The young man laughed whimsically. "Alas, I will never succeed as a novelist like my brother Wilkie. He has made more out of his *Woman in White* than I have made out of both my novels. My art lies in illustration, as you know. I am more of an artist than a writer, as was my father."

"Although I believe that your grandfather wrote?"

"Indeed, he did, sir. But had to leave his native Ireland to come to this country in order to earn a living as a picture restorer. Being no man of business, he failed to provide for his family."

"In that, we share a common background, Charley. That is what endears me to you. Moreover, I respect your critical opinion."

"Which brings us neatly to my point. You are clearly worried. I suspect it is about this novel that you have been working on of late. I was wondering why you have brought me to this unfamiliar Limehouse region, away from our usual London haunts, where we might bump into friends and colleagues."

Dickens sighed.

"Unfamiliar? My godfather, old Christopher Huffman, sold oars, masts, and ships' gear, just round the corner from here in Church Row. It was in old Huffman's house there that my father once placed me on the table and told me to sing to the assembled company—to show me off. No, Charley, this place is not so remote for me. Over twenty years ago I used some of this very area as background"—he waved his hand to encompass the surroundings—"as description in my book *Dombey and Son*."

Charles Collins was silent for a moment.

"But you are worried," he pressed.

Dickens compressed his lips for a moment and then nodded slowly.

"You are discerning, Charley. Yes. I am worried."

"About the new book?"

Again, his father-in-law nodded.

"Care to tell me what the book is about?"

"I have a character who has been left a fortune provided that he marries a girl. I've called the girl Bella. Bella Wilfer. My character, I've called him John, has been out of England for fourteen years. Now, while the fortune is attractive, John has decided to return to London under an assumed name to assess the situation. If John doesn't marry Bella, then a man called Boffin stands to inherit the fortune. John gets a job as Boffin's secretary. John becomes the mutual friend of Boffin and the Wilfers. In fact, I have entitled my draft *Our Mutual Friend*. The upshot is that John and Bella fall in love and John declares his real identity and inherits the money."

Charles Collins pulled a face.

"It sounds like a romantic comedy of deceit with a happy ending."

Dickens scowled and shook his head.

"No, that's just it. It seems to lack spontaneity. It's become a sordid tale of deceit and money. It's full of pessimism. I seem to hear the words of that confounded woman Mrs. Lewes, George Eliot, whatever her name really is, who said that I scarcely ever pass from the humorous and external to the emotional and tragic, without becoming as transient in my unreality as . . . oh, damnation!" He cut himself short. "She's right. It reads like a dry treatise on morals, not a story."

"Well, I have noticed that you have been growing increasingly pessimistic with life in general," observed his son-in-law seriously.

"The story is too dry and dusty," went on Dickens, ignoring the observation. "I need to insert some drama, some excitement, some mystery. . . ."

The door of the snug suddenly burst open, and a middle-age woman stood nervously on the threshold. She was a round-faced lady who was, in fact, the proprietress of the tavern.

"Lud!" she exclaimed in agitation. "Mr. Dickens, sir, I am all of a tremble."

The two men rose immediately for, indeed, the lady was suiting the words to the action and stood trembling in consternation before them. Dickens came forward and took the landlady by the arm.

"Calm yourself, Miss Mary." His voice held a reassuring quality. "Come, still your nerves with a glass of port and tell us what ails you."

"Port, sir? Gawd, no, sir. 'Tis gin that I would be having if drink be needed at all. But it can wait, Mr. Dickens, sir. " 'Tis advice I do be needing. Advice and assistance."

Dickens regarded her patiently.

"Pray, what then puts you so out of spirits? We will do our best to help."

"A body, sir. A body. Washed up against our very walls."

The tavern walls were built on the river's edge, and those dark, choppy waters of the Thames could often be heard slapping at the bricks of the precariously balanced building.

Charley Collins grimaced.

"Nothing unusual in that, Miss Mary," he pointed out, adopting his father-in-law's manner of addressing the landlady. In fact, every drinking man along the waterfront knew the landlady of the Grapes simply as "Miss Mary." "Dwelling along the waterfront here you have surely grown used to bodies being wash up?"

It was true that the Thames threw up the dead and dying every day. Suicides were commonplace; there were gentlemen facing ruin in various forms who took a leap from a bridge as a way out and the poor unable to cope with the heavy oppression of penury. Among the later sort were a high percentage of unfortunate young women, unable to endure the profession that was their only alternative to starvation. Often there were unwanted children. And there were bodies of those who had met their ends by the hands of others for gain, jealousy, and all manner of motives. The flotsam and jetsam of all human misery and degradation floated along the dark, sulky river. Indeed, there were also unsavory stories of waterman, "river find-ers," who plied their trade on the river, taking drunks from the river-side taverns to drown them in the Thames, though not before emptying their pockets of anything valuable, or to sell their corpses for medical dissection. Death and the river were not mutually exclusive. In fact, many along the riverbanks were called "dredgers," dredging coal or valuables lost overboard from the ships that pushed their way along the river to the London docks.

"I would send for a constable at once, Miss Mary," advised Dick-ens, about to be reseated. Whereupon the lady let out a curious wail-ing sound that returned him to a standing position with some alacrity.

"I would be doing that, but it be young Fred who be fishing out the body, and the peelers is just as like to say 'e robbed the corpse. Now, if you were there to see fair play . . . they'd respect a man like you, Mr. Dickens."

"If I recall a'right, Fred is your nephew?"

"Me own poor departed sister's son, gawdelpus."

Dickens smiled skeptically.

"What makes you think the police would believe that this corpse had been robbed?"

The landlady blinked and then realized what he meant. She looked defensive.

" 'E only looked to see if there were anything to identify 'im, Mr. Dickens. The corpse, that is. Bert, I mean," she ended in confusion.

Dickens raised a cynical eyebrow.

"I presume that there was no means of identification . . . nor any valuables on him?"

"Fred ain't no dredger, Mr. Dickens. " 'E's a lighterman. Makes a good living, an' all." There was a note of indignation in her voice.

Dredgers found almost all the bodies of persons who had been drowned and would seek to obtain rewards for the recovery of the bodies or make money through the fees obtained by bearing witness at inquests. But no recovered body and no corpse handed to the coroner would ever have anything of value on it. Dredgers would see to that.

"I am curious, Miss Mary," interrupted Charley Collins, "why do you think that a policeman, seeing this body, might want to accuse anyone of robbing it? Plenty of corpses are washed up without anything on them and often without means of identification."

His father-in-law looked approvingly at him.

"A good point. Come, Miss Mary, the question is deserving of an answer."

"The man is well dressed, Mr. Dickens, and Freddie . . . well, 'e thinks . . . that is, Fred thinks that 'e was done in, begging your pardon."

"Done in? Murdered?" asked Collins.

"Back of 'is skull bashed in, sez Fred."

"And why would the constabulary think Fred might be involved?"

Miss Mary sniffed awkwardly.

"Well, 'e did three months in chokey last year. Po'lis 'ave long memories."

Collins frowned. "Chokey?"

"Prison," explained Dickens. "I believe the derivation is from the Hindustani *chauki*. Well, Miss Mary, Mr. Collins and I will come and take a look at the corpse. Don't worry. Fred will have nothing to fear if he is honest with us."

They followed her from the snug. The tavern building had a dropsical appearance and had long settled down into a state of hale infirmity. In its whole construction it had not a straight floor and hardly a straight line; but it had outlasted and clearly would yet outlast, many a better-trimmed building, many a sprucer public house. Externally it was a narrow lopsided wooden jumble of corpulent windows heaped one upon the other as one might heap as many toppling oranges, with a crazy wooden veranda impending over the water, indeed the whole house, inclusive of the complaining flagstaff on the roof, impended over the water, but seemed to have got into the condition of a faint-hearted diver who has paused so long on the brink that he will never go in at all.

The snug, which they had originally settled to savor their port wine, was a curious little haven in the tavern; a room like a three-cornered hat into which no direct ray of sun, moon, or star ever penetrated but which was regarded as a sanctuary replete with comfort. The name "Cozy" was painted on its door and it was always by that name that the snug was referred to.

Miss Mary, the proprietess, pushed her stately way through the taproom and into the dark lane outside. It was a long cobbled lane whose buildings towered on either side, almost restricting the thoroughfare. It was appropriately called Narrow Street, running parallel with the River Thames and separate from it only by such buildings as the Grapes from which they had emerged. She took a lantern by the door and conducted them round the corner of the building, down a small slipway, which led to the bank of the river.

A young man was there, also with a lantern, waiting for them. At his feet lay a dark shape.

"Thank Gawd!" he stuttered as they emerged from the darkness. "Thought I were gonna be stuck 'ere."

Dickens and Collins halted above the shape at his feet. Dickens took the lantern from the young man and, bending down, held it over the shape.

The body was that of a man of about thirty. He was well dressed in a suit of dark broadcloth and a white shirt that had obviously been clean at one stage but was now discolored by the dark Thames water and mud with bits of flotsam and jetsam that adhered to it.

"Handsome," muttered Collins, examining the man's features.

"And a man who took a pride in his appearance," added Dickens.

"How so?"

Dickens raised one of the man's wrists and held the lantern near the well-manicured fingernails.

"The arms are not yet stiffening with rigor mortis, so he is not long dead."

He searched for a wound.

"Back of the skull, guv'nor? Head bashed in," suggested the young man.

"Fred, isn't it?" asked Dickens.

"That's me, guv'nor."

"How did you find this body?"

"Came down 'ere to empty the . . . the waste," he quickly corrected what he was about to say with a frowning glance at Miss Mary. "Saw him half in and half out of the water. Dragged him up and then called Miss Mary."

"And you searched him? Anything to identify him?"

"Not a blessed thing. Straight out."

Dickens could not hide his smile.

"Nothing on him at all?"

"Said so, didn't I?"

"Very well, Fred. You cut along to the police at Wapping Steps. That's the nearest station. Bring the majesty of the law hither as quickly as you can." He turned to Miss Mary. "You best get back to your customers. There is nothing that you can do here."

Left alone, Dickens began a thorough search of the man's pockets.

Collins smiled sceptically. "You don't expect to find anything, do you?"

"I never expect anything. In that way I am never disappointed. But it is always best to make sure."

"The dredgers will have got to him before now."

"Not so. This man is young. His body appears in good health and better dressed than most people in these parts. What dredger do you know who would leave the possibility of a reward for finding the body even if they have taken everything from the pockets? A rich person would obviously need an inquest, and there would be the fee from the coroner if they took it along. No, the man was killed and the killer went through the pockets before tipping the body in the river. Ah . . ."

Dickens suddenly pulled from an inside waistcoat pocket what appeared to be a piece of narrow ribbon. It formed a small circle, tied in a bow.

"A woman's ribbon?" asked Collins with a frown.

Dickens held it under the lamp.

"A piece of red ribbon. Mean anything to you?"

Collins shook his head. "A lady's hair ribbon?" he guessed.

"Come, man . . ." Dickens was indignant. "Think of law. This is the sort of ribbon a legal brief is tied up with. You'll see this ribbon is still tied in a bow as if it has been slipped off a rolled document, a brief, without being untied and thrust into our man's waistcoat. Now look at the suite he wears; it appears to be black broadcloth. The man is without doubt a lawyer of some type."

Collins gazed at his father-in-law in astonishment. "Next you will be telling me his name," he observed dryly.

"Easy enough—Wraybrook."

"Oh, come!" sneered Collins. "I can see the logic that leads you to guess that the man is a lawyer . . . that has yet to be proved by the way . . . but where do you get the name Wraybrook from?"

Dickens held the lamp up so that Collins could see that he had loosened the corpse's starched high white collar.

"Laundresses are invaluable these days. One of them has had the goodness to write the name on the underside of the collar with some indelible marker."

He refastened the collar and completed his search before standing up.

"Poor devil. A young lawyer, his skull smashed in and thrown into the Thames. I wonder why?"

"Robbery? That's the usual form."

Dickens stood frowning down for a moment.

There was a noise from the lane as a figure came hurrying around the corner of the tavern and down the slipway toward them. It was the figure of a heavy man. As he came into the light of their raised lantern, they could see he was dressed in the uniform of the Metropolitan Police. He carried a torch, which he shone on them both.

"I'm told there was a body discovered here?" he said gruffly.

Dickens smiled. "And you are . . .?"

"Sergeant, sir. Sergeant Cuff of Thames Division." The sergeant suddenly peered closely at him. "Beg pardon, sir, aren't you . . .?"

"I am."

"Did you . . .?"

"No. The landlady of the Grapes called us to have a look. A young man, Fred, found it. He works in the taproom of the inn."

"Ah, just so." The sergeant nodded. "He came to the station to tell us, so I cut along here smartish while he made a statement." The torch moved down to the corpse at their feet. "No need to bother you further, then—you and Mr. . . .?"

"My son-in-law, Charles Collins."

"Right then, sir. I'll take charge from now on."

"Then we shall leave you to it, Sergeant . . .?"

"Sergeant Cuff, sir. Thank you, sir."

They reentered the Grapes and returned to the "Cozy," and as Dickens handed back Miss Mary's lantern, he informed her that a police sergeant had arrived to take charge of things. To their surprise, a moment later Fred came in. He smiled with some relief.

"Gave 'em the statement and they told me to go," he announced in satisfaction.

Dickens nodded with a frown. Then he turned to Miss Mary and asked: "I don't suppose you have a *Kelly's Post Office Directory* to hand?"

"Matter of fact, Mr. Dickens, I do have such a volume," she said, and turning behind her bar, extracted the volume from beneath the counter.

Dickens took it into the snug, sat down, and began to turn the pages.

"Looking for Wraybrook the solicitor, I suppose?" observed Collins, finishing the decanted port and peering at his empty glass with regret.

"Except he is not listed. Let's see, this is last year's and would have been compiled the year before. That makes it two years out of date. Perhaps our man, Wraybrook, only established himself within the last year or two."

"Perfectly logically."

Dickens put down the directory, pages open on the table, and sighed.

Miss Mary entered the snug at that moment.

"I just came to see if you needed a new decanter, gentlemen." Her eyes fell on the directory. "Did you find what you were looking for, Mr. Dickens?"

Dickens shook his head. "Regretfully, I did not."

Miss Mary glanced slyly at the open pages.

"Lawyers, eh? Well, if you are in need of lawyers, there are plenty to choose from there. Personally, I always prefer to steer clear of them. My late husband said—"

"We were looking for a lawyer who does not seem to be listed there," interrupted Dickens, who had no desire to hear the wisdom of Miss Mary's late husband.

Collins nodded sympathetically. "Perhaps you can call in at the offices of *Kelly's*. They might have a listing for Wraybrook in their next year's edition."

Miss Mary started and stared at him. "Wraybrook, you say, sir? You don't mean Mr. Eugene Wraybrook?"

Dickens frowned suspiciously at her. "Do you know a lawyer named Wraybrook?"

"He's a young gent, sir. A solicitor right enough. But he's only been in the country six months. They say he's from India. Not that he's Indian, sir. Oh, no, English, same as you and me. Pleasant enough, young man. He has rooms at the top end of Narrow Street here and one of them is his office. Not that he gets much work, I'm told. Decent enough and polite and pays his bills prompt, like."

"Would you recognize Mr. Wraybrook?"

"I would, sir."

"And young Fred?"

"Fred, sir? I don't think so. Fred works in the evenings and Mr. Wraybrook only comes here for lunch now and again."

"Did you take a good look at the body on the slipway?" asked Dickens curiously.

Miss Mary shook her head. "Not I, sir. Can't stand the sight of corpses and . . . why do you ask, sir?" She frowned and then her eyes widened suddenly. "You don't mean that . . . that . . .?"

Dickens rose quickly. "Do you know where this Wraybrook has his rooms? What number in Narrow Street?"

"I only know it's the top end, sir. But—"

"Would you give us about fifteen minutes, Miss Mary, and then go out and tell the policeman who is loitering outside with the corpse where we have gone?"

Dickens hurried from the tavern with Collins hard on his heels.

At the darkened top of Narrow Street they came to a cluster of tall tenement buildings crowding over the cramped lane and shutting out all natural light. A few gas lamps gave an eerie glow, and beneath these were some street urchins playing "five stones." For a three-penny piece one of them indicated the tenement in which he knew the solicitor resided. The rooms were on the second floor. There was a single gas burner on every landing and so it was easy to find a dark door on which was affixed a small hand-written card bearing the name "E. Wraybrook, Bachelor of Law."

Dickens tried the door, but it was locked.

Collins watched with some surprise as Dickens reached up and felt along the ridge at the top of the door and grunted in dissatisfaction when his search revealed nothing. He stood looking thoughtfully.

"What is it?"

"Sometimes people leave a key in such a place," Dickens said absently. "I expect Sergeant Cuff to be here soon, and I do not want to force the door. Ah . . ."

He suddenly dropped to one knee and pushed experimentally at a small piece of planking near the door, part of the skirting board. It seemed loose and a small section gave way, revealing the cavity beyond. Dickens felt inside with his gloved hand and came up smiling. There was a key in his hand.

"Strange how people's habits follow a set course."

A moment later they entered the rooms beyond. There was a strange odor, which caused Collins to sniff and wrinkle his features in bewilderment.

"Opium? The smell of dope?"

"No, Charley," replied his father-in-law. "It's the smell of incense, popular in the East. I think it is sandalwood. Find the gas burner and let us have some light."

The first room was plainly furnished and was, apparently, an office for prospective clients of the solicitor. On the desk there was a rolled sheaf of papers. Legal documents. Dickens absently took from his pocket the red ribbon, rolled the paper, and slipped the ribbon over it. He shot a glance of satisfied amusement at Collins. He then removed the ribbon, put it back in his pocket, and examined the documents. It was not helpful.

"A litigation over the ownership of a property," he explained. "And a cover note from an agent offering a fee of a guinea for resolving the matter."

He returned the document to the desk and glanced around.

"By the look of this place, it is hardly used and indicates that our Mr. Wraybrook had few clients."

A door led into the living quarters. There was an oil lamp on a side table. It was a sturdy brass-based lamp, slightly ornate, and a very incongruous ornamented glass surround from which dangled a series of globular crystal pieces held on tiny brass chains.

"Light that lamp, Charley," instructed Dickens. "I can't see a gas burner in this room."

Collins removed the glass and turned up the wick on the burner, lighting it before resetting the glass. The crystals jangled a little as he picked it up.

Beyond the door was a sitting room. Collins preceded Dickens into the room. Again the furnishings were sparse. It seemed that the late Mr. Wraybrook did not lead a luxurious life. There was little that was hidden from their gaze. A tin traveling trunk at the bottom of the bed showing that its owner was a man recently traveled. The wardrobe, when opened, displayed only one change of clothes and some shirts. The dressing table drawers were empty apart from some socks and undergarments.

"Gene! I thought that . . . oh!"

A young woman's voice had spoken from the doorway behind them. They swung round. There was a young woman standing there. She was not well dressed and was not out of place among the residents of Narrow Street. She stared at them, slightly frightened.

"What are you doing here?" she demanded, silently strident. "Where's Gene . . . where's Mr. Wraybrook?"

Dickens assumed a stern and commanding attitude.

"We will ask the questions, young lady. Who are you?"

The girl seemed to recognize the voice of authority.

"Po'lis, ain't cher?"

"Name?" demanded Dickens officiously.

"Beth Hexton. I lives 'ere."

The East End accent did not seem to fit with the delicate features of the girl. Collins could see that whatever her education, she was very attractive, a kind of ethereal beauty that his artist's eye could see in the kind of paintings that Millais and Rossetti and Hunt indulged in. She would not be out of place as a model for an artist of the High Renaissance.

"Here? In these rooms?" he queried.

"Naw!" The word was a verbal scowl. "In this 'ouse. Me dad's Gaffer Hexton," she added, as if that might mean something.

"Ah, Gaffer Hexton." Dickens smiled. "And he might be . . .?"

"Owns two wagerbuts on the river. Thought all you peelers 'ad 'eard o' me dad."

A wagerbut was a slight sculling craft often used for races along the Thames.

"A dredger?" Dickens said softly.

"Ain't we all got a livin' t' make?" replied the girl defensively.

"How well do you know Mr. Wraybrook?" he demanded.

Her cheeks suddenly flushed.

" 'E's a friend, a real gen'leman."

"A friend, eh?"

"Yeah. What's 'e done? Where yer taken 'im?"

There was a movement in the other room and they swung round. They had a glimpse of a stocky, dark-haired man making a hurried exit through the door.

Dickens frowned. "Who was that?" he asked.

" 'im? That's Bert 'egeton." The girl spoke scornfully.

"And he is?"

" 'E's the local schoolteacher. Fancies 'imself. Thinks I fancy 'im. *I don't think!*" she added with sardonic humor. " 'E's out of 'umor since Gene . . . since Mr. Wraybrook asked me to step out wiv 'im."

Dickens glanced at Collins with raised eyebrows. Although Dickens was certainly no social prude, it seemed a little incongruous that a solicitor would "step out" with a dredger's daughter. But then, she was an attractive girl, and if a local schoolteacher was seeking her favors, why not a solicitor?

A movement at the door and a dry, rasping cough interrupted them again.

It was the thickset policeman, Sergeant Cuff.

"Well, Mr. Dickens . . . for someone who did not know the corpse, you seemed to have reached here pretty quickly."

There was a little scream from the girl. She had gone pale, the back of her hand to her mouth staring at the detective.

Dickens made an irritated clicking noise with his tongue. "Miss Hexton was a friend of Wraybrook," he admonished.

" 'E's dead?" cried the girl in a curious wail.

"Murdered, miss," the policeman confirmed without sympathy.

The girl let out a wail and went running out of the room. They heard her ascending the stairs outside.

"Congratulations on your diplomatic touch, Sergeant," Dickens reproved sarcastically.

Sergeant Cuff sniffed. "The girl's a dredger's daughter. Gaffer Hexton. He would rob a corpse without thinking any more about it. In fact, he was going to be one of my next port of calls. He and his daughter probably set up Wraybrook to be done in, if they didn't do it themselves. Wraybrook was a godsend to these river thieves. Whoever did him in has made themselves a fortune."

Dickens frowned. "You seem very positive that it was a robbery?" Then he started. "You've just implied that you knew Wray-brook and knew that he had something of value on him? Look around you, Sergeant Cuff, would a rich man be living in these frugal rooms?"

Sergeant Cuff had a superior smile. "We're not stupid in the force, Mr. Dickens. Of course I knew Wraybrook. Been watching him for some months. I recognized the body at once but had to wait for a constable to arrive before I came on here. I suppose that you haven't touched anything?"

"Nothing to touch," retorted Dickens in irritation.

"I don't suppose there would be. How did you come to know Wraybrook?"

"I didn't. His name was on his shirt collar. A laundry mark. I deduced he was a solicitor by the cut of his cloth and went to look him up in *Kelly's*. Miss Mary at the Grapes saved me the trouble, as she knew of a Eugene Wraybrook and indicated where he lived. It was as simple as that."

"Very clever. Had you confided in me that you had seen the name, I would have saved you the trouble of coming along. Wraybrook arrived in London six months ago from India. We had word from the constabulary in Bombay that Wraybrook was suspected of a theft from one of the Hindu Temples. The theft was of a large diamond that had been one of the eyes in the statute of some heathenish idol. But while he was suspected, there was no firm evidence to arrest the man. He was allowed to travel to England, and we were asked to keep a watch on him. It was expected that he would try to sell the diamond and make capital on it. He was a clever cove, Mr. Dickens. I suppose, being a solicitor and all, he was careful. Settled in these rooms and plied for business. Not much business, I assure you. Seems he was eking out some living from his savings. We're a patient crowd, Mr. Dickens, we watched and waited. But that's all. . . . Until tonight. I guess someone else had found out about the diamond. He must have kept it on his person the whole time because we searched these rooms several times, unbeknownst to him."

Sergeant Cuff sighed deeply. "I suspect the girl and Gaffer Hexton, and that's where my steps take me next."

He touched his hat to Dickens and Collins and turned from the room.

Dickens stood rubbing his jaw thoughtfully.

Collins sighed and picked up the lamp. Its crystal hangings tinkled a little as he did so. "That's that. I think we should return to our decanter of port."

Dickens was staring at the lamp. There was an odd expression on his face. "Let's take that lamp into the office where we can have a look at it under the gaslight."

Collins frowned but did not argue.

Dickens stood appearing to examine the dangling crystals for a while, and then he grunted in satisfaction. He instructed Collins to put the lamp on the table, turn it out, and then he bent forward and wrenched one of the crystals from its slight chain with brute force, wrenching the links of the chain open. He held up the crystal to the gas burner. Then it walked to the window and drew it sharply across the surface. The score mark had almost split the glass pane.

"And that, dear Charley, unless I am a complete moron, is the missing diamond. By heavens, it's quite a big one. No wonder anyone would get light-fingered in proximity to it. I suspect that on the proceeds of a sale to an unscrupulous fence, even allowing for such exorbitant commission that such a person would take, one could live well for the rest of one's life."

His son-in-law frowned. "What made you spot it?"

"Look at the crystals, clear, pure white glass. When this bauble was hanging by them, it emitted a strange yellow luminescence, a curious quality of light. If it was crystal, then it could not be the same crystal, and it is entirely a different shape. Round and yellow. When I peered closely at it just now, I saw that its fitting on the chain was unlike the others. My dear Charley, if you are going to hide something, the best place to hide it is where everyone can see it. Make it a commonplace object. I assure you that nine times out of ten it will not be spotted."

Collins grinned. "I'll tell Wilkie that. My brother likes to know these things."

"Well, let's follow the redoubtable Sergeant Cuff. I think that this will take the main plank out of his theory that Wraybrook was murdered for the sake of the diamond."

As they left the late Eugene Wraybrook's rooms, a thickset man was hurrying down the stairs. He moved so quickly that he collided with Dickens, grunting as he staggered with the impact. Then, without an apology, the man thrust him aside and continued on.

"Mr. Bert Hegeton," muttered Dickens, straightening his coast. "He seems in a great hurry. Oops. I think he's dropped something."

Indeed, a small thin leather covering of no more than 2½ inches by 3½ inches lay on the top stair where it had fallen from the man's pocket.

"What is it?" asked Collins.

Dickens bent and retrieved it. "A card case, that's all. Visiting cards. Not the sort of thing one would expect a schoolteacher in this area to have." He was about to put it on the wooden three-cornered stand in the corner of the landing when he paused and drew out the small pieces of white cardboard inside. He grimaced and showed one to Collins.

They were cheaply printed and bore the same legend as on the handwritten pasteboard on Wraybrook's door. Dickens smiled grimly.

They ascended the stairs. They could hear Sergeant Cuff's gruff tones and Beth Hexton's sobbing replies.

Sergeant Cuff looked annoyed when they entered the room unannounced.

"You'll excuse me, Sergeant." Dickens smiled, turning directly to the girl. "Does Mr. Hexton live in this tenement?"

The girl stared at him from a tear-stained face.

"Mr. Dickens . . ." began the sergeant indignantly, but Dickens cut him short with a gesture. "I need an answer," he said firmly.

"On the next floor above this," the girl said, trying to regain some of her composure.

"A jealous type?"

"Jealous?"

"Come, Miss Hexton. You said that he was attracted to you and you rejected him. Isn't that so? In turn, you were attracted to Mr. Wraybrook?"

The girl nodded. "Gene was a gen'leman."

"So you have told us. But Bert Hegeton was not?"

"He was a beast. Yes, he and Gene had an argument this morning over me." Her eyes suddenly widened. "Bert said he would do for Gene. 'E said that. Told Gene that he wouldn't stand for him pinching 'is girl. I was never Bert's girl. Straight out, I wasn't."

Sergeant Cuff was shaking his head. "Come, Mr. Dickens, this won't do at all. We know that whoever killed Wraybrook robbed him and the cause was . . ."

He stopped because Dickens was holding out his hand toward him. On his palm lay the diamond.

"It was where we could all see it, in the crystals of the lamp," explained Collins.

Dickens then held out the visiting card case. "Hegeton just brushed past me on the stairs and dropped this. I think he killed Wraybrook in a jealous passion, removed certain items from the corpse to make it look like the work of dredgers, and left him in the river. He came back here and then he found Sergeant Cuff and us in the house and panicked. Instead of hiding the things that he had taken from the body in his room, he decided to go to dispose of them in the river. Fortunately, for you, Cuff, he dropped Wraybrook's visitors' cards on the way out."

He paused while Sergeant Cuff digested his words.

"Jealousy, over the girl?"

"Exactly so."

Sergeant Cuff was thoughtful.

There came the sound of footsteps ascending.

"Then we won't have long to see if your theory is a reality," Sergeant Cuff said grimly. "I have had a couple of constables outside with strict orders not to let anyone leave the house until I gave permission. If Hegeton has Wraybrook's personal possessions on him, then he would have been unable to discard them, and he should still have them on him now."

They turned as a police constable came through the door, ushering the white-faced Hegeton before him.

"What's all this?" he cried angrily. "You can't—"

"I can and I do," Sergeant Cuff said calmly. "Empty your pockets."

Hegeton needed a little persuasion, but after a short while a number of items lay on the table before him, including a silver hunter watch. Cuff picked it up and glanced at it.

"Bert Hegeton? That's your name?"

The thickset man nodded resentfully.

"Then you would not be bearing the initials EW, would you. The inscription on the watch is 'EW from his friends, Advocates Club. Bombay.' You are right, Mr. Dickens. This is our man."

Beth Hexton gave a little scream and lunged toward the schoolteacher but was held back by Sergeant Cuff.

"You killed him, you swine. You killed him!" she cried.

Bert Hegeton turned a pleading face to her. "I did it to protect you, Beth. He wouldn't marry you. Not him with his high-and-mighty airs. He only wanted one thing. He would have discarded you after that. I love you, Beth. I . . ."

The girl again leaped forward, beating at him with her fists.

The constable and Sergeant Cuff separated them.

Half an hour later Dickens and Collins were back in the "Cozy" of the Grapes, sipping their port. Dickens had been frowning in concentration ever since they had returned. Suddenly his features dissolved into a rare smile of satisfaction.

"Damn it, Charley! I can feed parts of this little drama into my book and use it to make the tale come alive."

Collins was cautious. "You'll need to change the names, surely?"

"Nothing simpler. Bert Hegeton now . . ." Dickens paused in thought. "Why, I do believe that is easy enough. Hegeton in Old English means a place without a hedge. Do you know there is such a place-name in the county of Middlesex, which has now been corrupted into the name Headstone? So let us have Bert . . . no Bradley, sounds more distinguished, Bradley Headstone." He smiled in satisfaction.

"Eugene Wraybrook?" queried his son-in-law.

"Even easier. Just change the ending of Wraybrook into another word meaning exactly the same thing—brook becomes burn. Wrayburn. The name still means the place of the remote stream."

Collins grinned. His father-in-law enjoyed etymology and playing with words.

"So what about poor Beth Hexton?"

"Beth is Elizabeth, so we make her Lizzie. Hexton can become Hexam. And there we have my new characters. I can get on now, build up some enthusiasm about rewriting my book. I can even bring in Beth's father, the dredger. Gaffer Hexam. Ah, to hell with those critics who would say my work is becoming full of dry, moral rectitude. Away with such shadows."

He struck a pose. Collins knew that his father-in-law liked to perform.

*   *   *

"Hence, horrible shadow.

"Unreal mockery, hence. Why, so being gone.

"I am a man again."

Collins nodded slowly. "Well, there was no detective needed in *Macbeth,* but this has, indeed, been a neat piece of detection."

"These shadows passing before us, Charley, are the substance of the writer's craft," mused Dickens. "You can let time slip by you with its shadows, who have the agility of a fox, now you see them, now you don't. The writer must capture them before they disappear. Mind you, I think I can dispense with the character of Sergeant Cuff."

Charles Collins grimaced. "I felt sorry for poor Sergeant Cuff, off on the wrong track about the diamond and the reason for the murder." He suddenly grinned. "I'll have to tell this story to my brother, Wilkie. He's been saying that he wants to write a novel in which a policeman is called upon to solve a theft of some enormous diamond and subsequent murders. This might give him some ideas."

Dickens chuckled with a shake of his head. "A policeman solving crimes of theft and murder in a novel? I'll have to have a word with your brother. No one will believe a policeman as a detective hero."

"I seem to recall that when Sir James Graham set up his detective department twenty years ago, it was you who used your campaigning journalism to break down public hostility to having a dozen Metropolitan Police sergeants working among them in plain clothes solving crimes."

Dickens pursed his lips in irritation. "That's different," he snapped. "You are talking about a police detective in a novel. The reading public will never buy such a book."

𝔉agin's 𝔔evenge

BY BRENDAN DUBOIS

Brendan DuBois is the award-winning author of short stories and novels. His short fiction has appeared in *Playboy, Ellery Queen's Mystery Magazine, Alfred Hitchcock's Mystery Magazine, Mary Higgins Clark Mystery Magazine,* and numerous anthologies. He has twice received the Shamus Award from the Private Eye Writers of America for his short fiction, and has been nominated three times for an Edgar Allan Poe Award by the Mystery Writers of America. He's also the author of the Lewis Cole mystery series—*Dead Sand, Black Tide, Shattered Shell,* and *Killer Waves.* Other works include *Resurrection Day,* an alternative history thriller that looks at what might have happened had the Cuban Missile Crisis of 1962 erupted into a nuclear war between the United States and the Soviet Union, and which received the Sidewise Award for best alternative history novel of 1999. His latest novel, *Betrayed,* finally resolves the decades-old question of MIAs from the Vietnam conflict and their ultimate fate. Most of his works of fiction show his deep interest in political and military history throughout the world. He lives in New Hampshire with his wife, Mona. Please visit his Web site, www.BrendanDuBois.com.

❧

IN A SMALL village about thirty miles north of London, the manuscript collector sat at the edge of a muddy ditch, looking over the narrow country lane to the gated driveway that led up to the house that was his target tonight.

Though, of course, *house* was too simple a word to describe the large building. *Mansion,* perhaps, or *great estate,* or whatever such obscenely priced and overbuilt places were called in this lovely country. On both sides of the country lane, hedgerows and shrubbery rose up to the height of one's head, interspersed with old, thick trees. Before him were two granite pillars, holding up a wrought-iron gate. An electronic lock of a sorts was centered in the gate, and he sat still in the darkness, just waiting.

He shifted his weight, feeling the dampness of the soil against his dark, insulated military-issued clothing. Hanging around his neck was a set of Russian-made night-vision goggles. American or British issue were more efficient, but the Russian gear was cheaper and he was used to their operation. He waited some more, feeling a breeze tickle at his face and hands. It was a cold, damp night. Of course it was. What kind of other nights did they have in Britain?

He pulled back the sleeve on his coat, pressed the side of the watch, saw the blood-red numerals come into vision. Just after two in the morning. Not bad. Time to get moving. He stood up in the ditch, stretched his arms and legs, and looked up and down the narrow road. Nothing. Not a light, no movement, no sound of vehicles. Except for the electronic lock on the gate and the quality of the roadway, he could have been here, walking around, in the time of Charles Dickens. He was sure the old man—old Boz himself!—would have felt right at home in this place.

But what we're doing, he thought. Would Dickens feel right about that?

Pushing that question from his mind, he sauntered across the lane and went up to the gate. Lots of handholds and footholds, and in a matter of seconds he was over on the other side, now officially trespassing. He paused, waited, looked up the driveway to the great old house. Not even out of breath. Even though he was now a law-breaker, he felt safe enough. This poor old country was facing a wave of budget cutbacks, which meant that the people living out in the rural area no longer had police protection, reliable public transportation from one village to the next, or local health care. In that way, these places—save for electricity and safe drinking water—had gone back in time almost two centuries.

He took his time walking up the driveway, feeling confident in what was ahead, what his abilities were going to do for him tonight. This was his third visit to this impressive place but it certainly was going to be a different one. Both of his previous visits had been conducted under falsehood, pretending to be an American art professor, working on a coffee table book about the great houses of Britain, their glorious past, nervous present, and uncertain future. The owners of the place—a ruddy-faced overweight man who thought a coffee-stained ascot tied around his flabby neck was the height of fashion, and his botox-injected shrew of a wife—thought it was simply fantastic, brilliant, that someone would pay attention to their ancestral home. In his earlier visits the man had prattled on and on about his extensive line of ancestors who had built and lived in the house, and the woman had followed them from room to room, muttering requests through her gin-slurred voice for free copies of the book when it was published. Of course, what they really wanted was some extra attention so some American dot-commer might think about taking it off their hands, and when he left after touring the house twice, he was faced with a brief spasm of guilt: for what he had done by lying to them, and what he was about to do to them tonight.

But he had quickly gotten over the guilt. An American trait, he was sure.

By now he was at the house, looking up at its three stories, the fine stonework and tall windows illuminated by a quarter moon, up there in the sky. It looked impressive, and it wasn't the fault of the moonlight that it couldn't illuminate the old heating system, leaking roof, and rotting timbers. Grand homes always had grand problems, and by now, most of the grand families owning them no longer had grand bank accounts. He walked across toward the rear of the house, to the service entrances, and after a brief moment or two of wearing the night-vision goggles and working with a lock pick that he kept in a zippered case belted to his leg, he was now inside the home. He waited, goggles back around his neck, wondering if it was the nervousness or anticipation of what he was going to do that made him halt.

Whatever. Time to get moving.

He slipped the night-vision goggles back up over his face, saw the world snap into green-tinged focus, and he started walking. He was in the basement of the great house with its old kitchens and servant quarters, now closed and empty and dusty. It wasn't hard to imagine what it must have been like, to have been down here during the giddy times between the great wars, or during the turn of the previous century, when everybody had their secure place in their class, and when those who lived upstairs never had to worry where their food, clothing, and comfort was coming from. He wondered just how foul Dickens would have responded to such a place, seeing in the years after his own death, how the great gap still remained between the downstairs and the upstairs.

Well. Speaking of stairs, here we go, he thought.

He walked up, staying to the side of the stairs, so the wood didn't have as much chance to creak, continuously moving his head, back and forth, back and forth, knowing that he looked like some kind of giant mutant insect on the prowl. But night-vision goggles, though they were wonderful in opening up the night to one's eyes, were crap when it came to peripheral vision. He would hate to be going down one of the long hallways, while the master of the house stepped out from a dark corner with a cricket bat to whack him upside the head.

Wouldn't be nice at all.

Top of the stairs and he kept moving, listening as well, taking the next flight up to the second floor. But the house was still this night, the master and mistress no doubt dozing off somewhere after a bitter night of a small meal in one of the minor dining rooms, and then nodding off while watching *The Weakest Link* or something on BBC2.

Second floor. Rotated his head. Everything was as he remembered it from his previous two visits. To go left meant going down a long corridor with closed-off bedrooms and the master bedroom, and going right meant going down another long corridor, also with closed-off bedrooms, save for one door that was very important to him. He took a breath, moved, and—

Noise.

Damn, he thought. He looked to the left and saw a flash of light, and he closed his eyes and raised the night-vision gear. Another weakness: bright light from an open door or a flashlight could blind you for long seconds, long seconds when you were exposed and could be caught. There was movement and he looked around in vain for a hiding place, and then just stepped back down the stairs and flattened himself against the wall.

He was quite aware that his heart was racing well along. He thought about what might happen if he was going to be caught in the next few seconds or so. If he had successfully gone through that last door and got what he needed, he might have been able to bowl his way out. But not here, standing so exposed on the stairway. What could he say? Obviously the master and mistress wouldn't believe his tale of being a college professor, working on a book. Then, what could they believe? That he was a special correspondent from *Tatler* magazine?

Another noise. The flush of a toilet, and a hammering surge in the water pipes that meant a plumber should be here one of these days. A voice, replied by a louder voice, "Damn that curry, it's still giving me . . ." dribbling off as a door was slammed.

His fists had been clenched. How about that. He slipped the

night-vision goggles back on, took a breath. He counted to fifty and then went back up to the landing, and headed right, moving fast but knowing he still had to be quick and quiet. The master and mistress were awake, and he didn't want any strange noises to cause them to come out and investigate.

All right, he thought, here we go, and he went to the last door on the left, put his hand on the knob, and turned and walked in, gently closing the door behind him. Another breath, taking in the library and office. Another advantage of the night-vision gear. No need to turn on a light, use a flashlight—or torch, of course, have to be polite to the hosts tonight—or strike a match. Everything was exposed. Before him was a room lined on all sides by floor-to-ceiling bookshelves, the shelves crammed with leather-bound books, hardly any of which the master of the house read. He knew a lot about the man and his habits, and knew that he got part of the joy in his life from possessing old books and manuscripts, not actually reading the damn things. It was the possession that gave him the joy, not the pleasure of reading.

Near the center of the room was a wooden desk that seemed to be the size of small aircraft carrier, and he went around to the other side, down to the lower drawer. The master of the house's most prized possession, which was going to depart these grand surroundings in just a few seconds. He worked again at the drawer with his lock-picking gear, and the drawer slid out easily enough in just a few seconds. The thumping in his chest seemed to grow harder. In the center of the drawer, in a cardboard folder tied together by a string, was a pile of old papers. He lifted the folder and closed the door. The smell was the first thing he noticed, the smell of the old paper, and then the sheer excitement of holding what was in his hands.

He stood up, knew he should be getting the hell out of here, but he couldn't resist. He laid the folder down on the desk and carefully undid the string, opened up one side of the folder.

"I'll be damned," he whispered. It really was there, really did exist. He ran his fingers across the old paper, looked down at the crabbed handwriting and the old ink, and the scratch marks and jottings and everything else, that represented the master's most prized possession and jewel: the original and complete and unedited manuscript of Charles Dickens's second great work, *Oliver Twist*.

Without even having to look closely at the page, he knew what the very first sentences were: "Once upon a time it was held to be a coarse and shocking circumstance, that some of the characters in these pages are chosen from the most criminal and degraded of London's population."

Then, slowly and almost reverently, he closed the cardboard cover, tying the string back around the folder. Sure, he knew what the first and many other sentences of *Oliver Twist* were, but there were other things in this manuscript as well, hidden secrets that were about to be revealed, revealed in a way that he hoped the spirit of Dickens would appreciate.

Holding the stolen pages close to his chest, he left the office, closed the doors, and in a matter of minutes was back on the lawn of the old house, walking quickly back to the gate and what freedom waited for him.

⁓

A night later, in a quiet room in a bed-and-breakfast just south of where he had committed his crime of burglary, he finished rereading the manuscript. He held the old paper in his hands and then carefully started leafing through the book, taking out a page here and there, placing single sheets on the bed. He worked until the entire top of the bed was covered with sheets of the manuscript. His eyes ached from the work of trying to decipher the handwriting, trying to make sense of the scratches and cross-outs, tried to read the old paper and old ink. But besides the ache was the simple pleasure of reading something closing in on two hundred years of its life, and he reveled in reacquainting himself with the old and familiar characters: the innocent Oliver Twist, the criminal but amusing Artful Dodger, the hooker with a heart of gold, Nancy, and the dastardly Bill Sikes.

And not to forget the character that had brought him here, Fagin, the master thief, the corrupter of youth, and the head of a criminal gang.

But there was more to Fagin than just that. In reading the old words, the old phrases, what Fagin was and what he was called stuck with him, like a burr under a saddle, something painful and disquieting. Oh, he was under no illusion that the manuscript had to be politically correct, or even fair by today's standards. Dickens was a giant of his age, but he was also a man of his age, and he didn't begrudge how he had created Fagin and what he called him.

Still . . . what Fagin was called and what he did in the book was most certainly going to cause this priceless manuscript to be turned into ashes, in a very short time.

He knew he should feel guilty about what he had planned for the cherished words of Dickens, but instead, he almost felt at peace.

He looked at the clock on the nightstand. Time to get to work, yet again.

From underneath the bed he took out his suitcase and opened it up. In one corner of the suitcase, nestled among his clothes, was a shaving kit. It was heavy as he picked it up and went into the bathroom. He glanced in the mirror, saw the drawn face, the tired eyes, and looked away. No time to waste on beauty tips.

He unzipped the kit and removed a can of shaving cream. It felt heavy as well. He took the can back into his room, unscrewed the bottom. The bottom slid out, revealing a thick metal tube, fastened to the false bottom. He looked over at the clock. Two minutes to get it done. Two minutes. At the top of the tube he unscrewed the thick top, and then went to every sheet of paper. He upended the tube and a clear liquid oozed out. From one page to the next, he worked as fast and as careful as he could, smearing the top of each sheet with the liquid, until he was finished. He didn't look at the clock. Couldn't. When he was done, he screwed the top back on, put the fake can of shaving cream back together, and then looked at the clock.

Three minutes. Damn.

A brief bite of panic rose in the back of his throat, and he pushed it back. Nothing he could do now, except keep on going on. He returned the shaving cream to the shaving kit, washed and rewashed his hands in the sink, and then dried off his hands and went back out to the room. The damp marks on the top of each page were slowly drying. He waited until the sheets dried out, and then he collected them and put them back in order, and then put everything back where it belonged.

Then he left the room and went downstairs, to find the best restaurant there was in this small village.

⌒〜❧

A day later he was in London, at a private club in the Bloomsbury section of that great old city, within easy walking distance of the British Museum. He was in a small, private dining room, sitting across from a man he supposedly knew only as Mister Hale. Though he insisted on being called Mister Hale, the man was in fact a retired British Army officer and dressed the part, from his lean bearing to thin white mustache and impeccable dark gray suit with a regimental necktie of some sort. The room with its old polished wood paneling held just four tables, and the other three tables were empty. They ate a fine meal of sea scallops, washed down with a chilly French Chablis that seemed to match Hale's mood, and when they entered the coffee phase, Hale waved away the two older men in white jackets who had served them. The door closed behind them and Hale said, "Well. Here we are."

"That's right."

"You've done incredibly well. If, in fact, you have the merchandise in question."

He said nothing, just cocked his head, like a bird dog hearing the rustle of something in tall grass. Hale nodded in understanding and said, "This room has been, as is said, swept. There are no listening devices to concern you. So feel free to speak."

"All right. Hell of a nice necktie you got there. Where did you get it?"

Hale's face reddened some. "By serving in my regiment with honor over a number of years. Including fighting the Red Chinese in Korea, in some frightfully deep snow above the 38th parallel. Any other impertinent questions?"

"Not for the moment."

"Quite. All right, please open up that dispatch case of yours and show me that you have the merchandise."

He waited for just a second, like pointing out to Hale that if he had his way, he could take the dispatch case and just walk out, but instead, he reached under the white tablecloth-covered table, pulled out the leather case. He unzipped it and opened up a leather flap, then placed it across the table. Hale grunted and leaned over, now taking a magnifying glass out of his pocket to examine the pages. The older man slowly went through the pages, sucking his breath through his teeth every now and then, as the paper rustled and was laid down on the tablecloth.

In the meanwhile, he sat there, hands folded, to prevent them from shaking, for he wasn't sure if the treatment he had given the pages the other night was visible, but it didn't seem to be, so maybe this damn thing was going to work out after all.

Hale looked up. "You've done well."

"Thanks."

Hale glared, and then reached into another pocket, pulled out a cell phone. He manipulated the buttons with the ease and grace of an older gentleman whose VCR at home had been flashing "12:00" for three years, and then he said, "This is Hale. Complete the transfer."

The old man flipped the lid on the phone and returned it to his coat pocket, and looked over, as if saying, all right, sonny, it's your turn.

So it was.

He reached to his side, unclipped the Blackberry unit that was there, and idly thought, well, well, dueling electronic information systems. He worked the buttons with his fingers, and after a few minutes or so of dexterous work, he saw that in fact a numbered account in a bank in the Cayman Islands had just received an extraordinarily large deposit.

He looked up, nodded. "Then it looks like everything is well, isn't it?"

Hale took the manuscript and replaced it in the folder, and then, in turn, put it back into the leather dispatch case. He vigorously zipped it shut and said, "I suppose it is."

"Then you'd be quite wrong," he said.

Again, the older man's face reddened, as Hale carefully removed the dispatch case and put it on the floor next to him, as if afraid he was about to be thrashed about and have it stolen.

"I don't understand," Hale said. "Our agreement is complete. The manuscript for the funds. What else is there?"

He raised his hands up and placed them on the white tablecloth. "Let's talk about the manuscript, shall we? Do you have any idea what you now have in possession?"

"Of course I do," he shot back. "The Charles Dickens's original, handwritten manuscript of *Oliver Twist*. I've just verified it, you fool."

"Yes, perhaps I am a fool, but let's talk a bit more. There's more in those pages than just the original, handwritten manuscript. You should have noted, the original, handwritten, unedited manuscript. Correct?"

The color was still in the old man's face. "I have no idea what you're talking about."

"Oh, I think you do. For the manuscript in your hands contains words and phrases that never showed up in print or public, doesn't it."

Silence. All he could hear was the slow tick-tocking of a tall clock in the corner, and the murmur of traffic from below.

"I believe it's time for us to depart," Hale said.

"Nope."

Hale attempted a laugh. It sounded as sincere as a telemarketer trying to sell aluminum siding to an apartment dweller. "What are you going to do? Steal back the manuscript?"

He shook his head. "Nothing as direct as that. Perhaps a phone call to the Metropolitan Police after I leave here. Perhaps nothing is found on you, perhaps you skate free. But the humiliation and embarrassment, for a man such as yourself . . ."

Hale appeared to be trying to compose himself. His voice lowered, he said, "What the devil do you want?"

"Some questions answered, and that's that."

"In exchange for you not presenting me to the police? That doesn't seem particularly fair, especially if I manage to bring you along with me. Let's see which one of us is released by the police first."

He said, "Certainly. And let's see whose name gets more play in your tabloids."

The old man looked at him, eyes cold and icy, and then he relented.

"Go ahead," Hale snapped. "Make it quick."

"Let's get back to the manuscript," he said. "That's what makes it so valuable, doesn't it. The words and phrases that never appeared when the book was first serialized in that magazine, *Bentley's Miscellany,* or when it appeared in later editions."

A slight nod, that would have been missed if he hadn't been looking right at Hale's face. He went on. "You see, most people, when they hear *Oliver Twist,* they think of the stage musical, or the movie that won the Academy Award back in 1968. Songs about love and redemption. Young boys out on the street, playing at being thieves. Well-scrubbed and well-fed actors playing their parts. Happy endings. Most people hardly ever refer to the older movie that David Lean made in 1948, or the original manuscript. Correct?"

A grudging reply. "You may be right."

"Oh, I am right, and you know it. For that's the dirty little secret of *Oliver Twist,* is the character of Fagin, the master thief and head of a gang of boys. In Dickens's original words, Fagin is sometimes called just Fagin. But most other times, well, he's called something else. Am I right, Hale?"

The old man sighed. "You are."

"And what is he called?"

Two words. "The Jew."

He nodded. "That's right. The Jew. Or as Dickens described him in the book, a 'very old shriveled Jew,' or the 'wily old Jew' or 'crafty Jew.' Now, it's not fair to place our way of thinking and customs upon the people of a different time, but even after the story appeared in print, back in 1841, Dickens was criticized for being an anti-Semite. He received so much criticism that when the book was reissued many years later, he went through it and took out most of the references to Fagin as the Jew. He even atoned for what he wrote about in *Oliver Twist* by making the main character in his last novel, *Our Mutual Friend,* a sympathetic Jewish man. But still, the controversy remains. Remember that David Lean film I mentioned earlier, the one made in 1948? Sir Alec Guinness played Fagin, and his portrayal was considered so offensive and anti-Semitic, that it was nearly three years before it was shown in the United States."

Hale said, "If you have a point here, you are taking a dreadfully long time to make it."

"One of my many faults," he said. "The point is, if the original manuscript of *Oliver Twist* was in private hands, and if this manuscript showed that the original depiction of Fagin—one that never appeared either in its magazine serialization or in book form—was even more vile, more anti-Semitic, perhaps showing Fagin with an unhealthy interest in the young boys in his gang . . . well, then this manuscript might have a value for certain parties, correct?"

The older man sat there, glowering. He went on. "You asked me to call you Mr. Hale, but to be more polite, I suppose I should call you Colonel Hale, for your years of service to the Crown. Correct?"

"You have done your research," he said simply.

"That I have. And I've also found something else interesting, where you spent most of your postings. Oh, like you said, you did spend some years in Korea. And in Malaysia, as well. But the bulk of your service has been in places in the Middle East. Like Aden. Iraq, before the current troubles. Saudi Arabia. Places where there might be people . . . or groups . . . who would love to have this manuscript in their hands. Perhaps publish it and spread it around the area, showing how one of Britain's most beloved writers, a writer from a country allied with you-know-who, was actually someone deeply anti-Semitic. Or, from their vantage point, someone who had the correct point of view of a certain group of people. Quite possible, am I right, Colonel?"

"Are your questions done, young man?"

He shrugged. "Pretty much. I just have two more questions, Colonel. How does it feel that by giving this manuscript to a certain group of people, you'll be just adding more fuel to a fire of conflict that's been going on for generations? And why?"

The colonel glared at him. "I don't bloody care what they do to each other. Ignorant savages. And as for the other question, it's what I was paid for. Just like you. You're in the service of your master, whoever pays the piper."

He shook his head. "You see, that's the difference between you and me. I know who my master is. And it's not whoever's paying my freight that week. There's an old story, probably apocryphal, about one of your countrymen visiting a ranch in Texas, more than a hundred years ago. The Englishman came up to a cowboy, who was repairing a fence. The Englishman asked the cowboy, 'Could you direct me to your master?' And the cowboy looked at him and said, 'The sumbitch hasn't been born yet that'll be my master.' Get the point, Colonel? I may be hired, but I sure ain't owned."

Now Hale stood up, glaring, the dispatch case firm in his hand. "I'm leaving now. And I advise you to do the same, and leave my country at once."

He picked up a cloth napkin, dabbed at his lips. "Best advice I've heard all day."

But if the advice had been good, he had ignored it. Instead of leaving London, he stayed in a small hotel that was literally a stone's throw to the British Museum, and spent two days wandering through the immense wings and displays, not looking for anything in particular, just enjoying the relics of empires past. On the third day he walked from his hotel to Doughty Street in London, filled with old dwelling homes in the brownstone style, and spent an hour at the Dickens House Museum, where Charles Dickens had lived for a few years, and where he had written *Oliver Twist*. The home was small and the rooms were tight indeed, but he enjoyed the sensation of being in the same space where Charles Dickens had once lived and worked. But going to the museum was more than just paying homage to a writer he had long since admired; it was also a way of asking for some form of forgiveness. He wasn't sure what the spirit of Dickens would have thought of what he had done; he just hoped that somewhere, somehow, he'd be able to explain it to him.

Going out through the entrance to the museum, there was a cluster of school-aged children in uniforms, with plaid skirts and jackets, white knee socks, and polished black shoes. Each had an enormous notebook in her hands, and they were buttonholing tourists as they walked out. One serious-looking girl of about eleven or twelve said, "Excuse me sir, may I ask you a question? For a school project?"

He smiled down at her. "Certainly."

Her voice suddenly got serious as she read from a sheet of paper placed on the notebook cover. "After visiting the Charles Dickens House today, what do you think was the most important thing you know about Charles Dickens?"

So many answers to this one question, he thought, so many answers. As he was going through each possible answer in his mind, he found that his mouth was ahead of him. He said, "I think the most important thing about Charles Dickens was his care and defense for those who had little care and no defense. He . . . he hated poverty, hated violence, hated bullies, hated oppression, and in his works, you find that he had no patience for the tyranny of the church, tyranny of the state, or tyranny of those with small minds. He also—"

And then he stopped, as the young girl continued scribbling furiously in her notebook, and when he said, "Enough, young lady?" she was so intent on finishing what she was writing that she could only nod.

Leaving the Dickens House and walking the few short blocks back to his hotel, he felt odd at what he had just done, in touring the museum and speaking to the young British girl, a descendant of sorts of the time and place that Dickens had inhabited. What would Dickens have thought about what he had just said? He had no idea. But he also had a satisfaction of a job well done, of something that he had almost surely pulled off, and he was lucky indeed, there would be just one more step to be taken before he went to Heathrow and flew home to Boston.

And outside of the hotel, just as he was going up to the steps leading to the front entrance, is where they got him.

Part of him admired the smooth professionalism, how the white van—and amazing how many white vans existed in London—that cruised up to him, the doors sliding open, the beefy men coming out to the sidewalk and grabbing his arms and belt, and in a matter of seconds he was bundled into the van and driven away. There were five men—two up front and three in the rear—and the windows of the van were tinted. The men were breathing heavily and seemed wired, and he sat perfectly still.

The man in the passenger's seat up front—who seemed the oldest and also seemed in charge—looked back at him and said, "We'd prefer not to shackle you. So if you just stay still and do what you're told, we won't put the handcuffs or chains on you. Understood?"

"Yes," he said. "Thank you. I'll sit still and do what I'm told."

The man nodded and he sensed that the other men relaxed as well, as the van moved through the crowded London streets. He felt odd, out of place, not only because of the way he had been seized, but because seeing all those vehicles driving on the left just seemed to violate something deep inside of him, like the laws of nature were being breached. He was hopelessly lost and he looked around and then took a deep breath. What the hell. It was out of his hands, and about the only thing he had left was time. He had to make it work for him.

The van suddenly turned left, went down a dead-end narrow street, which was blocked at the end by a metal door, which slid open as the van approached. They entered a parking garage, and in another minute he was taken out and brought through a series of doors. Another breath. A quiet, polite processing took place. Photos were taken, as well as fingerprints, and his belt and shoes were removed. He was placed into a small room, with a wooden table, bolted to the floor, and three wooden chairs. The door slammed behind him, and there was a clicking noise as it was locked. The room was empty, the white ceiling tiles stained to a color of dirty ivory from all the tobacco smoke. On one wall was a mirror. He resisted the urge to stick his tongue out at his hidden watchers.

He paced around the room once, and then took all three wooden chairs and lined them up on one side of the table. He sat in the middle one and waited for a while, until he lost track of time.

Another breath. He closed his eyes, started rewatching *The God-father* movie in his mind's eye. He let his breathing ease as he sat there, and when it came to the point where Don Corleone was shot down in the street after buying fruit, and his son Fredo fumbled in trying to protect him, the door was unlocked and a man strode in.

He seemed to be in his mid-thirties, wore dark gray slacks, a white shirt, and a dark red necktie. His face was fleshy and his hair was black, cut crew-cut short, and he looked to be a man in charge.

Until he saw the way the chairs had been set up. He frowned, went over to the other side of the table, and dragged a chair back to the opposite end. He sat down, a manila file folder in his hands. The man cleared his throat. "The name is Guy Thomson. I'm with the Special Branch."

He nodded. "Pleased to make your acquaintance."

Thomson put the folder on the table, opened it up. "And you are . . . one Peter Dudley. Of Boston, Massachusetts. Correct?"

"Very correct," he said.

"Yes," the detective said, as if pleased with himself. "One Peter Dudley. Rare manuscript collector. Former U.S. Army sergeant. And thief."

"Nice research job," he said.

"Oh, it gets better. Mr. Dudley, are you familiar with Lord and Lady Winship? Are you?"

"Should I be?"

Thomson's eyes narrowed. "Let's stop the gameplaying, shall we? Twice you've entered their home under false pretenses. Pretending to be an author of some sorts. And you entered their house at least one more time, as a burglar. For they are now missing something quite valuable."

He folded his arms. What approach, he thought, what approach should he take?

Well, let's try this one.

"I'm afraid you have it all wrong," he said. "I did enter the house, but I never said I was a writer. I said I was hoping to become a writer, and that I wanted to do a book about—"

"Please," Thomson interrupted, his voice harsh. "That's so much bollocks, and you know it. They are both insistent that you claimed to be an American college professor. Otherwise, you would have never gained entry."

All right, he thought, let's try this one.

"I demand to see a representative of my embassy. And a lawyer."

Thomson smirked. "We'll get around to contacting your embassy one of these days. And in this country we call them solicitors, and whether you get one depends on how helpful you are. So, Mr. Dudley, do you want to be helpful today?"

"Depends on what you mean by meaning helpful."

Thomson leaned over the table. "Here's what I mean, mate. That you admit you were in Lord Winship's home. Admit you went there with the intent to burgle. Admit that you stole a rare manuscript, the handwritten manuscript of *Oliver Twist,* written by Charles Dickens."

He kept silent.

"Oh," the detective added. "And tell us where the manuscript is, and if you don't have it, tell us who does."

He nodded.

The detective said, "Well?"

"Sorry," he said, shaking his head. "Guess I don't feel like being helpful today."

Thomson smirked. "You will, one of these days."

And Thomson got up and left the room.

And the door locked shut again.

*   *   *

A routine of sorts was established. He was put into a small cell with a mattress, sink, and toilet. No reading material, no radio, no television. At odd times, here and there, he was brought out for a continuing talk with Detective Thomson. There were no physical threats, no physical abuse, but after a day or so, he was tired, he was achy, and he just wanted to get a good night's sleep in a comfortable bed, after a wonderful meal. For the food that was served in his cell at various times of the day and night were the worse clichés of British cooking: cold porridge, chewy beef sandwiches with stale bread, and cold toast and dry cereal. Nothing was warm, nothing was hot, nothing was particularly tasty, and through it all, as he waited, he sort of admired the indirect approach that they were taking.

He blinked his eyes, as he sat in the interrogation room. Because of the times he had been woken up and brought here, he wasn't sure how many days he had been kept. But it had to be at least a week.

Across from him, looking clean and refreshed and well fed, was Detective Thomson. Over the hours and days Thomson had worked alone, meaning sometimes he was the Good Cop, sometimes the Bad Cop. During the times he was Good Cop, Thomson promised lenient treatment, hot shower, clean sheets, if only he admitted that he burgled the home, stolen the manuscript, and gave up the name of the buyer. And when he was Bad Cop, there was a lot of blustering, yelling, and table pounding, ending with, "This ain't no *NYPD Blue*, sonny, you're in my town now, and we follow my rules!"

Today, it seemed like Thomson was playing Impatient Cop, for he kept on returning to the evidence the police had. "Come along, Peter. We have you dead to rights. The Lord and Lady have picked out your photo from an array. We know you aren't a writer. And your bloody fingerprints are all over the place, especially the places the Lord and Lady didn't escort you, like the south servants' quarters, where the lock had evidence of being picked. And the desk in Lord Winship's office."

He rubbed at the stubble on his face. "Sounds pretty serious."

"Oh, you have no idea how serious," Thomson said. "You're going to be here for quite a long time, until you give it all up. So let's start with another question. Where is it?"

He shrugged. "Don't know."

Thomson said, "Your hotel room, your luggage, the other rooms you stayed in, your hired car . . . all have been searched and searched again. So the manuscript is in somebody else's hands. So tell me, Peter, where is it?"

He touched his hair. Ugh. It'd probably take an hour of shampooing before it was clean. "May I ask a question?"

Thomson seemed surprised. "Sure. Why not. Ask away."

"What's the point?" he asked. "Why the effort?"

"Stupid question," Thomson said. "A crime has been committed, and that's all you need to know."

"Come on, that's not a good answer."

"Only answer you're going to get."

He said, "If you won't answer, maybe I will, then. I'd guess that the Lord and Lady have some influential friends in the government, in the ruling party. The pressure is on to take care of this case, solve it quickly, and have the manuscript back where it belongs. Am I right?"

Thomson said, "Tell me where the manuscript is, and I'll answer you."

"Can't help you there," he said. "But I'm sure I'm right. Political pressure, brought to bear upon a hardworking and dedicated detective. A detective who'd rather be out solving real crimes. Like assault or murder or rape. Not the theft of a dusty old manuscript. A detective pulled from his street work, street work that he cares about, and forced to baby-sit an American who loves books and old papers. *Tsk, tsk.* Puts one in the mood to write a strong letter to the *Times.*"

Thomson's face reddened. "Then think of this, mate. Maybe some pressure is there. I won't admit that. But I'll admit this. Maybe I'm here because I don't like the thought of some Yank coming in and stealing something that belongs to us, something that should stay on this island."

"Maybe Dickens belongs to the world."

"I don't care about the world," the detective shot back. "What I care about is that bloody manuscript, and where it's located. Understood?"

"Understood completely, Detective, and I'm sorry, I cannot be of any assistance."

Thomson snapped up the case folder with one strong hand. "Then be prepared to be here for a while. Or," he added, as he stood up from the chair, "do you expect a Dickens character to come to rescue you? Perhaps the Ghost of Christmas Past?"

And when Thomson reached the door, he said, "Actually, I'd put my trust in the Ghost of Christmas Future."

"Trust away, then," the detective said as the door closed behind him.

It was probably two days after that bout of interrogation that another man was waiting for him in the interrogation room. Despite knowing they were both under surveillance through the one-way mirror, he couldn't help but smile.

"Damn glad to see you," he said, sitting down across from him. "And did you know, you bear a striking resemblance to the Ghost of Christmas Future?"

The older man was heavyset, wearing a black suit, white shirt, and black tie. His jowls sat comfortably on his shirt collars, and he held a wooden cane in his gnarled hands. Except for a faint fringe of close-cropped hair around the top of his skull, he was bald.

"Not hardly," the older man said. "First, he wasn't an American. Second, I always thought he was an ugly tall thing in a black robe."

"You'll do."

The older man took a deep breath as he got up, leaning on the cane. "Maybe so, but it's time. Let's get out of here."

They left the room and went down the corridor, the men and women working in this place looking at them with ill-disguised anger and contempt. But no Detective Thomson. Too bad. He wanted to give him a cheerful good-bye.

He said, "Sure could use my belt and shoes back."

"Don't press it, Peter," he said. "It took enough horse trading and exchanging favors to get you out of here without a paper trail being left behind, not to mention dropping the entire issue of theft. Let them have your shoes and belt. We'll take care of it."

"I have no doubt," he said.

"Good."

Outside the air felt good on his skin, though it did feel odd to walk in stockinged feet out on the sidewalk. They were on the opposite side of the building from where he had been driven in, and he didn't mind the stares at all from the people passing by on the sidewalk. There was a black limousine parked before them, and he opened the rear door, allowing the older man to get in. It took a bit of huffing and puffing before the older man was settled in, and he sat down next to him, enjoying the plush interior, even enjoying the sound of the heavy door slamming shut. Before them was a Plexiglas window, separating the passenger compartment from the silent driver up front. Set in the middle of the seat backing was a wooden cabinet that looked as if it contained a liquor cabinet. He was terribly thirsty but decided against asking for a drink. There would be plenty of time for that later.

The limo moved out into traffic, and he settled back into the seat, feeling the best he had been for quite a number of days. The older man said, "Your cover hold?"

"Like a vise."

"Good."

"Mistreated?"

"Bad food, lots of yelling, not much sleep. Other than that, they were perfect hosts."

The older man murmured a laugh. "Then feel free to send them a thank-you card when you get home."

"And when's that?"

"Soon. We'll be in Heathrow in under an hour. There'll be a change of clothes, a shower, and a good meal waiting for you before you catch your flight. An Air Force executive jet, heading west."

"I thank you."

The older man turned to him, holding the cane in his hands. "No, I thank you. I was a skeptic, right from the start, especially when you told us about the manuscript and what would eventually happen to it when it got out on the market. About how you were sure a certain buyer could be found, and how a local representative to purchase the manuscript could be located. And the part about you staying behind in London, so you'd be arrested, to establish your bona fides to the buyers . . . that was brilliant."

There was a warm feeling surging through him, a nice feeling indeed. "So. Anything to report?"

The older man leaned forward, to the cabinet set before them. He opened the wooden door, revealing a small television screen. Underneath the screen was a number of buttons, and he pressed one, and then another. The television snapped into focus, and then a tape began playing. He looked at it intently. There were Arabic subtitles and an Arabic narrator. Showing on the television screen was a flat desert area. Two men in long, traditional robes were examining a scorched mark on the earth, as well as pieces of bent and twisted metal.

He watched, heart pounding, until the screen went blank. The older man said, "It came together. Again, I thank you. With the radioactive tracer dye you put on the manuscript pages, it was easy to follow the book when it left London and was transported overseas. To France,

Libya, and then to Yemen. We were able to follow it, right up to the point where we were able to identify the people we were looking for. Two days ago they went for a ride in Mercedes Benz, in a remote area of Yemen. They didn't get far."

"I see," he said.

"So you do," the older man said. He switched the television off, closed the cabinet door, and sat back heavily into the seat. "Now, then. What do you plan to do next?"

"Shower, eat, and sleep for a week."

"Sounds like a thorough plan."

"And afterward?"

"Haven't thought much about it," he said.

"I see." They drove in silence for a little while longer, and the older man said, "Dickens."

"Yes?"

"If he were alive, what do you think he would have felt about what we did with those old words of his?"

Good question, he thought. He remembered seeing the schoolgirl, a seemingly long time ago, at the Dickens House Museum. Remembered telling her how Dickens hated oppression, hated tyranny, and above all, hated bullies. . . . But he didn't want to fall into that familiar trap, of trying to superimpose one generation's problems and beliefs onto another.

He sighed. "Who knows. I'm too tired to think. All I know is that . . . well, I think he would have been horrified and amazed that his words still meant something. All these years later. And not just the frenzy that comes around, every Christmas, for Tiny Tim and Ebenezer Scrooge."

"Good answer."

"Only one I could come up with."

And then he stayed silent as they drove through Dickens's hometown.

Next Christmas at Dingley Dell

BY GILLIAN LINSCOTT

Gillian Linscott is best known for her series of crime novels featuring the suffragette detective, Nell Bray and an earlier series about Birdie Linnett. One of the most recent Nell Bray books, *Absent Friends,* was awarded both the Crime Writers' Association Ellis Peters Historical Dagger in the UK and the Herodotus Best International Historical Mystery Award in the USA. A former journalist, she lives in Herefordshire, England.

W E WERE WARM in the snug of the Blue Lion at Muggleton, roast beef and good punch under our waistcoats, coal fire blazing in the grate. The reflection of the flames was turning the bronze fender around the hearth to the exact color of the winter sun that had set over the Kent fields a few hours before, at the end of a November afternoon in 1870. A jealous wind was rattling the windows and doing his best to filch our warmth from us, sending thin fingers under the sausage-shaped draught excluder across the door. My companion got up to nudge the draught excluder with his foot. He was a good forty years older than I was, with a thatch of gray hair and a figure thin as a carter's whip. Still there was a forcefulness to his foot that must have bruised the east wind's thieving fingers. As he came back to his seat at the fireside opposite me, there was a rushing sound and a rattling of the windows more violent than anything the wind could manage. A meteor-trail of red sparks sliced the darkness in the window, between the half-drawn curtains. He picked up the long-stemmed clay pipe he'd lodged against the fender.

"Spoiled it, they did, the locomotives. Spoiled the trade and spoiled the traveling."

"Still, they're very convenient," I said.

I'd arrived by train that afternoon, traveling from London across miles of brown sodden furrows gleaming under a pale sun, the occasional glint of a holly tree already bright with red berries. Most of the way my conscience was nagging at me for spending time and money I could ill-afford on a chase that might prove as illusionary as the lost gold of the Incas. I'd been pleasantly surprised to find my man waiting for me on the station platform in his coachman's cloak, gaiters and low-crowned hat. My trail to him, through friends to acquaintances to strangers, from gossip to hint to faint hope, had been like a paper chase on a windy day.

"If convenient's what you want," he said, "you should have stayed at home—as the cannibal said to the missionary he was a boiling of in his pot."

The Cockney was there in his voice all right, but under a lot of other things. He delivered his joke with the self-satisfaction of a veteran actor, sure that what had pleased for forty years would please again.

"So you don't care for locomotives?" I said.

"Makes no odds whether I care or not. Like caring or not caring for the Alps or a hippopotamus. But they spoiled the trade of as good a race of men as you'll ever find on this earth, and they spoiled something else besides."

He made the old stage coachman' salute, a rolling round of the wrist, with the little finger thrown in the air. Again, there was a touch of the stage about it and he was looking at me sidelong. It struck me that he wanted my questions, was getting impatient with me for being diffident and roundabout in asking them.

"So what else did they spoil?" I asked. I was still dancing round why I'd come, like a bad boxer who won't drop his guard long enough to land his blow.

"Arriving's what they spoiled. Arriving and leaving. You'll never know it, you young'uns, the four-in-hand coming into the yard of an inn with the lamps blazing, through the gateway with no more room than you could put a rat's whisker on either side, dogs barking, stable boys running, passengers on top colder than if they'd been lost in the Arctic ten years, the landlord in his apron at the door, punch warming on the fire inside. There was nothing like it in this world and there won't be again."

"Was it like that," I said, "that Christmas you arrived here with him?"

"Yes, it was. Just like that, both the Christmases."

"What?"

From the way he was looking at me, he'd intended exactly the effect he'd produced. I felt at a loss, stumbling.

"But there was only the one Christmas at Dingley Dell, the famous one. The one in here."

For reassurance, I put my hand on the book on the table beside me. The pages were fluffed at the edges from much reading, the leather cover stained from many journeys.

"There only could have been the one," I explained to him, wondering if he'd even read it. "By the next year Winkle and Snodgrass were married, the Pickwick Club dissolved, and Mr. Pickwick retired to Dulwich and given up traveling. There was only the one Christmas."

I'd come to him for confirmation that the people and events in the book I'd loved since my father had first read it to me in the nursery had really existed and happened. *The Pickwick Papers* was at least as real to me as any of my friends and colleagues. I wanted him of all men to confirm that reality, and here he was attacking it.

"So you see, there was only the one Christmas," I pleaded.

He stared at me over the rim of his tilted glass. There was something in his eyes now that hadn't been there before, something cold and sad. A voice in me said that I should stand up now, this minute, call for my bill, pick up my book, and go straight home to London by the next train. He just sat there, looking at me. It was a look that was somehow both challenging and pleading, daring and asking me to stay and hear. That need and my quest had brought both of us in the whole whirling universe to this room and this night.

"There was only the one Christmas he wrote about," Sam said. "But there was the next one he didn't."

"Next Christmas at Dingley Dell?"

Dingley Dell. A mere two miles of wind and rain from where we were sitting in comfort. The old manor house, the candlelight and bowers of holly and ivy in the wood-paneled room, the fire crackling on the great hearth, the mistletoe bough, the laughter and the slide of dancing feet. They'd existed (I was sure they'd existed) just for that one Christmas forty-three years ago—long before I was born—and part of me hoped that if I took that two-mile stroll I'd find them still there. He was staring at me, still with that cold and sad look in his eyes.

"Next Christmas at Dingley Dell," he repeated. Then, with his long pipe in one hand and the punch glass in the other—taking a pull at the one and a sip of the other to punctuate the narrative—he told me this story.

"Two days before Christmas it was, the Christmas of 1828. Cold and frosty just like the year before, horses' hooves striking sparks off the roads, breath of the outside passengers trailing out behind like smoke from a dragon. Mr. P. inside and me on top. Coach to Rochester, then change to another coach for the fifteen miles to Muggleton, arriving here at the Blue Lion at three o'clock in the afternoon. The landlord showed him up to his room, he ordered dinner in half an hour and a brandy and hot water to be going on with. I carried up his bags. He was standing there, staring out of the window, still in his overcoat and gaiters. It was getting dark outside, being near enough the shortest day of the year.

"Sam," he says, "are there any other coaches expected tonight?"

"Nothing in the regular way," I said, knowing the times of coaches better than my ABC. "A lot of people traveling on their own account, mind. The stable boy says they're so crowded in the yard they're having to ask the horses politely if they mind chumming up with a friend."

"So you're already on gossiping terms with the stable boys, are you, Sam?"

He smiled, but it struck me there was something a touch strange about the smile. About the question, too. After all, by then I'd been working for him the best part of two years, so he surely knew *Keep yourself to yourself and mind your own business* has never been my family motto. Then I thought it was maybe indigestion or being tired from the journey, because he wasn't as young as he used to be after all, even though he could still kick up his heels and behave like a schoolboy if it suited him. So I said nothing and the girl came in with his brandy and hot water, put some more coal on the fire and lit the candles. When she'd gone I helped him off with his overcoat and gaiters and he sat down, stretched his legs to the fire, took a pull of the brandy, and gave a long sigh. Only it wasn't quite a contented sigh, as you might have expected in the circumstances.

"Sam," he said, "you'll see you get yourself a good dinner."

"Trust me for that, sir."

"You'd oblige me for keeping your ears open for any other travelers arriving here tonight."

I looked at him. "Anybody in particular, sir?"

"Oh, no, nobody in particular."

Well, I knew he was curious by nature, but there had to be more to it than that. Still, it ain't polite to ask too many questions, as Bluebeard said to the magistrates when they asked him what became of his wives, so I just said yes, sir, made sure he had all he wanted, and went downstairs to make myself comfortable in the servants' room.

"A convivial evening it was, too, table crowded, three or four ladies' maids who weren't painful to the eye, couple of private coachmen, two or three ostlers, everybody pretty happy at the prospect of good Christmas tips and enough to eat and drink. After the pie and ale we put together for a bowl of punch, and there were speeches and a comic song or two. But all the time I was keeping my ears open for comings and goings outside in the stable yard. By ten o'clock, when we were pretty well down to the bottom of the punch bowl and the maids had been called away to see their ladies to bed, the score stood as follows:

One young gentleman in a phaeton, racing a friend for a bet, swore at the grooms for not changing his horses quick enough, drank a bottle of port while he was standing there watching them, away in under twenty minutes.

One elderly gentleman in his own coach with two daughters and a terrier. Terrier bit the stable boy, daughter said it was the boy's fault, party shown to private room, grumbling.

One clergyman in a pony cart, thin as the heels of a pauper's stockings. Asked for a good feed for the pony, cheapest bed they had, and a veal pie for himself.

Another young gentleman in a terrible temper, the one who'd been racing the first young gentleman. Wheel had come off his vehicle a mile away. Wanted a wheelwright, a blacksmith, a couple of Derby winners for a change of horses. Got a pint of brandy, a lot of apologies from the landlord, and the share of a room with the clergyman.

Well, I slipped upstairs from time to time and reported all this as instructed. What I got every time was a "Thank you, Sam" and the statements that he didn't need anything, was entirely comfortable, and wished me to be happy with my friends downstairs.

It was quarter an hour or so after ten when the sharp man arrived, night black as Newgate's doorknocker, frost fit to crack your teeth. I happened to be out in the yard when he came bowling in like the devil's hounds were after him at a hammering trot, pulling up so sharp it was a miracle he didn't have the two horses straight over backward on top of him. Good horses they were, too, but sweating so much they were wet as herring and steam rising from them like a pair of kettles. When the boys came to take them out of the shafts, those horses were near leaning on the boys out of sheer weariness. Not that he noticed. He was out of the carriage before the wheels stopped turning, flinging the reins to the groom as if he didn't care whether they got caught or not. First proper sight of him I had was in the light from the doorway. He was wearing a long traveling coat and boots. Hair grizzled, cut so short you could have turned him upside down and used him for a scrubbing brush, chin and cheekbones fit to sharpen knives on, thin lips closed tight as a rattrap. Altogether a useful item to have around the kitchen—only not a comfortable one on account of those eyes. As near black as I've ever seen eyes and not giving out anything, only taking in. As soon as his boot was over the step he was shouting "Landlord!" And I thought, "Well, I'm bothered if he isn't a foreigner." Which was a puzzle to start with, what a foreigner would be doing, driving to a little out-of-the-way place like Muggleton on a dark night two days before Christmas, so fast that he'd come close to crocking up two good horses. So I waited a bit while the landlord came, regretting he had no private rooms left. If the gentleman would kindly consider sharing . . . Kindly or otherwise, the gentleman wouldn't. He didn't say much, but enough to show he wasn't a man accustomed to not getting his way. He spoke English as well as you or I, only with that accent. And he had a pocketful of English money, more than enough to make the landlord decide that he and his wife would move out of their own room and let the gentleman have it for the night. So while everybody was bustling round with sheets, coal scuttles, and warming pans, I went upstairs to report.

"There's a Frog arrived," I said.

The word had got round from one of the ostlers who'd once worked at a livery stables alongside the sea at Dover, so he reckoned he was an expert on France.

"A Frenchman, Sam? You're sure of that?"

He sounded startled, which wasn't surprising. It wouldn't be so singular now, finding a Frog at an English inn, but what you've got to remember is, this was forty-three years ago. That's only twelve years after we'd sent old Boney . . . all right, Napoleon Bonaparte if you want it fancy . . . only twelve years after we'd sent him packing for good, and as far as most of us were concerned, the right place for Frogs was on the other side of the Channel. So you could understand him being startled. Only it was more than startled. He was scared. Now, I'd been with him through law courts, riots, prison, women having hysterics, and lord knows what besides, and never known him scared. He might have been a year or two past his prime, he might have been carrying a pound or two more than a man in fighting trim, but you've read the book so you'll grant me he had a heart like a whole circus—full of lions. Isn't that the truth?"

Yes, I said. The fire had burned low and the draught excluder must have wriggled away from its duties again, because there was a chill in the room. Sam stood up, a bit stiffly, put a log on the fire, ladled us two more glasses of punch from the bowl in the hearth.

"Scared of the Frenchman?" I asked him. "Why?"

He made a long business of swallowing a mouthful of punch, as if still hesitating about whether to finish his story, but we both knew he'd gone too far to draw back.

"He tried to hide it, of course, spoke as if it was no more than curiosity.

"What does he look like, Sam?"

So I told him, but that didn't satisfy him, he had to have a look at the man. So out he goes onto the landing in his slippers, traveling shawl over his waistcoat, to look over the banisters. But as luck would have it, just as he steps out, the landlord and the Frog are coming up the stairs. Mr. P. steps back into his own doorway to let them go past, but as he does, his eyes meet Mr. Frog's. It's the Frog who speaks first, a few words in his own language, in a grating kind of voice like the rest of him. Mr. P. blinks, then comes back, good and hearty, "And a Happy Christmas to you, too, sir." Then Frog and the landlord have gone past and the two of us are back in his room in front of the fire. I can tell he's a bit shaken, but he's trying to hide it.

"What was that he said to you, sir?"

"Just wished me the compliments of the season, Sam."

Well, I thought, there's a bit more to it than that, as the crocodile said when he went for the arm and got the fingers. But he wanted to be left alone.

"That will be all for tonight, Sam."

"Early start in the morning, sir?"

We had it all sorted out already. Breakfast first thing, then walk across the fields to Manor Farm where his good old friend Mr. Wardle was waiting for him to start the Christmas celebrations. But he hesitated.

"I think not after all, Sam. I find myself quite tired from the journey. You may call me at eight."

Well, I thought to myself as I went downstairs, he's had a long journey and if he wants a good sleep, that's his business. But I felt twitchy as a cat in a dog kennel. I didn't sleep much. Because of the crowding I was chummed up with a couple of grooms and a bagman who snored like a leaking pump, but it wasn't that. About five in the morning I heard the skivvy coming downstairs to get the stove going in the kitchen and thought I'd see if I could persuade her into making me a cup of something warm. But she wasn't in a generous mood, owing to all the extra work, so I went through to the scullery for a chat with the boot boy. Having been a boot boy myself before I went up in the world, I thought maybe I could improve his mind with a few professional tips. Well, he was polishing away at a line of boots by the light of a tallow candle. I thought I'd show him how to do the thing properly and looked for Mr. P.'s soft-topped traveling boots. Only they weren't there. Soft boots, stiff boots, hunting boots, ladies' boots, old boots, new boots, any boots you like to name but not Mr. P.'s boots.

"You're missing a pair," I said to the boy.

He said something disrespectful to his elders and betters about having enough boots there to last him till suppertime and not wanting any more. So I thought Mr. P. must have just forgotten to put his boots outside his room for cleaning the night before and I'd nip up and get them. Only I had to find my own boots first. I was in stockinged feet, and the cold from the scullery floor was striking through. Well, you wouldn't know this, but in a nice kindly place, they let the servants leave their boots by the fire in the kitchen overnight so there's a bit of warmth in them when you put them on of a morning. I'd left mine there by the fire with the rest. They weren't there. All the other servants' boots were there, only my boots gone. So there was a facer, wasn't there? His boots gone and my boots gone. I ask you, what would you make of that?

He looked at me, cradling the bowl of his pipe in his hand, as if he really wanted my opinion.

"I suppose the Frenchman had taken both pairs," I said, "but I'm sure I don't know why."

"Which is exactly what I thought, too, only we were both of us wrong, as you'll hear in a minute."

He filled the pipe slowly, drew on it with eyes closed, making me wait.

"So I went running upstairs in my stockings with the candle, worried now, opened his door quietly, hoping to find him asleep as he should be. Empty. His room was empty. Bed still made up as if he hadn't slept in it, fire burned down to embers, everything quite tidy, no sign of a struggle, but no sign of him, either. His overcoat was gone. It had been hanging on the back of the door, but it wasn't there anymore. His hat and gloves that had been on the table, gone. Gaiters I'd left out on the sideboard to dry, ready for brushing in the morning, gone. All of them and him, too, vanished like the lady from the magician's cabinet but no roll of drums and lightning flash to bring him back again. I found the landlord still half-asleep collecting glasses in the snug.

"Up to him if he wanted to go out, as long as he comes back and settles his account," he said. "If he wanted to unbolt the door and—"

"Had somebody unbolted the door?"

"Somebody had, but that isn't my fault. An inn's what I run, not one of His Majesty's prisons."

So sometime in the dead of night he'd got up, dressed himself, and gone out. It came to me that if he hadn't been able to sleep (which would have been out of the common with him, though) he might have decided to walk the couple of miles in the dark to Dingley Dell and surprise his old friend Mr. Wardle by being there for breakfast. In which case he'd send somebody over with a message as soon as it got light letting me know and telling me to come on with the luggage. Very likely—only I didn't think so. I went back to the kitchen, grabbed my overcoat and any old pair of boots that would more or less fit, and went out.

*   *   *

Church clock striking six. Still dark as the inside of a chimney, no moon or stars and cold as a beggar's bed. Over the stile, along the footpath across the fields, no more than a black line against the frost on the grass. Every now and then I'd stop and listen for him up in front of me. Nothing. Now, that path goes right past the pond where they'd gone skating the Christmas before. Remember it? Yes, of course you do. Winkle making a fool of himself and Mr. P. sliding on the ice like a schoolboy and falling in. Well, just as I was getting near the pond I heard a shout, an almighty splash, and a lot of ducks quacking. I thought, "Bother me if he hasn't gone sliding again and fallen in again." So I shouted I was coming and started running. Now it ain't easy, running in the dark in somebody else's boots. I won't tell you how many times I fell over and how I cursed, but shouting to him now and then with what breath I'd got left to hold on, keep his heart up. Then I heard a voice from a clump of bushes to the side of the path.

"Sam. Is that you, Sam?"

His voice, a bit shaky. It jolted me because I'd been thinking of him down in the water.

"Was that you gone in again?" I said.

"Both of us, the Frenchman and me. He's drowned, Sam."

He came out from the bushes. There was just a touch of light coming into the sky by then, enough to see the dark shape of him and his face as white as the inside of a turnip, glasses gone. He put a hand on my wrist to steady himself, and I could feel the sleeve of his overcoat, sopping wet. His teeth were chattering from the cold.

"Back to the Blue Lion," I said, taking his arm and trying to pull him along. He wouldn't go.

"We've got to get him out, Sam."

It turned out that the bushes he was in were at the top of a little bank, just above the pond. You could see the ice now, with a great black jagged gash in the middle of it. I made him stay on the bank. I was half the weight that he was so the ice held me all right. The Frenchman was head down under the ice, just the end of his legs sticking out. I took hold of his ankles, pulled him out, dragged him back over the ice to where Mr. P. was waiting. Between us, we got him out on the bank. His hair was even more of a scrubbing brush by then, from the frost.

"We'll send a party out for him with a hurdle," I said. "He's in no condition to object."

Mr. P. stood looking down at him for a while. Then he said, "I'm sorry about your boots, Sam. They're in the coal cellar." And turned away. We didn't go back to the Blue Lion but on over the fields to Manor Farm. That was his idea. When we got there Mr. Wardle had servants scurrying, fires going, got him put to bed with a warming pan. He didn't say much. Mr. Wardle did most of the talking.

"A terrible accident. They must have gone out for an early walk together and went sliding on the ice like last year. You can see how hard Pickwick tried to save him—soaked through and quite worn out. He could have lost his own life, rescuing a man he hardly knew. But the water was too deep for him. A gallant heart, Sam. A true and gallant heart."

While this was going on, some of the workers from Manor Farm were out collecting the body and taking a message to the coroner. What with Christmas, it was several days before they assembled a jury and brought in death by misadventure. Mr. Pickwick had a shocking cold by then, but he gave his evidence like a good'un—how the monsieur had gone sliding on the pond and fallen through. And if any of the jurors thought it odd that the man had chosen to go sliding on a pond at dead of night, well he was a Frog after all and that was enough to account for it. Now, what was it you was wanting to say?"

I'd been trying to interrupt for the last minute, opening and shutting my mouth, probably enough like a frog myself.

"Mr. Wardle said the water was too deep? Too deep for Mr. Pickwick to rescue the man?"

"He did."

"But it wasn't."

"Oh, you was there, I suppose."

"No, of course I wasn't. I wasn't even born. But it's there in the book, when Mr. Pickwick fell in the year before. Listen. I riffled through the pages, found the familiar passage, and read . . . 'the fears of the spectators were still further relieved by the fat boy's suddenly recollecting that the water was nowhere more than five feet deep.' Mr. Wardle must have known that because he'd lived at Dingley Dell all his life. And Mr. Pickwick must have known from the year before that all he had to do was shout to the Frenchman to stand up."

Sam's eyes were bright with a look that could have been either relief or regret.

"So you know better than any of us who were there, do you?"

"I know what he wrote." I was still holding on to the book like a log in a shipwreck.

"And what do you make of it, then?"

I said, reluctantly, "I think Mr. Pickwick drowned the Frenchman. He made an assignation with him out there in the dark, somehow decoyed him onto thin ice, where he knew he'd fall through."

"So why would he do that, then?"

"Perhaps they loved the same woman once. Perhaps the Frenchman had decoyed her away from him, married her, and destroyed her, and Mr. Pickwick had been waiting all his life to avenge her. It would explain why he never married."

But Sam was shaking his head. "A pretty story."

"Had he defrauded him perhaps over some business deal?"

Mr. Pickwick had been a successful businessman before his retirement, though nowhere is it stated exactly what his business was.

"Warmer, but not there yet by a few furlongs."

"So it was a business affair?"

"Business of a kind."

"So what kind of business ends in . . ." I could only mumble the word ". . . murder."

Sam leaned forward and took the book out of my hand.

"You say you know what he wrote. It's all in here—or enough of it to tell you if you know what to look for."

"But what? There's nothing in it about a Frenchman."

"You're wrong, you know. What about that first day of the Christmas party at Dingley Dell? The first few minutes of it."

"There was no Frenchman there. They were all as English as you or I."

"Were they, though? You remember there was a girl there that gave one of Mr. P.'s friends a look so warm and welcoming it was enough to make the statue in the passage unfold his arms and hug her."

"Emma and Mr. Tupman. They weren't French."

"What about the statue?"

"The statue?"

The look on my face made him smile, though it was a sad kind of smile. He opened the book, picked his way slowly through the pages, and handed it back to me, marking the place with his thumb.

"Read that."

" '. . . and Emma bestowed a half-demure, half impudent, and all pretty, look of recognition, on Mr. Tupman, which was enough to make the statue of . . .' "

I pulled up short. Odd how you can read a book a hundred times, know it as well as you know your own life, and still miss something.

"Statue of who, then?" Sam asked.

" '. . . *statue of Bonaparte.*' "

"There's your Frenchman. English Christmas, English party, old English manor house, old English squire—and what has he got in his hallway? Not a statue of Admiral Nelson or the Duke of Wellington as you might expect. Just England's worst enemy. Old Boney himself, the Corsican tyrant, His Frogship Napoleon Bonaparte. Are you there yet?"

My head was sunk down in my hands. I shook it. When Sam spoke again it was as almost as much as to me to himself.

"We made the same mistake, you and me. We both knew him when he was elderly, me in person, you from the book. But any man who's elderly had to be young once, you'll grant that. So let's say he's what, sixty years old, in 1827, he must have been born in 1767 or thereabouts. So take him—say—just twenty-two years on from there, a young man starting out in life—what date do you get?"

"1789."

I made the calculation dejectedly in my head, not seeing where he was driving. Even so, the date had a resonance. I looked up and met his eyes.

"The French Revolution."

"The French Revolution. Now, you imagine a young man brought up in Paris, Frenchman for a father, Englishwoman for a mother, he's got to take one side or the other, hasn't he? And he being hotheaded like any young man, brave and generous by nature, as he always was, let's suppose he takes the side of the revolutionaries. I'm not saying it's right, mind, I'm just putting it to you."

"Are you telling me Mr. Pickwick was a French revolutionary?"

"You wait. Hold your horses. Because of this revolution, England and France go to war, right? That's a matter of history. Now, suppose you was one of the high-ups on the Frog side, you'd want to know what England was going to do, wouldn't you? Things like where the soldiers were billeted, how many warships there were in the Medway. And if you had a lively young man on your side, half English by breeding, speaking the language from his mother's knee, wouldn't it come into your mind that he'd be a darned sight more useful living quietly on the other side of the Channel finding out things you wanted to know instead of getting his brains blown out on the battlefield?"

"He came to England as a spy? No. Never, surely . . ."

But even while I was spluttering protests, thoughts were crowding in that pointed the other way. The book tells us little about Mr. Pickwick's background before that day in May 1827 when the Corresponding Society of the Pickwick Club was formed. He was a man with many friends but no trace whatsoever of a family of his own, not the merest distant cousin. He had enough wealth to look after his friends as well as himself, gained in a trade we're told nothing about. And . . .

" 'Mr. Pickwick was an enthusiastic admirer of the army.' "

The quotation came from me as a groan, but brought a wintry smile from Sam.

"It was one of his jobs, you see, keeping an eye on the army and navy, particularly round the docks at Chatham."

And the docks at Chatham are less than twenty miles from Mr. Wardle's hospitable home at Dingley Dell.

"Did Wardle know?"

"Of course Wardle knew. He was the man to whom Mr. P. used to send his reports."

"But the man was the very pink of an English squire. English as oak, English as roast beef, English as . . ." Comparisons failed me.

"There you go again, making the same mistake. In the book Mr. Wardle's an old gentleman. Now, you know what a republican is— somebody who wants to do away with kings and queens?"

"Of course."

"Now, you might find this difficult to believe, loving our dear queen Victoria the way I'm sure we all do, that back eighty years ago, when Mr. Pickwick and Mr. Wardle were young, there were men even in this country who thought cutting the heads off kings and queens wasn't the worst of notions. Now, I'm putting it to you, suppose Mr. Wardle was one of those and Mr. P. was under orders to come over here in a fishing boat by night and meet him."

"But they didn't meet properly until May 1827, at the military review at Rochester. Mr. Wardle says he's been to the Pickwick Club a few times, but he has to introduce himself."

"Yes, and invites the whole pack of them to visit his home straightaway. Didn't that strike you as rather out of the common?"

"The action of a fine hospitable English gentleman."

"Hospitable English humbug. That meeting was a sham. They'd arranged it so that they could be in public what they'd been for forty years on the quiet."

"Spies? Conspirators?"

"*Friends* is a kinder word."

The look in his eyes was pleading. He wanted me to understand, had kept this assignation with me toward the end of his life so that there should be somebody left in the world who did understand. But I didn't. I felt as if my best friend—a man I'd loved nearly all my life—had betrayed me. He saw that from my face, sighed.

"But it's not the kind words you're thinking, is it? It's the other words—*traitor, murderer,* and so on. Well, I said them myself once. Said them to his face that Christmas Eve when we was on our own. That's after he told me the story, between sneezes from the cold he'd taken going into the water. And I remember every word of it, just as if he was sitting there now."

⁓

And Sam told me, sitting there in the firelight with the look of a man who's just put down a burden at the end of a long journey. And as he told it to me, an odd thing happened. Perhaps it was shock from what I'd heard, or tiredness from a long day, or the punch, or a combination of all three of them. Whatever the reason, as I listened, the whip-thin figure of Sam seemed to melt away into the chair and out of the chair came somebody entirely different. A plump man of sixty of so, a mostly bald head with a soft little fringe of hair above the ears, rounded legs in old-fashioned buff tights stretched toward the fire, eyes gleaming from behind round glasses with such a mixture of sadness and benevolence that the shock and anger drained out of me and it was all I could do not to get to my feet and embrace the old friend of my childhood, the companion of my life. The voice had changed, too, from Sam's brisk voice with its lingering trace of Cockney to an orotund tone, with the leisure of a slower-paced time than this steam-age of ours.

"I would not deny that I was influenced by human passions, and human feelings—possibly by human weaknesses—and yet above all things the desire to benefit the human race was my guiding principle. It drove me, as a very young man, half English and half French, to embrace those principles of Liberty, Equality, Fraternity, which seemed to better intellects than mine the dawn of a new world and happiness for all men. I wished to take up arms for those principles, but so utter and complete was my belief that I even agreed for their sake to take on the role of . . . yes, my old friend, I shall admit the word . . . of spy in the country of my mother's birth. More than spy, agitator. I was sent across the Channel and into the Estuary of the Thames one foggy night in a ship loaded with a cargo of gold bars. The gold was for delivery to a fine and generous-hearted Englishman who believed as we did in those three great principles. The intention was that the gold should be used at the proper time to finance a rising against King George, so that England and France could go together hand in hand, brother and sister republics—leading the world to a future when there should be no more ignorance, distress, or want."

The eyes behind the glasses gleamed with the fire of a much younger man, then grew sad again.

"Alas, as time went on, the news from France convinced both

Mr. Wardle and myself that far from leading the world to better things, our revolution had sunk to a state of bloodshed, bad faith, and cruelty the like of which the world had not seen since the barbarous ages. So we ceased to send our reports to Paris, ceased to stir up rebellion against King George. We expected retribution from our masters in Paris for our falling-off, but nothing happened, nothing whatsoever. We concluded that those masters had fallen victim to the cruelty that they themselves had helped to generate. So there we were, Mr. Wardle and I, two men whose great aim in life had vanished like a ghost at cockcrow, possessors of a shipload of gold bars (stowed safely in the cellars at Dingley Dell) of which only a small fraction had been expended for the purpose intended. So what did we do, my friend? What would you have done?"

I couldn't answer. I may, I think, have stretched out a hand to him, pleading for I didn't know quite what, because he smiled.

"You have hit it, my friend. We decided to give it away. To devote our lives to spending, for the purposes of philanthropy, gold intended for rebellion and bloodshed. At first we used it discreetly to relieve the distress of refugees who had come over from France. Then—as the years went by and there was still no word of my old masters in Paris—we spent it for any purpose that seemed good to us, from relieving the cares of our friends to benefiting men and women we should never know or see. There are poor crofters in the Highlands, sir, whose very roofs over their heads depended on that French gold, debtors who walked dazed from prison into the loving arms of their families, orphans taught trades, girls slipping from the paths of virtue brought safely home to their own firesides."

"So you spent it all," I said.

"Not entirely. We were prudent custodians, and when we met openly that Christmas at Dingley Dell—the one in the book I see you holding—we had a few thousand pounds left for disposal. We made a careful choice of who should receive it, causes particularly dear to us, the end that would crown all our work. That second Christmas—the one that is not in the book—I came here on my own to take the last of the gold bars for distribution. But alas, as Sam has told you, another man came, too. As soon as I saw the Frenchman I recognized him as the son of my old spymaster." As he said it, his expression changed into the nearest it could come to a sneer. "The bad son of an infamous father. They had flourished in other people's misfortunes. But France fell on hard times and the family with it. From either need or covetousness the son must have remembered his father's story about the gold sent to England so many years before. He had, I learned later, been tracking us for years the length and breadth of the kingdom. Here, at this very inn, he found me at last."

"And you drowned him?"

"Yes, my friend, I led him to the pond and drowned him. Believe me, if it had been only myself involved, I should have said, 'Do what you like with me. I've lived my life and don't regret a moment of it.' But Wardle had a family, a reputation. Should I—while there was a brain in my head or an ounce of strength in my arm—not act to save his daughters' tears, his infant grandchildren's disgrace? If I did wrong, then I am content that the one who will judge us all shall judge me according to my deserts."

The figure stretched an arm to the hearth, lifted up a glass of punch in what looked like a toast. And as he did it, he merged somehow back into Sam performing the same action, so which was toasting the other I couldn't have said. Sam took a sip.

"So there you have it, young'un. And whether you write it down or not, I leave it to you."

I'm still wondering.

A Tale of One City

BY ANNE PERRY

Anne Perry is the worldwide best-selling author of two Victorian detective series, the Thomas Pitt series and the William and Hester Monk series, each taking a different look at the English society in which they are set. She is also writing another acclaimed historical series set during the French Revolution, and consisting of the books *A Dish Taken Cold* and *The One Thing More*. Besides this, she has also written a fantasy duology, *Tathea* and *Come Armageddon*. In her spare time she lectures on writing in such places as the cruise ship the *Queen Elizabeth II*. She makes her home in the highlands of Scotland.

SYDNEY CARTON SAT alone at a table near the door of the Café Procope, staring at the dregs of the red wine in his glass. He did his best to ignore the voices shouting, laughing, swearing around him in the suffocating heat. It was the seventh of July, 1793, and Paris was a city oppressed by hunger and fear. In January the Convention had sent the strangely dignified figure of Louis XVI to the guillotine. Predictably, by February France was not only at war with Austria and Belgium, but with England as well.

In the Place de la Revolution the scarlet-stained blade rose and fell every day, and tumbrels full of all manner of people, men and women, old and young, rich and poor, rattled over the cobbles on their last journey. The streets smelled of refuse piled high and rotting in the heat. Fear was in the air, sharp like sweat, and people along the Rue St. Honoré complained because the streets stank of blood. You could not drive cattle down them any more because the stench terrified them and they stampeded out of control, mowing down passers-by and crashing into house and shop windows.

All that Carton cared about was Dr. Manette's daughter Lucie, whose husband was locked up in the prison of La Force, with no hope of escape. Carton would have done anything he could to ease her distress, but he was utterly helpless.

The café door was wide open to let in a little air, and he did not notice anyone coming or going until a small man with tousled hair and a cheeky, lopsided face sank into the chair opposite him, having ordered wine from Citizen Procope as he passed.

"At least there's still wine, even if there's no bread," he said with a grunt. "Do you know what they're charging for a loaf now?" he demanded Carton's attention. "Three sous! Twelve sous for four pounds! That's more than a carpenter earns in a day, and twice a week's rent. And the laundresses down at the river are creating hell because there's no soap! Never mind a Committee of Public Safety! What's the point of being safe if the sides of your belly are sticking together?"

"I'd keep a still tongue in your head, if I were you, Jean-Jacques," Carton replied dryly. "If you criticize the good citizens of the Committee, your belly'll think your throat has been cut, and likely it'll be right!"

Jean-Jacques's wine came; he thanked Citizen Procope and handed him five sous. He sniffed the bottle and pulled a face. "Not bad," he observed. "Want some?"

Carton never refused wine. "Thank you." He held out his glass.

Jean-Jacques filled it generously. "You know my sister?"

"Amelie?"

"No, no! Amelie's a good woman, she never does anything except what she's told. Marie-Claire." He drank half of his glass. "I wish I had some decent cheese to go with this."

Carton liked Jean-Jacques. There was a good humor about him, an optimism, misplaced as it was, that lifted the spirits. He was pleasant company.

"What about Marie-Claire?" he asked, to be civil. He did not care in the slightest. To tell the truth there was very little he did care about. He had no belief in himself, nor any in justice or the goodness of life. Experience in London as a lawyer had proved his skill, but it had not always led to victory, acquittal of the innocent, or punishment of the guilty.

Jean-Jacques leaned forward over the table, his round eyes bright, his face alive with suppressed excitement. "She has a plan," he said softly. "To get a whole crateful of cheeses, and not just any cheeses, but perfectly exquisite, ripe Camembert! And a side of bacon!"

In spite of himself Carton's imagination was caught. Even the bare words conjured up the fragrance of rich, delicate flavor, food that satisfied, that filled the nose and lay on the tongue, instead of the rough bread and stew with barely any meat in it that had become the common fare. Even though these days one was glad enough to have more than a spoonful or two of that. "What sort of a plan?" he said dubiously. Marie-Claire was an erratic creature, younger than Jean-Jacques, probably not more then twenty-two or three, small like him, with wide brown eyes and wild hair that curled just as hectically as his, only on her it was pretty. She had been one of the women who had marched on the Palace at Versailles demanding food and justice in the early days of the Revolution when the King was still alive— fruitlessly, of course. The King had listened to everybody, and then done whatever he was told by the last person to speak to him, which was always some minister who did not listen at all.

Jean-Jacques was still smiling. His teeth were crooked, but they were very white. "There is a particularly large and greedy fellow called Philippe Duclos on the local committee," he replied. "The man with the cheeses, whose name I don't know, has hidden them so well no one knows where they are, except that they are somewhere in his house, of course. Marie-Claire is going to use Philippe to put his men there, so that the good citizen can no longer get to his cheese in secret." He smiled even more widely. "Only he is, of course, going to warn Citizen 'Cheese' beforehand, so he will have the chance to move them. Then . . ." He clapped his hands together sharply and made a fist of the right one. "We have them!" he said with triumph. "Half for Philippe, half for Marie-Claire. She will eat some, and sell some, which I will buy." He opened his hands wide in a generous, expansive gesture, and his irregular face was alight with pleasure. "In two days time we shall dine on fresh bread, I have some decent wine, not this rubbish, and ripe Camembert! How is that, my friend?"

"Unlikely," Carton replied ruefully, but he did smile back.

"You are a misery!" Jean-Jacques chided, shaking his head. "Are all Englishmen like you? It must be your climate: it rains every day and you come to expect it."

"It doesn't rain in London any more than it rains in Paris," Carton answered him. "It's me." It was a confession of truth. His general cynicism stretched beyond his own lack of worth to include everyone else.

"Cheese," Jean-Jacques said simply. "And more wine. That must make you feel better!" He reached for the bottle and poured more for both of them. Carton accepted with a moment of real gratitude, not so much for the wine as for the friendship. He thought the plan was doomed to failure, but it would be pointless to say so.

Carton deliberately put the cheese out of his mind. Even in Paris torn apart by the violence of revolution and sweating with fear, it was necessary to earn a living. He could seldom practice his usual profession of law, but he had a superb gift of words, even in French, which was not his own language, and Paris was awash with newspapers, pamphlets, and other publications. There was the highly popular, scurrilous *Père Duchesne* edited by the foul-mouthed ex-priest Hébert, which slandered just about everyone, but most particularly the Citizeness Capet, as Queen Marie Antoinette was now known. The latest suggestion was that she had an unnatural relationship with her own son, who in the normal course of events would now have become Louis XVII.

And of course there was *L'Ami du Peuple,* edited by that extraordinary man, Jean-Paul Marat, who liked to be known as "The Rage of the People." Someone had had the audacity, and the lunacy, to haul him up before the Revolutionary Tribunal in April. He had stormed in, filthy and in rags as usual, carrying the stench of his disease with him. The whole body of them had quailed before him, terrified, and he had been carried out shoulder-high in triumph. There was now no stopping him. The Paris Commune was his creature, to a man.

Carton always took good care to avoid him. Even though Marat lived here in the Cordeliers District, as did most of the revolutionary leaders, it was possible to stay out of his way. Instead Carton wrote for small, relatively innocuous publications, and earned sufficient to get by.

So it was that two days later on July 9 he sat in the Café Procope again, near the door in the clinging, airless heat. He was eating a bowl of stew with rough bread—more than some could afford—when Marie-Claire came in. Even before she turned toward him he could see the fury in her. Her thin little body was rigid under its cotton blouse and long, ragged blue skirt, and her arms were as stiff as sticks. She looked left and right, searching, then turned far enough to see Carton and immediately came over to him. Her face was white and her eyes blazing.

"Have you seen Jean-Jacques?" she demanded without any of the usual greeting.

"Not today," he replied, clearing a little space on the table so she would have room for a plate. "But it's early. Have some stew while there still is some. It's not bad."

Her lip curled. "What is it? Onions and water?" She sat down hard, putting her elbows on the table and both hands over her face. "I've lost my cheeses! That son of a whore took them all! It was my idea, my plan!" She looked up at him, her face burning with indignation. "He didn't even know about them, Fleuriot, until I told him!"

Carton was disappointed. He realized he had been looking forward to the richness and the flavor of cheese. It seemed like a long time since he had eaten anything that was a pleasure, not merely a necessity, although he was aware how many had not even that. The crowds pouring out of the areas of factories, abattoirs, and tanneries, such as the Faubourg St. Antoine, with their acid-burned, copper-colored faces, hollow-eyed, dressed in rags and alight with hatred, were witness enough of that. They were the people who worshipped Marat and gave him his unstoppable power.

Citizen Procope came by, and Carton requested a bowl of soup and bread for Marie-Claire. She thanked him for it, and for a moment the rage melted out of her eyes.

"Forget the cheese," he advised regretfully. "There's nothing you can do anyway. It's gone now."

Her face hardened again. "The pig! Slit his throat, and he'd make a carcass of bacon to feed us for a year! He won't have got rid of all that food, he'll have it stored somewhere. The Committee could find it, because they'd take his house apart, if they had to."

Carton's stomach tightened. "Don't do it!" he said urgently. "Don't say anything at all! It'll only come back on you. You've lost them—accept it." He leaned forward across the table, stretching out his hand to grasp her thin wrist. "Don't draw attention to yourself!"

She glared back at him. "You'd let that pig get away with it? Never!" Her teeth were clenched, the muscles tight on her slender jaw. "I'll make him sweat as if the blade were already coming down on his neck. You see!"

Citizen Procope brought her soup and Carton paid for it.

She took the bowl in both hands, as if it might escape her. "You see!" she repeated, then picked up the spoon and began to eat.

The next morning Carton was again sitting at his usual table at the café with a cup of coffee that tasted like burnt toast, and possibly bore a close relationship. At the next table three men were laughing uproariously at the latest joke in *Père Duchesne,* and adding more and more vulgar endings to the tale, when Jean-Jacques came storming in through the open door, his hair tangled, his shirt sticking to his body with sweat. His face was white and he swiveled immediately toward Carton's table and staggered over, knocking into chairs.

Carton was alarmed. "What is it?" he asked, half rising to his feet.

Jean-Jacques was gasping for breath, choking as he struggled to get the words out. "They've arrested her! Marie-Claire! They've taken her to the prison! You've got to help me! They'll . . ." He could not bring himself to say it, but it hung in the air between them.

Carton found his own voice husky. "What have they charged her with?" It was all unreal, like a fluid fear turned suddenly solid. He knew when Marie-Claire had spoken of it that it was a bad idea to seek revenge, but this was different, it was no longer thought but fact, shivering, sick and real.

"Hoarding food!" Jean-Jacques said, his voice rising toward hysteria, as if he might burst into mad laughter any moment. "She doesn't even have the damn cheeses—or the bacon! Philippe has!"

"I don't suppose that makes any difference," Carton sank back into his chair and gestured for Jean-Jacques to sit down also. It was always better to be inconspicuous. They did not want anyone looking at them, or remembering.

"That's enough to send her to the guillotine!" Jean-Jacques obeyed, the tears running down his face. "We've got to get her out of there! You're a lawyer—come and tell them that she wasn't even there! It's Philippe, because she reported him! You've got to hurry. If someone stands up for her, we can make them realize it's him. They'll catch him with the cheeses, and that'll be proof."

Carton shook his head. "It won't be so easy." In spite of the heat there was a coldness settling inside him. "Philippe will have thought of that. . . ."

Jean-Jacques half rose to his feet, leaning forward over the table. "We've got to do something! We've got to help! She didn't take them. There has to be a way to prove it!"

Carton rubbed his hand wearily across his brow, pushing his hair back. "It isn't about taking them," he tried to explain. "It's about reporting Philippe. The cheeses are gone. He can't afford to be blamed, so he's blaming her. If they can't find them, who's to say which one is guilty?"

Jean-Jacques straightened up with a jolt. "Exactly! No one at all! Come on! We've got to hurry. For that matter, who's to say there ever were any? Citizen Fleuriot can't admit to having lost them without admitting to having had them in the first place! It's perfect. Hurry!"

Carton stood up and went after the rapid and highly agitated figure of Jean-Jacques. There was a kind of logic to it. The only trouble was that logic counted for very little in Paris these days.

Outside the street was hot and the sour smells of rubbish and effluent assaulted the nose. The air itself tasted of fear. A wagon rumbled by, half empty, a few casks in the back. An old newspaper stirred a little in the gutter and settled again. There was a group of Revolutionary Guard at the corner, laughing at something, muskets slung idly over their shoulders, red, white, and blue cockades in their hats.

Jean-Jacques was almost at a run, and Carton had to increase his pace to keep up with him. They had not far to go; there were district headquarters and prisons all over the place. Carton's mind was racing, trying to think what to say that would help Marie-Claire now, and not simply make it worse. He would have to offer some explanation as to why Philippe was blaming her. And it would have to be a story that left no guilt with him! If only Jean-Jacques would slow down and allow more time to think!

They passed a woman on the corner selling coffee, and a group of laundresses arguing. There were people in queues for bread. Of course they were far too late! Or perhaps it was for the candle shop next door, or soap, or any of a dozen other things one could not buy since spring.

Then they were at the prison. A huge man with a red bandanna around his head stood outside the doorway, barring their entrance. Jean-Jacques did not even hesitate. "I have business with Citizen Duclos," he said confidently. "Evidence in a case." He waved his arm in Carton's direction. "Citizen Carton is a lawyer. . . ."

"We have no need of lawyers!" the man with the bandanna spat. "Justice gets no argument here."

"Never say that, Citizen," Jean-Jacques warned, glancing over his shoulder as if he feared being overheard. "Citizen Robespierre is a lawyer!"

The man with the bandanna rubbed the sweat off his face and looked nervously at Carton.

Carton cursed Jean-Jacques under his breath. "We have our uses," he said aloud.

"Go in, Citizen." The man ushered them past.

Jean-Jacques obeyed with alacrity, Carton with great reluctance. The place seemed to close in on him as if the walls were human misery frozen solid. Their footsteps had no echo, and yet there were sounds all around them, snatches of voices, cries, someone weeping, the clang of a door slamming shut. He had been here only minutes, and he was already longing to leave, his body trembling, his stomach knotted tight. He thought of Charles Darnay locked in the prison of La Force nearly a year now, not knowing if he would ever leave, and Lucie outside, every day trying to see him, imagining his suffering, helpless to affect it at all.

Jean-Jacques had reached the official in charge and was speaking to him. He was a lean, ferret-faced man with a scar on his shaven head, and most of his teeth missing. What hunger and injustice there had been in his life one could not even guess. He gestured to Carton to come forward.

Carton obliged, his hands slick with sweat, his shirt sticking to him. How had he ever allowed himself to get caught up in this? It was insanity! He stood in front of the man with the scar and forced himself to speak.

"Citizen, I have certain information you may not have been given regarding a matter of hoarding food. Cheeses to be exact."

"We know all about the cheeses, and the bacon," the man replied. "We have the hoarder in custody. She will be dealt with. Go about your business, Citizen, and leave us to do ours."

Jean-Jacques was fidgeting, wringing his hands, moving his weight from one foot to the other. It was hopeless, but Carton was terrified he would say something, and so involve both of them. It did not need much to make people suspicious.

"Ah!" Carton burst out. "Then you have recovered the cheeses! I was afraid you would not!" He saw the man's expression flicker. "Which would mean you had not caught the principals in the act."

Jean-Jacques froze.

The man scowled at Carton. "What do you know about it?" he demanded.

Carton's brain raced like a two-wheeled carriage cornering

badly. "I think you are a just man and will need evidence," he lied. "And if goods are in the wrong hands, then the matter is not closed until that is put right."

The man leaned toward him. He smelled of stale wine and sweat. "Where are these cheeses, Citizen? And how is it you know?" His eyes were narrowed, his lip a little pulled back from his gapped teeth.

Carton felt his body go cold in the stifling heat. Panic washed over him, and he wanted to turn on his heel and run out of this dreadful place. Memories of past prison massacres swarmed in his mind like rats, the priests hacked to death in the Carmes in September of ninety-two, and the women and children in the Salpetriére. God knew what since then.

"We know where they were taken from, Citizen, and when!" Jean-Jacques broke in. "If we put our heads together, find out who knew of them, and where they were, we can deduce!"

The man scowled at him, but his eyes lost their anger, and interest replaced it. "Wait here," he ordered. "I'll go and find out." And before Carton could protest, he turned and strode away, leaving them under the watchful eyes of two other guards.

The minutes dragged by. There was a scream somewhere in the distance, then dense, pulsing silence. Footsteps on stone. A door banged. Someone laughed. Silence again. Jean-Jacques started to fidget. Carton's fists were so tightly clenched, his nails cut the flesh of his hands.

Then there were more screams, high and shrill, a man shouting, and two shots rang out, clattering feet, and then again silence.

Jean-Jacques stared at Carton, his eyes wide with terror.

Carton's chest was so tight he was dizzy. The stone walls swam in his vision. Sweat broke out on his body and went cold when his wet shirt touched him.

There were footsteps returning, rapid and heavy. The man with the scar reappeared, his face bleak. He looked at Carton, not Jean-Jacques.

"You are wrong, Citizen lawyer," he said abruptly. "The woman must have been guilty. Maybe she gave the cheeses to a lover or something."

"No!" Jean-Jacques took a step forward, his voice high. "That's a lie!"

Carton grabbed his arm as the man with the scar put his hand to the knife at his belt. Jean-Jacques pulled away so hard he lost his balance and fell against Carton's side, stumbling.

The man with the scar relaxed his hand. "It's true," he said, staring at Jean-Jacques. "She attacked Citizen Duclos, then tried to escape. The innocent have nothing to fear."

Jean-Jacques gave a shrill, desperate cry. It was impossible to tell if it was laughter or pain, or both.

Carton's lips and throat were dry. "Did you get them back?" He had known this would be hopeless, whatever the truth of it. He should never have come. "Maybe she was just . . ." He stopped. There was no air to breathe.

The man with the scar shrugged. "It doesn't matter now Citizen. She was shot running away. Your job is finished." He smiled, showing his gapped teeth again. "I guess you won't get paid!"

Jean-Jacques let out a howl of grief and fury like an animal, the sound so raw even the man with the scar froze, and both the other guards turned toward him, mouths gaping.

"Murderers!" Jean-Jacques screamed. "Duclos stole the cheeses, and you let him murder her to hide it!" He snatched his arm away from Carton's grip and lunged toward the man with the scar, reaching for his knife, both their hands closing on the hilt at the same time. "Her blood is on your soul!" He had forgotten that in Revolutionary France there was no God, so presumably men had no souls, either.

The other guards came to life and moved in.

Suddenly Carton found his nerve. He put his arms around

Jean-Jacques and lifted him physically off the ground, kicking and shouting. His heels struck Carton's shins and the pain nearly made him let go. He staggered backward, taking Jean-Jacques with him, and fell against the farther wall. "I'm sorry!" he gasped to the man with the scar, now holding the knife with the blade toward them. "She was his sister. It was his responsibility to look after her." That was a stretching of the truth. "You understand? He doesn't mean it." He held Jean-Jacques hard enough to squash the air out of his lungs. He could feel him gasping and choking as he tried to breathe. "We're leaving," he added. "Maybe we didn't really know what happened."

Jean-Jacques's heels landed so hard on his shins that this time he let go of him and he fell to the ground.

The guards were still uncertain.

Philippe Duclos could appear at any moment, and Carton and Jean-Jacques could both finish up imprisoned here. Ignoring his throbbing leg, Carton bent and picked up Jean-Jacques by the scruff of his neck, yanked him to his feet, and gave him a cuff on the ear hard enough to make his head sing and—please heaven—rob him of speech for long enough to get him outside!

"Thank you, Citizen," he called to the man with the scar, and half dragged Jean-Jacques, half carried him to the entrance and the blessed freedom of the street.

He crossed over, turned right, then left down the first narrow alley he came to before he finally let go of Jean-Jacques. "I'm sorry," he said at last. "But you can't help."

Jean-Jacques shook himself. "Let me go back and get her." His voice was thick with sobs. "Let me bury her!"

Carton seized his shoulder again. "No! They'll take you, too!"

"I haven't done anything!" Jean-Jacques protested furiously. "For what? For coming for my sister's corpse? What are you, stone? Ice? You English clod!"

"I am alive," Carton responded. "And I mean to stay alive. And yes, coming for her corpse would be quite enough for them to blame you for, and if you used a quarter of the brain you've got, you'd know that."

Jean-Jacques seemed to shrink within himself.

Carton was twisted inside with pity. He refused to think of Marie-Claire's bright face, her vitality, the dreams and the anger that had made her so vivid.

"Come on, friend," he said gently. "There's nothing we can do, except survive. She'd want you to do that. Come and have some wine, and we'll find a little bread, and perhaps someone will have onions, or even a piece of sausage."

Jean-Jacques lifted up his head a little. "I suppose so." He sighed. "Yes—survive. You are right, she would want that."

"Of course she would," Carton said more heartily. "Come on."

They started to walk again, crossing the river and turning south for no particular reason, except that neither of them was yet ready to sit still. Finally they came to a wine shop with the door open. The smell of the spilled wine inside was inviting, and there was room to sit down.

The proprietress was a handsome woman with a fine head of black hair, long and thick like a mane. She stared at them, waiting for them to speak.

"Wine?" Carton asked. "Start with two bottles. We have sorrows to drown, Citizeness. And bread, if you have it?"

"You would feed your sorrows as well?" she asked without a smile.

"Citizeness . . ." Carton began.

"Defarge," she replied, as if he had asked her name. "I'll bring you bread. Where's your money?"

Carton put a handful of coins on the table.

She returned with a plate of bread, half an onion, and two bottles. Half an hour later she brought another bottle, and half an hour after that, a fourth. Carton kept on drinking—his body was used to it—but Jean-Jacques slumped against the wall and seemed to be asleep.

Citizeness Defarge remained, and in the early evening brought more bread, but by then Carton was not hungry.

Jean-Jacques opened his eyes and sat up.

"Bread?" Carton offered.

"No." Jean-Jacques waved it away. "I have worked out a plan."

Carton's head was fuzzy. "To do what?"

"Be revenged on Philippe Duclos, of course! What else?" Jean-Jacques looked at him as if he were a fool.

Carton was too eased with wine to be alarmed. "Don't," he said simply. "Whatever it is, it won't work. You'll only get into more trouble."

Jean-Jacques looked at him with big, grief-filled eyes. "Yes, it will," he said with a catch in his voice. "I'll make it work . . . for Marie-Claire." He stood up with an effort, swayed for a moment, struggling for his balance. "Thank you, Carton," he added formally, starting to bow, and then changing his mind. "You are a good friend." And without adding any more he walked unsteadily to the door and disappeared outside.

Carton sat alone, miserable and guilty. If he had really been a good friend, he would have prevented Marie-Claire from setting out on such a mad plan in the first place. He had spent his whole life believing in nothing, achieving pointless victories in small cases in London, and now here writing pieces that did not change the Revolution a jot. It carried on from one insane venture to another regardless. The Paris Commune, largely ruled by Marat, whatever anyone said, made hunger and violence worse with every passing week. France was at war on every side: Spain, Austria, Belgium, and England. Since the hideous massacres last September when the gutters quite literally ran with human blood, Paris was a city of madmen. Charles Darnay was a prisoner in La Force, and Lucie grieved for him ceaselessly, every day going to wait outside the walls, carrying their child, in the hope that he might glimpse them and be comforted.

And here was Carton sitting drunk in Defarge's wine shop, sorry for himself, and ashamed that Jean-Jacques called him a friend, because he had no right to that name.

Two days later, July 12, Carton was back in the Café Procope, taking his usual midday bowl of soup when two soldiers of the Revolutionary Guard came in, red, white, and blue cockades on their hats, muskets over their shoulders. They spoke for a moment with the proprietor, then walked over to Carton.

"Citizen Carton," the first one said. It was not a question but a statement. "You must come with us. There is a matter of theft with which we have been informed that you can help us. On your feet."

Carton was stunned. He opened his mouth to protest, and realized even as he did so that it was totally pointless. It was his turn. Sooner or later some monstrous injustice happened to everyone. He had been informed on and there was no use fighting against it. He obeyed, and walked out between the guards, wondering what idiotic mistake had occurred to involve him. It could be something as simple as the wrong name, a letter different, a misspelling. He had heard of that happening.

But when he got as far as the Section Committee prison where Marie-Claire had been shot, and walked along the same stone corridor, with the same smell of sweat and fear in the air, he knew there was no such easy error.

"Ah—Citizen Lawyer," the man with the scar said, smiling. "We know who you are, you see?" He nodded to the soldiers. "You can go. You have done well, but we have our own guards here." He gestured toward three burly men with gaping shirts and red bandannas around their heads or necks. In the oppressive heat their faces and chests were slick with sweat. Two had pistols, one a knife.

The soldiers left.

"Now, Citizen Carton," the man with the scar began, taking his seat behind a wooden table set up as if it were a judge's bench. Carton was left standing. "This matter of the cheeses that were stolen. It seems you know more about that than you said before. Now would be a good time to tell the truth—all of it. A good time for you, that is."

Carton tried to clear his brain. What he said now might determine his freedom, even his life. Men killed for less than a cheese these days.

"You don't have them?" He affected immense surprise.

The man's face darkened with anger and suspicion that he was being mocked.

Carton stared back at him with wide innocence. He really had no idea where the cheeses were, and he had even more urgent reasons for wishing that he did.

"No, we don't," the man admitted in a growl.

"That is very serious," Carton said sympathetically. "Citizen . . .?"

"Sabot," the man grunted.

"Citizen Sabot." Carton nodded courteously. "We must do everything we can to find them. They are evidence. And apart from that, it is a crime to waste good food. There is certainly a deserving person somewhere to whom they should go." The place seemed even more airless than before, as if everything which came here, human or not, remained. The smell of fear was in the nose and throat, suffocating the breath.

Along the corridor to the left, out of sight, someone shouted, there was laughter, a wail. Then the silence surged back like a returning wave.

Carton found his voice shaking when he spoke again. "Citizen Sabot, you have been very fair to me. I will do everything I can to

learn what happened to the cheeses and bring you the information."
He saw the distrust naked in Sabot's face, the sneer already forming
on his lips. "You are a man of great influence," he went on truthfully,
however much he might despise himself for it. "Apart from justice, it
would be wise of me to assist you all that I can."

Sabot was mollified. "Yes, it would," he agreed. "I'll give you
two days. Today and tomorrow."

"I'll report to you in two days," Carton hedged. "I might need
longer to track them down. We are dealing with clever people here. If it
were not so, your own men would have found them already, surely?"

Sabot considered for a moment. Half a dozen revolutionary guards
marched by with heavy tread. Someone sang a snatch of the Marseil-
laise, that song the rabble had adopted when they burst out of the
gaols of Marseilles and the other sea ports of the Mediterranean, and
marched all the way to Paris, killing and looting everything in their
path. Carton found himself shaking uncontrollably, memory nause-
ating him.

"Tomorrow night," Sabot conceded. "But if you find them and
eat them yourself, I'll have your head."

Carton gulped and steadied himself. "Naturally," he agreed. He
almost added something else, then while he still retained some balance, he turned and left, trying not to run.

Back in the room he rented, Carton sank down into his bed, his mind
racing to make sense of what had happened, and his own wild promise to Sabot to find the cheeses. He had been granted barely two
days. Where could he even begin?

With Marie-Claire's original plan. She had intended to have
Philippe tell Fleuriot that he was going to post guards, so he had
moved the cheeses and the bacon to a more accessible place. Only he

had done it earlier than the time agreed with Marie-Claire. Presumably his plan had worked. Fleuriot had moved the cheeses, and Philippe had caught him in the act, and confiscated them. Fleuriot had said nothing, because he should not have had the cheeses in the first place. So much was clear.

Marie-Claire had heard of it and attempted to accuse Philippe, but either she had not been listened to at all, or if she had, she had not been believed, and Philippe had silenced her before she could prove anything. According to Sabot, no one had found the cheeses, so Philippe must still have them.

Maybe Carton should begin with Fleuriot. He at least would know when the cheeses had been taken, which—if it led to Philippe's movements that day—might indicate where he could have hidden them. Carton got up and went out. This was all an infuriating waste of time. He should be working. His money was getting low. If it were not his own neck at risk, he would not do it. All the proof of innocence in the world would not save poor Marie-Claire now. And it would hardly help Jean-Jacques, either. No one cared because half the charges made were built on settling old scores anyway, or on profit of one sort or another. Those who had liked Marie-Claire would still like her just as much.

He walked along the street briskly, head down, avoiding people's eyes. There was a warm wind rising, and it smelled as if rain were coming. Old newspapers blew along the pavement, flapping like wounded birds. Two laundresses were arguing. It looked like the same ones as before.

He went the long way around to the Rue St. Honoré, in order to avoid passing the house where Marat lived and printed his papers. He had enough trouble without an encounter with the "Rage of the People." A couple of questions elicited the information as to exactly which house Fleuriot lived in, next to the carpenter Duplay. But Fleuriot was an angry and frightened man. The loss of a few cheeses was nothing compared with the threatened loss of his head. He stood in the doorway, his spectacles balanced on his forehead, and stared fixedly at Carton.

"I don't know what you're talking about, Citizen. There are always Revolutionary Guard about the place. How is one day different from another?"

"Not Revolutionary Guard," Carton corrected patiently. "These would be from the local Committee, not in uniform, apart from the red bandanna."

"Red bandanna!" Fleuriot threw his hands up in the air. "What does that mean? Nothing! Anyone can wear a red rag. They could be from the Faubourg St. Antoine, for all I know. I mind my own business, Citizen, and you'd be best advised to mind yours! Good day." And without giving Carton a chance to say anything more, he retreated inside his house and slammed the door, leaving Carton alone in the yard just as it began to rain.

He spent the rest of the afternoon and early evening getting thoroughly wet and learning very little of use. He asked all the neighbors whose apartments fronted onto the courtyard, and he even asked the apothecary in the house to the left, and the carpenter in the yard to the right. But Philippe was powerful and his temper vicious. If anyone knew anything about exactly when he came with his man, they were affecting ignorance. According to most of them, the place had been totally deserted on that particular late afternoon. One was queuing for candles, another for soap. One woman was visiting her sick sister, a girl was selling pamphlets, a youth was delivering a piece of furniture, another was too drunk to have known if his own mother had walked past him, and she had been dead for years. That at least was probably honest.

Carton went home wet to the skin and thoroughly discouraged. He had two slices of bread, half a piece of sausage, and a bottle of wine. He took off his wet clothes and sat in his nightshirt, thinking. Tomorrow was July 13. If he did not report the day after, Sabot would come for him. He would be angry because he had failed twice, and been taken for a fool. And what was worse, by then Philippe himself would almost certainly be aware of Carton's interest in the matter. He must succeed. The alternative would be disaster. He must find out more about Philippe himself, where he lived, what other places he might have access to, who were his friends. Even better would be to know who were his enemies!

He finally went to sleep determined to start very early in the morning. He needed to succeed, and quickly, for his own survival, but he would also like to be revenged for Marie-Claire. She had not deserved this, and in spite of his better judgment he had liked her. It would be good to do something to warrant the friendship Jean-Jacques believed of him.

In the morning he got up early and went out straight away. He bought a cup of coffee from a street vendor, drank it and handed back the mug to her, then walked on past the usual patient queues of women hoping for bread, or vegetables, or whatever it was. He passed the sellers of pamphlets and the tradesmen still trying to keep up some semblance of normality at what they did: millinery, barrel-making, engraving, hair-dressing, or whatever it was, and retraced his steps to the local committee headquarters. It was a considerable risk asking questions about Philippe Duclos, especially since he was already known and Philippe would be on his guard. He knew he had taken the cheeses and would see threat even where there was none. But Carton had to report to Sabot by midnight tonight, and so far he had accomplished nothing. It was not impossible that in his fear of Philippe, Fleuriot had already warned him that Carton was asking questions.

Affecting innocence and concern, Carton asked one of the guards where he might find Citizen Duclos, since he had a personal message for him.

The man grunted. "Citizen Duclos is a busy man! Why should I keep watch on him? Who knows where he is?"

Carton bit back his instinctive answer and smiled politely. "You are very observant," he replied between his teeth. "I am sure you know who comes and goes, as a matter of habit."

The man grunted again, but the love of flattery was in his eyes, and Carton had asked for nothing but a little harmless information. "He is not in yet," he replied. "Come back in an hour or two."

"The message is urgent," Carton elaborated. "I would not wish to disturb him, but I could wait for him in the street near his lodgings, and as soon as he comes out, I could speak with him."

The man shrugged. "If you wake him you'll pay for it!" he warned.

"Naturally. I am sure his work for liberty keeps him up till strange hours, as I imagine yours does, too."

"All hours!" the man agreed. "Haven't seen my bed long enough for a year or more!"

"History will remember you," Carton said ambiguously. "Where should I wait for Citizen Duclos?"

"Rue Mazarine," the man replied. "South side, near the apothecary's shop."

"Thank you." Carton nodded to him and hurried away before he could become embroiled in any further conversation.

He found the apothecary's shop and stood outside it, apparently loitering like many others, occasioning no undue attention. People came and went, most of them grumbling about one thing or another. The pavements steamed from the night's rain and already it was hot.

Twenty minutes later a large man came out, bleary-eyed, unshaven, a red bandanna around his neck. There was a wine stain on the front of his shirt, and he belched as he passed Carton, barely noticing him.

Carton waited until he had gone around the corner out of sight, and for another ten minutes after that, then he went under the archway into the courtyard and knocked on the first door.

A woman opened it, her sleeves rolled up and a broom in her hand. He asked her for Philippe Duclos and was directed to the door opposite. Here he was fortunate at last. It was opened by a child of about eleven. She was curious and friendly. She told him Philippe lodged with her family and he had one room. Carton asked if Philippe were to be given a gift of wine, did he have a place where he could keep it.

"He could put it in the cellar," she replied. "But if it is a good wine, then one of the other lodgers might drink it. It would not be safe." Was there not somewhere better, more private? No, unfortunately there was no such place. Might he have a friend? She giggled. The thought amused her. She could not imagine him trusting a friend, he was not that kind of man. He did not even trust her mother, who cooked and cleaned for him. He was always counting his shirts! As if anybody would want them.

Carton thanked her and left, puzzled. Again he was at a dead end. He went back to the neighbors of Fleuriot to see if he could find anyone, even a child or a servant, who might have seen Philippe's men moving the cheeses, or if not cheese, then at least the bacon. One cannot carry out a side of bacon in one's pocket!

He spoke to a dozen people, busy and idle, resident and passerby, but no one had seen people carrying goods that day, or since, with the exception of shopping going in. Even laundry had been done at the well in the center of the yard, and the presence of the women would have been sufficient to deter anyone from carrying anything past with as distinctive a shape as a side of bacon, or odor as a ripe cheese.

He saw only one rat, fat and sleek, running from the well across the stones and disappearing into a hole in the wall. Then he remembered that there was a timber yard next door, belonging to the carpenter Duplay. Shouldn't there be plenty of rats around?

What if no one had seen Philippe move the cheeses because he hadn't? They were still here—the safest place for them! Fleuriot would guard them with his life, but if Sabot should find them, then Fleuriot would take the blame, and Philippe would affect total innocence. He would say he knew nothing of them at all, and Marie-Claire, the only person who knew he had, was dead and could say nothing. It made perfect sense. And above all it was safe! Philippe simply took a cheese whenever he wanted, and Fleuriot was too frightened of him to do anything about it. Certainly he would not dare eat one or sell one himself.

Carton walked away quickly and went back to the Café Procope and ordered himself a slice of bread and sausage and a bottle of wine. He sat at his usual table. Every time the door swung open he looked up, half expecting to see Jean-Jacques, and felt an unreasonable surge of disappointment each time it was not. He had nothing in particular to say to him, apart from to forget his plan for revenge, whatever it was, but he missed his company, and he hurt for his grief. Perhaps he even would have liked to talk of Marie-Claire and share some of the pain within himself.

If the cheeses were still in Fleuriot's house, then it would take a number of men, with the authority of the Commune itself behind them, to search. The local authority was no good, that was Philippe himself. How could Carton get past that? He stared into his glass and knew there was only one answer—the one he had been avoiding for the last half year—ask Marat! Marat was the Commune.

There must be another way. He poured out the last of the wine and drank it slowly. It was sour, but it still hit his stomach with a certain warmth. So far he had avoided even passing the house in the Rue des Medicines where Marat lived. He had rather that Marat had never even heard of him. Now he was about to ruin it all by actually walking into the house and asking a favor! Never mind drunk, he must be mad! He upended the glass and drained the last mouthful. Well, if he were going to commit suicide, better get on with it rather than sit here feeling worse and worse, living it over in his imagination until he was actually sick.

He went outside and walked quickly, as if he had purpose he was intent upon. Get it done. The fear of it was just as bad as the actuality. At least get this achieved.

He was there before he expected. He must have been walking too rapidly. There was an archway on the corner leading into a cobbled yard with a well in the center, just like any of a thousand others. At one side a flight of steps led up to an entrance, and even from where he stood Carton could see bales of paper piled up just inside the open doorway, boxes beyond, and printed newspapers ready to deliver. There was no excuse for hesitation. It was obviously Marat's house.

He took a deep breath, let it out slowly, then walked across and up the steps. No one accosted him until he was inside and peering around, looking for someone to ask. A plain, rather ordinary woman approached him, her face mild, as if she expected a friend.

"Citizeness," he said huskily. "I am sorry to interrupt your business, but I have a favor to ask which only Citizen Marat could grant me. Who may I approach in order to speak with him?"

"I am Simonne Evrard," she replied with a certain quiet confidence. "I will ask Citizen Marat if he can see you. Who are you, and what is it you wish?"

Carton remembered with a jolt that Marat had some kind of common-law wife—Marat of all people! This was her, a soft-spoken woman with red hands and an apron tied around her waist. "Sydney Carton, Citizeness," he replied. "It is to do with a man hoarding food instead of making it available to all citizens, as it should be. Unfortunately he has a position in the local committee, so I cannot go to them."

"I see." She nodded. "I shall tell him. Please wait here."

She was gone for several minutes. He stood shifting his weight from foot to foot, trying to control the fear rising inside him. It even occurred to him to change his mind and leave. There was still time.

And then there wasn't. She was back again, beckoning him toward her and pointing to the doorway of another room. Like one in a dream he obeyed, his heart pounding in his chest.

Inside the room was unlike anything he could conceivably have expected. It was small, a sort of aqueous green, and the steam in it clung to his skin and choked his nose and his throat. The smell was ghastly, a mixture of vinegar and rotting human flesh. In the center was a tin bath shaped like a boot, concealing the lower portion of the occupant's body. A board was placed across it on which rested a pen, inkwell, and paper. Even through the heavy steam Carton could see Marat quite clearly. His toadlike face with its bulging eyes and slack mouth was almost bloodless with the exhaustion of pain. There was a wet towel wrapped around his head. His naked shoulders, arms, and upper chest were smooth and hairless.

"What is it, Citizen Carton?" he asked. His voice was rough and had a slight accent. Carton remembered he was not French at all, but half Swiss and half Sardinian. The stench caught in his throat and he thought he was going to gag.

"Would you rather speak in English?" Marat asked—in English. He was a doctor by profession and had held a practice in Pimlico in London for some time.

"No, thank you, Citizen," Carton declined, then instantly wondered if it was wise. "Perhaps you would indulge me should my French falter?"

"What is it you want?" Marat repeated. His expression was hard to read because of the ravages of disease upon his face. He was in his fifties, a generation older than most of the other Revolutionary leaders, and a lifetime of hate had exhausted him.

"I believe a certain Citizen Duclos has discovered a quantity of exceptionally good food, cheeses and bacon to be exact, in the keeping of a Citizen Fleuriot, and has blackmailed him into concealing that food from the common good." Carton was speaking too quickly and he knew it, but he could not control himself enough to slow down. "Citizen Duclos is in a position of power in the local committee, so I cannot turn to them to search and find it."

Marat blinked. "So you want me to have men from the Commune search?"

"Yes, please."

Marat grunted and eased his position a little, wincing as the ulcerated flesh touched the sides of the bath. "I'll consider it," he said with a gasp. "Why do you care? Is it your cheese?"

"No, Citizen. But it is unjust. And it could be mine next time."

Marat stared at him. Carton felt the steam settle on his skin and trickle down his face and body. His clothes were sticking to him. The pulse throbbed in his head and his throat. Marat did not believe him. He knew it.

"A friend of mine was blamed for it, and shot," he added. Was he insane to tell Marat this? Too late now. "I want revenge."

Marat nodded slowly. "Come back this evening. I'll have men for you," he assured. "I understand hate."

"Thank you," Carton said hoarsely, then instantly despised himself for it. He did not want to have anything in common with this man, this embodiment of insane rage who had sworn to drown Paris in seas of blood. He half bowed, and backed out of that dreadful room into the hallway again.

*   *   *

He returned to his rooms and fell asleep for a while. He woke with a headache like a tight band around his temples. He washed in cold water, changed his clothes, and went out to buy a cup of coffee. He would have to think about something more for publication soon, as he would run out of money.

It was half past seven in the evening. He had not long before he would have to report to Sabot.

He was almost back to Marat's house when he heard shouting in the street and a woman screaming. He hastened his step and was at the entrance archway when a Revolutionary Guardsman pushed past him.

"What is it?" Carton asked, alarm growing inside him.

"Marat's been killed!" a young man cried out. "Murdered! Stabbed to death in his bath. A mad woman from Calvados. Marat's dead!"

There were more footsteps running, shouts and screams, armed men clattering by, howls of grief, rage and terror.

Dead! Carton stood still, leaning a little against the wall in the street. In spite of all his will to stop it, in his mind he could see the ghastly figure of Marat in that aqueous room, the steam, the shriveled skin, the stench, the pain in his face. He imagined the body lifeless, and blood pouring into the vinegar and water. And with a wave of pity he thought of the quiet woman who for some inconceivable reason had loved him.

He must get out of here! Maybe he would be lucky and the widow would not even remember his name, let alone why he had come. He straightened up and stumbled away, tripping on the cobbles as he heard the shouts behind him, more men coming. Someone let off a musket shot, and then another.

All his instincts impelled him to run, but he must not. It would look as if he were escaping. A couple of women accosted him, asking what was wrong. "I don't know," he lied. "Some kind of trouble. But stay away from it." And without waiting he left them.

When he finally got inside his own rooms and locked the door, he realized the full impact of what had happened. Marat, the head of the Commune, the most powerful man in Paris, had been murdered by some woman from the countryside. The revenge for it would be unimaginable. But of more immediate concern to Carton, he did not have Marat's men to search Fleuriot's house for the cheeses. And Sabot would expect an answer tonight or Carton himself would pay the price for it. He would have to do something about it himself, and immediately.

He dashed a little water over his face, dried it, put his jacket back on, and went outside again. The one idea in his mind was desperate, but then so would the result be if he did nothing.

Rats were the key. If he could not get Marat's men to search Fleuriot's house, than he would have to get someone else to do it. The carpenter Duplay, with his wood yard next door, was at least a chance. He could think of nothing better.

He walked quickly toward the Rue St. Honoré, hoping not to give himself time to think of all the things that could go wrong. He had no choice. He kept telling himself that—no choice! It was a drumbeat in his head as he strode along the cobbles, crossed to avoid a cart unloading barrels, and came to the archway at the entrance to the carpenter's house. He knocked before he had time to hesitate.

It was opened within two minutes by a young woman. She was small and very neat, rather like a child, except that her face was quite mature, as if she were at least in her middle twenties. She inquired politely what she could do to help him.

"I believe the Citizen who lives here is a carpenter," he said, after thanking her for her courtesy.

"Yes, Citizen. He is excellent. Did you wish to purchase something, or have something made, perhaps?" she asked.

"Thank you, but I am concerned for his stock of wood, possibly even his finished work," he replied. "I have reason to believe that food is being stored in the house next door—cheese, to be precise—and there are a large number of rats collecting. . . ." He stopped, seeing the distaste in her face, as if he had spoken of something obscene. "I'm sorry," he apologized. "Perhaps I should not have mentioned it to you, but I feel that the Citizen . . ."

There was a click of high heels on the wooden stairway and Carton looked beyond the young woman to see a man whose resemblance to her was marked enough for him to assume that they were related. He was about thirty, small and intensely neat, as she was, almost feline in his manner, with a greenish pallor to his complexion, and myopic green eyes which he blinked repeatedly as he stared at Carton. He was dressed perfectly in the manner of the Ançien Regime, as if he were to present himself at the court of Louis XVI, complete with green striped nankeen jacket, exquisitely cut, a waistcoat and cravat, breeches and stockings. It was his high heels Carton had heard. His hair was meticulously powdered and tied back. He fluttered his very small, nail-bitten hands when he spoke.

"It is all right, Charlotte, I shall deal with the matter."

"Yes, Maximilien," she said obediently, and excused herself.

"Did you say 'rats,' Citizen?" the man asked, his voice soft, accented with a curious sibilance.

With a shock like ice water on his bare flesh, Carton realized what he had done. Of all the carpenters in Paris he had knocked on the door of the one in whose house lodged Citizen Robespierre, and apparently his sister. He stood frozen to the spot, staring at the little man still on the bottom stair, as far away from him as he could be without being absurd. Carton remembered someone saying that Robespierre was so personally fastidious as to dislike anyone close to him, let alone touching him. He had constant indigestion for which he sucked oranges, and anything as gross as a bodily appetite or function offended him beyond belief.

"I am sorry to mention such a matter," Carton apologized again. He found himself thinking of Jean-Jacques and his grief, and how alive Marie-Claire had been, how full of laughter, anger, and dreams. "But I believe Citizen Fleuriot next door is hoarding cheese, and it is unfair that he rob the good citizens of food by doing so, but it is also a considerable danger to his immediate neighbors, because of the vermin it attracts."

Robespierre was staring at him with his strange, short-sighted eyes.

Carton gulped. "I have not the power to do anything about it myself," he went on. "But I can at least warn others. I imagine Citizen Duplay has a great deal of valuable wood which could be damaged." He bowed very slightly. "Thank you for your courtesy, Citizen. I hope I have not distressed the Citizeness."

"You did your duty," Robespierre replied with satisfaction. "The 'Purity of the People' "—he spoke as if it were some kind of divine entity—"requires sacrifice. We must rid France of vermin of every kind. I shall myself go to see this Citizen Fleuriot. Come with me."

Carton drew in his breath, and choked. Robespierre waited while he suffered a fit of coughing, then when Carton was able to compose himself, he repeated his command. "Come with me."

Carton followed the diminutive figure in the green jacket, heels clicking on the cobbles, white powdered head gleaming in the last of the daylight, until they reached Fleuriot's door. Robespierre stepped aside for Carton to knock. The door opened and Fleuriot himself stood in the entrance, face tight with annoyance.

Carton moved aside and Fleuriot saw Robespierre. A curious thing happened. There could not be two such men in all France, let alone in this district of Paris. Fleuriot's recognition was instant. He turned a bilious shade of yellowish-green and swayed so wildly that had he not caught hold of the door lintel he would have fallen over.

"I have been told that you have some cheeses," Robespierre said in his soft, insistent voice. "A great many, in fact." He blinked. "Of course I do not know if that is true, but lying would make you an enemy to the people. . . ."

Fleuriot made a strange, half-strangled sound in his throat.

Carton closed his eyes and opened them again. His mouth was as dry as the dust on the stones. "It's possible Citizen Fleuriot does not own the cheeses?" he said, his voice catching. He coughed as Robespierre swiveled around to stare at him, peering forward as if it were difficult to see. Carton cleared his throat again. "Perhaps he is frightened of someone else, Citizen?"

"Yes!" Fleuriot said in a high-pitched squeak, as if he were being strangled. "The good citizen is right!" It was painfully clear that he was terrified. His face was ghastly, the sweat stood out on his lip and brow, and he wrung his hands as if he would break them, easing his weight from foot to foot. But the fear that touched his soul was of Robespierre, not of Philippe Duclos. He gulped for air. "The cheeses are not mine! They belong to Citizen Duclos, of the local committee. I am keeping them for him! He has threatened to have my head if I don't. . . ." His voice wavered off and he looked as if he were going to faint.

Robespierre stepped back. Such physical signs of terror repelled him. The Purity of the People was a concept, an ideal to be aspired to, and the means to achieve it was obviously fear, but he did not want ever to think of the reality of it, much less be forced to witness it. "Philippe Duclos?" he asked.

"Yes . . . C-Citizen . . . R-Robespierre," Fleuriot stammered.

"Then Citizen Carton here will help you carry the cheeses out, and we will give them to the people, where they belong," Robespierre ordered. "And Citizen Duclos will answer with his head." He did not even glance at Carton but stood waiting for an obedience he took for granted.

Carton felt oddly safe as he followed Fleuriot inside. Robespierre was a tiny man with no physical strength at all—Philippe could have broken him with one blow—but it was not even imaginable that he would. Robespierre's presence in the yard was more powerful than an army of soldiers would have been. Carton would not even have taken a cheese for Sabot without his permission.

When the food was all removed, the yard was completely dark, but Robespierre was easily discernible by the gleam of his powdered hair. Carton approached him with his heart hammering.

"Citizen Robespierre?"

Robespierre turned, peering at him in the shadows. "Yes, what is it? You have done well."

"Citizen Sabot of the local committee is a good man." His voice shook, and he despised himself for his words. "I would like him to have an opportunity to be rewarded for his service to the people by receiving one of the cheeses."

Robespierre stood motionless for several seconds. He drew in his breath with a slight hiss. "Indeed."

"He works long hours." Carton felt the blood thundering in his head. "I must report to him tonight, to show my honesty in this matter, or . . ." he faltered and fell silent.

"He does his duty," Robespierre replied.

Carton's heart sank.

"But you may be rewarded," Robespierre added. "You may have one of the cheeses."

Carton was giddy with relief. "Thank you, Citizen." He hated the gratitude in his voice, and he could do nothing about it. "You are . . ." he said the one word he knew Robespierre longed to hear, ". . . incorruptible."

He took the cheese and went to the local committee prison. Sabot was waiting for him. He saw the cheese even before Carton spoke.

Carton placed it on the table before him, hating to let go of it, and knowing it was the only way to save his life.

"I found them," he said. "Citizen Robespierre will arrest the hoarder. You would be well advised to take this home, tonight— now! And say nothing."

Sabot nodded with profound understanding and a good deal of respect. He picked up the cheese, caressing it with his fingers. "I will leave now," he agreed. "I will walk along the street with you, Citizen."

Philippe protested of course, but it availed him nothing. Fleuriot would never have dared retract his testimony, and apart from that, there was a sweetness in having his revenge on Philippe for having stolen his hoard, and then terrified him into guarding it for him, adding insult to injury.

Reluctantly Sabot was allowed his one cheese in reward. It was all over very swiftly. Robespierre was not yet a member of the Committee of Public Safety, but it was only a matter of time. His star was ascending. Already someone had whispered of him as "The Sea-Green Incorruptible." Philippe Duclos was found guilty and sentenced to the guillotine.

Robespierre never personally witnessed such a disgusting act as an execution. The only time he ever saw the machine of death at all was at the end of the High Terror still a year in the future, when he mounted the blood-spattered steps himself.

Carton had not intended to go, but memory of Marie-Claire was suddenly very sharp in his mind. He could see her bright face under its tumbled hair, hear her voice with its laughter and its enthusiasm, as if she had gone out of the door only minutes ago. Half against his will, despising himself for it, he nevertheless was waiting in the Place de la Revolution, watching with revulsion Citizeness Defarge and her friends who sat with their knitting needles clicking beside the guillotine when the tumbrels came rattling in with their cargo of the condemned.

As usual they were all manner of people, but not many of them wore the red bandanna of the Citizens' power, and Philippe was easy to see.

Carton felt a joggle at his elbow, and turning for an instant, he thought it was Marie-Claire. It was the same wide, brown eyes, the tangle of hair, but it was Jean-Jacques, his face still haggard with grief. He looked at Carton and his cheeks were wet.

Carton put out his hand to touch him gently. "I'm glad you didn't try your plan," he said with intense gratitude. He liked this odd little man profoundly. It was stupid to have such a hostage to fate, but he could not help it. Afterward they would go and drink together in quiet remembrance and companionship. "It would never have worked," he added.

Jean-Jacques smiled through his tears. "Yeah, it did," he answered.